The White River Killer

The White River Killer

Stephen Wilson

ISBN: 978-0-692-38729-0

1: Prologue

GOOD DRIVING IS ITS OWN REWARD

THE SAFEST DRIVERS ON THE ROAD are those hauling a corpse to a discreet location while avoiding the notice of law enforcement.

Luis Espinoza slowed the blue pickup and used the pale glow of a streetlamp to check his newly acquired Rolex. He pulled back the ragged cuff of his faded blue winter coat; it was almost three a.m. The heavy storm was slowing their progress. Luis would have preferred to wait for clear skies, but he had no choice. The man said the body needed to disappear, and if Luis wanted this gig, well . . .

He pressed the accelerator and he and Pablo Sanchez continued to move through the flooded streets of the Latino barrio of Hayslip, Arkansas, a small farming community.

The battered truck, jacked yesterday afternoon, entered foamy water swirling in a narrow intersection just as a streak of lightning revealed Luis's hands trembling on the steering wheel. Ashamed, his eyes darted sideways toward Pablo.

His young partner seemed oblivious to the risk they were taking. He stared, expressionless, at the rising water while clutching a folded sheet of paper in his left hand. With the other hand, he tapped a knife rhythmically on his knee like he was the drummer in an imaginary band.

Luis met Pablo six months ago on a night as desolate as this. The boy was curled up, whimpering on a gravel bed next to an empty freight car in Guatemala. Pablo had lost a fight with a burly railroad guard, his bloody arms still trying their best to block the blows from the watchman's metal baton. Feeling an unexpected sympathy, Luis crept up behind the big man, zeroed in on a spot on his balding head, and slammed a heavy rock against the guard's skull. Pablo was duly grateful, and Luis delayed his departure by a week so that his sister could nurse his new friend back to health.

Uncertain how Pablo would manage on the drive this evening, Luis had written up a step-by-step plan to help him keep his wits. He was trying his best to manage the barely sixteen-year-old. Their night work until now had been limited to minor break-ins and rolling drunks, nothing of this magnitude. Luis worried the boy would crack under tonight's stress. In mocking irony, it was Luis, eleven years older than Pablo, who was overwhelmed. His chest throbbed as if it were being squeezed by a tight metal band.

A small fortune in cash was within their reach—if he could keep his wits.

As they neared the town center, the road cleared of standing rainwater. Main Street, coming up now, marked the most hazardous leg of their journey, a necessary evil due to high water that prevented a more circumspect route. They would sprint along this well-lit road for two hundred yards before they could return to the relative safety of a dark two-lane.

Luis glanced at the rear view mirror. The thick carpet roll was too long for a short-bed Dodge, and flopped over the tailgate. He tried to return his focus to the road, but not before he caught a glimpse of his dark eyes in the mirror. He knew he looked angry. Well, why shouldn't he be angry? There was a time when his family would have been the one giving the orders, telling others to do the dirty work. Not now. No, *he* was the one saying 'yes sir'. It wasn't right. He wasn't like Pablo. He had an education. He grew up with fine things. *Hell yes*, he was angry.

Luis slowed the vehicle, hesitating in the safety of the shadowy intersection, four blocks north of the town square. They remained there, studying the street warily.

Pablo's nervous Spanish was barely audible over the rain pelting the roof. "Is the cop still there? Can you see his car? I can't. He should be gone by now . . . Is he?"

"Hold on. I can't see anything," Luis said, squinting in an effort to see through the foggy windshield. The wipers squeaked noisily on each pass, battling the downpour.

Pablo leaned forward, his brow raised in fear as he pointed a switchblade in front of him. He used one of the few English words he knew, his voice cracking, before he returned to his native language. *"Stop!"* His knife was directed at the twenty-four-hour *Git It N Go* convenience store located on the corner, across the road from where the pickup idled. "He's there. His patrol car. See?" He tapped the windshield with his blade.

Luis grabbed the .38 under his seat. *"Put the knife down . . .* Where?"

"The bastard parked *behind* the store tonight. *Why?* He never does that. It's a trap!"

Luis prided himself on knowing the routines of Hayslip's tiny police force. It allowed them to do their work in peace. "How could it be a trap? I don't see his . . . *Christ!* How many times have I told you that you need glasses? That's the girl's car, not his, and it doesn't look *anything like a patrol car!* Don't lose it, man."

Pablo pouted. He fell back in the seat and flicked his knife open and closed several times.

The interior of the cab had grown humid and Luis wiped sweat from his forehead with the palm of his hand. Returning his attention to the small store, he spotted the curvy figure of the young cashier through the plate glass window as she picked up a magazine from a rack in front and then returned to the rear of the building.

A new understanding made Luis panic, his breaths became rapid. *No . . . no . . .* His thinking about tonight was all wrong. It would be better to know where the cop was when they were in transit, rather than delay until late at night to miss him at the store.

Hayslip's deputy dawdled each evening inside the *Git It N Go* to mess with a girl at the register. But with the deputy gone at this hour, he could be anywhere. It would have been much smarter to arrive when his attention was on the girl, not his duties. Now there was a chance they would run into him on Main Street.

He surveyed the length of the broad avenue. Nothing moved along the gloomy corridor except silver sheets of rainwater. Traffic signals, fried by the storm, blinked red warnings in all directions.

Luis needed time to think. *Did the cop go back to the jail to sleep?* He didn't know what the redheaded fool did this late at night when dawn approached.

"Let's take off," Pablo said.

"I'll say when we go. I'm—"

There was a flash of white light in the rear view mirror just before a vehicle plowed into the truck's tailgate, Luis's head snapped backwards and then the force of the crash slammed him against the steering wheel. For a painful moment, he was disoriented by the harsh jolt.

Regaining his wits, Luis shouted a war cry that was a confused mixture of profanity and terrified gibberish. He flung open his truck door and leapt out.

Pablo bounded out the passenger door after Luis, waving his arms. "Luis *don't* . . ."

Luis shielded his eyes from the blinding headlights, too enraged to hear the warning. Harsh bile burned his throat. The stolen pickup, a body in the rug; there was too much to explain away. This singular opportunity for a return to the good life was ruined. Cursing the deputy to hell, he fired four rounds at the hazy outline of the patrol car. His fourth shot went wild and smashed the vehicle's left headlight. A second later, the remaining lamp shorted out, issuing a soft pop of complaint as it died.

Luis wiped icy droplets from his face and realized that he had been fooled by a mirage. Like a nightmare, a gray Oldsmobile, with chrome fenders and a vinyl top materialized. No one was sitting inside the idling car, either dead or alive. After a moment of uncertainty, he took small steps forward, Pablo behind him.

Low thunder rolled overhead as the Olds driver—about Pablo's age—rose somewhat unsteadily behind the dash.

Behind him, Luis heard Pablo whisper, "Un niño." A kid.

The lighted dashboard tinted the boy's features an eerie teal. Almost in slow motion, the youth slid behind the steering wheel, wide-eyed, as the men approached. His mouth opened partially, perhaps to cry out, maybe to plead.

Raising his pistol, Luis aimed at the center of the driver's blue-green head. But his gun hand quivered, and his vision turned cloudy. The trigger resisted the pull of his finger.

With nothing to lose, the boy slapped the Olds's gear shift into reverse. The rear tires spun loudly on the wet street and then gained traction.

Pablo pointed at the retreating vehicle. "Stop him. Do something."

Pulling back from the two men standing in the front of the car, the vehicle made a wild retreat, barely staying between the ditches.

Luis lowered the gun as a porch light flicked on down the street. He ran for the truck. "We've got to get out of here." He flung open the truck door and jumped in, grabbing the steering wheel.

Pablo's arms flailed against the rain in wordless fury, but he sprinted after Luis and leapt into a vehicle already pulling away.

As they took off, Luis looked back and saw the Olds careen into a parking lot and crash backward into an automatic car wash. It then pulled forward, the metal siding on the building crashed to the ground, and the vehicle raced away in the opposite direction.

Luis accelerated toward highway 281.

After they had gone almost a mile, Luis berated himself in Spanish for panicking with a mournful wail of frustration. "*Goddamn!* I thought it was the cop. Why . . . did . . . I . . ."

Staring at the muddy floor mat underneath his feet, Pablo was silent.

Luis drove on, squinting into the rain until he made out an unmarked trail connecting to the highway. He turned to Pablo, who still clutched the plan in his hand. "Where are we? What number? Read it."

Pablo opened the sheet of paper, pulled a small flashlight from his pocket, and recited aloud. "Nine. Exit the highway at the fourth dirt road. Unmarked. Count each road."

"Was that the first or second road?" Luis asked. His mind was racing so fast everything was jumbled.

Pablo looked up, shrugged his shoulders and turned off the light. "I don't know."

"You're supposed to be counting. Count."

"Yeah . . . *I think* that was the first." Pablo put the sheet of notebook paper on the seat beside them and pointed to the right. "That's the second."

They had passed the crude turnoff before he finished the sentence.

"Second," Luis said. "Okay, two more." Luis shoved the gun back under the seat.

They noted a third trail that looked so vague it appeared to be more a memory of a cow path than a route.

"Okay . . . It's coming up at the top of this hill," Pablo said.

Luis turned onto a narrow dirt path that first cleaved a line of pine trees, and then divided an open meadow into two sections. Farther away from the highway, the terrain on either side of the road transformed into impassably thick undergrowth dotted with scrub trees.

Luis leaned to his left to fully view the side mirror. No headlights pursued them in the night. They had done it. The ache in his chest eased.

As they splashed through water hiding potholes in the road, Pablo fidgeted in his seat and eyed the dark cottages on their route. The primitive structures were cloaked in shadows by brambles and pine foliage. "Are you sure they're all empty?" Pablo said. "How can there be so many houses and no one living in them?"

Luis pointed to a shack on the right. "No electricity. No running water. Rotten floor boards. They call this place Shanty Town. They're old sharecropper shacks—nothing here but an abandoned ghost town. I've been here a few times before. It's a good place to hide things."

"Hide things? What have you put out here?"

Luis ignored the question. Veering off the meager road, he headed for the drop-off spot. The truck struggled to make it up the muddy rise, slippery with rain. He parked next to a drainage canal, barely visible in the overcast night. Luis turned off the headlights, plunging them into darkness. They sat for a full minute to let their eyes adjust.

"When do we leave? Pablo asked. Tomorrow? That dude might have recognized us or we could run into him again. We can't stay here."

"We'll handle him if we run into him again."

"But—"

"No . . . I've been thinking," Luis said. His voice was a whisper. "There's more money to be made from this . . ." Luis's head tilted to the rear to indicate the unmoving passenger in the truck bed. "This is the start of something very bad. A pillar of the community won't want to deal with the details. He has too much to lose."

"Pillar . . . of the . . .what?"

Luis shook his head. "Never mind. I just think we can make more money before we leave . . . I've got uh, some things I need to take care of."

After an uneasy moment of quiet, Pablo asked, "What are you going to do with your share of the money?"

Luis considered the question before deciding to answer it. "I haven't told you this, but my sister just arrived. I'm going to help Maria get settled. I promised I'd take care of her."

"Maria's here? In Hayslip? " Pablo then separated Maria's name into three lovely parts, wrapping each syllable in a verbal caress, "Ma—ri—a."

Luis's eyes narrowed, and his lips pressed together into a scowl. *Maria turned men into fools.* He glowered at Pablo.

Smiling apologetically, Pablo turned his attention to the particulars of the miserable weather outside the door window. He edged closer to the glass as his hand swept back and forth, wiping away condensation. "*Shit . . .* Some guy is watching us. He's standing by that tree. Look!"

The tightness in Luis's chest returned, squeezing the air from his lungs. Struggling to breathe, he slid closer to Pablo's window to see through the gray mist. After several tense seconds, he returned to his former position. "It's only a shadow. Yes, it looks like a man, but it's not. You need glasses."

"But I saw him move. He walked—"

"*Glasses.*"

Pablo folded his arms around his chest and his bottom lip jutted out.

After their breath had fogged the windshield completely, Luis said, "Okay, let's go."

11. Use side rails to get into truck bed. Don't leave footprints on wet ground.

Stepping onto slick side rails, they climbed into the cargo area. The men stood on either side of the rug, staring down at it expectantly as if it might suggest how best to move it.

"Did he tell you who's in the rug?" Pablo asked. "Do you know? What did he do wrong?"

"Don't know. Don't care," Luis said. "Let's lift it."

Crouching down, they tried to lift the carpet, but discovered it was too heavy to pick up. The long downpour had soaked it for several hours after they took it from the mansion to hide it until nightfall in the woods. Now, filled with both water and a body, the dead weight stuck to the truck bed as if glued. After minutes of futile strain, both of them were breathing heavily. They sat across from each other on the sides of the truck bed to catch their breath.

"The goddamn thing won't budge," Pablo said. He straightened and put a hand on his back.

Luis struggled for air. "Give me a minute." He realized that he had unintentionally reverted to English and returned to their native Spanish. There was too much at stake to trust Pablo's rudimentary English skills. "Let me think."

"Maybe we drop the tailgate, go real fast, hit the brakes, and let it slide out the back."

"That wouldn't make it slide out. It'd come forward if it moved at all."

"I mean *real* fast."

Combing his fingers through his thick black hair several times, Luis tried to focus his thoughts.

A nighthawk's nasal *peent* came from a leafless tree. Pablo pulled at his collar to shield himself from the rain now reduced to drizzle. "I'm cold."

The muffled snap of a wet branch silenced the bird as a nocturnal creature moved toward them through the undergrowth. Pablo turned to survey the dark terrain behind him and grabbed the knife in his pocket.

Luis glanced up. "Stop looking around! There's no one out here. *Focus.* If dumping a body was easy, he would've hired children, not us. We've got to open the rug and pull him out. There's no other choice."

Pablo put his hands up fingers spread apart, to emphasize his opposition to the idea. "No. I told you. I'm not risking that. You get cursed if you touch a dead person who didn't have last rites, and you become the next to die, *damned for eternity.*"

"That's a superstition."

"No, it's not. *It's true.* The old men in my village said the curse can follow you for years. But when it tracks you down—you're dead, just like that." Pablo snapped his fingers. "No, I won't do it. I respect the dead." He made the sign of the cross.

"Those old men were just . . ." He needed a new approach. "Then what do you suggest?"

"We drop the tailgate, go fast, and hit the brakes."

Luis released a long sigh and became quiet. Storm water cascaded through the large ditch beside them and the echo of a diesel truck floated through the trees from the highway. Considering the problem of unloading their freight, he bit his bottom lip in concentration. Finally, he got down by the carpet and tried to ignore the cold metal floor soaking his clothes in rainwater. He burrowed his arm underneath the rug. This close to the rug, he could see stubborn traces of sawdust still lodged in the weave of the braided rug despite the rain. "Get on the opposite side, facing me, and push your arm underneath it—hurry."

"What does that do?"

"Just do it . . . *Quick.*"

Pablo took his time stretching beside the rug and then strained to get his arm under the dead weight.

"Okay, on the count of three lean up."

"What?"

"Look at me. Do as I do."

"What are you going to do?"

"*For God's sake,* just follow me."

Luis bent at the waist like a lever, and the rug rose. Pablo, on the other side, got the idea. Miraculously, they achieved a seated position with the carpet on their shoulders. Pablo looked as if he had learned the secret to walking on water.

"It works," Pablo said.

"Thank Archimedes."

"Who?"

"Now let's stand up," Luis said.

That portion of the miracle did not work as well. Luis was almost to his feet, but then fell hard, landing on his knees and crying out in pain.

Pablo couldn't make it to his feet and remained seated.

The carpet on his shoulder, Luis shuffled on his knees to his left, agonizing with each small sidestep. "Slide to the side of the pickup and we'll dump it over."

"But if we go fast—"

"Move!" Luis barked. The heavy pressure on his knees became

unbearable and he flung the carpet toward the trench with a loud grunt of effort.

Pablo saw it flying at him too late.

The airborne rug pushed Pablo toward the truck wall, coming to a stop when his neck struck its curved edge with a resounding thud. The carpet roll bent around the boy's head. Luis pushed the floor covering off Pablo and it fell over the side.

Collapsing on the truck floor, Pablo cradled his neck with his hands, and curled his body into a ball. "My neck is broken . . . My neck—*bro-ken!*"

Luis stood and saw blood through a ripped pant leg. "*Shit.* These were new." He glared at Pablo and his hand slashed through the rain in frustration. "Don't be a baby. If you broke your neck you'd be paralyzed. We can't stay here." Luis limped to the side of the truck and slid down to the side rail.

Pablo tilted his head up. "Is my nose bleeding?"

"No! Get up now—or I'll drop the tailgate, go real fast, hit the brakes, and let you shoot out on the highway." He got behind the steering wheel and slammed the truck door.

Once inside the cab, Pablo's fingers sought the bridge of his nose. "How long before they find the rug?"

"Who knows? But when they do, the Hayslip paper will have more than the latest soybean prices on the front page."

As they drove off, their numbered plan was folded neatly on the seat between them.

13. Cover the rug in brush or trash. Hide it completely.

2

THE BOY KING

JOHN RILEY HUBBARD SAT on an old Harvester tractor listening to the slow grinding of the starter. He released the key, leaned back in the seat, and cast a long string of profanities into the frigid morning air, throwing in a couple of boot stomps to make his meaning crystal clear.

When he had finished venting, he sighed and looked into the predawn sky. He was losing whatever advantages his early morning start gave his workday. Successful farming was as much about timing as it was about rain, and completion of critical work on Hubbard's irrigation depended on the ancient machine performing today as if it was 1980, the year it was manufactured.

His cell phone's sharp ring was jarring. Thrusting his hand into the pocket of his green barn jacket, he tried to mask his annoyance. "Hullo."

The male voice on the line was loud, almost shouting at Hubbard. "Guess what Deputy Pine found in that big ditch that runs through Shanty Town?"

Hubbard felt an unexpected ripple of tension course through him when he heard *Shanty Town*. He didn't recognize the voice immediately, but then he realized that the call's timing provided all the identification he needed. Only the *Boy King*, sometimes known as Tony Andrews, would phone before daybreak, and assume he'd receive a gracious reception.

"Just a minute," Hubbard said. Unwelcome as the interruption was, he had to be courteous; the Boy King's newspaper, owned by the Andrews family for multiple generations, provided one of his two sources of additional income. There were months when one or the other of his two part-time jobs—covering high school games or selling burial insurance—kept the lights on. He was like every other small farmer he knew. He depended on the support of a small paycheck from other sources to keep his farm running.

He leapt off his tractor, landing in one of the shallow pools of standing water that dotted the lawn. Icy water surged through a gash on his leather work boot. Frowning, he picked his right foot up and tried ineffectually to shake the water out. He mouthed a silent 'goddamnit'.

Hubbard pulled the phone away from his ear and took advantage of his lanky frame to make a couple of lengthy strides toward a squat tree stump—a cedar island rising a few inches above the soaked lawn. He climbed on top of the stump and put the phone to his ear, clutching his coat collar to his neck in the surprisingly chilly April morning. Hearing road noise on the line, Hubbard guessed Andrews was calling from his Suburban's speaker phone.

"Er, say again? What did Eddie find?"

"Dep-uty Pine," the Boy King said.

"Yes, Dep-uty Pine." Eddie Pine comprised exactly half of Hayslip's thin blue line; Sheriff Toil was the other half.

There was a pause in the story, possibly a dramatic flourish meant to provide significance to whatever was to follow.

"Deputy Pine found a body." The Boy King's high-spirited voice made it sound as if Deputy Pine discovered Blackbeard's treasure chest. "He was on patrol overnight and on his way home when—"

"On his way home?" Hubbard said. "That's not on—"

The Boy King charged on. "Sheriff Toil's there now—*right now*. Anyway, it gets better."

"Better?"

"The dude, the body, uh, the *victim*—that's the word—was murdered. Straight up! Shot with a shotgun. Both barrels! He was wrapped up in an old rug and tossed into the ditch. This could be the White River Killer?"

There was a hint of a question tacked on to the Boy King's excited speculation, as if he were market testing how an unlikely connection to the White River Killer might play among the readers of *The Hayslip Union Democrat*.

"The White River Killer?" Hubbard said, trying to discern the Boy King's reason for making a wild connection to a serial killer presumed to be dead for almost a decade. He then braced himself for the news that someone from Hayslip had been murdered. "Who was it? Someone from town? Who?"

"What! Do you think I'd get this pumped if someone I knew had been murdered? Am I like that? Am I? Tell me. Am I?" People in town said Andrews had two speeds: high or low. Obviously he was in high mode today.

Hubbard lied. "No. No, of course not." As the sky brightened, he could dimly see the expanse of his bare acreage, seemingly begging for his attention.

"This is *so* big," the Boy King continued with undiminished zeal. "The victim was a college student from UA Monticello—apparently an Arab. The kid's wallet was filled with Arab stuff, writing and such. Just about nothing in English 'cept his driver's license and student ID. Anyhow, we're lucky today's Monday. We could get it in the paper this week if we start right away."

There was one place Hubbard knew he would not be visiting this morning—Shanty Town. When he was twelve, he spent an entire summer stalking ghosts supposedly haunting those abandoned shacks. Unfortunately, his youthful quest didn't turn out the way he expected. At the bitter close of that miserable season, he swore he'd never go near those hovels again.

The Boy King spat out an order. "Pull to the side, jerk wad!"

Taken aback by the command, Hubbard realized belatedly that

Andrews was talking to another vehicle on the highway. He heard the SUV's big engine whine and assumed the Boy King was passing the slower-moving car.

As the motor noise decreased, Andrews restarted the conversation so casually it was as if he hadn't left it. "So, how 'bout it? This is front page material."

"Isn't there someone else you can send out for this? I'm really—"

"The *Union Democrat* is a lean, mean machine. I've got eight stringers. Three didn't answer their phones, Mary Bernhart claimed she had the flu and had a hundred and one fever, Tomlinson said he was still in mourning for his wife—Did something happen to his wife?—and the rest said they had to get their kids off to school. Everyone just thinks about their own needs, it's so disappointing. You're my only hope."

"I'm sorry, I just can't. March was just too warm and wet this year and I'm way behind. Rupert told me the other day that he's got his tomatoes in the ground, while I got a few hundred *Pink Lady* seedlings in my hot house that have yet to see dirt. There's no way."

"I see. And how much work are you getting done in the mud today? Not much, I'd guess."

Hubbard's tractor was at his right—a study in still life. "Well, I'm looking at my tractor right now."

"Okay, I'll add forty to your usual fee; that makes it almost two hundred! Just like a day at the Farmers' Market, only less work." It was typical of Andrews to pull out his wallet to win a disagreement. The Boy King used money like a sledgehammer, smashing anything in his way.

"Look, I'm just a guy who makes extra money as a high school sports reporter for a small town weekly. I don't know anything about covering a murder. Give me a Timberjack's basketball game and I'm your guy."

"John Riley, this happened in our town. All I need is forty column inches . . . Oh, I see what this is about. I'll go a full two hundred dollars. Cash."

"*Cash?*" Hubbard was startled by the unexpected offer. Cash was good; the amount would almost cover the delinquent electric bill.

The Boy King pounced on the opening. "Yeah, cash. I don't like to pay off the books, but for this . . ."

Hubbard was quiet, thinking about tractor repair expenses, child support, and every other bill stacked on his kitchen table.

"It's important to keep the town informed," the Boy King said. "Do you know how many years it's been since we've had a murder in Hayslip?"

Hubbard's voice turned cold. "Yeah. I remember."

The Boy King stammered, "Oh God. I'm um, a, sorry. I wasn't meaning to . . . I wasn't referring to . . ."

On the line, Hubbard heard brakes squeal and then the repetitive thumps that sounded like the ones created by a highway rumble strip. Andrews screamed like a teen actress in a slasher flick. Next, tires screeched across wet asphalt. Whatever was happening, the Boy King was not in control of the huge SUV. How fast was the idiot going?

Andrews cried out a rapid-fire mantra. "Oh, God. Oh, God. Oh, God. Get-outta-the-way. Get-outta-the-way."

A new threat barged into the sound mix—an air horn blaring on a diesel rig.

Hubbard was blind to what was going on, but tried to help by throwing out advice for every driving emergency he could envision. "Ease off your brakes! Don't over-correct. Keep your wheels straight! Get back in your lane."

The big truck's horn became deafening, blotting out everything else. Hubbard squeezed his eyes shut, steeled for the carnage. He pulled the phone a few inches away from his ear, his pulse racing.

Unexpectedly, the air horn's roar peaked and diminished. Its confrontational blast downgraded into a rude insult as it trailed away.

The previous commotion faded and Hubbard heard the Suburban's tires crunch over the gravel on the highway shoulder and come to a stop. He realized he'd been holding his breath. He inhaled with relief, stepped off the tree stump and squished across the grass.

After another moment, the Boy King came back on the line. "Are you still there? Can you believe that guy? What was he thinking? He could have gotten us both killed. Some drivers just can't think fast. Just a minute . . ." There were more sounds of unknown things being jostled about in the cabin.

"Well, this sucks. I dropped my coffee and it spilled over everything. That damn poultry truck came within inches of hitting me. But get this: just as we passed, I looked up onto that trucker's red face peering down at me. I could tell he was yelling something—but, you know, by then it was too late for his apology—that doesn't help anyone. What I need is for that fool trucker to take driving lessons before he kills somebody."

"I think you've hit the nail right on the head." Hubbard said, hoping his sarcasm went undetected. "And why are you out on the road so early this treacherous morning?"

"Highway Commission meeting."

Hubbard started to laugh at the absurdity, but with effort caught himself. "Well, that's a coincidence. By the way, was there a vote on the interstate extension?"

Andrews's chuckle sounded forced. "Um, no, but I keep pitching. Never give up."

It was a lame effort at positive thinking. The Boy King's three-year term on the commission was due to end, which meant the new roadway wasn't going to happen. *Hayslip can't catch a break.*

"So, what about it, Hubbard? Can you help me out? Isn't this what I pay you to do?" There was a note of undisguised frustration in Andrew's voice.

Hubbard pulled his ball cap down toward his eyes. He couldn't afford to lose this job. He'd have to find a way to handle his Shanty Town memories and not let his life spin out of control.

"Okay. For a full two hundred and fifty dollars, I'll do my part. I'd hate to let you down."

"What? Two hundred and fifty? It wasn't a double homicide, just a single."

Hubbard and Andrews were silent on the line.

"Okay." Andrews gave in. "Sometimes you're just like your uncle R.J."

Hubbard frowned in the emerging daylight. Was Andrews dragging his uncle into the conversation to goad him? "Thanks, but I'm nothing like my uncle," Hubbard said. "Oh, and cash, right?"

"Yes. Cash. Two hundred and fifty dollars. I got it. Do you usually demand unmarked, non-sequential bills? You'll have to excuse the question; it's the first time I've been blackmailed."

"A personal check is fine. I trust you."

"Hmm."

"Any other thing you want?" Hubbard asked. He looked down, his other boot leaked, too. He shook his head in resignation.

"Focus on the White River Killer angle. It's a natural. And get plenty of photos. Hurry, they're waiting on you."

"They're waiting on me? You want photos of a dead body in the *Union Democrat?* And what about the *White River Killer?* Why do you think—? Hello?"

The Boy King was gone. Hubbard pulled the phone from his ear, looked at its blank screen and returned it to his pocket. He glanced up at the pink-blue sky, took a deep breath and slowly released it.

Shanty Town . . . Two years of sobriety . . . I'm so screwed.

3

BIG FISH ON SMALL RIVERS

THERE WAS NO TIME TO WASTE if Hubbard was going to arrive at the crime scene before the state police got there and shut out the press. Why was Andrews taking this story on? Usually, Mrs. Welsh doled out the assignments. He dashed through his house, grabbing a camera bag and notebook. Returning to Shanty Town after all these years seemed so goddamned unreal.

He stepped onto his front porch, pulled off his damp baseball cap and shielded his eyes from the bright sunlight. Minutes before, the sun had been peeking over the horizon. Now it was resting on the treetops.

Once underway, the truck flew down the highway toward the two rows of desolate wooden shacks. Leaving the two-lane, he followed an unpaved route through a line of pine trees and across a small pasture.

He eventually came to the first of several ancient cabins. Except for scattered patches of faded paint still clinging to its rough siding, it was the color of kindling with a roof of rusted tin. His childhood memories were nothing like the landscape today. Surrounding acreage, last cultivated during a long-ago summer, had devolved into feral wilderness. Scrub trees, kudzu vines, and thorn-covered brush tracked and pulled at the ruins, slowly devouring them.

At the end of the lane, he spotted Sheriff Toil and Eddie, his young deputy, at the top of a slight rise. Their hands stuffed into their coat pockets, they stared into the drainage channel that eventually emptied into the White River. Toil was wearing a regulation uniform, but Eddie had on a hunter's orange-colored jacket.

Toil turned when he heard Hubbard's truck. For a moment, Toil was transformed in Hubbard's imagination into old Sheriff Conklin, waiting on the Hubbard family car as it approached on a mid-summer day. Hubbard shook his head to clear it. *Different time, different dirt road, different murder.*

Hubbard gave a cursory wave to the policemen when they looked up, and then reached for his camera bag, reproaching himself for still hauling his father's old Nikon along with the newspaper's camera. *Carrying his old camera doesn't get it fixed.* But somehow, having it with him, like his old tractor, kept a connection to his father alive. He got out of the truck.

Sheriff Toil was a middle-aged man with a receding hairline and an expanding waist. Eddie Pine was twenty years old, a recent escapee from high school, rail-thin, with red hair that couldn't be tamed. Both men held these undemanding law enforcement jobs in Hayslip because the town's lenient work schedules allowed them spare time to run their small farms.

"John Riley Hubbard, what're you doing here?" Eddie made it sound as if they had just bumped into each other walking along the beach at Gulf Shores.

Sheriff Toil's head tilted back and his lips compressed with sudden concern. Based on his earlier conversation with Andrews, Hubbard surmised that Toil had pocketed a nice finder's fee for calling this in. Evidently, he had not considered how he would explain Hubbard's unexpected appearance.

That presented a problem. Toil probably held off calling the state police too. The sheriff was engaging in unethical behavior, even for

Hayslip. And how exactly was Hubbard to explain his arrival? The justification, "Just driving by" didn't seem convincing for this remote location. Andrews should have warned him.

Hubbard gave Eddie a slight punch on the arm. "Hey, Eddie, it's good to see you, man."

"I saw your uncle R.J. at the Hunter's Den the other day," Eddie said. "He was buying a whole bunch of stuff. Is he going huntin'?"

Hubbard shrugged his shoulders. "I don't know. We don't talk much."

"He was at Rotary on Tuesday," Toil added.

Hubbard's uncle was a man who never went unnoticed. The standard conversation opener, at least to his nephew, seemed to always include a recent sighting of R.J., no matter how insignificant—walking down the street, washing his car—nothing escaped comment.

Eddie glanced down at Hubbard's writing pad and camera. "How did you hear about us finding a body?"

Hubbard looked to Toil for help, but the sheriff refused to meet his gaze.

"I thought you wrote only about high school games."

"Timberjack games and uh, major crimes. Both topics." *Please drop this.*

Eddie's brow furrowed as if he was trying to solve a complex math problem. "Only me, the sheriff, and the state police know about the murder."

Hubbard's mind raced. Eddie wouldn't stop until he came up with some explanation, no matter how lame. For a moment his mind was blank, and then he saw a way out. "Oh, *well,* I have a police scanner. You just can't stand on your heels in the news business, you know." He sounded like Clark Kent. He hoped Eddie wouldn't ask him why a part-time, high school sports reporter was so dedicated that he listened to a police scanner at the break of day.

Now it was Eddie who looked concerned. "Did you have your scanner on a week ago Monday night, a little after midnight?"

Hubbard turned to the sheriff, who was staring intently at the tops of his shoes. He glanced back at the deputy. "Last week? Monday night? No. Why? Something happen?"

Eddie's smile vanished—a rare event. "No. Nothing happened. Not a thing. Just wondered."

Eddie walked a few dejected steps away before bending down to scoop up a small stone, which he chucked into the air.

What the hell happened last week? thought Hubbard.

With Eddie out of earshot, Hubbard looked at Toil and turned his hands up. He whispered. "You could have warned me ahead of time that I needed to come up with a story."

Toil cleared his throat. "Don't get mad . . ."

Hubbard sighed. "I'm not like that anymore." *Will the town ever let it go?* "I just wished you said something."

Toil's head bent. "I didn't think it through . . . If you're going to get any shots, you better start now. When the state police arrive, they'll chase you out of here and confiscate the paper's camera to prevent unauthorized photos in the media. And the way Connors operates, you'll probably never get it back."

"Okay, okay," Hubbard said. "Let me get a shot of you boys in front of the ditch."

"Hurry," Toil said.

Hubbard arranged both men in front of the channel. He glanced toward the highway, expecting each cool breeze to carry the wail of an approaching police siren. Hubbard raised the camera and sized them up in the screen. He lowered the camera.

"You know, Eddie, I think smiling for the camera is the wrong choice right now."

Toil glared at Eddie, who immediately dropped his grin. Hubbard snapped a photo and reviewed it. Now the lawmen looked unnaturally dour, like suspects caught at the scene.

"Do you guys have the *Do Not Cross* tape they use on cop shows on TV? If you guys could hold on to it at each end, I can get a shot of it with the ditch just beyond."

"Okay," Eddie said.

"Yeah," Toil said, "but we left the tape back at the office. Oh, we've used it a couple of times, but the state police think we always do it wrong. There doesn't seem to be much point in going to the trouble." Toil's words barely concealed his bitterness. He used his right thumb and forefinger to squeeze the bridge of his nose.

"Are you okay, Sheriff?" Hubbard asked.

Toil waved the question away. "Yeah, I'm okay. I'm just tired, but I got to be ready for Sergeant Connors."

Toil and the state police were engaged in a never-ending battle for mutual respect. Hubbard heard stories about the conflict in town, but this was the first time he'd seen it played out in person. Toil, who'd recently replaced Sheriff Conklin, had scant background in law enforcement. He'd served in the Army's military police decades ago, but only took the low-paying job for the extra cash he needed to keep his farm running. No one else had applied for the job.

Time was running out for Hubbard. He wheeled in a tight circle and took photos of the sheriff's truck, the road, the nearest tin-roofed shanty, the rough terrain, and a blurred photo of Eddie walking to his car.

Hubbard didn't want to do it. But he'd been ordered to get a shot of the body. "Okay so, I guess the body's in the ditch?"

Hubbard fiddled with the paper's digital camera while Eddie walked toward the ditch in advance of them like a tour guide. He made a broad sweep of his arm. "Right this way."

They followed behind him like tourists. There was a long carpet roll that rose above the top of the ditch at one end, while the other end sloped downward. At the lower end, a body had slid out. It was gruesome.

The moment felt too familiar. *Different year . . .*

Below them in the mud was the body of a young man wearing an expensive-looking blue suit, white shirt, and a red-patterned tie. There was a rough crater of dried blood and bone in the center of his chest. The bottom half of his tie was missing below the gaping hole. A lock of black hair curled across his forehead like a comma. Hubbard took a breath, trying to keep his nausea at bay.

There was a moment of quiet as storm water at the bottom of the ditch worked its way to the White River. Several footprints in the mud surrounded the floor covering, probably made by Eddie or Toil, opening the carpet upon its discovery and then returning it to an approximation of its original, rolled-up state. If the state police, coming from Monticello, knew what was happening to their crime scene, they would be speeding here with the same urgency as Pony Express riders of the Old West.

Hubbard fired off three photos of the carpet roll and murder victim, although he couldn't imagine the graphic shot finding a spot in the local paper. Mrs. Welsh, the editor, wouldn't allow it. She was the only one in town who could tell the Boy King "no" and make it stick.

Eddie ran back to his car to answer a radio call.

"How long before they get here?" Hubbard asked.

Toil checked his watch. "Any minute I guess." He rubbed his eyes with the back of his right hand.

"Any idea how long he's been dead?"

"Eddie didn't think he's been out here very long by the looks of him," Toil said. "No more than a day. Killed yesterday morning? Um, Sunday morning? Yeah—Sunday."

"Okay, so how did Eddie stumble on this?"

"He was uh, on patrol," Toil said. It was a lie and the sheriff didn't sell it well.

Hubbard raised an eyebrow in disbelief—Eddie wasn't on patrol among a bunch of abandoned shacks. But Toil didn't flinch, so he let it pass.

Eddie finished his call and trotted up to them.

Toil said, "Was that anything?"

"Nah. Somebody reported that a couple of drunk Mexicans got into some kind of scrap on Main Street last night. No one was reported hurt."

Toil shook his head with a resigned air. "Well, we'll look into it after this. Probably kids raising some hell. But if they were illegals in a scrap, we'll never hear from them." Toil turned to his deputy.

"Eddie, we've got to find those Mexicans working the still in the deer woods."

Eddie nodded, but shrugged as if the moonshiners were the phantoms of the forest.

Hubbard recalled Andrews's serial killer theory. He looked down at the carpet roll. He knew that Andrews wanted him to check out his ridiculous theory, and he reminded himself he was being paid to do so. Was there a way to ask the question and not sound half-witted? He came up empty.

"So, ah, do you think it's the work of The White River Killer?"

Sheriff Toil looked at him and blinked several times as if he was having trouble understanding the question.

Eddie's forehead furrowed like a field of freshly planted corn and he looked down at the brown braided carpet like he had never seen one before.

"Th—The White . . . River Killer?" Toil asked.

"The rug's wet 'cause it was raining last night," Eddie said. "I don't think it were in no river."

Toil shook his head. "The White River Killer's victims were all young women. They were strangled, cut up, and shoved into some kind of plastic bags used in hospitals. They found those bags scattered along the banks of the White River up around Pine Bluff." He pointed at the carpet roll with the detached air of a college professor. "Our victim is a dude who was put down with a shotgun. He was wrapped in a carpet with all his body parts still attached and tossed into a ditch."

"In Hayslip, not Pine Bluff," Eddie said, finishing the mercy killing of the lame theory. "But if you drive ten minutes or thereabouts, you could get to our neck of the White River," the deputy added the last part with southern diplomacy.

The sheriff ignored Eddie and examined Hubbard intently. "The crimes are nothing alike. Why do you think the White River Killer did this?"

"Yeah, I know. It looks unrelated." Hubbard paused. "And how do you know the victim is a student at Monticello College, an Arab?"

Eddie perked up. "How'd *you* know he were a student?"

"I . . . uh, heard it on the scanner."

Eddie's brow creased, probably trying to imagine a radio call providing so much information.

Toil pulled a wallet from his coat pocket. "Eddie got his ID when he discovered the body."

Toil flipped it open. It was thick with credit cards and cash, a student identification card, and miscellaneous papers with Arabic writing. The young man's name was Amir Abadi. His driver's license indicated he lived off-campus in Monticello. Hubbard recognized the address as being in an area where large homes were being renovated into high-end duplexes.

In the ID photo, Abadi displayed a shy smile and wore a yellow polo shirt. His brown eyes were directed away from the camera; eyebrows raised in amusement, as if someone were trying to steal his attention. Hubbard spotted the date on the license. It was issued in May of the previous year. He was twenty-one years old. *He was just a kid . . . just a damn kid.*

Eddie looked toward the highway. "What's taking the state police so long? This is a crazy-long time to wait, even for them."

Toil avoided eye contact with Eddie. "Well, there were certain delays in contacting them."

"There were?" Eddie asked. His brow creased and his eyes shifted back and forth between Toil and Hubbard as if he suspected there was something going on that he wasn't privy to.

Hubbard looked at the two policemen-farmers. They weren't going to solve anything. Neither were the state police—crimes in rural and poor southeast Arkansas didn't get the same focus as those committed in the more metropolitan central or northwest Arkansas. The killer would get away with dumping the body here and just walking away.

Hubbard's father's murderer did the same walk eighteen years ago. It was the summer that Hubbard turned twelve.

On the rare occasions old Sheriff Conklin agreed to discuss the killing with Hubbard, the grizzled lawman said he believed the killer was a local. Only someone from Hayslip could find the remote location and also know that Frank Hubbard would be there alone. Conklin was so sure of his theory he passed his certainty on to Frank Hubbard's son. Hubbard never let it rest. For years, he pestered Conklin about the investigation or called the state police in Monticello, sometimes continuing all the way up the chain of command to Little Rock, trying to ensure that his father's case was not forgotten.

Hubbard told himself he'd know the killer's identity one day. In his dreams, he saw it play out. He would surprise the murderer, kill him, and leave him where he fell.

Some nights, the dark expectation of vengeance was all he had inside him. As he neared thirty, with so many years elapsed, even that hope was fading.

Police sirens were barely audible in the distance.

Toil looked at Hubbard. "You'd better get out of here."

The sheriff turned north, in the direction of the highway. The view of the distant two-lane blacktop was obstructed by undergrowth and a thick line of pines. In unison, their heads tracked the wail of police sirens as they approached on their left, and continued past the approximate point where the caravan should have turned, and followed them as they sped on, sirens fading in the west.

Toil sighed loudly, "So much for GPS. Eddie, go up to the highway and guide them in. I'll get on the radio and let those idiots know they missed the turn."

Eddie ran to his patrol car and headed for the highway. Toil went to his vehicle to get on the radio.

Taking the opportunity to return to his truck, Hubbard knew he should be driving away now. It would be the sensible thing. He grabbed his camera bag, but paused to think about what he was doing. He wanted to see—no, *had* to see—how the state police would handle the murder investigation. He couldn't leave here without knowing that justice would be done. He glanced at Toil talking on the radio to the police caravan. The officer took a deep drag from a cigarette that curled upward from the grip of his index finger. Dark circles under the sheriff's eyes revealed his fatigue. *Why are you doing this job?*

Hubbard returned the camera bag back to the truck. He would stay and risk the consequences.

After a few minutes passed, Eddie had the state police approaching. Hubbard joined Toil and they walked closer to the road.

Toil jabbed his thumb toward the ditch behind them. "You know, we get one week of training each summer to do this, just one damn week each year, to prepare us for that." He took a deep breath, but released it in a shallow smoker's cough. He looked directly at Hubbard, but struggled to find the words. "I'm so goddamn tired . . . Every night, I work under the lights in my fields past midnight, and then I can't fall asleep when I get to bed . . . The next morning I'm back doing this. I can't think straight anymore. But if I'm going to keep my farm . . ."

Toil faced Hubbard. "How did Conklin do it? He was sheriff for decades and kept working his farm the whole time. Before he died, he saved enough money to become part-owner of a radio station. How? How does that happen? What was his secret?"

"I don't know," Hubbard said. "Times were different."

Toil's expression turned sour, as if he taken a bite from a lemon. "Yeah that's it—times were different. I can't wait until the geniuses at the state police arrive . . . Please, don't tell them your theory about the White River Killer. You don't want to mess with Sergeant Connors."

Eddie's patrol car, followed by several state police vehicles, rounded the final bend. Their sirens, jarring on a normal day, were more like a sense memory from the past.

The shriek was chilling.

Toil's voice rose in volume to compete with the clamor from the police caravan. "Connors better not make me look like a fool in front of those damn troopers of his again. I've had it. If he pushes me too far about how Eddie and I handled this, well, you just watch what I do."

Hubbard's mouth parted in surprise.

Toil pointed, as if he was marking a spot on the ground in front of them. "Right here, right now, I'll clean his clock in front of God and everybody." Toil chuckled with anticipation and pressed his right fist into his hand.

Hubbard glanced in the direction of the approaching sirens.

I'm standing next to a redneck that doesn't have a clue about the trouble he's about to make for himself.

4

YOUR STATE TAX DOLLARS AT WORK

SIRENS BLISTERED THE AIR as three white state police sedans, a black coroner's van, and Eddie's tan police cruiser crawled toward the crime scene, slowed by the bumpy, pockmarked road. For some reason, Eddie had added his own vehicle's siren to the din. Hubbard hoped the deputy was displaying a previously unnoted sense of black humor. But most likely, Eddie was taking advantage of a rare opportunity to drive with it blasting loud enough to blow the bark off trees. Since other troopers were using their sirens, he could use his without fear of being rebuked by the sheriff. Hubbard covered his ears. Toil appeared immune to the pandemonium.

The procession fell silent as it rolled to a standstill. Troopers, technicians, and Eddie jumped out of their vehicles, grabbed equipment, and marched briskly up the rocky grade to the drainage channel. The uniformed group hesitated at the top of the modest slope, turning to look down at the only police car still occupied.

Hubbard regarded the unmoving team. "What are they waiting for?"

Toil followed Hubbard's gaze. "I expect Connors treats them just like us. Dammed if they proceed without his blessing, and cursed if they wait for his instructions."

Hubbard put his hand on Toil's shoulder, trying to find a way to steer Toil away from a confrontation he would surely lose. "I don't think it's a good idea to start a dust-up with the sergeant. He'd slap cuffs on you so quick that . . ."

Toil's eyes were focused on the narrow road. "Just look at him— Princess-Sergeant of the State Police," he sneered.

Hubbard looked down the hill at the patrol car. So far, the pace of the investigation was providing little reassurance that things would change once the professionals arrived. Sgt. Connors's placid features gave the impression he didn't have a care in the world as he reviewed papers on a clipboard, taking time to rub his chin in slow reflection. At last, he pulled a microphone close to his mouth. His thick Delta drawl echoed through the air, relayed by every radio on the road. "Show us, ten-six, at location. I don't have an address. Last mile-marker was one-four-eight."

"Ten-four," a garbled female voice responded through static.

Hubbard continued observing the officer, fascinated by the man's self-absorption when a dozen lawmen were waiting on him to begin a murder investigation. In this moment of suspended activity, a purple martin announced its spring arrival at the top of a scraggily oak tree, a surreal opposition to the body in the ditch.

Connors came to life and reached across the seat to grab his "Smokey" hat. His foot pushed his car door open, and he stepped onto the road. Connors stood just over six feet, almost Hubbard's size. In a ceremonial manner worthy of a Japanese admiral, he placed his hat like a crown atop his blond crew cut. Next, he adjusted the Sam Browne belt across his barrel chest. When he was done, he looked up. The members of his team waited expectantly, like hunting dogs straining upon the leash.

"Don't stand around!" Connors snapped. "You know what you gotta do. Get goin'!"

The assembled troopers scattered to begin their work. Hubbard smiled as even Eddie sprang to attention, walking first one way and then another before slowing to a reluctant stop, a ship without a port. He stood uneasily with his hands at his side, strumming both sets of fingers against his legs, searching for some way to contribute.

Connors approached Toil and Hubbard with the grace of a bull-dozer, stomping his way up the hill toward them. "So, this is Shanty Shacks?"

"Shanty Town," Toil said.

Connors shook his head and rolled his eyes. "*Whatever.* After all the stories I've heard, I was expectin' something more. What's the matter, Sheriff? Did the spooks take one look at you and fly off?" He noticed Hubbard. "Toil, I see you're expandin' the Hayslip Crime Busters Squad."

Surprised, Toil looked at Hubbard and turned back to Connors. The sheriff began to correct him, but the trooper didn't wait for his response.

"Well, let's see what you screwed up." Connors headed for the ditch.

It took a moment for Hubbard to understand why Connors thought he was Toil's second deputy. He glanced at Eddie who was wearing a non-regulation winter coat over his khaki shirt and badge. Eddie also had on blue jeans and boots, making him look similar to Hubbard in a superficial review. Toil's badge was attached to his city-issued heavy coat. Both men probably left their police hats in their vehicles. The informality of the Hayslip law enforcement dress code was helping Hubbard slip underneath state police radar.

Toil shrugged. "Let him think what he wants." The sheriff swung on his heel and followed Connors to the channel, folding his arms across his chest. With each step forward, Toil and Connors edged away from each other.

Hubbard followed several paces behind them, marveling at the apparent tension. He began to scribble notes as he followed.

At the rim of the ditch, several technicians were at work taking photos, starting on their reports and engaging in a variety of myste-rious measurements. They had already inserted tiny red flags into the ground, forming a Lilliputian barrier around the body.

Connors glowered down at footprints in the mud surrounding the carpet roll. "Did my people do that?"

A young technician stood up. "No, sir. We've taken photos and we're planning on making casings of those footprints."

Eddie saw his opening into the investigation. He came up behind Hubbard and pointed to the incriminating tracks. "Those are our footprints. There weren't any footprints when I found the body . . . Honest." Eddie sounded like a little boy explaining where he was when the cookie jar was robbed.

"Ooo-kay," Sgt. Connors said. "It appears like you boys had a dance lesson down there. You learnin' swing dance, Deputy? Tell me, Sheriff, what part about securin' the crime scene do you not understand?"

The words shot out of Toil's mouth like bullets. "Eddie didn't know it was a crime scene until he opened the rug and saw the body. Exactly how was he supposed to get down there without using his feet? Fly?" Toil folded his arms.

Hubbard turned to look behind him and tried to imagine Eddie's patrol car on the road. How did Eddie spot the small part of the nondescript carpet that was visible? This was not adding up. He looked at the other troopers. No one seemed to be interested in the bickering between the two men. *Maybe they've seen Connors in action too many times.*

Connors flicked a hand in Toil's direction like he was sweeping crumbs off a table. "Deputy, what was it about this rug that made you want to get out of your vehicle and open it up?"

"I thought I could use it," Eddie said meekly. "You know, at home."

"This filthy thing?" Connors asked. "You were going to put this piece of shit in your home?"

Eddie's ears glowed crimson. "Well, I was going to soap it down in the car wash. I bet it cleans up real good."

"Yeah, if your home's at the trash dump," Connors said.

Eddie looked down at the ground and slunk away from Connors like a frightened cat.

Toil's right hand balled into a fist.

Hubbard noted Toil's reaction. He shook his head. *Don't do it.*

Pacing back and forth, the sergeant monitored the team's work. He stopped, taking a long look at the body. *"Jesus.* How close does a shotgun need to be to make that tight of an entry wound?"

An older man with gray-streaked hair and a black windbreaker with the word "Coroner" applied to its back stood, his hand pressed against his back. He was so portly that he couldn't close the jacket around his mid-section. "Point blank. No more than an inch away. I've seen people killed by shotguns, but not once when the killer pressed two barrels right up to the victim's chest and let him have it. And I've been doing this for thirty years."

The heavy-set man began changing into a new pair of latex gloves.

"So, what do you—" Connors's question was interrupted by a call on his radio. He returned to his car.

Hubbard felt a palpable decrease in the tension among the team of troopers when Connors was gone. Toil and Eddie were called away to provide statements to a trooper making notes on a clipboard. Hubbard looked down at the coroner; he was examining some substance between his thumb and index finger before sealing it in a plastic bag. He handed it to a younger technician with a bad case of acne, who was probably his assistant. "Number it and write in the notes 'gathered from quadrant one of the rug'."

The assistant nodded and took the sample.

Hubbard couldn't contain his curiosity. "What was that?" He called down to the coroner.

The coroner didn't look up. "Sawdust. Doesn't look like pine. I'll find out later. Traces of it are all over the rug. I guess some of it was too deeply embedded to get washed off by the rain."

"Was this a suicide?"

The coroner took his time before looking up at Hubbard and seemed to be evaluating him. Evidentially, Hubbard passed inspection because he answered the question. "You can't commit suicide with a shotgun. The barrel's too long. Your fingers can't reach the trigger on the gun. You can do it if the barrel's sawed off or you remove a shoe and use your toe to pull the trigger, but . . ." He indicated the Arab's—Abadi's—two dress shoes. "And after you kill yourself, you don't wrap yourself up in a rug and drive to . . . whatever you call this place."

"Yeah, good point" Hubbard grimaced at his dumb question. "It's called Shanty Town, by the way."

The coroner nodded and surveyed the abandoned shacks on the road. "Uh, yeah, I can see why."

Hubbard forced himself to examine the corpse. Amir Abadi's hands were professionally manicured and looked unmarked. "But it's a natural reaction to push a shotgun away before it gets anywhere near your chest, to fight like hell to survive. Was he unconscious? Were his hands tied?"

"No marks or other indication that his hands were restrained. He could have been drugged. We'll check for that. But I can tell from the entry wound he was standing. And he stayed upright for at least two heartbeats after he was shot and then he just fell backward like a cut tree. There's a significant contusion on the back of his head."

"Was he hit?"

"Nope—it was made by a fall. His head landed on something hard—like concrete. I might be able to pick up a trace of what he hit when I put him up on the rack at my shop."

"Up on a rack?" This all seemed more like an exercise in record keeping than a true investigation.

The coroner waved his hand. "Not really, just my way of talking . . . Yep, I'm guessing he stood there for a moment with one hell of a surprised look on his face. A shotgun only knocks you down in the movies. Two faltering heartbeats and he tipped over like a giant redwood—dead."

"How do you know it was only two heartbeats?"

"Thirty years' experience." The coroner arched his eyebrow. "You got thirty years to spare? Jump down here and I'll tell you all I know about corpses."

"No offense. Just curious."

The coroner nodded. "We're all new once, but this is the last question. After the heart stops beating, you stop bleeding. You drain out some, but the amount of blood and its trail is different. A wound of this size would've created a gusher of blood—if he had lived long." The coroner pointed at Amir Abadi's chest. "See how it's a tight semi-circle, with stuff that looks like wet mud? Most of the blood you see beneath the wound is just drainage."

Hubbard felt his stomach turn over. He took a deep breath.

The old man had his second pair of gloves on. "Yep, I've seen more blood than the Red Cross." He seemed amused by his own joke. "It talks to me."

It was a struggle to stay, but Hubbard needed to know that this investigation would lead somewhere. "Does it give you an idea about who the murderer was?"

The coroner's face lost any trace of humor. He glanced at the corpse and then back to Hubbard. "Yeah, it does. It tells me that the murderer must be one sick, smooth-talking son-of-a-bitch. I think he somehow conned this boy into not defending himself."

Looking at the corpse was beginning to drain Hubbard.

You okay, kid?" the coroner asked.

"Sure. Thanks for the info," Hubbard said. He left the water conduit, taking deep breaths. The memory of another blood stain, the one on his father's blue denim shirt seventeen years ago, invaded his thoughts. Hubbard leaned over, putting his hands on his knees, trying to breathe.

Things were quiet on the hill while Connors was gone and the crew worked in peace. Upon returning, however, he resumed his routine of criticizing his team's performance.

Eddie continued to try to help the technicians, only to be shooed away each time. Toil remained on the sidelines, glowering at Connors. Hubbard hadn't met Sgt. Connors until this morning, but his own animosity toward the man had risen as quickly as an August thermometer. The lead trooper was not only baiting Toil and Eddie, but also members of his team. Protected by his rank and uniform, he was nothing but a bully.

Hubbard was too aware of his own weaknesses to not realize his precarious position here. When someone pushed him, he always pushed back. It was only a matter of time before Connors tried something with him. He was turning his life around, and didn't want it to take a detour here. He made his first step to leave when Connors decided to return to his performance.

Connors looked like a one-man parade as he swaggered across the length of the marked area. "Boys, this has been another outstanding performance by the Hayslip Police Department. This crime scene is so corrupted by the locals, if we found a written confession from the killer it wouldn't hold up in court."

Toil's head jerked backward, as if he had taken a blow straight to the chin.

If the other troopers found the sergeant funny, they didn't react. Hubbard could see their sideward glances but none of them looked up. He was surprised to discover that his right hand had become a fist of its own volition.

"I think this here mess calls for a contest. The man who can list the most procedure violations made by the locals wins a free breakfast at City Café. Sheriff Toil here will be our impartial judge."

"You goddamn son-of-a-bitch," Toil roared back. "Why don't you come over here and say that to me?"

The crew stopped their work, and stood to witness the altercation. None of the troopers interceded, probably hoping the sheriff would land a lucky punch on their boss. Eddie's mouth fell open and he looked to Hubbard for his help.

Hubbard shrugged his shoulders. *What do you want me to do?* he mouthed.

Eddie tilted his head and his eyes turned doleful like a beagle in distress and he mouthed back *please*.

Hubbard's brow furrowed. The deputy must think Hubbard had some of his uncle's magic ability to order people around, but his first instinct was only to insert himself into this fight—which would only serve to land him in jail.

Ten or fifteen years younger than Toil, Connors didn't seem to have any reservations about using the out-of-shape sheriff as a punching bag. The son-of-a-bitch was closing in on the sheriff with a challenging, sadistic grin. After the fight was over, the state police version of events would become the official account. Connors's team might hate him, but they wouldn't contradict his story to avoid the taint of perceived disloyalty and ostracism from their fellow state troopers. Any conflicting testimony offered by the locals, Eddie and Hubbard, would be ignored as biased. Toil couldn't win this battle. He would be finished as sheriff and might end up spending time in jail.

Think of something.

Perhaps a different target for Connors's ridicule would do the trick? He couldn't believe he was about to utter these words:

"So, Sergeant, do you think the White River Killer was behind this? Should the paper warn the folks in Hayslip that a serial killer is on the loose?"

Hubbard knew this was not the smooth conflict resolution that Eddie was expecting, but it was the best he could come up with. The deputy swung his arms back and forth in front of his chest, waving Hubbard off. Toil's shoulders flew up as if a bucket of cold water had been dumped on him. The local lawmen had warned him not to mention the White River Killer theory to Connors, but Hubbard thought the idea was bizarre enough to disrupt the encounter. He was right.

Connors turned back, a sour expression on his face, to examine Hubbard. "The White River Killer? And I thought it was Jack the Ripper all this time." He glanced at Toil. "I should have known one of your deputies would crack the case. Toil, how long has *this idiot* worked for you?"

"He's not my deputy," Toil said.

"Then who is he?"

"He's a reporter," Eddie said.

Connors's face twisted as if he wanted to spit out the words. "A reporter! Jesus. What the hell is a reporter doing here? How did somebody from the Little Rock media get here before we did?"

"Not Little Rock; the *Hayslip Union Democrat*," Hubbard said.

Connors shook his head in confusion. "The—The weekly shopper?"

"No, it's a real newspaper," Eddie said. "They've got stories on anniversaries, high school sports, spelling bees, crop reports, and more."

Hubbard offered the sergeant a pleasant half-smile, but he was burning inside. "Even better, every story is written on the sixth-grade level—you'd like it." *Settle down. Two years. Don't throw it away.*

The sergeant's back straightened and the belt tightened across his chest. "Boy, how'd you like to spend tonight in county lockup?"

On the other side of the road, doves rose from their hiding place in the tall grass and took flight.

"Connors, have you met *R.J. Hubbard's* nephew?" Toil interjected. He enunciated R.J.'s name carefully as if he was talking to a foreigner. "This is John Riley Hubbard," he concluded, his head tilted toward Hubbard.

"What? Who? Ah . . . um." Connors looked pained, as if he had just brushed against an electric cattle fence. "Mr. Hubbard is your uncle? Hubbard Farms? . . . Um . . . respectfully, I'll have to ask you to leave."

The troopers and technicians masked their smiles. Only the old coroner, standing by the body, laughed outright.

Connors stared at his crew, and they made a quick show of their intense concentration on their tasks. The coroner kept his smile; arms folded in relaxation. The old guy continued to stand there, as relaxed as a man standing at the ocean shore, until the sergeant gave up trying to stare him down and he returned to his work.

Connors angled his head toward the ground, closed his eyes, jaw muscles visibly twitching. He raised his head and opened his eyes a second later, forcing a smile to appear on his face. "Nice guy, Mr. Hubbard. Nice guy. I helped him with that trouble he had with his girlfriend."

Hubbard's brow furrowed. "What trouble? . . . What girlfriend?"

Connors grimaced and looked at Toil. Toil bent down and energetically plucked the tops off tall weeds as if he had just been appointed the official gardener of Shanty Town. Eddie spun on his heel and left to pull up a section of tape that had fallen down.

Connors held up the index finger on his right hand. "Um, wait, I got that wrong. I was thinking about another Hubbard down in Pine Bluff."

There was a long awkward pause. The convenient Hubbard in Pine Bluff sounded like a lie. So what if his uncle had girlfriend troubles? What's the big deal? How could Connors help with that? Hubbard sighed. Why would they think he was interested in any of this?

The whine of a diesel truck echoed up from the interstate. Connors's eyes seared at Hubbard from under the bill of his hat.

"I've got everything I need," Hubbard said. "I guess I'll be going."

He'd only made it a few steps when Eddie called out to him. "All the *Do Not Cross* tapes are up, if you want to get some more photos before you leave."

"Eddie. *Oh, Eddie.*" Toil rubbed his forehead and then looked up at the sky. His tone reflected a disappointment going all the way down to the bone.

Eddie bit his lower lip.

"Photos?" Connors almost choked on the word, but it had the same effect as spurs on his sides. "Hubbard! Stop right there. You can't leave here with that camera."

"Eddie, step this way." Toil gestured for Eddie to follow him. They walked a short distance and then huddled together, heads bowed, Toil's hand gripping Eddie's coat lapel.

Hubbard pressed the outside pocket on his coat as he pleaded. "Sergeant, I really need these photos. Andrews specifically asked me—"

"Corporal Thomas, will you come here?" Connors called. His eyes bore into Hubbard.

The corporal trotted up.

"Yes, Sergeant Connors?"

"Stay with me. I may need a witness on this. I want this to go by the book."

"Yes, sir."

The two troopers approached him, Connors in the lead. "Young Mr. Hubbard, you have taken unauthorized photos of a crime scene and I am confiscating your camera in accordance with Arkansas state law. Please surrender it now, or face the consequences."

"Can't we talk about this?" Hubbard pleaded. "I need these shots. I can't give them up." His hand remained on his coat pocket.

"Mr. Hubbard, you leave me no choice but—"

"Okay, okay, okay," Hubbard said, reaching into his coat. "Don't get excited. Here it is."

Hubbard handed the camera to Connors, who tossed it to Thomas. He began to pat down Hubbard's other pockets. The sergeant pulled out Hubbard's notes, extra batteries, and a second lens. He glanced at them and handed them back.

"Empty your front pockets."

With an exasperated sigh, Hubbard drew out the contents: a set of keys, a white handkerchief, and a pocket knife. He displayed them in both hands.

"If that knife was a couple inches longer, I could arrest you for carrying a concealed weapon," Connors said.

"That's good to know."

Connors chin raised a notch. "Thank you, *young Mr. Hubbard*. I hope you have a very nice day. Tell your uncle that you'll get it back at the end of the investigation." Connors took Hubbard's camera from Thomas. "You can leave now."

Hubbard remained there for a moment and then walked to his truck, shoulders lowered. He kicked the mud off his boots, got behind the wheel, nodded to Toil and Eddie, tried to suppress a smile, and drove away.

Eddie turned back to the sheriff, shaking his head, keeping his voice low. "Why did Hubbard provoke Sergeant Connors? That's risky business."

Toil was surprised that Eddie didn't see it. "The way he handled himself, did he remind you of anyone just now?"

Eddie shook his head. "You mean like on TV?"

"Blood will tell, Eddie," Toil said. "At the end of the day, blood will tell."

"Whose blood? I don't get it."

Toil sighed. "Okay. Ask the other troopers if they need anything from us and let's get out of here." While Eddie made the rounds, Toil watched Connors high step back to his crew. The capture of Hubbard's camera seemed to inflate the trooper's ego to the size of a Macy's parade balloon. His chest was extended, and his walk was a bantam strut. "And that's how you deal with rich boys. Did y'all see him run with his tail between his legs?" He raised Hubbard's camera above his head like it was his trophy. "Too bad he had to leave his camera behind. I hope we don't lose it."

Connors lowered the camera and turned to the sheriff. "Toil, you and Hubbard should've known better than to try a stunt like this on me. I may not be able to prove it, but I know you tipped Hubbard off." Connors twisted the lens back and forth as if he was trying to crack open a safe.

"Hey, don't break the camera," Toil said, trying to grab it from Connors. "It's not a toy."

"Can't the Hayslip paper get something better than an old Nikon?" Connors peered through the viewfinder. "It may have been something in its day, but film cameras are obso—"

"You should see the other camera he used," Eddie said. "It's digital and got all the bells and whistles. I saw the picture he took of us. We looked sharp!"

"Oh, Eddie," Toil moaned. "Can't you just shut up for once? Just once?"

"What do you mean?" Connors said. "This *is* Hubbard's camera.

This is the one he . . . gave me . . ." He lowered the Nikon to his side.

A technician behind Connors whispered something. Several other troopers turned away, their backs trembling with suppressed laughter.

Connors face turned red. He took a few paces, stopped, and hurled the camera like a fast ball toward a large rock standing a few yards from the ditch. The camera shell shattered on impact, throwing bits of casing and broken lens glass in all directions. The back cover sprang open, tossing a yellow film roll onto the ground.

"No one plays the Arkansas State Police like that. I don't care what his last name is. I'm gonna make the *young Mr. Hubbard* regret the day he tried to make a fool out of the law."

Toil snorted. "The law? I don't think *the law* looked like a fool."

Several troopers laughed outright, ignoring Connors's glare.

As the laughter died down, everyone's eyes were drawn to the scattered remains of the old Nikon and one yellow film canister.

5

BROKEN AND ENTERED

START. STOP. START. STOP. Damn these school buses. Hubbard's hands gripped the steering wheel, his index fingers tapping away to release pent-up frustration. Each of his attempts to pass the lumbering yellow transports that were clogging 281 was thwarted by heavy morning traffic. His eyes traveled restlessly from the road, to the side view mirror, and back again, expecting to see a state police cruiser's blue lights any moment.

How long before Sgt. Connors uncovered his bait-and-switch? Seeing an opening, he gunned the truck's V-8, waving to the children in the bus windows as he passed

Finally reaching town, Hubbard turned onto Main Street and headed for the town square which consisted of an expanse of clover-filled lawn with a small concrete pad hosting a granite memorial to Hayslip's fallen and a couple of park benches. The Hayslip business district surrounded the green space, looking much as it did mid-century, when Hayslip proclaimed itself the "Tomato Capital of the World."

Main Street split off into a circuit around the square. Hubbard slowed for several City Café customers who had stopped to greet friends in the middle of the street. Reluctantly, they moved to the sidewalk. He made quick turns around the square and parked in front of the *Hayslip Union Democrat* offices. He retrieved the digital camera from the bag and got out of the truck.

Most of the businesses on the square were yet to open, but he knew he could rely on the formidable Mrs. Welsh, his former English teacher, now grandly-titled as the Editor-in-Chief of the *Union Democrat,* to be at work. When Hubbard tried the front door he found it unlocked as he expected.

Buoyed by his successful arrival with the photos, Hubbard breezed into the office, camera in hand. "I'm here!" he called out, as if he was the last arrival at a party coming to a boil.

Just beyond the bunker-like sales counter at the entrance, Mrs. Welsh was sitting at her desk, which was surrounded by eight smaller desks. All the other work stations were unoccupied. The oak office furniture, small and utilitarian, combined with the pressed tin ceiling, gave the workplace the Spartan feel of a 1920s operation. The plaster walls of the large room were lined with framed *Union Democrat* front pages from the past—last year's flood, bumper crops, twenty-pound tomatoes, and President Franklin Roosevelt's motorcade driving past Hayslip on his way to Louisiana in 1936.

Mrs. Welsh glanced up from her computer and examined Hubbard over the top of black-framed glasses. She slowly twisted around to check the time on the wall clock behind her and then back to Hubbard. "Are you just getting here?" she asked, in a manner that could be interpreted several different ways. Was she tepidly welcoming him? Incredulous that he might have been in the office before this moment without her noticing him? Or hinting subtly at his unaccountable tardiness?

Probably all three, Hubbard decided, as he nodded and said. "Yes, ma'am."

She leaned forward and commenced a series of pointed questions. "You know Mr. Andrews would like to include your story in the paper—for this week? *Not* next week? *And* today is Monday? *And* our deadline to send your story to complete the paper's layout is noon today? Those young men who are waiting in India for your story have only so much time to lay out the paper before they have to e-mail their files to the Little Rock printer. Then the printer has to meet the mail drop deadline. Everything depends on you finishing this story in a timely manner. *You know that.*"

"Yes, ma'am."

"Is your story done?"

"No, ma'am."

"Then how do you plan to submit your assignment?"

"Don't we have until the noon deadline?"

"*I* have until noon, yes. You do not."

"Yes, ma'am."

"Brinkmanship, Mr. Hubbard. Haven't I cautioned you about brinkmanship?"

"Yes, many times. Don't worry; I can knock something out fast. So here's the camera. Can you download the photos and see if I got anything you like?"

"Yes, yes, yes," she replied in an irritated voice. Her attitude seemed to indicate that she doubted finding anything acceptable.

Hubbard glanced toward the rear of the building where Andrews's office was situated. The Boy King's executive space bore no resemblance to a place where work was actually done. The walls showcased bizarre tribal masks, meant to scare evil spirits, that he had purchased during a trip to Africa. The globe-trotting Andrews never sought out the typical tourist destinations. After a trip to the Amazon, Andrews once whispered that he had learned the "how to" of making shrunken heads and other lost arts from the "holy man" of a river tribe. Hubbard refused the offer to view his examples. Andrew's interest in the macabre might explain his hope that the recent murder had some connection to the White River Killer.

"Did the Boy King make it to the highway commission meeting in one piece?"

"Please, don't call Mr. Andrews that. He knows everyone uses that hateful term behind his back. Please remember, words can hurt."

Hubbard recalled the same three-word slogan on a poster hanging in her classroom years ago. "Yes, I'm sorry. I should be more thoughtful."

"What did he tell you about the meeting?" Her brows knitted in casual interest, but her voice lowered like they were sharing a secret.

"Nothing. Why? Just that he had a meeting."

"Oh, only that." Mrs. Welsh nodded. "He's going through so much right now. At the very moment when he was going to prove to that family of his . . ." She connected the camera to her computer, shaking her head.

"What's his big problem? Does one of his race horses have a cough?" Hubbard said.

"Shouldn't you be writing your story?"

In was a mystery how the erratic Andrews found a tender spot in the heart of the invulnerable Mrs. Welsh. Perhaps it was because Andrews needed her continual supervision to be a fully functional adult and she never lost her love of teaching. Whatever the reason, they had a very unique relationship that resembled a stern mother and her wayward son.

"Did the state police tell you they had any leads at this point?"

Hubbard shook his head and flipped open his notes. At the top of the first page was Amir's address. "I don't have a lot of hope in those guys in the Smokey hats—especially Sergeant Connors—"

"Sergeant Connors! *Oh no, not him.* Why did they ever give that awful man a badge?"

"I don't know. Anyway, the victim wasn't from around here so there won't be any locals nipping at their heels to keep the case open. They've got too many open cases in Pine Bluff; I think they'll just finish their work here and work the local cases that will keep everyone happy."

Mrs. Welsh took his arm and tried to turn him toward a computer. "Well, when you finish your job, everyone will be happy with you too."

Hubbard took a step and stopped as a bitter realization crashed down on him. Why was he complaining about the state police and Sgt. Connors? He didn't want to do any more work than they did—

just the minimum and collect a paycheck. *If he cranked this article out like a Timberjacks' game summary, he'd be no better than any of them.* Years ago, the state police blew off his father's death despite Hubbard's relentless badgering for justice. It couldn't happen again. He raised the notebook and looked at Amir's address once more.

He made a decision.

"Well, just a couple of things you need to know, Mrs. Welsh. The state police may be barging into this office in the next few minutes to confiscate the camera you're holding—" Hubbard raised his hand to calm her. "Everything's okay. There's just something about news-paper photos and crime scenes that don't play nice. If you want to have any pictures in the paper, you mustn't dawdle getting them downloaded."

"I never dawdle," Mrs. Welsh said, although she quickened her efforts. "Dawdling slows the mental faculties. I don't know why we want to waste the entire front page on a dead body in Shanty Town. Someone should burn those filthy buildings to the ground. They're empty and nothing but a breeding ground for snakes, rats, and disease."

Hubbard nodded. "Yeah, good idea—I wouldn't object to seeing them burn." He headed for the door.

"Where are you going?"

"That's the second thing. I have to make one more stop before I can write the article."

Mrs. Welsh's voice rose sharply in surprise. "*What's that?* I thought you were fully prepared."

"Um, no, I have to go the victim's apartment. See if there's a next-of-kin and get a statement. You know, the Boy . . . um . . . *our Tony* is always interested in the human angle."

"But he didn't say anything about—"

"Now, isn't that just like him?" Hubbard waved goodbye to a confused Mrs. Welsh. He let the door bang shut behind him. As he walked away, he thought he heard her muffled voice: "brinkman-ship."

Why was he doing this? He sighed in frustration.

Even if you somehow catch the killer, even if you lynch him from the war memorial in the town square for all to see, it won't change the past. No ripples of justice traveling backward through time to make things right. The dark corners never go away. Grow the hell up.

Hubbard exited Main Street and was quickly on his way to Monticello. Unlike 281, the road to Monticello was an undivided four-lane. Hubbard interpreted the speed limit as a mere proposal for consideration. Barreling down the highway, he skidded to another frustrating delay when traffic stopped to allow a highway department gravel truck drop its load. Hubbard glanced at his Timex. *Will Connors be as late to the victim's home as he was to the crime scene?* Less than a minute later, he was waved through.

He passed through a cleared right of way, which extended on either side of the Monticello highway as far as the eye could see. Designated as the route for the future extension of the Pine Bluff interstate, it perpetually waited for state funding to be completed. If this road project was finished, it would reverse Hayslip's fortunes. The town was situated at the mid-point of the nascent route, and would reap an economic windfall from new restaurants, hotels, and other retail businesses.

Andrews's appointment to the state highway commission, almost three years ago, had been Hayslip's best hope for shifting the gears of the commission from park and into drive and getting the new route to Shreveport, Louisiana, constructed finally. The Boy King's term on the state board was coming to an end, and as he had told Hubbard on the phone this morning, he was "still pitching" in his efforts to get the project going.

Hubbard was forced to slow as he approached Monticello's town square. Amir lived on West Fifth Street, a right turn at the end of the square. Hubbard pulled onto a street of refurbished Victorian homes, all freshly painted, displaying lush lawns thanks to automatic sprinkler systems at work despite the recent rain. If the college student was living here, he must have come from a wealthy family. Saudi Arabian oil money? Kuwait?

Hubbard cruised by the front of Amir's building, a dusty red-

and-cream frame residence with a large turret—a former mansion now finding new life as expensive apartments. He scanned the street and driveway for police cars or the vehicles of possible tenants in the house. He couldn't spot any sign of movement along the row of large homes basking in the morning sun.

At the corner, he turned and parked a short distance down the block. He got out of his truck and checked the address in his notes. Since the home was a duplex, the entrance to Amir's apartment, "B", would be probably at the rear or side of the house. Hubbard walked down the narrow alleyway that split the block lengthwise.

The dark rose turret of Amir's Victorian home became visible over the top of the brick privacy fence to his right. The back gate was unlocked. He hesitated, looking around at the multiple rear windows of the surrounding houses to see if anyone was watching from any of them. He knew that he would look plenty suspicious to any neighbor peeking at him from behind a curtain. He took a deep breath and pushed open the gate.

Once he entered, things weren't as simple as he hoped. There were more entrances into the house than he anticipated. Two un-marked doors were at the rear of the house, opening to a large wooden deck that extended the length of the structure. These doors weren't identified in any way and didn't seem to be intended as primary entrances. Hubbard strode to the side of the residence near-est the driveway. He saw a door with a mailbox marked "C" next to it. No luck. He retraced his steps, glancing furtively at the windows of the surrounding Victorian homes and went behind the house to the other side, where he found another entrance with a mailbox marked "B".

Splintered wood surrounded the door handle and frame, and a small pile of ragged wood chips spread across the door mat. Above the mat, the round lock had been crudely pried off. He paused four feet away from the door and surveyed the area. *A break-in?* He ex-amined the front of the mahogany door and pushed his hair off his forehead.

Okay. How long ago did Toil say the murder occurred? A day? Yesterday morning?

It was unlikely the murderer still would be here. If Amir had roommates, it was impossible to imagine they didn't notice this. Most likely, Amir lived alone. The apartment was empty. This was a high risk opportunity. With the state police absent, and the door busted, he could snoop around inside and see . . . what? Hubbard couldn't come up with what might reasonably be in there, but still, it was too tempting.

Of course, there was also another possibility; his speculation was wrong in its entirety. He could traipse blindly inside, be discovered by someone residing in Amir's apartment, and be shot dead as an intruder. There were no legal consequences for shooting anyone breaking into your home under Arkansas law.

He took five steps backward to get a better view of the backyard. The four stalls in the remodeled garage were vacant. He checked his watch. The morning was burning away. The street was quiet. Residents were probably at work or in classes at the college. He returned to the door. He rationalized, Amir's main entrance wasn't properly shut, almost open. *Can't leave it like that.*

He tapped the door with his boot, it held, so he tapped it again, harder this time and it swung open. *See, almost open.* He glanced nervously toward the street. Anyone would stop and helpfully secure a neighbor's open door. *It's an act of courtesy.*

He remained on the stoop and leaned his shoulder against the door frame so he could get a better view of the interior. The luxurious residence had an open floor plan. To the left was a high-tech kitchen, and just beyond was a well-appointed dining room. The dining table held a translucent blue vase that contained fresh flowers. The beautiful arrangement reflected the artful efforts of a florist, not a grocery store. Did Amir have a girlfriend? The walls held several oversized photos, expensively framed and matted, close-ups of wild flowers and a stunning image of a river that looked a lot like the White at morning. A silvery mist hovered eerily above the water.

Hubbard took in as much as he could. He hadn't tried to envision Amir's living conditions before now, other than the crude furniture of a college dorm. But if he had, it certainly would not have been this grand style. Who was this guy?

Then Hubbard saw something that looked out of place. Resting on the thick beige carpet that began on the other side of the kitchen's tile floor was a small white rectangle. The arctic white paper looked like the back side of a photograph. The possibility of seeing the image was tempting. Hubbard listened intently for any sound of human activity in the house. Nothing.

He should leave. Obviously, there would be no one here to interview. This could be the murder scene. Or, could it? The older homes were all packed together. Large homes built on narrow lots. The discharge from a double-barrel shotgun wouldn't go unnoticed like the relative quiet of his door lock being pried off did. After hearing the thunderous discharge of a gunshot, the tenants in the house or the neighbors would jump up and call 9-1-1.

He looked back at the bright rectangle floating starkly atop the beige rug. It seemed to beckon him.

Four steps away? Just four steps, take a quick glance at it and four steps out. Perhaps it's just a piece of paper. No, it's not. It's a photo.

"Hello," he called to anyone who might be inside, "I noticed your door was open." Don't shoot, he wanted to add. Without more thought, he took five steps, not four, to reach the white rectangle. He was correct. It was a photo of three costumed girls at a Halloween or New Year's Eve party. The trio assumed the "Charlie's Angels" pose, holding imaginary guns for whoever held the camera—Amir? It looked like a typical sorority party: raucous, drunken. The girls were pretty, but all wore neon-bright colored wigs, flapper styled, making it difficult to differentiate their faces. Once again, Amir was not living a life Hubbard would have predicted.

Above him, the second floor groaned softly. His eyes shot up toward the ceiling. He stood motionless for several breathless seconds and listened, biting his lower lip in concentration. *How would I explain my presence here?* Older homes often made noises. Perhaps there was someone in one of the other units? He slipped the photo into his pocket.

A wave of cool air blew against the back of his neck. His left arm rose in defense, and he spun around in time to see the unit's back door, which he now saw led to the outside deck, slam against the wall of the apartment. He shook his head wryly. Apparently, the door hadn't been properly latched. He stepped to the door, and in order to avoid leaving fingerprints, he used his elbow to knock it closed. He leaned back against it until it clicked shut, and he sighed in relief. From this new vantage point, he could see stairs at the far end of the apartment. *This is a two story apartment?* Then his eyes were drawn to the floor.

About four feet to his left, near the dining table; three boxes crammed with photos, photo albums, at least two cameras and a Mac computer were all thrown together in a sloppy rush. He considered the boxes. Were they left behind during the break-in? He tried to imagine what might have happened here. Perhaps Amir interrupted this burglary and—

Hubbard jumped away from the door. The sound of approaching footsteps on the wooden deck was as startling as it was distinct. Were the state police here? No deafening sirens filled the air, and those guys probably used them for a doughnut run. His pulse quickened in realization as he glanced back at the boxes. He was wrong. The containers hadn't been placed there a day ago.

The break-in is still going on.

He turned to leave by the door he came in from, but stopped. *Are you going to run? Let him get away with it?* The familiar rage returned, undiminished by time. He lowered into a crouch, his eyes focused on the door. This would be just another fight, he assured himself, and he knew how those worked. He would take that son-of-a-bitch's shotgun and twist it around his neck like a noose. Amir would have justice, unlike his father. His heart raced as his focus narrowed on the brass doorknob as it twisted ineffectually back and forth. The knob stopped moving, and the door creaked as the man leaned his weight into it. It wouldn't be long before the door gave way, but the element of surprise was on Hubbard's side.

"Open up." It was a man's voice, filled with frustration.

Who is he talking to? Hubbard suddenly remembered the creak of the floorboards on the second floor of the apartment. *Oh, shit—*

The apartment's back door shifted sideways and the floor bent. His knees buckled as the room tilted up as if he was on a ship cresting a wave during a storm.

He opened his eyes, not remembering closing them. No longer focused on the door of the apartment, he inspected the carpet at close range. The lush pile was difficult to see, even though it was no farther away than the end of his nose. His bruised head throbbed. What the hell hit him? *Who* the hell hit him? The rest of his body was like a lead weight, dumb to his commands to rise. What was that irritating noise? Either his head was buzzing, or it was the wail of approaching police sirens. And who was talking? It sounded like the man on the other side of the door, speaking Spanish in a whispered rush.

Hubbard's Spanish was rusty at the best of times. He was so much stronger in French after years of study. *C'mon, speak French,* he thought groggily. *Parlez- vous Francais?*

He caught a Spanish word he understood—*matale.*

"Kill him," the man said.

6

THE FIVE WS AND HOW

SPRAWLED OUT ON THE FLOOR of Amir's apartment, Hubbard's haze cleared as he felt a cool spring breeze blowing through the open back door. Outside, multiple police sirens peaked in decibels and then fell silent. Their ear-splitting approach had scared the intruders off, likely saving his life. A jolt of adrenaline surged through his body as he realized the troopers might find him at a second crime scene. Damage to the front door clearly signaled a break in—an offense that Sgt. Connors would be happy to charge him with.

He moved one limb at a time until he made it to a seated position. He rose unsteadily to his feet. The open door at the rear of the apartment led to the deck and revealed the two thugs' escape route into the backyard. Hubbard used it for the same purpose.

As he stepped onto the deck, Hubbard discovered a trail of photos, scattered across the lawn like fat breadcrumbs, the farthest near the back gate. He ignored the ache at the back of his skull and made it as quickly as he could to the alley. Here the incriminating line of photos evaporated. No one was in sight.

Why would the thieves steal photo prints when there were things of real value all through the place? He looked down at the last of the fallen images—yet another eight-by-ten-inch shot of an empty, weedy field. At the right top corner of the photo, someone had written *NW32* in blue ink.

Hubbard recalled the professional camera lens on the dining room table in the apartment. *Why was Amir taking photos of empty fields? And who would want them this badly?*

Hubbard peered back around the fence toward the Victorian. There was no activity inside or around the house that he could see. Where were the troopers? *Of course—they're waiting on Connors, just like last time.* Support for his assumption came from a new siren, approaching from the west. Sgt. Connors's vehicle arriving finally from Hayslip. Hubbard pictured a group of cops and technicians, impatiently standing at the front of the house, waiting for Connor's barked approval to begin their work. He hoped they wouldn't find any evidence of his presence. They shouldn't—he had left everything as he found it. Hubbard gingerly touched the blood-matted hair on the back of his head as he hurried back to his truck. The troopers might not notice his pickup down the block immediately, but given time . . .

He took Second Avenue to get to the highway to ensure that he didn't pass Connors on the way back. Once the siren faded, he got back on the main road to Hayslip.

Hubbard glanced at the clock on the dashboard. It was past ten o'clock. The sun dominated the sky, quickly heating the day. Bright sunlight reflected off the road and he blinked in pain, flipping down the windshield visor. Sweat trickled down the side of his face; his head throbbed. He shrugged off his coat but as soon as he threw it to the back seat, his cell phone, still in a coat pocket, rang. It had to be Mrs. Welsh, reminding him of the perils of brinkmanship. He reached back for it, continuing to steer with his free hand.

"Don't worry. I'm on my way—"

"Mr. Hubbard? This is Mrs. Fincher," the elderly voice quivered on the line.

Hubbard's heart sank. *Not today.*

"Hello, Mrs. Fincher. It's odd that you called—I'm coming back from Monticello and I just passed the road to your place."

"Oh, perhaps you could turn in on your way. I may be coming into some money to start my insurance back up." Her voice was hopeful.

There was an extended back and forth as Hubbard gently explained why he couldn't see her now. He didn't know if she fully understood his explanations, but in the end, they had set up a time to meet to discuss her burial insurance. Hubbard reminded her to write their appointment down on the pad by her wall phone and then he hung up.

It wasn't as easy to find a parking spot on the square as it had been earlier. Hubbard drummed his fingers on the steering wheel impatiently as he waited for a car to pull out from a space in front of the Hayslip municipal building and parked. He jogged across the square to the *Union Democrat* offices, using his right hand to explore a nice-sized bump on the back of his head.

When he entered the news office, his reception was not what he expected. Instead of rising up with panicked recriminations concerning the missed story deadline, Mrs. Welsh slouched low in her chair, an unfamiliar pose for a woman who favored starched white blouses for their professional decorum. She stared despondently at her computer screen, her face a sickly pale.

He walked around the sales counter and approached her with caution. Was this a diabolical guilt-trap?

Mrs. Welsh was the first to speak. "You didn't say the student was A-mir." Her voice broke on his name.

Hubbard crouched down beside her, surprised by the rare show of sentiment. "I'm sorry. I didn't know you knew him."

"He worked on a project for Mrs. Andrews as a photographer. He would come by and wait for his late afternoon meetings with Mrs. Andrews, and then they'd leave to work on their project. She was always late, so we'd talk about photography, flowers, everything. He was a sweet boy, very charming. *Always on time.* Who could do such a thing to him?"

"I don't know."

"We can't run these photos of him. They're all too coarse. He deserves better."

"I understand. I didn't think you would . . . Did he do anything for the paper? I don't remember seeing his name on a photo credit."

"We never used him here at the *Union Democrat*. I think he worked on a brochure for the college or other things. "

"Did Tony know him?"

"Yes, of course. I told you—he did his work for the Andrewses. He was a very talented."

"Yes, he was."

Mrs. Welsh turned to him. "You're familiar with his work?"

"I think I saw some of his photos on the walls of his apartment." Hubbard explained.

Her eyes widened. "You went in?"

"Yes . . . the door was open . . .sort of."

"Did he live with anyone? His girlfriend? He said he found someone, but he couldn't talk about it."

"He may have had one, but I think he lived alone."

Mrs. Welsh turned suddenly toward the wall clock. "Oh, my goodness. The time. The deadline. You'll never make it."

"I write fast."

"No one can write that fast."

"Call your young men in India and tell them we'll be just a little late."

"I simply can't do that. In the ten years I've done this, I've never missed a deadline."

"That's why they'll have no problems waiting for you. It's the first time in ten years."

Mrs. Welsh's shoulders drooped. "Can you get it done by 12:30?"

"12:45."

Mrs. Welsh nodded, spiritless. "Amir was *so young* . . . Well, you have your pick." She indicated the three desks reserved for freelance staff.

Hubbard rose and turned toward the nearest desk.

"My God! What happened?" Mrs. Welsh cried out, rising to her feet.

Hubbard spun back to her. "What?"

"Your head!"

Startled, Hubbard brought both hands up to his face. "What's it doing?"

She spun him around to examine him. "No goose! Your head is bleeding."

"Oh, that . . . I . . . I ran into a door."

"Backward?" Mrs. Welsh raised an eyebrow and put her hands on her hips. "Were you fighting again? One day your anger will kill you"

"I'm not that person anymore. I've been peaceful . . . and sober for two years."

"So how did this happen, young man? Something about your uncle again? That's only hateful gossip. Your mother was a fine woman. And your uncle . . . has lots of friends. Pay no mind to small minds."

"It wasn't about my mother, father, *or* uncle. It was nothing like that."

"Well, what was it then? I want the truth."

Hubbard sighed. He gave Mrs. Welsh a quick summary of what happened at the apartment trying to downplay the drama, which proved to be impossible. As she listened, Mrs. Welsh's facial expression degraded from concerned to terrified as she listened to him summarize events at Amir's place. Her obvious distress made Hubbard reflect, for the first time, on how close he had come to a nasty end pursuing a $250 article. "*Kill him*," the man had said. What had possessed him to take that risk? When he finished his tale, he was as disturbed by his foolhardiness as Mrs. Welsh. Embarrassed he had behaved so recklessly, he didn't wait for her to chastise him but went to a computer and logged on.

"What are you doing? You can't write now. You need to go to a doctor right away."

"I'm fine. If I had a nickel for every time I've been hit on the head . . ."

Mrs. Welsh began to wring her hands. "You *must* go to a doctor. You could have a concussion. There might be internal bleeding. Your brain could be swelling as we speak. There's no time to waste.

Why in the next minute, you might fall over dead!" Mrs. Welsh's voice rose with each syllable.

Hubbard was taken aback by Mrs. Welsh's display of raw emotion—probably a side effect of Amir's brutal murder. He shouldn't have let her see the photographs of the body.

"Mrs. Welsh, if this is your idea of a pep talk before I begin writing—it needs work."

Making a sound like an agitated crow, Mrs. Welsh threw up her arms in disgust. "Awwwk! Don't come running to me when your head explodes!"

She stormed off and got on the phone to her young men in India. Hubbard imagined their surprise when they read the grisly story of a murder in a small town paper usually dedicated to golden anniversaries, school lunch menus, and "Sunday School Roundups."

He turned his attention to the blank screen, and fought a wave of anxiety about how to start—never mind finish—this story. He was an amateur. His coverage of local sports was based on a formula he repeated time and again: "Timberjacks Corral Mustangs." But his sports template didn't transfer easily to a murder story: "Local Killer Bests Visiting Arab."

The flashing cursor seemed to taunt him. Mrs. Welsh sat motionless at her desk, waiting for him to start typing. He could sense her eyes on his idle hands, lolling on the keyboard as if his fingers were on summer vacation. An image of the blank front page of the Union Democrat floated through his mind. He had to start writing something—anything. By the time his article appeared mid-week, the murder would have been covered in a variety of news outlets. But *Union Democrat* readers would still be interested in a feature focusing on the local angle that Little Rock media would ignore.

He would begin with whatever came to mind after the fifth blink of the cursor. His words might be schlock, but they would be words.

The countdown began. Five . . . four . . . three . . . two . . . one . . .

Hubbard typed as fast as he could, refusing to stop for either cliché or hyperbole. In spite of the rush, he tried to provide some order by telling the story in a chronological manner. Mrs. Welsh startled him when she came up behind him and began dabbing the back of his head with a swab from a first-aid kit. He plowed on despite the distraction.

Almost an hour later, Hubbard checked the story's word count, and was surprised to find that the end was in sight. But there was no satisfactory ending. Without an arrest, there was no final score.

The second part of this investigative series will appear next week. Why did he write that? Someone else could do the follow up; he had a daughter to think about. He did a spell check. He then sent the article to Mrs. Welsh who was now engrossed in her own project.

"Okay," Hubbard said. Mrs. Welsh's computer pinged. He was surprised that the story's arrival at her computer didn't get a stronger reaction.

She turned to him. "They stole Amir's Rolex."

"They what?"

"Look at this," Mrs. Welsh said pointing to her computer.

Hubbard went to her and bent over her shoulder to see the computer screen. Mrs. Welsh had blown up one of the images, turning it into a close-up of his left arm.

"Amir owned a gold Rolex. It was his pride and joy. It's gone."

Hubbard inspected the photo. Amir's shirt and suit cuff had risen up revealing a slight tan line by the wrist. But no watch.

"Nice job Mrs. Welsh. It's odd though; Sheriff Toil showed me money that was still in his wallet. Why not steal it all?"

"Some people can't pass up the prestige that comes from showing off an expensive watch."

"Maybe—but I don't think this was a robbery. Someone put a shotgun against Amir's chest and pulled the trigger. A thief carrying a shotgun as his weapon of choice is hard to imagine. And if the guys who broke into Amir's place were part of this, why were they interested in his photographs?"

Mrs. Welsh suddenly stood up. "The deadline."

In a flurry of activity, she printed out the article and retrieved her red pencil. As she read the article she peppered Hubbard with comments and questions.

"You make Sheriff Toil and Eddie sound like Batman and Robin."

"That's called the home team advantage. Everyone likes to root for the locals.

She frowned. "And did that nasty sergeant from the state police really say, 'Another outstanding job by the Hayslip Police Department.' That doesn't sound like him."

"It's a direct quote. He said it front of about twelve people," Hubbard said.

"And the state police got lost trying to find Shanty Town? Sergeant Connors is not going to like reading that."

"I'm just a simple reporter trying to serve the public."

After she completed her interrogation, Hubbard was dismissed from duty. When he stepped out to the sidewalk it was almost one p.m. It had been a surreal day, and it was only half complete. Now he was back in the real world, comprised of a broken tractor and tomato plants that still needed to see dirt. Someone else could take it from here. He took a deep breath and released the tension from his shoulders. As he walked across the square, he gazed into a beautiful blue sky with only a few scattered clouds. The remainder of the day should be straight up from this low point. The worst was over.

His cell phone rang. Hubbard drew the phone from his pocket and looked at the name on the display.

It was his ex-wife.

The sun slid behind a gray cloud.

7

TRUST ME. I KNOW.

THE NAMEPLATE ON THE DESK READ *Dr. Henry Thomas, Neurosurgery*. Inside the private office, R.J. Hubbard, the uncle, some said *notorious* uncle, of John Riley Hubbard, waited patiently in the leather wingback chair across from the surgeon's desk. He could see Thomas through the partially open door as he waved his arms, giving instructions to his staff in the hallway. The doctor snapped at a young nurse, telling her that he had an important meeting with Mr. Hubbard and the patients could wait.

He leaned back in the chair, trying to be patient. His left hand adjusted the crease in his black wool slacks. Satisfied, his hand returned to the arm of the chair and his fingers lightly strummed the burgundy hide. R.J. took great pride in his appearance. He was a striking figure; some people noted that he looked like a 'patriarch' in a Ralph Lauren advertisement.

R.J.'s cell phone rang. This was not a good time, but out of habit, he pulled it out of his tailored tweed jacket and looked at the screen. Juan—one of the few men he trusted and his longest-serving employee. Juan knew where R.J. was and what he was doing. The call had to be important.

R.J. stood and closed the office door. Thomas could wait, just like his patients.

He clicked on the phone. "Yes Juan?" R.J. listened and his day got a little worse—if that was possible. After a moment, he couldn't contain his reaction. "A front page story? Is he crazy? What's Andrews doing? Sheriff Toil called me about finding Abadi's body early this morning. We don't need this now. Andrews doesn't understand what John Riley is like. He never lets go of anything—never— never—never. He'll keep digging . . . He never let up on my brother's murder. The state police said he drives them crazy with questions even now . . . No. I'll handle it. I'll find a way to get my nephew off this—but it won't be easy . . ." R.J. felt the room begin to spin and he sat down in the chair. He took a deep breath, while trying to understand the pampered weasel's motivations. No wonder the Andrews family kept the Boy King out of Little Rock— afraid of what the nut job would do. "He's one weird son-of-a-bitch, but he's a *smart* son-of-a bitch. He's got a reason for playing up this story and I'll figure it out—and when I do . . . Okay, I'll talk to you later. I've got to meet with our little medical miracle, Dr. Thomas."

The muffled buzz of conversation in the hallway continued. The doctor was canceling surgery scheduled for later in the day. Perhaps he was anticipating a conversation that would take a long time? This wouldn't take much time all. R.J. glanced down at the large envelope that he had leaned against the chair leg. Nine years ago, when Thomas was in deep shit, R.J. knew that having a doctor indebted to him would be valuable one day.

The doctor was from Hayslip. It helped that he was aware R.J. Hubbard was a villain of Cain and Abel proportions. Thomas's opinion of R.J., however, hadn't prevented him from requesting aid from the gentleman farmer when he needed to hold on to his medical license. Almost five years earlier, the elder Hubbard entertained Thomas's tearful appeal and mulled it over before offering terms for his help.

Attempting to perform an abortion on your underage girlfriend is never a good idea. Especially one conducted without any medical staff in support. The girl's parents had found out about what the doctor had done and the whole story was heading for the evening news and the prosecuting attorney. Only R.J. Hubbard could stop something like this before it became a media firestorm in Arkansas. In the end the storm passed by, causing no damage. After significant cash gifts from R.J, the girl's parents were placated.

R.J. Hubbard's tarnished reputation never stopped anyone from asking for assistance. Especially when the need was great and the challenge deemed impossible. R.J. helped people he liked all the time at no cost. Those he didn't like, he charged dearly. As repayment for this, he wouldn't take money. Thomas's debt would have a different currency.

One day, and it would be *someday*, he had emphasized to the doctor. He would require a favor from Thomas as compensation. Hubbard didn't know what he would ask for in the future, but it would be significant. When asked, the doctor would do as he requested. Compliance on this point was not discretionary. If Thomas understood the terms of the deal, he'd be fine.

If not . . .

Today was that someday.

There was a knock on the office door.

R.J. shook his head with a muted wry smile—the man was knocking before entering his own office door. "Come in," R.J. said.

Thomas entered and then closed the door. He wore a white lab coat with a stethoscope protruding from his outside pocket. He smiled and opened his mouth like he was going to say something, but seemed to change his mind. He went behind his large desk and sat down. His eyes glanced toward Hubbard, but refused to meet his gaze directly. His hand patted the thinning brown hair on the top of his head nervously. "Mr. Hubbard, would you like some coffee?" Thomas asked.

"No—"

R.J. was interrupted by a stressed conversation taking place just outside the door; a patient was running a high fever.

Thomas stood. "Get away from the door. I'm in conference with Mr. Hubbard." He returned to his seat. "I'm sorry."

The conversation subsided as the women moved down the hallway. The doctor turned back to R.J.

"You have patients waiting on you," R.J. said. He reached down for the envelope. "I'll get to the point. Do you know why I'm here?"

"I—I think so. I know I owe you a lot and—"

"You owe me everything." R.J. pointed to the Oriental rug on the floor, the sailing trophies lining a bookshelf, the photos of Thomas's family. "This office, your lifestyle, your marriage . . . and your freedom."

"I know that. I'm happy to repay you, any amount. Wh—What do you want?"

"A week from this Friday, you are performing surgery on a man with a brain tumor . . ."

"What man?" The doctor flipped opened his laptop and began to frantically scroll through various screens. "Who? I'm a surgeon. I have surgeries every day. I don't know—"

"Don't interrupt."

The apology sounded like it came from a frightened boy. "Sorry." He closed the laptop, returning his focus to R.J.

R.J. paused for dramatic effect. "I will determine the outcome of that surgery."

"The outcome? I don't understand."

"If certain conditions are met, I want you to do the best job you can. Save him if possible."

"Conditions? What conditions?"

Hubbard continued, ignoring Thomas's questions. "And if my conditions are not met, he won't survive the operation."

Thomas's mouth fell open and he pushed himself away from his desk as if it had become toxic.

Hubbard held up a finger in the casual manner of a dog trainer regaining the attention of a border collie. "Don't," he said quietly. "Use the trash can by your desk if you're going to become sick. I'll wait."

"If you're asking me to . . ."

"I'm not asking."

Thomas froze in his chair; his expression looked as if the man was trying to remember how to breathe. Finally, he gathered himself, shaking his head broadly. "It's impossible. The operating room is filled with people; nurses, an anesthesiologist, and techs coming in and out. All of them are watching every move I make. It can't be done. Even if I agreed to such a monstrous thing, it's impossible."

"Not if you plan ahead. Create a distraction and the knife will slip. I know there's a specific nerve cluster in that area of the brain that leads to the heart. I've done my homework."

"There will be an autopsy. I'll be arrested and charged with murder. Don't you see?"

"There won't be an autopsy. It's a risky operation as it is. The family will insist on a quick burial. I've already taken care of that."

"The family knows about this?"

"You know what you need to know."

Thomas became teary-eyed. "What kind of monster are you?"

The side of Hubbard's mouth turned up in a sarcastic grin. "The worst kind. The kind you'll see in your nightmares, if you don't honor our deal. It wouldn't be difficult for me to arrange for all the sordid details surrounding that poor young girl's abortion to see the light of day."

The color drained from Thomas's face. "I'm going to be sick."

"Not yet. Not until we're finished."

"Please, no."

"You don't have a choice. You know that. You know who I am. What I can do. You made this deal with your eyes open."

"Who is it? "Thomas's head bent down, and he pressed his hand against his eyes.

Hubbard remained silent, waiting for Thomas to regain his composure. After a long minute, Thomas looked up. His eyes were red.

"I don't think I can do it." Thomas pleaded.

R.J. noted the change in Thomas's voice. It was the response of a beaten man. This had been surprisingly easy. It was time to ease the man's anguish. "We all do things that we don't think we can do when there's no other choice. Trust me. I know."

"What day is his surgery? I can't remember my schedule. Who is it? Who do you want me to . . . *to kill?*"

Hubbard didn't respond immediately. *There's no other choice.* After a moment, he responded. "Me . . . I guess I need to make an appointment. You'll have to bump a patient to another day."

He handed Thomas the X-rays in the envelope.

Over an hour later, R.J. was in the medical center parking deck searching for his car. His hand raked through his silver hair as he tried to remember; was his Jaguar on the seventh or eighth level? Nothing looked familiar. *Goddamn this thing in his head.*

Thomas reacted as R.J. expected, and the elder Hubbard had his bittersweet victory. There was still more to accomplish, and very little time to do it. He had to close things out.

R.J. strolled down the concrete ramp to the seventh level of the medical center deck. His cell phone rang. He walked to the short exterior wall before answering.

"Hello, this is R.J."

"Oh, I am so glad we finally reached you."

He recognized the warm voice of Carlos Rodriguez's wife. "Hello, Mrs. Carlos. I had my cell turned off for a while. I'm in Little Rock. How can I help you?"

"We had a call from John Riley and we know how you like to be kept up to date. He wants us to find a housekeeper for him. He needs someone to be at his home when his daughter comes home from school and during the summer."

R.J. didn't reply for a moment, trying to absorb the new information. "Emily? She's going to live with him now? My nephew is having a very busy morning."

"I don't know how it happened. He said he just found out. John Riley's very nervous about having her at home. He says he doesn't know what to do with a little girl. He works all the time and he couldn't bear the thought of her coming home to an empty house. He said he did that growing up. Wasn't his mother there after his father died?"

R.J.'s voice became softer, more reflective. "It's . . . complicated. I think I get it now." His attitude became businesslike. "Well, he doesn't understand how expensive it is to have a housekeeper. I've tried to teach him about money—"

"Your nephew said it would be just for a couple of months until he could figure things out. He'd get a loan from the bank. Did he ask you for help? Do you know about this?"

"No. He didn't call me. He never asks for my help. You did right by telling me." Sometimes John Riley acted like he had stopped growing at twelve. "What does he want his new housekeeper to do?"

"He didn't really know. Be there for Emily was most important. He said maybe she could make Emily lunch."

"That's more like something for a nanny or a mother. If he'd just get married again . . . Okay, sounds like you're going to have to create a list of duties for her. But it doesn't matter. He can't afford a housekeeper."

"Do you want me to tell him that?"

Hubbard held up his hand before he realized that Mrs. Carlos wouldn't be able to see his gesture. "No, if he knew I was against this he'd just want it more . . . Okay, this may work out for all concerned. I want Luis Espinoza's sister for this job."

"*Maria?* But John Riley wants an older woman, someone maternal. He said mature several times. Maria looks like she belongs on a magazine cover."

"Well, I don't care what *he* wants. *I* want her there. Maria is it. I need her in his house."

"But, Mr. R.J. . . ."

"I have my reasons. You've found his housekeeper: *Maria.* Okay? Tell Mr. Carlos I want him to sell this for me . . . Now, as for Maria's salary, we're going to finagle this and here's how we're going to work it . . ."

At the end of the call, R.J. looked out at the beautiful afternoon. Maria would be inside John Riley's house. He could ask Luis to get updates from his sister on what his nephew was up to. Depending on what happened on the operating table, he could handle the rest after that. He gazed down at the blooming dogwoods lining Markham Street below him. *Surgery.* It was hard not to wish for a lucky break on a spring day.

———————◆◆◆———————

Over forty years ago Carlos Rodriguez arrived in Hayslip, and like Columbus found the natives to be friendly. In those days, filled with dreams for his new home, he planted a metaphoric Guatemalan flag and claimed the rural area for his people. Since that time, Mr. Carlos, the name he always went by, used his property and his many mobile homes to serve as a major U.S. entry point for immigrants from his country. He made a nice living, providing cheap labor to dozens of local companies until his charges found better jobs elsewhere. There was always a fresh wave of illegal workers in the pipeline.

But where was Mr. Carlos now? That was the mystery that the younger Hubbard wanted to solve. He had told Mrs. Carlos he would wait for her husband at the City Café while she tracked him down.

He arrived at the restaurant door just as Sheriff Toil was exiting with a to-go coffee. Hubbard noticed that Toil hadn't taken the time to shave this morning. He looked even more tired now.

Toil spotted Hubbard and grabbed his arm. "You know what that son-of-a-bitch Connors wants me to do? It's his investigation, he should do it. We're supposed to stand back at this point."

"No. What does he want you to do?"

Toil tugged at Hubbard's sleeve to emphasize each point. "Connors told me I had to get hold of the parents and tell them what happened to their son since the boy's body was found in Hayslip. Do you know how hard that's going to be? Call parents and break the news that their child has been murdered?"

"No, I can't imagine that. I'm sorry he put that on you."

"*Yeah, me too.* Anything to make my world a little darker."

"Have you seen Mr. Carlos?"

"Not today."

"I've got to get something settled. If you see him, tell him I'm at City Café," Hubbard said.

"Will do." Toil said. He turned and shuffled slowly across the street as if he was a condemned man walking the last mile carrying a to-go coffee.

Hubbard entered the café, which was usually empty by this time in the afternoon. Today was no different. The seating area was vacant, save for a single waitress topping off ketchup bottles at one of the tables. Joe Sinclair, the owner, was sitting on a bar stool behind the cash register at the entrance, playing a game on his iPhone. He looked up as Hubbard entered.

"It's two o'clock. We're closing in thirty minutes. The stove is off for the day," Sinclair said.

"Just need coffee."

"To go?"

"For here. I'm waiting for Mr. Carlos."

"We're closing—"

"In thirty minutes. Got it."

Sinclair directed Hubbard toward the long lunch counter on the far wall next to the kitchen. The counter's original linoleum top was worn clean of its original design, now it was a milky white color with a reddish border. Hubbard took a stool, and Sinclair returned with a cup and saucer and a pot of coffee. "This may be stout."

"That's how I like it."

Sinclair shrugged, set the cup down and poured. "Your uncle had lunch here on Friday."

Hubbard nodded without comment.

Sinclair sat down beside him and changed the subject. "Hey, did you hear about the dead Arab Eddie found in Shanty Town?"

"Yeah, I did."

"I bet he was up to no good. They say he was from the college. I wonder if it was that kid who came here all the time with Mrs. Andrews."

"I don't remember seeing—"

"They would come at the end of the day when business has died down. They usually sat close together in the back booth over there, looking at photographs, laughing at nothing—and making me close late." His hand raked over the upright hairs on his steel-gray crew cut. "She's married. She ought to be more concerned about how things look. Haven't seen them together in about a week . . ." Sinclair paused and his brow creased. "What?"

Hubbard didn't realize his expression had changed. He had thought he had put the murder behind him. But just the suggestion of a romantic connection between the student and the Boy King's wife drew him in again. It reminded him that Andrews had said nothing about knowing the student. He felt a burning in the pit of his stomach. "Nothing . . . It just sounds like it probably was him. I didn't realize they met here."

"I could tell you stories about what happens in here after the lunch rush. Well, enjoy your quick cup of coffee." He walked away with the pot, brow creased, eyeing the brew with concern as if he thought he saw something in its murky depths.

Behind him, he heard the restaurant door open. He swiveled around and was relieved to see Carlos Rodriguez entering. Over the years, the Guatemalan's increasing success was matched by his expanding girth. His body now resembled an over-stuffed teddy bear.

Sinclair pointed Rodriguez toward Hubbard, then to his watch, and informed him of the nearing closing time, as if it had the same urgency as a rocket launch.

Rodriquez approached Hubbard. He used a handkerchief to wipe sweat from his brow and smiled broadly. He reached out his hand.

"And how are you, my friend? I'm sorry that I was unavailable when you called," Rodriquez said.

"That's okay, Mr. Carlos. I got an unexpected call from my ex-wife and I'm trying to get ready."

"I heard. Your daughter is returning home. That's wonderful. Emily is a sweet girl. How old is she now?"

"Ten."

"I remember. You were just out of high school. We thought you'd be going to Europe. *France*, wasn't it? Quite a surprise when you stayed."

"Yes. Things happen."

Mr. Carlos shook his head reflectively. "Now she's almost grown. It goes much too fast, doesn't it?"

"I know that's right. So, did your wife tell you that I need an older lady to be with Emily until I can come up with a permanent solution?"

"Yes, she did. I think I may have someone."

Hubbard felt himself relax. Mr. Carlos was a miracle worker. "Someone mature? Good natured? A jovial woman?"

"Jovial? I don't . . . I think she's very mature. Her name is Maria Espinoza."

"What's Mrs. Espinoza's situation? Has she raised kids? Is she a widow?"

"No husband, sadly. She is in one of my trailers until she gets settled here. I know she loves kids. All the young children are drawn to Maria like she's a magnet—most especially the boys."

"How old is she? Emily is a very active little girl."

"John Riley, don't you know you never ask a woman her age? I promise you. You'll fall in love with her the moment you see her."

"Well, you've been doing this a long time. I trust your judgment. Now the hard part, can I afford her? I'm thinking about getting a loan to make this work." Hubbard took a breath. "Let's talk money."

The negotiation went well. Mrs. Espinoza was surprisingly affordable. A couple of extra sales of burial insurance each month and Hubbard could manage. He would pay Mr. Carlos directly, and Mr. Carlos would pay Mrs. Espinoza. The circuitous salary trail was necessary to hide the payments from immigration authorities.

Hubbard stood and reached out and the two men shook hands.

Once again, Mr. Carlos came through for him. "When I was a kid, you came by the house twice a week to give me the allowance from my uncle or just to check on us. I could count you when there was no one else . . . I just want you to know . . . I think you're a good man."

Rodriguez didn't produce his usual smile. "Sometimes I'm happy when I can do a good thing. Other times, I just do as I'm told."

It seemed like a curious thing to say.

8

ONE NIGHT IN SHANTY TOWN

HUBBARD SPED DOWN THE HIGHWAY toward Monticello, thinking he was a lucky man. The maternal Mrs. Espinoza seemed perfect. Perhaps she could teach Emily the things women liked to do? Cooking? Hubbard only knew how the timer on the microwave worked. Cross-stitch? Hubbard smiled at his old school thinking. Bring it up to the twenty-first century: Advanced science and math? Bricklaying? He doubted Mrs. Espinoza would be the source of much guidance on those subjects.

It was difficult not to over think this. It was too important. Until now, his ex had tried to keep Emily out of his reach, first by moving to Memphis, before eventually returning home to Little Rock. But he had managed, with the help of R.J.'s lawyers to get Emily home for the summers the past three years. Asking for his uncle's assistance was a last resort, but it had come with strings. Thanks to R.J., she had spent her days at a summer academy in Monticello learning Spanish, R.J. deeming the French language "useless". Now, with regular school in session, maybe he could provide her with a more traditional home life. But could he do it? The answer to that question was uncertain in his mind. What did he know about a normal family? That would be Mrs. Espinoza's charge, helping him give his daughter something he had never seen in practice. He took a deep breath and let it out. There would be time to worry about that tomorrow . . . and the next day after that . . . and the day after that.

With that concern on hold for now, his mind drifted back to the events of the day. He thought about the Boy King's very young queen. Trish Blankenship—now Trish Andrews—knew Amir well enough to spend afternoons at City Café with him, looking at photographs and laughing about nothing as Sinclair said. Why not? They were about the same age. In the photograph, Amir looked attractive enough, thick black hair, brown eyes, a bit thin, but normal for that age. Was there anything going on between Amir and Trish aside from photography?

It would be difficult for Hubbard to approach the pretty blonde and ask her about the relationship. Hubbard knew her too well. During the time when he was making mistakes as quickly as a shot glass could be filled, he bumped into Trish and several of her friends out for a night on the town. A bit late, he learned the group comprised her bachelorette party. She never said a word about it in the back seat. Trish married Andrews the next weekend. Their chance meetings since then had been awkward, with Trish ducking away at the first opportunity.

When he drank, most of the nights he could remember he wanted to forget. From his brief encounter with Trish, he could understand how the former cheerleader might drive a man insane with jealousy at the thought of losing her to another man. Even now, Hubbard's memory of holding her that night still lingered.

But the idea of Tony Andrews pressing a shotgun to someone's chest and pulling the trigger in cuckolded fury seemed too ludicrous to imagine. Shooting Amir, disposing of the body, and covering up the crime would have been a lot of work for an aging *Boy King* to undertake.

Andrews had a checkered history with his wives. His money could only go so far in holding a marriage together. Two other women had married Tony Andrews and left him after the pre-nup terms were satisfied. Not one to learn from mistakes, Tony retained his fondness for cheerleaders fresh from the field of play. Trish was his third wife, and as he told everyone who would listen, this was his last marriage.

Hubbard reminded himself that all of this was none of his concern. He had gone as far on this murder story as he was going to go.

The remainder of the afternoon was consumed by a futile search for a single valve, reverse stroke fuel pump and a non-compact starter suitable for his old tractor. The guy at *Crantz Auto Parts Barn* thought he was joking when he asked if he had a source for the obsolete parts.

"If you know Henry Ford, he might pull them off a Model T for you," the smartass replied.

The long trip turned out to be unsuccessful. Hubbard was disappointed but not surprised. He knew he'd have to give up on his father's tractor one day. Maybe now was the time. Nearing the end of the long drive home, Hubbard approached the turnoff leading to Shanty Town. He wanted to ignore it. It had been a hell of a day and there was more to be done tomorrow. But this was where his day began and there were still too many unanswered questions. Was Amir murdered in Shanty Town? If so, were there witnesses? The empty shacks were never occupied by transients; the rotting structures were more likely to collapse than provide shelter. Besides it would take a vehicle to reach the remote location and once you arrived at the godforsaken place you would probably prefer to spend the night in your car, stretched out on the back seat, rather than in those decrepit buildings.

Hubbard pulled off the highway and rolled to a stop on the gravel shoulder at the turn to the lane leading to the ghost town. He sat for a moment, his truck idling. There was another possibility. Perhaps the moonshiners in the Deer Woods had relocated here, afraid that the Sheriff or Eddie might stumble across them in a moment of blind luck, after over a year of searching. The still had started after Hubbard had sobered up, so he had no idea where it was. Its hiding place was a small mystery in town; maybe the young student snooped it out and wanted a byline in the paper. Moonshiners, usually armed when working, wouldn't take kindly to the unexpected arrival of a young Arab toting a camera. Did the state police, earlier this morning, take time to search for potato peels or corn cobs piled somewhere in the brush—the remains of distilling? If they were here, did the Mexicans running the still let some evidence of their presence remain? Evidence they would retrieve from here as soon as possible?

No, don't do this. He wasn't a cop. Investigating this would do nothing for him. *You're picking at an old wound.* Once more he reminded himself that he had a daughter to think about and a crop to plant.

In spite of his reasoning, he knew exactly what he would be doing in the next minute.

His path through the pines and across the meadow was well lit by the moon. It was quiet this spring night, well before the summer's deafening uprising of crickets and cicadas. In the lifeless silence, his truck, bumping and creaking along the road, could be heard from far away. No reason to announce his arrival to skittish moonshiners. He parked a short distance from the first rough structure. He retrieved a flashlight from the glove box and began to hike the twists and turns of the nineteenth-century road.

Hubbard rounded a bend in the road and saw the dim profile of the first abandoned dwelling, empty and forlorn. The old road curved ahead of him, making it impossible to see all the remaining hovels of Shanty Town. He trudged on.

A gentle but persistent spring wind funneled through the shacks, making a soft sound like shallow breathing. Unexpectedly, there was part of him that was twelve once more, walking this same road in a search for answers in a village of the dead.

Each dark shanty sprang to life in his imagination as ivory moonlight entered through holes in the roof, illuminating window-eyes and doorway-mouths, animated when he was directly in front, and returning to darkness with a sigh as he passed. The wild undergrowth surrounding the buildings created long shadows that stretched across the road, adopting forms both human and inhuman. He had reached the same spot on the road where, years ago, on the last day of summer . . . He shook his head. Ghosts were just a trick of the subconscious mind.

It was an extended walk before he rounded a sharp curve and the last four shacks of Shanty Town came into view. Hubbard stopped abruptly and switched off his flashlight.

He wasn't alone.

Through dense foliage, he could make out an indistinct glow of yellow light, definitely man-made, and hear the muffled melody of a love-sick country ballad that seemed to originate at the end of the row.

His pace slowed, becoming careful and deliberate. A few more yards and he saw the source of the light: a window in the last shack. The small cabin faced south toward the drainage channel. It was about a half-football field distant from him. The cabin's interior light flickered, as if someone was moving around inside.

He considered his options. If he left, he wouldn't know who had taken up temporary residence here. Maybe it was a witness. He had come all this way and he couldn't turn back now. Edging closer, he decided he could steal a quick look at the occupant and then go.

Choosing each step carefully to avoid making noise, he neared the window, his heart pounding. More of the interior came into view. A kerosene lantern was perched on a step ladder creating an amber glow. He spotted a cot, pushed against a wall. If he got any closer, he would be forced to step out of the dark and into the window's pool of light.

A new thought occurred to Hubbard: What if the thugs from earlier in the morning were inside? But why would they be here? What would . . .

From the darkness behind him, the unmistakable sound of the hammer on a pistol locking into place caused his heart to jump. He froze.

"Okay, you son-of-a bitch . . . You've been walking on that road for too long . . . I got you now, and I'm going to put you in the ground where you belong. Let's see if you bleed red, just like the rest of us."

The gunman's voice had a rural twang and a stark tremor. There was something about the voice Hubbard recognized, but competing against the music on the radio it was difficult to distinguish it. He raised his hands over his head. "Yes, sir . . . I'm raising my hands . . . Neighbor, I'm sorry if I startled you, just out for a little night air, stretching the legs."

"I know that voice," the gunman said, his voice relaxing.

Hubbard turned around, as relief and anger flooded over him. "Eddie?"

"John Riley Hubbard, what're you doing here?" Eddie said. He returned the pistol to his holster. "Sorry about the gun and all."

Hubbard didn't respond immediately. He walked around in a wide circle, hands behind his head, fingers laced, breathing deeply. After his initial anger, Hubbard recognized his own role in creating this near-disaster. "It's cool. Everything's okay. Just give me a minute."

When Hubbard dropped his arms and nodded a greeting, Eddie returned to his open, if somewhat embarrassed, self and graciously invited Hubbard inside.

Hubbard followed him up the fragile steps into the shack. "Andrews said you found the body on your way home. I guess I understand now."

Eddie turned off the radio as Hubbard surveyed the primitive interior.

"Um, it's cozy. I guess . . ." Hubbard was at a loss for words.

Much of the wooden slat ceiling had fallen over the years, revealing a surprisingly sturdy tin roof overhead. Eddie had obviously taken a broom and mop to the place, industriously cleaning decades-old dust. A cool breeze wafted through the room.

In the main room, Eddie had dragged a camp cot, two lawn chairs (did Eddie have guests?) and an impressive array of camping equipment. All of Eddie's additions were colorful, but seemed out of place when set against the driftwood-textured floor, walls, and ceiling. The only trace remaining of previous tenants was a wall calendar from the year 1967 nailed to the slat wall.

The deputy had probably let the yellowing artifact remain due to the large cover photo of a young blonde in a pink bikini sitting on the hood of a lime green Ford F-150. She wore a smile so radiant and heartfelt that it could encourage any sensible man to consider the Ford product line for his next purchase. Eddie's two lawn chairs faced it like it was a flat screen TV.

All of Eddie's stuff could be expected to be found at the site of a weekend camp site, but this was Shanty Town, far away from Eddie's double-wide trailer, his wife, and small baby, Eddie Jr.

"So, Eddie—" Hubbard began, settling into a lawn chair.

Eddie held up his hand, and pointed to the ice chest. "Do you want something to drink?"

"Oh, no, I'm fine. I just, um . . ." Hubbard's fingers strummed the arms of the chair as he searched to a conversation topic. He didn't want to ask Eddie what had split up his family. Too many people seemed to relish the gossip surrounding Hubbard's family for him to imitate them.

Eddie seemed intent on fulfilling his offer. "No, you'll like this. I promise. It's as good as any drink at the Capitol Hotel bar."

Hubbard didn't want to add rudeness to his intrusion. *You can handle this. Just take one drink and you're out the door.* "Okay, sure. Thanks . . . Um, Eddie, you're in town a lot more than me. Do you remember ever seeing that Arab kid before now?"

Eddie crossed to the red and white ice chest on the floor positioned directly below the calendar. He paused to consider the question. "You know. I thought he looked familiar. I may have saw him, or someone who looked like him talking to R.J. in the alley behind the square one afternoon."

It took a moment for Hubbard to process that bit of information. "R.J.? I didn't know that he knew—"

Eddie turned back toward Hubbard, concerned he might have said the wrong thing. "I didn't get a good look. It was dark. I might be wrong. It could have been another Arab kid."

Hubbard held up his hand to reassure him. "It's no big deal. I'm sure Abadi knew plenty of people. Um, were they doing anything, or just talking?"

"Nothing special. The Arab kid handed R.J. a big envelope and R.J. got into his big Lincoln and drove off. That's all I saw. It was already getting dark, so I didn't get a good look."

Hubbard nodded and tried to smile reassuringly. He wondered if that big envelope contained photos like the one he saw at the student's apartment. But why would R.J. have an interest in photos of empty fields?

The deputy pushed the ice away from whatever he buried at the bottom of the chest, Hubbard gazed up at the time-traveling girl smiling back at him from the "Swinging Sixties." She was impressively built, with coiffed hair and long legs ending in red high heels..

Eddie grabbed two plastic cups and gently shook the ice water off a jar filled with clear liquid. Any male who grew up in the rural south would recognize the contents. It was as unnecessary to identify his prize as it was to expound on the significance of the Stars and Stripes at a tractor pull. Eddie had visited the Mexicans in the deer woods.

If there was any troublesome conflict between his official role and his leisure activities, it didn't show. Perhaps he reflected the town's ambivalence toward the illegal still. "Better to have a moonshine still than a meth lab," everyone said with a certain amount of civic pride.

Eddie crossed back and sat on the lawn chair beside Hubbard and handed him a cup. "Cheers." Eddie raised his cup.

Hubbard elevated his drink in return. Eddie took a sip. Hubbard glanced furtively into the cup. The plastic container seemed clean enough and Eddie was a very generous bartender. He brought it to his lips and carefully took a sip, ready to eject at the first taste of trouble. The white lightning was ice cold and free from the pungent taste of high octane alcohol. In fact, there was no bitterness at all. He swallowed. No burning as it went down. Hubbard felt a calmness spreading throughout his body that warmed and cooled simultaneously. The Mexicans in the Deer Woods were craftsmen. *Was there anything Mexicans can't do?*

"You see?" Eddie said, with the raw enthusiasm of a cult's new member.

"I do see." Hubbard took another sip. "So, do you go into the Deer Woods to get this?"

"Well, not in uniform I don't. I don't want to be shot." Eddie chuckled at the thought.

"No. I wouldn't think."

The two men sat in silence. Their eyes returned to the only girl in the room. Hubbard now understood why Eddie let her remain on the wall. It was an excellent decision. She had a kind face and a joyful smile. Best of all, she seemed quite sane. He took another sip, a bigger one this time.

"You got to wonder where she is now." Eddie was wistful.

Probably in a nursing home, Hubbard thought, but he didn't want to break the reverie. "I don't know. I hope she's happy."

"Yeah," Eddie agreed. "She deserves to be happy."

"Oh, she certainly does." Hubbard sighed.

"Happy," Eddie summarized in a whisper, his head bobbing in agreement.

This wasn't Eddie's first drink of the evening, nor his second.

"So, Eddie, I got to ask. What're you doing here? Why aren't you at home? You've got a wife and a baby."

Eddie's eyes began to fill with tears and his chin lowered to his chest. "I know I should be home. I screwed up. I messed up bad."

"Well, what happened? Maybe I can help?"

"I'm in the shitter. I'm really in the shitter this time . . ."

Hubbard let the silence continue. It was Eddie's story to tell.

"You know, Sophie? The girl who works at the Git It N Go?

"Oh . . . yeah," Hubbard said. He had noticed a certain pouty quality about her.

"Well, um, one night, a few weeks ago, I stopped in there about one a.m. on a Saturday night—well, Sunday morning, really. And, uh, she asked for help moving some stuff back in the stock room. And, uh, we went back there, and so . . . and so nature took its course. "Oh, John Riley," Eddie moaned, "nature took its course!" He repeated the final part as some sort of self-indictment.

It took a moment for Hubbard's brain to process "nature taking its course" in the *Git It N Go* stock room.

Eddie's lifted his head, shamed, coming uncomfortably close to a full crying jag. Hubbard was immediately uncomfortable, but patted Eddie on the shoulder as a stop gap. "Well Eddie, how old are you? Nineteen? Twenty? Sometimes hormones . . ." Hubbard stopped. Was he going to tell Eddie about the birds and bees? Besides, the story didn't explain why Eddie was living in an abandoned shack.

"But that weren't enough for me. I kept coming back. And somehow, Mona must've heard something from somebody. She came to the store after midnight and my patrol car was parked outside. The store doors were locked and she couldn't see anyone inside, so she knew it were true. She got on my police radio and told the world about the low-life, cheating bastards the Hayslip Police Force hired. I think she was mostly talking about me."

"Most likely," Hubbard agreed.

"The state police heard someone talking trash on our police radio and they made a federal case out of it. But the sheriff and I are telling them that it didn't come from us. I don't think they believe it. You won't tell, will you?"

"No, of course I won't."

"Mona threw me out of the trailer on my mom and dad's farm. My parents agreed I needed to learn my lesson and told me to leave. So, I'm out of my home sweet home and staying here . . . Anyway, that's how I saw that rug. My headlights lit it up when I was turning around."

"Why here? Why not stay with a friend or at the Hayslip Motor Court?"

"I don't want anyone to hear about this. The deacons at my church would kick me out of the congregation if they knew. It's too small a town to be staying at someone's house. People would want to know why I wasn't at home. I tried to stay at the Motor Court, but too many folks from town are out there at night. You know Mike Fortinbras? He lives in a room out there. And I almost bumped straight into Mrs. Andrews one night at the ice machine. And you know that—"

"Wait. What? Mrs. Andrews? Why would people from town want to spend the night at . . . Ah, I see. Okay. I'm with you."

"I love Mona, John Riley. I really love my family."

"I know you do. She'll come around. Just stay away from the Git It N Go."

"I don't go anywhere near it."

Hubbard took another drink. "You didn't happen to see anyone with Trish, did you?"

"Who?"

"Um . . . uh. Mrs. Andrews." Hubbard looked at an almost empty cup. "Jesus. What's in this?"

"It's good, isn't it? It helps me forget my par-tic-u-lar situation."

"Yeah, I can see that. Um, but was Mrs. Andrews with anyone when you saw her?"

"No. She was just getting a bucket of ice, didn't see anyone else."

Hubbard nodded, took a drink and stood. "Well, it's time for me to get home . . . uh, go home. But now, tell me one thing, Eddie. And shoot it to me straight."

"Okay."

"Those things you were saying, when you had a gun on me—"

"I'm sorry about that, I didn't—"

"That's okay. But I have to know something. You said I'd been walking on that road for too long. You wanted to know if I'd bleed. Nobody walks on that road and we all bleed. Except for . . . Have you seen a ghost out here? Is that what you thought I was? A ghost?"

"Spooks? Heck, no. That's just people's imaginations running off with them. There's no such thing as ghosts. I'm not ignorant, you know." Eddie tried to laugh and failed. His chuckle turned into a hacking cough.

"I saw one out here, a long time ago."

"You did?" Eddie paused, swallowing hard. He gave a sidelong glance out the front window opening as if he was afraid of being overheard. His voice fell to a whisper. "He walks the road at night."

"I know."

Hubbard's simple confirmation seemed to alarm Eddie even more. He jumped up from his chair like a jack-in-the-box and rushed to the doorway and stood next to him. He grabbed Hubbard's arm, his voice filled with urgency. "What did you see?"

Hubbard had never told this story to anyone, but strong moonshine was loosening his lips.

9

EVERYONE HAS A STORY

HUBBARD COULDN'T SEE ANYTHING past the dim circle of light surrounding the shack. The formless night summoned old memories. Eddie left the cabin doorway and returned to his lawn chair in the main room.

Hubbard turned to face him. "I heard all the tall tales about ghosts, just like you. Everyone knows someone who claims he saw a dead relative or friend walking that dirt road. You can't grow up here without those damn stories finding a place in your head."

Hubbard took a drink from the cup. He noticed that Eddie had locked his hands on the aluminum arms of the chair, squeezing so hard his knuckles were white. "After my dad died, everything fell apart at home. My mom took to her bed . . . and she never really left. The doctor said it was clinical depression. But Mom always had a different reason, a different complaint. And my uncle R.J. didn't come around again for a long while. I felt so . . . alone."

"What happened to R.J.? That doesn't sound like him."

An animal scurried through the undergrowth about twenty yards from Hubbard, its quick footsteps breaking the deadly quiet. Startled, Hubbard turned to find the source of the noise. In the next moment, he smiled wryly, amused by his case of nerves. He turned back to Eddie. "That summer sucked. Two weeks after we buried my father, R.J.'s best friend, Tom Cole, died in some kind of fishing accident on the White River. I don't think they ever figured out how it happened. He may have slipped on some wet moss and hit his head on a rock. That part of the river is treacherous as it narrows by the cliffs. Anyway, when R.J. did the eulogy, he started crying and couldn't stop. I guess it was all too much for him—losing his brother and best friend, all in the space of two weeks."

Eddie shifted in his seat. "God, I'm sorry, man."

"Yeah . . . And it got worse. There were some stupid stories going around town about . . . my family. So, I kept to myself, away from my friends, afraid of what people might say to me, and what I'd do to them in return. About this time, uh, I started getting into fights here and there."

Hubbard stopped. Why was he even telling Eddie this? He had bottled it up inside him for so long. It must be the moonshine.

"I was a stupid kid. I thought that if there were ghosts in Shanty Town, maybe my dad was here too. Perhaps there was some part of him still on this earth." Hubbard pointed to the road. "I'd find my dad out there and he'd tell me who killed him—and I'd do the rest. I'd get justice done."

Uncomfortable with how much he revealed, Hubbard looked longingly at the ice chest on the floor and the moonshine it contained. He held his empty cup aloft. "If this keeps up, one day Mexicans will be on the moon."

"Illegally," Eddie said. He rose with a nervous chuckle. After Eddie had poured Hubbard another drink he returned to the lawn chair. "But what happened? What did you see?"

Hubbard took a drink before he replied. "Eddie, if you ever tell anyone this—"

"I won't say a word. I promise," Eddie said. "Didn't your mom ever wonder where you went at night? What did she think—?"

Hubbard's reply was sharp. "No, she didn't ask." He softened his tone. "Maybe she didn't know. Like I said, she was in bed. She was hurting. It wasn't her fault . . . Nobody's fault . . . Nobody . . . Understand?"

Eddie nodded earnestly. "So did you see your dad's *actual ghost?*"

Hubbard noticed that the blue plastic cup in Eddie's hand was crumpling under the pressure of his grip. Hubbard stalled, taking a deep drink, afraid of Eddie's reaction. But he decided to go on, to say his story aloud, and see if it sounded real.

"I was out here every night, eavesdropping on crickets and tree frogs and fighting off mosquitoes. I got about a thousand chigger bites that made me look like a goddamn pin cushion and I was just about to give up. All I wanted was for God to let me say goodbye to him. Throw the dog a bone, you know?"

Hubbard took a sip. It felt too good. It made him remember why he stopped drinking.

"One evening, at the end of the summer, I was sitting on the rotting steps of one of these abandoned shacks. That night was like every other one—nothing happened. I got up to walk back home when the temperature began falling, getting cooler, like a storm was coming. I looked at the sky, but there weren't any clouds, just stars. The tops of the trees began to sway, rocking back and forth like a cradle, but there wasn't any wind. And then, everything got quiet—the crickets, everything. It was so silent, I thought I went deaf." Hubbard's hand reached up by his ear as he remembered. "I snapped my fingers to check my hearing. Then the hairs on my neck stood up like paint bristles . . . You know, sometimes you wait too long for something to happen, and when it does—*I just wasn't ready* . . . I felt him behind me on the road . . . I took a deep breath and turned to face . . . him . . . it . . . whatever."

Hubbard was surprised at how calm he sounded describing the event that still visited him in nightmares. Even now, he controlled his emotions with effort. Maybe it was good to talk about it. Confession was good for the soul they said. "And there he was—the shape of a man. But that's all there was, all I could see was just his outline, a silhouette, and nothing else, no face, just darkness. Every time I thought I could see his eyes, in the next instant, they faded away. He was a man with nothing inside of him."

"Jesus Christmas! What happened?" Eddie put his hand on his hair as if he feared it might stand on end.

"It kept coming toward me. He got so close I could touch him—a shimmering black form, but alive somehow. I got so cold, my teeth started chattering."

Eddie's eyes grew wider. He jumped out of his chair and high-stepped around the cabin. "Oh, God, I would've crapped in my pants. Did you have a weapon?"

Hubbard's brow creased. "No, I didn't have a gun. I was twelve."

Eddie shrugged, shaking his head as if he didn't see the problem with an armed twelve-year-old hunting a ghost during the dead of night.

Hubbard rubbed his face. He couldn't tell him everything. How could he tell Eddie that he begged the dark figure on the road, an apparition that he knew had to be his father, to reveal who had shot him? Recount to Eddie his childish promise of vengeance? Justice, he then believed, was the only way to save his mother. With the killer known to everyone, she could leave the house without fear of what people might say. "I've got to find him. It's the only way to save Mom!" he had cried out that night. The mute figure approached him without words, gliding forward to touch him on the shoulder. It was an unnaturally cold hand—a dead hand.

Hubbard turned to Eddie and revealed his darkest secret. "I was a kid . . . I ran. I ran before I learned the truth. Everything that followed from that day forward is on me." He shook his head. "All the time I spent out here, a whole summer, every single night, the heat, the mosquitoes, all for nothing. I still think about it."

Eddie threw his empty cup to the floor and the plastic container bounced once and then rolled in a tight circle before coming to rest. "But, you don't know if it were your father. Hell, your father would have let you know it was him, gave you a sign or whatnot. He wouldn't have scared the shit out of you. I would've run, too. Anyone would've."

"Don't you understand? I could've ended it. I could have saved my mother if I talked to him."

"Like a conversation? I never heard of a spook wanting no conversation. Hellfire! Haunting us is bad enough. We gotta talk, too?" Eddie turned slightly, angling his body toward the road, raising his voice. "I got nothing to say to no ghost. I'm good."

Hubbard attempted a smile. But after another moment, his head fell back in full laughter. Eddie smiled.

Hubbard's laughter wound down and he finally stopped. He wiped a tear from the corner of his eye and patted Eddie on the back. "Thanks for listening." He handed Eddie his cup. "Well, I got to go. It's late." Hubbard turned away and tried to find the top step, but stumbled and fell to the ground.

Eddie came to the edge of the porch and teetered for a moment. "Are you okay?"

"Never better." Hubbard got up, brushing himself off. "That 'shine is off the charts. I'm heading back to my truck."

"Wait a minute." Eddie went into the cabin and returned with Hubbard's flashlight and handed it to him. He glanced down the dirt road. "Where'd you park?"

Hubbard oriented himself, and pointed in the general direction of the highway. "That way."

"Are you going to be okay?" Eddie asked. "Maybe you shouldn't be driving?"

"I know a way to get home that won't put me on the road."

"What if you see that thing again?" Eddie pointed into the night. "Maybe it's the hard corn, but I've seen something standing out there almost every night. It's as if he's waiting for someone. I'm taking no chances. As long as I'm stuck in Shanty Town, I'll sleep wearing my holster."

Hubbard shook his head dismissively. "The mind plays tricks on you, Eddie. There's nothing out there but shadows. If something was out there once, it's long gone now."

As he started off, Hubbard was less concerned about spirits on the road than the spirits in a sloshed Eddie, armed with both a gun and a heightened fear of things that go *boo* in the night. Hubbard turned and saw Eddie still standing on the steps of the shack, hand on his holster, squinting in his direction, ready to spring into action if needed.

Hubbard considered how an inebriated Eddie might react if a deer unexpectedly bolted across the road. Would he draw his gun and fire into the night, killing Hubbard in the process? He remembered he was carrying the flashlight in his right hand, unlit. Would a surprising burst of unexpected light look like the specter of a ghost, and send Eddie over the edge? Hubbard almost could feel the bullets slamming into his back. His thumb traced a slow circle around the edge of the switch, round and round and round.

He made it to the first bend in the road and was no longer in the direct path of any well-intentioned bullet coming from the shack. Eddie was a good friend to be so willing to help him battle the phantoms of the afterlife if the need arose. But Hubbard had no expectations of needing his help tonight.

By the time Hubbard reached his truck, his head seemed clear, but he knew better than to risk the highway. At the back of the large pasture, there were two worn tire paths made by generations of tractors harvesting hay. They made a passable route at this time of year and again at the end of summer after the final harvest. His truck would take a beating in tall grass, but the drive home would be safe.

It took a little more than fifteen minutes to take this improvised route at a crawling speed. After following the tractor path, he connected with another unpaved road that led to his farm.

Entering his house, he saw it how Emily would see it: cold, empty and dark. Maybe he could spruce the place up a bit. His ex-wife had taken most of the things when she left. Now it was a bit too Spartan. Too many bare gray walls. Why did he think he could make a home for Emily? He wanted her to always see a smile when she walked in the door. Could he even provide her with that small gift?

Hubbard made it to his bedroom, and emptied his pockets onto the dresser. He pulled out the photo of the young women he found on the floor of Amir's apartment making the "Charlie's Angels" pose. He had forgotten about the party girls. He studied the image. The female trio smiled back, perhaps a little tipsy, as a squadron of frat boys gathered around them, waiting to pounce. But there was something else that tugged just beneath his consciousness, like a fish breaking the water's surface for a second before submerging again, leaving only a ripple. In a different environment, without their costumes, vamp makeup, and neon plastic wigs, he knew those girls, all three of them. Where?

He dropped the photo on the dresser, crossed to the light switch and flicked it off. He kicked off his boots and fell across the bed fully clothed. *I'll remember them tomorrow . . .*

Asleep, the night vision returned. His dad's truck, save for a single bullet hole through the windshield, was unmarked. Hubbard stood beside the vehicle, watching paramedics toss a sheet over his father's body on a gurney. As it settled over him, Hubbard could see his mother walking away from the scene, weeping.

R.J. caught up to her and placed his arm around her shoulders in an effort to comfort his sister-in-law. Immediately, she pushed him away, her finger pointing at him accusingly, saying something he couldn't hear. R.J. stood there, dumbstruck, and then he began to whisper to her, his face turning red with emotion.

Young John Riley Hubbard stared at the adults, astonished by the scene. He swung around to note the sheriff's reaction. Conklin had lowered his clipboard and folded his arms around his chest, an attentive audience of one.

Panicking, Hubbard spun back to warn them, but his mother and uncle were gone from view.

Hubbard awoke with a start, surprised to find he was standing with his hands outstretched as if he was pushing against a wall. He lowered his arms and staggered to the hallway bathroom. He flipped on the light, and became violently ill.

10

WHAT'S GOING ON?

LYING ON HIS BACK, EYES OPEN, Hubbard saw the first rays of morning light brightening the bedroom. He groggily recalled the surreal images that roused him from sleep minutes ago and stared up at the white ceiling as if it were a movie screen suitable for the projected images from his dream.

In his dream, it was a summer night. He was trying to guide his family's truck down a bleak river flooding the shanty town road. In the bed of the truck, there was a carpet roll that was similar to the one that held Amir's body. It was difficult to see anything but blackness in front of him as the crack in the windshield had blossomed into a thousand different veins. But still, he knew where the current was taking him—toward the dark spirit that he met here on that long ago summer. Unexpectedly, he was distracted by feminine laughter coming from his left. He turned and saw the three costumed party girls standing on the front porch of an ancient shack, their nylon hair glistening in the moonlight.

Cleopatra and her gun-toting flappers called seductively, beckoning him. Their arms strained for him, enticing him further with moonshine poured into a golden cup.

Hubbard wanted the intoxicating drink they offered, but he was drifting past the sirens like Odysseus. Unlike the Greek hero, he tried to steer toward them but failed. Frustrated, he stretched for their extended hands, but the nubile girls were beyond reach.

They evaporated into the mist.

It was only a dream, but it had substance that felt like a memory; his reaching for them, their lovely arms wanting him in return. Hubbard rubbed his eyes and tried to ignore his throbbing hangover. He didn't know why, but the Arab's murder was turning out to be his own personal Pandora's Box. The nightmares, the doubts, and the anger from the past were refreshed and released, swirling around him like demons. The two murders—one old, one new—were unrelated. Why were they melding together in his head? Why couldn't he walk away from Pandora's bullshit box?

He rose with a sigh, walked to the dresser, and picked up the photo. The girls seemed so familiar. Why didn't he recognize them? He dropped the picture on the dresser and walked to the window to check the morning weather.

It looked like another clear day was on tap. Perhaps the fields would be workable soon. He stopped and looked down at the lawn, an empty expanse of green. His mouth dropped open. Where was his tractor? In the rush to leave yesterday, he'd left the machine in the same place where it had died. Now it was gone. Shit!

He threw on a t-shirt and jeans, grabbed his phone and bounded barefoot down the stairs and out to his backyard. The tractor wasn't in sight. *Why the hell would somebody steal . . .* He noticed faint impressions in the grass caused by the tractor's wheels rolling across the soggy ground in the direction of the barn. He followed the tracks and flung open the door of the farm building. There it was, once again in its proper spot.

Had his memory gotten this bad? First it was the girls and now he couldn't recall putting his tractor in the barn? No. The machine was pushed here. Not an easy process to steer and push; he would remember that struggle. Then he saw a note, duct-taped to the tractor seat. He pulled it off and read—

*Rebuilt fuel pump and starter busted. <u>Very old</u>. Found an-
other in Mexico. Here in few days. Juan.*

Juan handled a myriad of operational details for his uncle. Whatever his sources south of the border, Juan could always find whatever repair supplies for the old John Deere. But the frail man couldn't
have pushed the tractor by himself. Apparently his uncle's men had
been here too and helped shelter the tractor for the night. R.J. always seemed to know what was going on in Hubbard's life without
being told. This was yet another mysterious example.

His cell's ring tone broke the morning quiet. Hubbard drew it
from his pocket.

"John Riley?" The male voice on his cell was almost a whisper.

Hubbard recognized the voice, always hoarse from years of smoking. "Sheriff?"

"Are you alone?"

Toil asked him the question with such urgency, Hubbard found
himself glancing over his shoulder before he responded. "Yeah."

"I had to call you. You're the only one who'd understand. I called
overseas yesterday and it got freaky real quick."

Hubbard walked out of the barn, closing the door. "What got
freaky? I don't understand. What're you trying to tell me?"

"I've got to talk to you. It's about the Arab. But not on the
phone, in person."

He didn't want to be involved with this, but now he found he
couldn't pass up an opportunity to learn more about the murder.
Hubbard took a step, stopped abruptly, grimaced, and sighed. He
lifted his foot to see what he stepped in. "I could come by your
office later. I'm going—"

"No. Someplace else. Not my office."

"Um . . . okay." Options were limited in Hayslip. "How about
the City Café?"

"Yeah, that'll work. How quickly can you get here?"

Hubbard was becoming concerned about Toil's apparent case of
nerves. "I don't know. How's an hour sound? Sheriff, are you okay?"

"An hour. City Café. Act like nothing's up. We're just having coffee. I'm not supposed to be talking." Toil hung up.

Hubbard lowered his cell. Was he missing something? They were going to meet at City Café and drink coffee while acting like they were just drinking coffee. What the hell was all that about?

Hubbard gazed out at his field. There was much to do, but without a tractor . . . Maybe he could stop by the Kubota dealership in town. *Stop holding on to the past.* It was past time for a new tractor.

It was unexpectedly difficult to find a parking spot at the town square. He spotted a car pulling out on the far side of the square and gunned his truck around the loop and grabbed it. As he got out of his vehicle, he saw four TV crews and several people he guessed were reporters. This was more interest from the Little Rock media for a murder in southeast Arkansas than usual. Perhaps it was the Arab angle that brought them here.

All the media folk were grouped within the confines of a make-do fence consisting of *Do Not Cross* tape strung around empty barrels. A state police trooper was standing between the reporters and the short flight of steps that led up to the sheriff's office. The cop's hand rested on his holstered gun as if he expected bored members of the press to transform into an angry street mob at any moment.

His attention on the reporters to his right, he collided with someone directly in front of him.

"Hey, watch—" Tony Andrews's hands pushed Hubbard back.

Hubbard turned and saw Andrews lowering his outstretched arms. Andrews was a tall man whose face had a slightly Teutonic appearance and framed a long, aquiline nose. His thinning sandy-colored hair drew attention to the top of his balding head. People in town had noted that when the Boy King was angry or embarrassed his partially exposed scalp turned bright red. It appeared almost purple this morning. "Oh sorry, I should watch where I'm going." Hubbard indicated the crowd to his right. "I guess we should've expected—"

"I don't know why I should pay you for that reporting job you did."

"What? Oh well, I told you that all I knew was sports—"

"Mrs. Welsh showed me your copy. Where was the White River Killer? *No mention of the White River Killer.* Didn't I ask you to include—"

Hubbard nodded. "And I followed up on it with Toil. There doesn't seem to be any connection between this murder and—"

"A good reporter doesn't take no for an answer."

"I don't know what that means, so I guess I'm not—"

Andrews shook his head. "Don't worry, I'll handle it. I'll make it work."

"I still don't understand . . ." The words trailed away when Hubbard noticed Andrews's expensive shooting jacket with a padded right shoulder. "Hey, I didn't realize you hunted."

For a moment, Andrews seemed confused by the question then he waved it away. "Oh, the jacket. I don't hunt, I do shoot competitively. Our team was regional skeet champs two years ago. There's a competition tonight at the Remington range in Little Rock. I've got a new shotgun I'm breaking in. German model, very expensive, you probably haven't heard of it."

Aside from Andrew's boast about how much he spent on his new gun, this was interesting news. The Arab was killed by a shotgun. If Andrews found out that Amir and Trish were having an affair . . . A second later, Hubbard said, "Oh. You know I've been thinking about getting a shotgun. Would you be interested in selling your old—"

Andrews ignored the question. "Here's your check." He reached into his pocket and pulled out an envelope. "I was going to mail it, but since you're here . . ." Andrews tossed the envelope at him. "Next time, listen to my instructions . . . or I may not need your services anymore."

There was a split-second when Hubbard felt the old anger rise up. He stopped himself before he took the check and threw it back into Andrews's face. *Get a grip. Emily doesn't need to arrive in town and hear about her father getting into a fight in the town square. There are enough embarrassing stories without adding to the list.* Hubbard clenched his jaw.

"Well, I've got to get to Monticello." Andrews bumped him as he passed.

"Yeah." Hubbard struggled with his immediate instinct to grab the Boy King by the arm and spin him around. Instead, Hubbard watched him depart taking calming breaths. Was Andrews trying to tie Amir's murder to the White River Killer to shift attention from himself? But if the Boy King wanted to keep a low profile, why would he parade across the town square wearing a shooting jacket in broad daylight? But in the next moment Hubbard remembered Eddie's comment about seeing Trish at the motor court by the ice machine. She certainly didn't leave her mansion to spend the night in a dive like the motor court all by herself.

When he reached the diner, the high level of clatter in the packed restaurant surprised Hubbard. At the entrance, five small groups stood in front of the cash register, waiting to pay their bills. Several other customers waited along the foyer wall. Dill Foxcroft—the local road construction baron—was a bear of a man. He was just a bit older than Hubbard's uncle and was leaning across the front counter in an intimidating way, jabbing a finger in the direction of Sinclair.

"I've got meetings with a total of five work crews today at my place and you promised me box lunches for all the men. It's an important organizational day," Foxcroft said. His voice was low and threatening.

"You'll have them. It's just that my computer system screwed up my order to my suppliers. If you could just be a little flexible with the menu."

"I want what I want. I don't bend and I don't break."

Hubbard almost laughed at the self-important declaration, but Sinclair nodded energetically. "I'll get it done."

Dill Foxcroft, rich and imperial in manner, had an enviable position with state road contracts in Southeast Arkansas. If a contract was awarded—he got it.

"Good. That's what I want to hear. Now, I hope I don't have to go through all this with the church dinner—"

Hubbard didn't have time to wait through a renewed tirade. He cupped one hand close to his mouth to be heard over the hubbub. "Have you seen the sheriff?"

Sinclair looked up, but he seemed too interested in placating the road czar to speak to him. Foxcroft turned around to see who had the gall to interrupt. He mouth turned downward when he saw Hubbard.

"Hubbard." Foxcroft said the name as if it was a bitter taste in his mouth. "Tell your uncle to stay out of my business."

Hubbard's frowned. He didn't know Foxcroft well enough for the obvious negative reaction. It must mean that Foxcroft and R.J. had a recent run-in. "R.J.'s not in the road business."

"He'll know what I mean."

Sinclair tilted his head in the direction of the dining room. "Sit anywhere," he called. "Computer system acted up last night."

Sinclair seemed to think that was an answer to Hubbard's original question. "But is the sheriff here?"

"Any open table is good. The others waiting are a party of eight. We're getting them set up now."

Hubbard walked into the congested dining area. Waitresses and busboys were crisscrossing the floor, weaving through a sea of tables carrying loaded trays and coffee pots. Someone waved, catching his eye. Toil was by a booth on the north wall. Hubbard waved back and made his way toward the sheriff. Toil was halfway through a cup of coffee by the time he got to the booth.

Hubbard sat across from him and looked out at the crowded restaurant. "What's going on? It's usually quieted down by 8:30."

"Hell, who knows. You know most restaurants run by the seat of their pants. It's like all food joints are run by gypsies."

Hubbard's brow furrowed as he tried to follow Toil's hopscotch logic.

Sarah, a waitress who dyed her hair jet-black like a middle-aged Goth, arrived at their booth and set a cup down in front of Hubbard and paused, holding the coffee pot in her other hand.

Hubbard looked up and nodded. She filled his coffee cup.

"So, how's the best-looking man in Hayslip doing today?" the waitress asked, her lips forming a coy smile.

Hubbard shrugged. "I don't know. How're you doing today, Sheriff?"

Toil rolled his eyes.

"Your uncle had lunch here on Friday," Sarah said, putting a hand on her hip. "He had the meatloaf."

Hubbard sighed. "Can't go wrong with meatloaf."

"Did y'all hear Eddie found a dead Arab in Shanty Town?" Sarah asked.

Toil's back straightened. "Sarah, I'm the sheriff. Of course I heard. It's my job."

"Just making conversation. Everyone's talking about it. Jake Tyler heard the police think he was part of some terrorist group."

Toil leaned in. He arched an eyebrow as if he was getting angry. "Sarah, *I am the police.*"

Sarah didn't seem convinced. "Are you two big spenders getting something to eat or are you going to be draining coffee cups all morning?"

"Nothing for me," Toil said. His jacket was open and he patted his large stomach in support of his decision.

Hubbard looked up. "Two eggs over medium. Dry toast. Bacon. Hash browns. And a side of grits."

Sarah whisked off to another table.

"So what couldn't you talk about on the phone?"

Toil looked down at the table and rubbed his hand across his mouth and then looked around the large room. Hubbard followed his gaze and surveyed the diners as well. No one seemed to be paying attention to them.

"Yesterday afternoon, I tried to call Amir's parents overseas. A hell of a lot of numbers, but it was the home phone number the school listed for him in Egypt."

"I wondered what country he was from," Hubbard said. "So, how did the conversation go? I know it must have been a difficult—"

"No. You don't understand what happened on the call."

"I guess I don't."

"So, I called and a guy talking Arab answers. And I think: how am I going to get through to this rag head and make him understand? So, I talk real slow, like—I—am—the—sheriff—of—Hayslip—Arkansas—in—the—United—States—"

Hubbard put up one hand. "I got it. So what happened?"

"Well, this went on for a few minutes. He'd say something in Egyptian gobbledygook, and I had to back up and begin again. Until finally . . ." Toil paused inexplicably to take a sip of coffee.

Hubbard's bobbed his head to encourage him to finish his story. "Finally?"

"The Arab started talking English, but with a Boston accent." Toil did a poor imitation of an accent that seemed far from Bostonian. "He's says, 'Will ya hold da line for a moment?' So he puts me on hold and I hear elevator music. Would somebody tell me *who* on earth likes that classical music?" Toil looked almost as if he thought the classical music was the strangest part of the call. "Then another guy comes on the line. He says, 'This is Staff Sergeant Charles Harshaw, United States Marines. You are on a secure line. Please identify yourself.' "

Toil was silent.

"Wow," Hubbard said, almost as a whisper. His single word response was inadequate, but he couldn't think of anything better. "And?"

"Well, I tried to tell him who I was. But he stopped me and asked for my mother's maiden name."

"Didn't he believe you were a sheriff?"

"Hell, I don't know. He wanted to know how I got the number and why I was calling it. He had an attitude like I did something wrong. It kinda pissed me off."

"Did you tell him why you were calling?"

"Yeah, of course. I told him that we had a dead Egyptian student and I was calling the contact number for his parents. He asks me if it was a car accident. I tell him no, Amir Abadi was murdered."

Toil took another sip of coffee.

Hubbard placed his hands on the table. "And you're killing me now. So, what happened then?"

"Well, he puts me on hold again and the damn classical comes back on. The Marine returns and says I wasn't to go anywhere because I'd be getting a phone call from the FBI in Washington within thirty minutes. I asked him if he needed my phone number, but he said—get this—he said that he has my office number, my cell and my home number. But before he gets off, I ask him where the hell I called? After some huffing and puffing, he says I called a special phone line into the United States Embassy in Cairo, but it would be deactivated as soon as we hung up so don't call it again. Anyway, he says for me to shelter in place."

Hubbard tried to make a reasonable connection from the Arab student to a secure line into the U.S. embassy in Egypt, but came up empty. "So what'd you do?"

The sheriff seemed embarrassed. "Well, I . . . uh . . ."

Hubbard tried not to smile. "You called that phone number again to see if he deactivated it like he said?"

Toil was sheepish. "I couldn't resist. But he was right. Just dead air."

"And did the FBI call you?"

"Yeah, about forty-minutes later the phone rings. My caller ID says it's from Washington. It's some guy who says he's some sort of big deal with the FBI, assistant director or some such thing, and wants me to identify myself again. I try to give him my mother's maiden name, but he says he wants me to tell him what elementary school I went to. I tell him. Then he asks for my social security number. Well, I'm not going to just give out my social security number over the phone. So, he goes so far as to tell *me* the number and asks me to confirm if it's correct or not."

"What'd you say?"

"I uh, told him he was correct?"

"So, where did all this end up?"

"He said an FBI team was on its way from Washington and I wasn't supposed to talk about either the call or the student to anyone else *under the penalty of law.*"

"And have you said anything to anyone? I mean, in addition to me?"

"No, of course not. The only people I've told have been you, Eddie, my wife, and my sister. I know how to keep a secret."

"That's good," Hubbard said. *Hasn't the FBI ever been in a small town?*

"When do they get here?"

"Maybe today, but why does the kid's home phone number connect to a U.S. government facility with people pretending to be his family answering?"

Sarah returned with Hubbard's breakfast. They watched in silence as she placed his food on the table. After she filled both their cups again, she left and they resumed the conversation.

The sheriff kept trying to put the pieces together. "Where are his parents? Why agents? Murder isn't a federal offense. They don't have jurisdiction on this. Why aren't they sending people from Little Rock?"

"Good questions. Well, you're right. It's pretty freaky."

"Damn straight it's freaky."

"Is Sergeant Connors in your office? I saw a trooper standing outside."

"Yeah, he is. I told the Feds a murder is handled by the state police, not me. I think Connors expects me to say something to him about the FBI, but I'm not going to give him the satisfaction—"

He was cut off by Eddie, who rushed up to the booth, breathing hard. "Sheriff, the you-know-who is here."

In one fluid motion, Toil was on his feet. "Well, I gotta run. C'mon Eddie, let's go." Toil bolted from the table.

Eddie remained behind, rubbing the back of his neck and shifting his weight from one foot to another. It looked as if he wanted to say something but was having trouble finding the words. "You know, about last night. When you were walking away, right before you made the first turn, uh, uh, I know you're not going to believe this, um, but I swear to God, coming up behind you on the road I saw—"

"Eddie!" Toil shouted from the far side of the room. Startled patrons turned to look at the deputy.

"Talk to you later." Eddie left in pursuit of the sheriff.

"Later." Hubbard frowned. What did Eddie see? *Moonshine plays tricks on your mind.*

He didn't want to hear another ghost story.

A few minutes later, he paid his bill and exited the café, squinting in the bright morning sun. *Don't get tied up in this. Emily is arriving in just a few hours. Stay focused. Go buy a new tractor.*

Across the square there were six large vehicles that hadn't been there earlier. Three Suburbans and three panel vans, all black with tinted windows, were parked in a row in front of the sheriff's office. It appeared the FBI wasn't interested in making a low-key entrance into Hayslip.

The arrival of the FBI energized the members of the news media. They stood behind the yellow tape and badgered the trooper with questions.

One reporter's shouted question floated across the town square. "What's going on?"

Yeah. What is going on?

11

YOUR ACTION NEWS TEAM

HUBBARD WAS STILL ON THE SIDEWALK in front of City Café when he heard a voice coming from his left.

"*Hey* . . . Hey, buddy! Help me out, please." It was a man's voice filled with desperation. Hubbard turned around to see a middle-aged man chugging down the sidewalk. The pudgy man's face was red, and covered in sweat. His appearance was so strained that Hubbard thought the man was having a heart attack.

"Are you all right?" Hubbard asked, trying to remember CPR.

The man caught up with him and grabbed Hubbard's arm, holding him while he caught his breath. A second man, somewhat younger, with a video camera in one hand and a canvas bag slung over his shoulder, was following behind him. Hubbard noticed the sweat-stained writing pad in the first man's hand.

"Can I help you?"

"Please . . . please," the man said, between breaths.

The cameraman behind the reporter was in a much better shape. When he joined them, he looked up at the sky, shielding his eyes in the bright sunlight, and then took a few steps to the left, putting the sun behind him. He placed the camera on his shoulder and pointed it at Hubbard.

The panting man had recovered somewhat, although his shirt collar was soaked with sweat.

"We've got to feed an interview about the murder of the student back to the station within five minutes for the noon news," the reporter said.

Hubbard looked at his watch.

The reporter held up his hand. "I know it looks like we've got time. But we've got to put the whole thing together. Do my VO, send it, and they have to assemble it . . . It takes time. I need a comment from a local on the murder . . . any local will do and you're right here."

"Well, I don't really know anything. The folks in the municipal building are probably your best source of—"

"Oh, no. I just need a comment from a resident. You live here, don't you?"

"Well . . . yeah," Hubbard said. An old man, Mark Stillings, caught his eye from across the square. The elderly man loved to talk. In fact, he hated to stop talking. "I'll tell you who'd be good. See that gentleman over there—"

"If I have to run across this square, I'll die. I'll literally die. No joke," the reporter pleaded. "It's just a couple of questions, nothing big. Thirty seconds of your time. Do unto others, you know? Your name?"

"John Riley Hubbard . . . Okay, thirty seconds, and that's it."

"God bless you," the reporter said. "I'm Ben Silverman. I'm with Channel Five's 'Total News Now' news team."

"Nice to meet you."

"So, do you know what to do in an interview?" Silverman made a hand gesture to the cameraman.

"Uh . . . I answer your questions?"

"Well, that's a good start. But I mean you need to answer with full sentences, not just 'yes' or 'no.' Like if I ask something like . . . Are tomatoes an important crop for Hayslip? You'd answer, 'tomatoes are a very important crop to Hayslip' . . . or whatever you thought. Got it?

"Uh . . . yeah, I guess that makes sense."

"Okay, let's begin with an easy one."

Hubbard nodded. He wondered if this was a good idea.

"There's talk around town about the death of a young Arab man with a mysterious background, a loner with few friends. I've heard some people believe his death may be associated with terrorist activities. Do you think it's understandable that some people are thinking about terrorism? Or do you disagree with the talk about terrorism?"

Hubbard took a moment, struggling with the question. "I . . . uh . . . guess . . . I disagree?"

The reporter sighed. "Remember full answers." He tried another question. "Do you think stronger gun controls could've done anything to prevent this murder?"

"Um . . . I don't . . . wasn't he killed by a shotgun?"

The reporter closed his eyes. "Jesus," he said softly.

"I'm sorry I don't know if I'm very good at this," Hubbard said.

The reporter tried again. "Tell me about the sense of outrage the town feels now."

"Outrage?" Hubbard noticed that the reporter frowned. "I guess we all feel a sense of outrage. When anyone is murdered, it's natural to be outraged, I guess."

"There have been complaints in the past about the state police in southeast Arkansas. What do you think about the way the state police is handling the investigation?"

"I don't know what the state police are doing. I don't think anyone in town does. They haven't given out any information. I guess they'll make some announcement later today."

The reporter turned to look at the cameraman, who shrugged in response.

"Okay," Silverman said. "That'll have to do. Thank you."

Before Hubbard responded, the two men were running back to their truck. Hubbard stepped off the curb and spotted Eddie running back toward the café.

Eddie waved at he approached. "The FBI folks left Washington early this morning and they got some real empty stomachs. I gotta pick up their order." He came to a stop in front of Hubbard. "And guess what?"

"What?"

"They got a female FBI lady with them and she's a looker and a half!"

Hubbard began a warning. "Now, Eddie—"

Eddie shook his head in a broad motion. "Oh, no! I've learned my lesson the hard way. I'm live bait for women. I know that now."

"That's good. Any leads? What are they talking about in there?"

"Nobody's talking about anything—they're all yelling like they're on late-night radio."

"Really? What are they yelling about?"

"I'm Southern Baptist. Baptists can't say the words the FBI man used without guaranteeing a spot in hell. My preacher says that it's better to bite your tongue than fall off the precipice into the fiery inferno."

"I don't want you to be damned for eternity on my account. Just give me an idea of what they're saying . . ."

Eddie's eyes turned up and his brow creased in concentration. "Let's see . . . the *blankety-blank* corrupted crime scene evidence . . . and whose *blanking* footprints are whose in the police photos . . . and why Connors allowed a *mother-blanking* reporter on the scene. And how the hell did the reporter find out about the murder in the first place?"

Head bent, Hubbard listened intently to Eddie's summary, surprised Connors rather than Toil, was blamed for the bungled crime scene.

Eddie picked up speed as he got into a rhythm. "And the amateur way Connors runs an investigation and why does Connors try to blame everything on the sheriff and why'd it take so long to stop *blanking* around and get a team to the Arab's apartment."

Eddie stopped talking with an expectant look on his face, apparently waiting for Hubbard's reaction.

Hubbard couldn't help but smile. "Well, I guess I agree with the FBI's summary of events."

Eddie nodded. "Well, I've got to get going or they'll be yelling at me about why I took so *goddamn* long to bring them their hamburgers."

Eddie realized he used the base language of a sinner, his voice lowered in dejection. "Well, look at me. I'm talking like I'm a special agent with the FBI."

Hubbard patted Eddie on the shoulder in an effort to console him as the deputy went into the café.

Across the square, the reporters were still waiting for some kind of statement from the sheriff, state police, FBI, or whoever might be running the show. Hubbard had his own questions. Taking the long way to the municipal building, Hubbard passed the row of FBI vehicles, all empty save one. Behind the wheel of an SUV, an agent in the familiar blue jacket held a cell phone to his ear. His face was colored by emotion. To Hubbard, it looked like he was begging for understanding from someone who didn't give a hoot about his emotional distress. The agent's left hand was on the steering wheel and Hubbard saw the gold band. *Ah, marriage.*

Hubbard was now at the rear of the building. Back at mid-century, during Hayslip's golden years, the entire city building was filled with town and county offices. As cheaper imported tomatoes flooded the market, Hayslip declined in size, and so did the number of public servants. Instead of letting large sections of the building remain vacant, private businesses leased office space. One of those businesses was the *Pink Lady Beauty Parlor.* The shop's entrance was located at the rear of the large building. He knew the shop's owner, Sally Place, would accommodate a man in need.

The *Pink Lady's* door and the sign above were adorned with a painted illustration of a tomato, since the business's name was a reference to a popular tomato type, not a blushing woman. Hubbard paused before he went in, coming up with phony details to justify his request—if pressed.

As he entered, the happy chatter of women, comfortable in their domain, greeted him. He was inside for only a moment before their conversations diminished, hair dryers were lowered, scissors fell silent, and heads turned toward him. The women brazenly examined him, looking him up and down. It was disconcerting.

Sally Place came out of a room at the back of the salon and appeared surprised to see Hubbard standing at its center. She glanced at her hairdressers and tapped her watch with emphasis. "Back to work," she said. Sally approached Hubbard and examined him like he was a yard sale find.

Hubbard began his prepared explanation. "I was wondering if I could cut through your shop to get to the uh, facilities. You see—"

"Sure, go ahead. You know the way."

It took a moment to accept the easy victory. "Thanks," he said.

Hubbard headed for the door leading to the interior of the building. The long corridor would pass by the back door into Toil's office.

He slowed as neared the sheriff's office. He didn't know what he hoped to discover on this scouting mission. But if the venetian blinds in front of the glass in the door weren't fully closed, he could view the office unseen, getting a glimpse of a map, or some photos of persons of interest, or a list of key insights into the nature of the crime taped to the wall, as was done in the hundreds or so TV dramas he'd seen. Then he'd be on his way.

The view wasn't as exciting as he hoped. Most of the agents had abandoned their coats and wore white shirts with ties. The eldest agent, a Latino man with silver streaks in his hair, had appropriated Toil's desk.

Eddie had made good time and when he entered carrying a box full of lunch sacks, most of the agents pounced on the box.

Hubbard brought his attention to Calvin Connors. The sergeant was the farthest away, directly opposite Hubbard. He sat alone on a straight-back chair. His eyes were vacant. His only sign of life was his chest rising and falling. Under his arms, dark patches of perspiration stained his khaki shirt. He didn't seem interested in lunch.

One agent, tall and skinny, with a bald spot on the rear of his head, stood in front of a white board. Hubbard noted the thin agent's wire-framed glasses when the man turned his head to say something to the senior agent at the desk. The older agent didn't react, so he returned his attention to something written in bold red marker on the board. Frustratingly, only a few letters were visible, the complete sentence was blocked from Hubbard's view by the agent at the board. If Hubbard was going to gain anything from this excursion, the man needed to step aside.

Hubbard counted the agents in the room. The total was fewer than the vehicles parked out front. Maybe Hubbard was wrong—at least some of Feds were inspecting the crime scene or tracking the killer.

He heard a toilet flush, followed by a second and third—maybe all agents were here still. The amount of time available to Hubbard was reduced to the time required to wash hands.

Hubbard issued a thought command to the skinny guy at the white board. *Move!* Were the Feds looking at the murder the same way he was? For Hubbard, evidence for a possible motive was provided by the blue suit the Arab was wearing that morning.

What were these professionals thinking?

The agent put the marker down on the tray. His small movement revealed two words—*Find the . . .*

The man continued to stand motionless in front of the white board.

Find the what? Find the what!

The fed paced to a nearby chair, revealing the last crimson word—*images*. A list of photo-sharing sites was listed underneath. Images? Did they mean digital copies of the photos stolen during the break-in? How did they know about them? Why were they important?

There were two other points, scrawled sloppily on the side and difficult to read. He didn't have time to decipher them; it was time to get going.

Hubbard became aware of another person in the corridor watching him. He slowly turned to face a petite young woman with straight black hair, dressed in a black blazer, matching slacks, and a silver blouse. Her arms were folded and an FBI badge was attached to her belt. She was coolly evaluating him from a few feet away.

Hubbard tried to bluff. "Excuse me. Can you direct me to the restrooms?"

From her bemused reaction, it wasn't going to work.

"Let me guess. You're the reporter who messed up our crime scene and jeopardized our case. We've heard all about you. Are you the man with the strung-out name? John-Riley-Hubbard."

"I don't know if I'm jeopardizing anything, but I'm Hubbard."

She nodded. "I'm Special Agent Lisa Longinotti with the Federal Bureau of Investigation. Would you like to step into the sheriff's office for a moment?"

"Do I have a choice?"

"No."

"Then I'd love to." He held out his arm toward the door, allowing her to go first.

Agent Longinotti opened the door and strode through, making an oversized announcement as if she was a magician preparing the audience for the unexpected rabbit. "Look who I found wandering about."

Hubbard made a tentative entrance, uncertain of the rabbit's duties on stage.

Sgt. Connors bolted up from his chair as if he'd been goosed. His hand shot forward, pointing at Hubbard. "That's him," Connors said. "He's that son-of-a-bitch Hubbard. *He's* responsible for this mess."

The agents in shirt sleeves sprang from their chairs, looking as if they wanted to tackle Hubbard. Fortunately, they waited for instructions from the man behind the desk.

There were too many people in the room to focus on them all, so Hubbard turned to the middle-aged agent. "Hi, welcome to Hayslip, Arkansas. We're glad you're here."

"That's on the sign coming into town," Connors said.

"It bears repeating," Hubbard said.

The senior agent let his pen drop on the pad. He leaned back in his chair and sized up Hubbard. The agent let the tension build and do its work on Hubbard, like solvent on a rusted bolt. The older man was good. So skilled at this interrogation tactic, it took a moment for Hubbard to find his bearings. Why was his act so familiar? Hubbard looked down at his work boots and sighed quietly. The man behind the desk played the game well, but R. J. Hubbard wrote the book.

"You're the reporter with three names," the agent said. "I was expecting someone more ominous from your description." He glanced at Connors, and then returned his focus to Hubbard. Putting great emphasis on each name, he said, "John-Riley-Hubbard, I am Thomas-Antonio-Eduardo-Ramirez, Special Agent-in-Charge for the Federal Bureau of Investigation."

Hubbard was silent, but it seemed like Ramirez wanted a response before proceeding. "I like your names. You beat me by one."

Ramirez ignored Hubbard's comment. "Under the tenets of the Patriot Act, I can put you in jail right now, without charges, and keep you there for as long as I want."

Connors eased up beside Agent Ramirez like they were co-captains of the team. He broke into a grin so wide; it was like the Arkansas Lottery had called his number.

Ramirez looked at one of the agents standing behind Hubbard. "Agent Ryan, contact the Little Rock office and see how long it will take them to get prisoner transport to come to Hayslip."

Connors beamed broadly and looked like he wanted to dance a jig.

There was a momentary hesitation in the voice coming from behind Hubbard. "Y—Yes, sir." Hubbard turned around to watch the agent leave. He glanced at Toil and Eddie, their expression of horror was unmoving, locked in place like the hardened ash forms of faces uncovered at Pompeii.

"How does the Patriot Act apply? Are you saying that the Arab kid was a terrorist? Or that he was killed by terrorists?"

Ramirez head went backward slightly, as if he was surprised by the pushback. He leaned forward. "I ask the questions. You answer them."

Hubbard realized that he needed to dial back any perception that he was challenging Ramirez's authority. "Yes, sir. Fair enough."

Hubbard's prepared for his role in the coming drama. It would be challenging, Ramirez was experienced. Hubbard's advantage was that Ramirez had no time to prepare. And his subordinates, as demonstrated by Agent Ryan's momentary hesitation, were inexperienced.

Ramirez's instruction to get prisoner transport was bullshit.

Longinotti walked to a chair to the right of the desk and sat down. Connors had made a move for it, but stopped when Longinotti grabbed it. He remained standing behind Ramirez, arms folded, smirking.

Hubbard looked down at the floor, his mind hoping for the best outcome possible. *Please don't tell Connors to leave. Please don't tell Connors to leave. Please don't tell Connors—*

"Have a seat," Ramirez said, indicating that he wanted Hubbard to sit in the worn oak chair at the front of the desk.

Hubbard sat down.

Longinotti was relegated to the sidelines for this, but she was more troubling for Hubbard than Ramirez. She seemed to size him up quite differently from her boss. Her expression was set, and her eyes narrowed into a laser-like focus. Hubbard prayed she had the good sense not to interrupt her agent-in-charge boss.

Ramirez leaned back into his chair, appearing confident and relaxed. "Well, for a reporter at a small town weekly newspaper you seem to be quite dedicated to your job. Up and at 'em quite early in the morning, are you?"

Hubbard's eyes flashed toward the trooper and his head tilted in a nod so subtle it was almost subliminal. He hoped it looked like Connors had communicated through an expression visible only to Hubbard, perhaps encouragement. He needed for this to last for a moment longer before Connors exploded in outrage. He returned his focus to Ramirez.

"I'm a farmer. I get an early start every morning," Hubbard said.

"But yesterday morning, how did you know a body had been discovered in Shanty Town?"

Connors shifted forward in his seat causing the old chair to creak.

Hubbard pretended to be distracted by the squeak. A slight furrow in his forehead appeared, a trace of a grimace, trying to convey the idea that he was concerned that Connors might be reacting nervously to the interrogation, giving them both away. His face returned to the innocent expression that a child assumes when he is caught with his hand in the cookie jar.

Longinotti looked away from Hubbard for the first time and leaned back to check out Sgt. Connors.

"Police scanner." Hubbard turned to Connors. "Cal, tell them a police scanner can pick up the state police."

Connors seemed startled by the stupid question. "Yeah, of course it can. Everyone knows that."

Hubbard was pleased by his support. "Thanks. See?" he said, in as warm a voice he could create.

Connors scowled.

"Oh, come on, Mr. Three Names," Ramirez said. "You've got someone local here that's feeding you information about the crime. We're going to close up that leak. Close it up, permanently."

Hubbard eyes grew wide in faux fear. He stared at one of Connor's shirt buttons then looked at Ramirez. "P—Please I have a daughter. If you think we're working together—"

"We?" Ramirez said. His eyebrows rose in showy curiosity. The reporter wouldn't be hard to break.

"Well, I thought that's what you meant. Didn't you? *Are you playing me?* What do you already know?" Hubbard acted like a desperate man and tried to appear like he was struggling to not look at Connors for guidance.

Hubbard's eyes flashed in the direction of Toil, still sitting, but sweating profusely. The sheriff looked like he was trapped in a sauna fully clothed. Fortunately, Hubbard and Connors were the two lead players in this drama and had the focus of the audience.

"I really don't want to lock you up," Ramirez said. "I didn't know you had a daughter. How old is she?"

"Ten," he said. "She needs her dad."

"I have a daughter, too. Tell me who told you about the murder and you'll be home tonight."

"I'm not working with anyone. If you think Cal and I are . . ."

Connors had been rocking back and forth on his feet like a tea kettle in a cartoon. He boiled over. "It's a lie."

Hubbard looked at Connors like he was an ally. He nodded vigorously. "Damn straight it's a lie," he told Ramirez, nodding at Connors. "We both categorically deny it. I consider Calvin a friend, a good friend. But he never gave me any information about the Arab's murder that morning."

"That's another lie," Connors bellowed. His denial felt as strong as a gale-force wind.

Hubbard's face became concerned by Connors admission.

Connors realized that his outburst worked against him. "I didn't mean it the way it sounded."

"Small towns, I hate them all." Ramirez said. "Everybody's somebody's cousin. I'll never get to the bottom of this and you're all wasting my time. Connors, get out of here. We'll be out there in a minute."

"But . . ." Connors said, wanting to begin a renewed defense of his innocence.

"Out. Right now. Ramirez pointed at the door. "Not another word or I'll call your captain to complain about your professionalism."

Connors seemed struck by fear. A complaint by the FBI's Special Agent-in-Charge to his boss would probably join a long list of existing grievances. Connors trudged for the exit.

Ramirez pointed to the remaining agents. "The sheriff and deputy will show you every entrance to this building. I want them all secured."

Toil, Eddie, and the remaining agents headed out the rear exit. When the office door closed, Ramirez turned back to Hubbard. "Look Riley, or Riley John. I'm going to give you a break because you have a daughter. I know you're going to write something for the local paper, but don't get in our way again. And, of course, if you find out anything about the murder, I expect you to inform us. This is a federal investigation. Understand me?"

"Yes sir."

"Now, to show you how easy it can be to work with me," Ramirez pointed to a file on top of a side table and nodded at Longinotti. "We're going to provide you with a photo of the victim for your paper before it's released to any other media outlet. You can tell your editor that your paper is the first to receive it. We'll be releasing it a little later to everyone else."

The advance release didn't make much difference to a weekly newspaper, but Mrs. Welsh would be pleased that the FBI acknowledged her paper's importance to the community.

"Thank you," Hubbard said.

Longinotti seemed to have problems handing over the photo to Hubbard. "But sir, I thought—"

Ramirez appeared irritated by her tentative objection. "Get it."

Longinotti got up and went to retrieve the folder.

Ramirez turned back to Hubbard. "All we have now is the Arab's driver's license photo, but were trying to track down other images."

Longinotti handed him a small envelope from the folder. She also handed him a card. "Here's my business card. Send me an e-mail and I'll get the Little Rock office to send you a digital copy."

"Thanks," Hubbard said, and began to open the clasp on the small yellow packet.

"We've got to get to work. Let's go." Ramirez reached for his coat on the back of the chair and headed for the front door. He stopped at the door to deliver one final threat. "I'm telling you once. No more unofficial releases of information under strict penalty of federal law. You were lucky this time. Next time, it'll be different." Ramirez exited.

Hubbard looked at the photo. As Ramirez had said, it was Amir's driver's license photo, the same one that Toil showed Hubbard at the ditch. In the photo, Amir, wearing a yellow polo shirt, stared directly into the camera . . . *with no trace of a smile.*

They had doctored the photo, transforming the Arab into a close, but not exact replica of the student. Amir didn't look like Amir anymore.

Hubbard felt his brow creased in confusion, and quickly tried to hide his reaction. He returned the photo to the envelope. He looked up and met Longinotti's intense gaze with as blank a face as he could manage.

She met his eyes directly. He might not have been able to disguise his reaction, but she couldn't hide the thoughts behind her concerned expression either—she knew that Hubbard realized the photo had been altered.

After an uncomfortable moment, she left the office in Ramirez's wake.

Hubbard was now alone in the office and sighed in relief. The hallway door sprang open, and Sheriff Toil and Eddie burst into the room, still unsettled by the confrontation.

Toil was breathing hard; one hand was on his chest. His other hand wiped the sweat from his brow with a handkerchief. "Oh man, I thought they were going to send you to Guantanamo Bay. What happened?"

Hubbard shrugged. "Ramirez told me to be quiet about the case under penalty of law."

Eddie grinned. "Us too," he said.

Hubbard smiled back. It was as if they all had been inducted into a secret club. He looked at his watch. Emily would be home within minutes.

This was going to be a day to remember.

12

THE SURPRISING MRS. ESPINOZA

TEN MINUTES BEFORE HIS EX-WIFE was scheduled to drop Emily off, Hubbard parked his truck at the side of his house. By the time it became twenty minutes after one p.m., he was pacing nervously on his front porch. His ex-wife was frequently late, and he tried not to read more into her tardiness than necessary. But still, he could never be certain about anything that involved the ex-Mrs. Hubbard.

From the porch, he heard Anne's Honda Accord turn off the dirt road onto the farm's gravel driveway. Hubbard waited expectantly, and a moment later he saw the sedan as it rounded the row of pine trees. The car left the farm's driveway after another thirty yards, and parked on his lawn facing the porch.

Thanks, he thought. His lawn needed some new tire ruts. No matter what she did, and he knew it would be galling, he couldn't lose sight of the goal—Emily at home.

Hubbard tried to see what was going on in her vehicle. Bright sunlight reflected blue skies and white clouds on the glass, obscuring the car's interior. He could tell Anne was sitting behind the wheel, but there was a stranger in the passenger seat. Emily had to be in the back seat.

The couple seemed to be having an argument. He remembered

many such lively conversations with her. He became impatient waiting for them to resolve their conflict and stepped off the porch.

Anne's door opened, followed by Emily's. The trunk lock was released and the lid popped up.

Emily didn't have her usual smiling face, her bottom lip was
pressing against the upper one as if she were steeling herself for a
vaccination shot. She marched toward the house, dodging Hubbard's outstretched arms. "I hate you," she said to Hubbard, and
went inside, letting the screen door slam behind her, venting her
ten-year-old fury.

Hubbard cleared his throat and turned to Anne who was carrying
a child's suitcase. It was a very small bag, considering she was to be
here for at least the summer.

Hubbard pointed at the pink suitcase. "Is that all of Emily's
things you brought?" He tried his best to make the question sound
light, happy, and free from frustration. As if bringing none of her
clothes was an inspired idea.

Anne produced a smile that managed to show a remarkable number of white teeth. At one time, he thought she had a great smile.
Now her bared mouth looked like an alligator's grin.

"She's growing so much; I thought you'd probably want to buy
her a new wardrobe that fit her. I'm keeping the rest of her stuff at
home. A young girl needs the reassurance of having a secure home
with her mama."

"Yes, of course. I see what you mean. It makes perfect sense. Um
. . . Why is Emily so upset?"

"Children can always tell, can't they? They have a remarkable
sense about people. They can see into the dark troubled soul of an
adult and just—*know*." Anne made a gesture toward Hubbard as if
he was the example that illustrated her point.

Hubbard took a deep breath, releasing his tension. He turned
back to her car, trying to see through the reflections on the windshield to the man still inside.

"Why doesn't your friend get out? I'd like to meet him." *And give
him my condolences.*

"Oh, no. I'm not making that mistake again. You end up destroying all my relationships."

Hubbard's eyebrows knitted together in confusion. "How do I—"

"Don't play innocent with me. As soon as any of my men meet you, everything starts to fall apart. They say they don't think you're as bad as I told them: You're not a monster, they say—ha! Then they begin to think there's something wrong with me. I won't make that mistake again."

Hubbard paused to make a measured reply. "I don't think meeting me is the reason they'd think something's wrong with—"

"Well, what else could it be? Now let's talk about child support."

"I thought you would pay me the same amount I was—"

"Oh, no. I'm not doing this to make things worse for me." Anne pointed at the farmhouse. "I can go in there and drag Emily back to her loving home." She took a step toward Hubbard's front door.

Hubbard reached out for her. "No, no, no, you'd don't have to pay any child support. I got it. No problem."

"In fact, I was thinking your payments would just continue." Anne looked at Hubbard intently.

Hubbard was stunned. "I—I don't have that kind of money . . . You know that."

"I figured you'd pull a stunt like that . . . Okay, I'll carry you for a while, but we'll talk about it again at the end of summer."

Hubbard's mood soared. It was the first time Anne had hinted Emily's stay might continue past summer. "Sure . . . sure." He reminded himself to keep his mouth shut. He made a gesture toward her car and its occupant. "I'm happy things are going so well for you."

Anne put her hand on Hubbard's arm, squeezing his bicep. "He's just as strong as you are. Maybe stronger."

An indistinct noise came from the car. It was muted, like a dull thump.

Hubbard glanced at the mirror-like windshield and pulled his arm away from her. "What're you doing?"

"My man can be very jealous . . . and he's not afraid to fight for me. Maybe if you'd fought for me more we'd still be . . ." She shrugged her shoulders.

Hubbard only thought his reply. *I never fought for you. You just caused a lot of fights.*

Her face became a portrait of pity mixed with sorrow. "A woman wants a man who's willing to die for her. You'll never understand us, will you?"

"No, I suppose not."

Anne smiled at his admission. "Okay. I'm off. Jay and I are going to use this time to explore our love, our passion. I've never known a love like this—ever. I've just outgrown you."

Hubbard nodded. "You do seem taller. I wish you both the best."

Anne sashayed back to her car and stopped at the door, glancing back at Hubbard, he assumed, to see if his eyes were on her ass. She flashed her smile-of-many-teeth in farewell. In a moment, Anne and her barely visible man were behind the trees and on the road for home.

Hubbard remained on the lawn, trying to decompress from the encounter. His ex-wife could be a walking public service announcement on the dangers of excess drinking.

Inside the house, Hubbard climbed the stairs carrying Emily's pink suitcase. He had a fair amount of trepidation about Emily's mood. He didn't know what Emily was told about her sudden return to Hayslip, but apparently the news was not meeting with her approval.

Emily was sitting on her bed, her back against the headboard, her arms folded across her chest. Her braided ponytail draped over her shoulder with a purple bow at its end. She stared at her fluorescent purple canvas shoes, clicking her toes together absentmindedly.

Hubbard set her suitcase on the floor and sat beside her. "I'm so glad you're here—"

"All my friends are in Little Rock."

Hubbard nodded. "I understand. It's rough to leave your friends. But the good news is that you have friends here, too. You always see them when Mom lets you come down for a visit."

"But everybody's got *school* friends. I won't fit into a group at school coming in this late. Even if I make friends, Mom will pull me out at the end of summer and take me back to Little Rock— until she gets a new boyfriend and then I'll be back here again. I don't want to have to make new friends every time mom changes men. It's not fair."

"No, you're right. It's not fair. Would it help if you were here fulltime?"

"Mom won't let you."

"We'll see if we can work it out. I have an idea and sometimes I can be pretty persuasive."

Emily looked at him like she wasn't convinced. "What if you get a new woman?"

"I'd only date a woman that you approved of. And I'd marry her, too. So there would be no more new women for you to worry about after that."

Emily looked like she was considering what he had just said. "Do I get to approve of her? Mama doesn't let me do that with her men. They just show up in the morning at breakfast. I don't like any of them. You promise I get to vote?"

Hubbard winced when he heard about his daughter's breakfast discoveries. He held out his hand to make a bargain. "Deal?"

Emily examined his face then examined his hand. She spit on her right hand to make their agreement contractually binding. "Deal."

Hubbard spit on his own hand. This had become serious. Where did his daughter learn to negotiate like that? What did he just agree to in a bout of guilt?

They shook hands in silence.

"In the meantime, I need your help to get Mrs. Espinoza all settled in."

"Who's Mrs. Espinoza?"

"Well, she's a nice lady who will be working here for a while and helping me take care of things. I need you to show her how we like things: The kinds of cookies we like, the things we love to snack on, our favorite games—that sort of thing.

"Don't you know my favorite cookie?"

"Well, I sure do, but Mrs. Espinoza doesn't."

Emily eyed him suspiciously. "Okay, daddy, what's my favorite cookie?"

Hubbard froze. He should know this.

Emily saw him hesitate. "Mama knows my favorite cookie."

"Well, so do I. You like uh, . . . daddy cookies."

"Daddy cookies? What're daddy cookies?"

"They're like gingerbread men expect they're thinner, younger and better looking—and they're made of chocolate—lots and lots of chocolate."

Emily burst out laughing. "Oh, daddy! You're so silly. Can she really make daddy cookies? Are those real?"

"When you're sitting down with a plate of daddy cookies and milk, you can tell me if you think they're real or not."

Hubbard heard a vehicle's wheels crunch down his gravel drive. He stood and looked out Emily's bedroom window. An older Chevy truck, white with some rust, came around the pines. It drove down the driveway and followed the recent tire tracks made by Anne's car onto the grass. He sighed.

He pointed out the window. "Look she's here."

Emily hopped off the bed and ran to the window. No one had gotten out of the truck.

"I don't see her."

"Well, she's probably getting her things together. Some older women carry stuff like medicine, mints, and handkerchiefs in their purse. Her brother drove her here."

"Is she a nice lady?"

"Well, I haven't met her. But I bet she loves kids. Now remember, we've got to be gentle with her, no roughhousing. Neither of us can climb on top of her. Okay?"

"Okay," Emily said, laughing again.

"But you can still climb on me. Hop on my back and let's go welcome Mrs. Espinoza."

By the time that Hubbard and Emily came outside, the truck's passenger door was open. A Latino teenager with eyeglasses, wearing a white neck brace, was standing beside it. The boy was speaking with someone inside the vehicle, but turned toward them when he heard the screen door slam. His head jerked backward when he spotted Hubbard. He grimaced in pain and brought his hand to his neck. One eyebrow arched as he examined Hubbard with obvious disdain.

Hubbard let Emily slide off his back and crossed to the driver's side of the truck. Another Latino man, older than the teenager, was in the driver's seat. He also seemed unpleasantly surprised by Hubbard and viewed him with apparent reservations, one eyebrow arched in distrust.

Did the two men come alone? Where was Mrs. Espinoza? As he neared the truck, he saw a small figure sliding off the truck's bench seat on the opposite side of the truck.

The Latino driver spoke English without an accent. He sounded as if he thought he had made a wrong turn. "Is this the Hubbard place? The home of the nephew of Mr. R.J. Hubbard?"

Hubbard tried his half-smile to ease the man's obvious nervousness. "Yes, you found us. I'm John Riley Hubbard."

"I'm Luis Espinoza. I—I work for your uncle."

"Oh, I thought I recognized you," Hubbard said. The man's discomfort seemed to increase. "Were you able to bring . . . um . . . your aunt? Grandmother?

Emily was talking to a young girl on the other side of the truck. R.J. was right. His daughter had a natural gift for languages and spoke easily with her. Emily's Spanish was fluid, without any grating stops and starts.

"Aunt?" Luis snorted. "Maria is my sister."

Hubbard nodded. "I see. Will she be able to come today?"

"She's here," Luis said, tilting his head at the passenger side of the truck.

Hubbard took a step to his left, ignoring the angry teenager with the injured neck, who was still staring daggers at him, and focused on the female visiting with Emily. She must be older than he thought, obeying some alternate rules of aging. "Mrs. Espinoza?" The young woman straightened to face him.

Hubbard sucked in some air and he took an involuntary step back. She was no one's idea of a grandmother. Her eyes were a deep, rich brown that made you forget watery blue eyes. Long eyelashes formed magnificent frames around those wonderful orbs.

Fortunately, Luis began to blather, allowing Hubbard time to recover from the surprise. "This is my sister Maria. She doesn't speak English . . . I told her that English would be more useful to learn. But what can you tell a woman?" There was more, something about "good with children" and "taught school" and other sentences that just floated in the air like lost balloons.

At long last, complete thoughts stormed their way into Hubbard's head—*What-the-hell? I mean what-the-hell?* More meaningful concepts followed: *Your mouth is open. Close it.* What had Mr. Carlos done to him? He had expected a woman with a careworn face who would dispense motherly advice and help nurture Emily. Instead Mr. Carlos sent him a beautiful young woman? What kind of bait-and-switch was that?

Her hair was cropped shorter than most Latino women he had met, dancing lightly across her neck and shoulders. Her legs were long, almost endless . . .

She was a terrible disappointment.

Hubbard realized belatedly that Luis stopped speaking. He forced his eyes away from the surprising Mrs. Espinoza, and nodded a greeting to her. "How ya doing?" he mumbled, and turned back to Luis.

Luis Espinoza glared at him with an expression that Hubbard interpreted as: *You son-of-a-bitch, I know what you're thinking about my sister.*

Hubbard attempted a facial expression that countered that implied message with: *I'm not thinking anything. Just greeting a new employee like any employer would.* He gave up on that.

The girl had to go. He needed an older woman—an unattractive woman in her twilight years would be perfect. "You know, on second thought," Hubbard said, hoping he'd find an easy way to do this.

A glint of sunlight off metal drew Hubbard's eyes to Luis's left wrist. He glanced first, and then did a double take, as if he doubted the reality of what he had just seen. Luis brought his left arm down quickly behind the door, out of sight.

Hubbard focused on Maria's brother, trying to read his furtive expression. Luis shifted his eyes away, avoiding his gaze. "Do you have the time?" Hubbard asked.

Maria's brother looked at the watch on Hubbard's arm.

"My watch is slow," Hubbard explained.

Luis snapped his fingers and pointed at the seat. "Pablo," he said.

Hubbard stepped closer to the door. "Is it three, yet?" He glanced to his left. Emily was leading Maria Espinoza into the house. They were chattering in Spanish like old friends.

Luis started the truck and it was moving away, even though Luis's nearsighted buddy had barely gotten into it.

Luis called from his open window as he drove off. "We'll pick Maria up at six."

Hubbard watched the truck crunch down the gravel drive and tried to visualize what he saw for only a split-second. Was Luis wearing a Rolex? A twenty-four-karat gold, $50,000 watch? Just like the one taken from Amir's body?

13

KILLING TIME

HUBBARD WATCHED LUIS'S TRUCK grumble down the rocky driveway until it was hidden by the pine trees lining the road. His previous notion that Luis sported Amir's Rolex on his arm seemed absurd. No one was so damn stupid that he'd take an expensive watch from his victim and wear it brazenly around town.

It wasn't a Rolex. It was something else. Nevertheless, to be sure, when Luis returned to pick up Maria; he'd make it a point to see the gold timepiece again.

How did things get so messed up with this girl-woman in his house? He replayed the conversation with Mr. Carlos from the previous day. He didn't recall anything that might've warned him "Mrs. Espinoza" was not what he expected. Usually, Mr. Carlos had a knack for putting the right person in the correct position. He really screwed up this time.

Hubbard headed inside to see what Emily and *Mrs. Espinoza* were doing. It didn't seem wise to let Emily get too attached to the Guatemalan girl since he'd be letting her go.

Excited giggling floated through the screen door. Well, what did he expect? The young woman was probably close to Emily's age.

In the kitchen, the two females had removed several bowls from the cupboards. Flour and other baking ingredients from the pantry were spread across the kitchen table. Emily was holding a glass measuring cup with awed reverence, as if she had been entrusted with the Holy Grail.

And Mrs. Espinoza—it was crazy to think of her as Mrs. Espinoza. Did she marry in grade school only to be widowed in high school? No. It was *Maria* who was checking out the kitchen drawers.

Emily flew to Hubbard and grabbed his hand, pulling him to the kitchen table. His daughter looked as if she was about to come apart at the seams from glee overload. "Guess what we're doing, Daddy?"

They parted as Maria came between them carrying a set of measuring spoons in her hand. She flashed a smile at Hubbard that produced unexpected results. He felt blood rushing hither and yon in his body, assembling for action.

He looked away and focused on Emily. "I don't know. What?"

"We're making Daddy Cookies!"

Hubbard's forehead creased. "You're making what?"

"Daddy Cookies!" Emily seemed pleased she surprised him, nodding as if she felt the need to confirm the reality of the wonderful news. "They have those cookies in Guatemala."

"They do?" Hubbard looked at Maria, puzzled. The girl-woman glanced at him in a charming way, shy, yet flirtatious, which was disconcerting. Did she intuitively understand that Hubbard had made them up? Are Daddy Cookies a real thing in Guatemala? He warned himself to avoid looking directly at her, especially into her eyes. Her eyes were nothing but trouble. *Keep your mind on the game, Hubbard.*

He returned his attention to Emily. "How can you make cookies without a cookie dough tube from the store?"

"I don't know, but Maria knows how."

Hubbard wanted to ask her how she could do that trick. But she was leaning over the table opening a sack of flour. The neckline of her blouse revealed . . . *You have to get out now. Your daughter is in the house.*

"I've got some work that needs to be done right away. Emily, I want to talk to Maria's brother when he comes to pick *her* up . . . Maria . . . Up."

Emily looked at him quizzically. "Okay."

Hubbard left the kitchen and made his escape. When he was safely on the small wooden back porch, he took a deep breath.

Now he had to find something to do. He would fill the time by adjusting the valves on his two water pumps to increase their pressure so they would have enough power to push water across wide fields.

As he hiked toward the irrigation equipment, he remembered his conversation with Emily about the parade of new male visitors she encountered at her mother's breakfast table. He blamed himself that Emily had to deal with these strange men coming and going from her life.

During the divorce proceedings, he had been so unsure of his ability to raise Emily properly that he didn't fight hard enough for her. His only option now was to force a rematch; and there was only one man who could help him accomplish that miracle: His uncle.

His stomach churned as he considered asking R.J. for help. He had avoided all of his uncle's offers of support since he was old enough to be on his own. In fact, the last time he asked for R.J.'s assistance was when he was seventeen and begged to go to Montreal for an entire summer to improve his French, a key part of his plan to escape from Hayslip.

Today would mark the first time he went to that bottomless well since the trip to Canada. He took a heavy breath and expelled air through pursed lips. He pulled his cell phone from his pocket. It lay heavy in his hand.

He hoped he had gained a temporarily reprieve when his call went unanswered through several rings. He was about to click off when his uncle came on the line.

"This is R.J." The voice was smooth and assured, as if it was your lucky day to be speaking to him.

"Hi, uh, this is—"

"Kid, I know who you are." Hubbard heard a smile behind R.J.'s words.

"Yeah . . . I don't know why I said that. Um . . . listen . . . uh . . ." Hubbard cleared his throat.

"Are you all right?"

"Yeah, of course." Hubbard's mouth went dry.

"Good . . . I'm fine, too."

"Um . . ." Hubbard swallowed hard and began. "Remember back when I was getting a divorce and you said I could hire a nice, respectable lawyer that I could afford, or retain a hired gun that was a world-class son-of-a-bitch."

"Yeah," R.J. dragged his reply out, like a singer holding a song's ending note. His uncle knew where this was heading.

Hubbard sucked in some air and jumped from the high diving board. "Will you hook me up with the son-of-a-bitch?"

There was a pause on the line. Hubbard wondered during the long silence if R.J. was going to play the "I told you so" card.

Instead, R.J. said, "What took you so long?"

When the call was over, Hubbard returned the phone to his pocket and gazed across a field of soybeans at an orange sun beginning its descent. His hand rubbed the stubble becoming a shadow on his chin. He knew the forthcoming terms for payback would be dear.

A deal was a deal. A daughter was a daughter.

———————◆◆———————

For almost two hours, Hubbard adjusted the pump pressure up and down, trying to find the sweet spot on the valve. Unfettered, the machines pulling spring water from a large pond behind his house were powerful enough to overfill and burst a fire hose.

Emily called from the back porch. "Dad-dy, the cook-ies are read-y!"

Hubbard looked at his watch, then back at Emily. She was about fifty yards away, hopping back and forth from one foot to the other, almost as excited as if she had been awarded the honor of announcing the victorious outcome of a great battle that saved the nation.

"O-kay," Hubbard shouted back. When was the last time he had seen her so happy about anything?

Hubbard entered the house and washed his hands before going into the kitchen. He tried not to laugh when he saw that his daughter's face, hands and clothes were covered in a fair amount of white flour. He glanced at Maria, who was washing dishes. His gaze drifted to the curves of Maria's backside until he became aware of Emily, studying her father's face with too much interest.

He looked down at columns of daddy cookies, aping their pose from gingerbread men. He had to admit, they did look better-looking and somewhat younger than the traditional cookie-men.

"The ones at the edge of the plate are still hot," Emily warned.

"Did you make all these?"

"With Maria's help," Emily said, graciously including the other member of the team.

Hubbard picked a cookie off the plate and under Emily's attentive gaze took a bite. Maria swung around from the kitchen sink, drying her hands on a towel, monitoring his reaction as well.

The cookie was hot, moist, and chocolaty, not the chewy concoction he typically burned in the oven during his rare attempts as a chef. "Wow," he said, genuinely impressed. "These are way good. Why do people use cookie dough tubes? Does Pillsbury know about this?"

He glimpsed Maria, and he knew he needed to say something. "Tres bien . . . Bueno," he said. He corrected himself again. "Mucho Bueno."

Emily apparently felt compelled to translate his rotten Spanish. When Emily finished, Maria smiled at Hubbard and nodded. Hubbard picked up the cookie plate and he offered it to Maria, "Um . . . s'il vu . . . por favor."

Emily started to interpret again, but stopped when her dad flashed an exasperated expression in her direction.

Maria took a cookie. Hubbard noticed her long fingers tapered to a conclusion of pink nail polish.

Emily tugged at his shirt several times to get his attention.

"Daddy . . . Daddy, did you know there's a man who looks just like you on TV?" Emily's head bent to the side, peering around Hubbard.

"Who? What?" Hubbard swung around. The TV was visible through the kitchen doorway, playing silently in the den. There was a shot of the Hayslip town square that cut to a two-shot of Hubbard and the sweating reporter from earlier in the day. A title graphic appeared underneath his image: John R. Hubbard, Hayslip Farmer.

"That *is* you," Emily cried out, pointing at the TV, and bouncing up and down with excitement.

Hubbard grabbed a TV remote control lying on the kitchen table and turned up the volume. As the sound level increased, he could hear the reporter's voiceover. "Some residents expressed disappointment at the pace of the investigation."

Hubbard's was next. In a new angle, his back was to the camera. "I guess we all feel a sense of outrage."

The live version of Hubbard's mouth fell open.

"Why are you outraged, Daddy?"

A tight shot of Hubbard's face appeared on the screen. "I don't know what the state police are doing. They haven't said anything."

Hubbard didn't remember being angry, but he sure looked pissed on TV.

"Why aren't the state police saying anything? Saying anything about what?"

A truck horn announced Luis's arrival. Maria took off her apron and grabbed a sheet of paper off the white-tiled kitchen counter. She handed it to Emily, whispering something that made Emily grin. Maria brushed past Hubbard smelling like chocolate and wantonness.

It took a moment for Hubbard to regain his senses. "Um, nothing, honey. They made it sound like I said something I didn't really say. It's nothing to worry about. Probably no one watched it."

The kitchen wall phone rang sharply. Hubbard jumped a bit.

"Do you want me to answer it?" Emily ran to the Caller ID display box on the kitchen counter. "It says 'Ark State Police'."

Hubbard rubbed his chin. "Um, no, let's not answer it. Give me a minute."

"Maybe they heard you were outraged at them and they want to say they're sorry and make up."

"May—be," Hubbard said.

Emily looked at the paper in her hand. "We need to get all this at the store."

"Get what? . . . What store?" He took the sheet from Emily and saw a long column of Spanish words.

"I can translate for us," Emily said. "It's a grocery list. Maria says we've got to have food in the house if we're going to eat."

Hubbard couldn't remember the last time he made anything that required ingredients and instructions rather than the mindless punching of numbers on a microwave. He nodded. "Well, I suppose she's right."

"The phone's still ringing."

"Ignore it."

Emily grabbed the list back from his hand, and took a deep breath, as if she was preparing to translate. The screen door slammed, and Hubbard remembered Maria was leaving. He clasped Emily by both of her shoulders. "You need to say goodbye to Maria," he said, spinning her around and aiming her at the front of the house. "She'll be upset if we don't wave goodbye."

Emily hopped, skipped and jumped to the door. Hubbard followed. Outside, Maria was in the old truck, sitting next to the surly teenager. The thought that she was romantically involved with the boy arose unexpectedly and he felt an unwelcome twinge of jealousy. Why the hell did he care?

Standing outside his truck, Luis's left hand rested on top of the pickup. In contrast to his earlier visit, Luis smiled and talked leisurely with his two passengers, as if Hubbard's farm was a tropical resort he hated to leave. Hubbard kept a good pace, trying to get there before Luis pulled his arm down. When he was only a few feet away, Luis turned to him and smiled.

"So, how was Maria's first day?" Luis said.

"Fine, I guess," Hubbard said.

"Maria's great!" Emily waved at Maria.

Hubbard nodded in polite agreement as his eyes focused on Luis's big watch and its gold metal band, gleaming in the last rays of sunset. Its large dial was gold as well.

It was a Seiko, not a Rolex. *I must've imagined it . . . Or did I? . . . No . . . Maybe.*

"Maria's a very good cook," Luis said. "She took classes at the finest—"

Emily looked up at Luis. "She made us Daddy Cookies."

"Daddy Cookies? What're those?" Luis said, his brow furrowing at the interruption.

Emily described the imagined pastry to Luis, while Hubbard revisited his memory of Luis's watch.

His attention, however, was drawn away by the passengers in Luis's truck.

Maria beamed at Emily; she seemed to enjoy watching the little girl's animated discussion of cookie baking with the disinterested Luis.

Her brother's friend, Pablo, sitting beside her, stared boldly at him. Hubbard returned his sharp glare, arching one eyebrow.

Was the boy this challenging to everyone? It was difficult to take him seriously. Wearing a thick neck brace, he looked like a Latino *Pez* dispenser.

Pablo shifted awkwardly in his seat, twisting both of his shoulders to gaze at Maria's profile. *He's jealous . . . Of me? . . . Why?*

Searching for something to say, Hubbard complimented Luis on his impressive mastery of English. Luis told him, that unlike Pablo, he been educated at a school for Guatemalan elite destined for government service.

It sounded like fantasy. Luis's membership at the top of society was difficult to imagine. Maria, *oh yeah*, she would be at the top of anyone's list, anywhere in the world. But, Luis?

Hubbard attempted a convoluted strategy to work a discussion of

Rolex watches into their conversation, but Luis ignored him. He got into his truck, and they drove away.

Hubbard watched them depart, deep in thought. The blue vehicle was on the other side of the trees when he realized he'd failed to fire Maria.

"Damn it," he whispered.

The watch Luis wore distracted him: the Seiko was not reassuring.

"I'm hungry," Emily said.

"I thought you ate cookies?"

"I did, but I'm still growing."

Hubbard patted her shoulder. "Yes, you are. Let's go into town and grab something fast. Pretty soon all you'll get to eat is home-cooked meals. No more junk food for you, young lady."

"Can we drive through *The Big Grape?*"

"Might as well, it's the most unhealthy stuff I can imagine."

"Junk food is my favorite kind of food."

"Mine too."

Hubbard decided during their drive, and over Emily's vocal protests, the best course of action was to go to *Piggly Wiggly* first. Whoever replaced Maria would need a fully-stocked kitchen, and the shopping list, written in her delicate hand, was better than anything he could devise.

At the grocery, Emily seemed to forget her hunger pangs when she became commander of their shopping expedition. Very quickly, the simple errand evolved into a grand scavenger hunt. They wove through the aisles, Hubbard pushing the cart and Emily charting their path. Emily's head bobbed up and down as she read and then surveyed the store shelves, stopping to point with delight when she spotted a prize from the list.

Hubbard nixed the vegetables on Maria's list. He had plenty of them stored in the large concrete bomb shelter that his grandfather built behind their farmhouse during the Cuban Missile Crisis. Inside the formidable concrete structure, which always remained cool, there were two rows of large wood slat baskets filled with root vege-tables packed in sawdust.

The agri-contents of the family bomb shelter reflected his hope, despite all contrary signs, that his life would one day find one sem-blance of normalcy: A farmer feeding his family from the harvest of his fields.

After he had loaded all the bags in back of the truck, Emily in-formed him that she was practically starved to death, and if they didn't eat right away she would faint.

Hubbard agreed this was an emergency situation and they hur-ried toward *The Big Grape.*

Their destination was a purple-colored, concrete block and neon-bedecked building on 281. The restaurant specialized in every type of food that could be deep fried, and was most popular at night when the journey to Monticello seemed too daunting. He joined a short line of vehicles waiting to order at a speaker entombed in a giant fiberglass grape that bore a toothy grin and faded eyes.

"So, what looks good to you?" Hubbard asked, as they examined the menu board positioned alongside the bloated fruit.

"Can I get the *Onion Life Raft* with chili and cheese?"

"Are you sure you can handle it? It's quite stout."

"It's my favorite. And a *Cherry Swamp Water* soda, please."

"You're a brave little girl."

When he began their dinner order, a familiar voice interrupted him.

"Is this John Riley?"

"Missy? . . . How're you? Is Carla Jo working tonight? And uh, uh . . ."

"Amy?"

"Yeah . . . Amy."

Missy affected a cultured accent. "Amy is on her continental tour, dah-ling. She's vacationing in Europe 'til fall. It's the social season, you know."

"Must be nice."

Missy's drawl returned to its roots. "*You bet your ass.* I didn't know there was so much money in pouring asphalt. She didn't even give us a clue that she planned to go to Europe until she woke us both up about a week ago, and said—"

A new voice purred over the speaker, "Hello, John Riley. How's that big farmer man tonight?"

"Carla Jo?"

"We're graduating in May," Carla Jo said, and playfully added, "We're legal now. You don't have to worry about—"

Speaking quickly, Hubbard said, "And I'm here tonight with my precious daughter, Emily."

The girls didn't miss a beat.

"Hello, Emily. We've missed seeing you," Carla Jo said. "How old are you now?"

"Ten and almost half, more or less."

"Ooooh, you've grown up," Missy said.

"Pretty much," Emily agreed. "Most of what they teach me in school I already knew." The college girls made appropriate sounds of awe at his daughter's expansive knowledge.

Ignoring parental prudence, Hubbard ordered two *Onion Life Rafts* with the works. The Hubbard family stomachs would share the same digestive fate tonight, sinking or swimming together.

At the window, Hubbard had his customary trouble reaching down from his supersized truck to a drive-through service window designed to serve shorter, portion-controlled vehicles of the 1950s. He leaned out the door window, trying to retrieve the cardboard tray that Missy held aloft. With her lithe body and graceful arms arching up to him, she looked like a ballet dancer taking a star turn in a southern-fried pas de deux.

Hubbard regarded her hazel eyes.

This seemed so familiar it felt like déjà vu.

Missy's head tilted. She batted her long eyelashes in response to Hubbard's new interest.

It all clicked.

"And I thought I'd never find you . . . Hello, *Cleopatra*."

Cleopatra blushed.

"I think we may have a friend in common. Could I come by sometime and visit?"

14

HOUSES KEEP SECRETS, EX-WIVES DON'T

ON THE DRIVE HOME FROM *The Big Grape,* Hubbard sidestepped Emily's questions as deftly as he could. He could tell her ten-year-old mind was churning away, trying to understand his unusual interest in the pretty girls at the drive-in. He couldn't tell her that these girls could provide the key to understanding the reason for Amir Abadi's murder.

"Daddy, why did you call that girl 'Cleopatra'?"

"Because she wore a Cleopatra costume on Halloween."

"So, why do you need her phone number?"

"I want to talk to her about a boy who went to her school and get some information to help his parents."

The thrust and parry of questions and answers continued until sleepiness overtook his daughter. By the time they got home, Emily's eyelids were fluttering. It was well past bedtime, she needed to eat quickly and get some sleep.

Hubbard grabbed the items needing refrigeration and left the other sacks in the back of his pickup to retrieve later.

When he closed the freezer door in the kitchen, he noticed Emily had polished off her *Life Raft* dinner at the kitchen table. The only bit remaining was her chili-colored mustache.

"Okay, wash your face and get ready for bed."

She nodded, stood, and with eyes blinking and her arms drooped to her sides, she used the minimum amount of energy necessary to propel her from the kitchen.

Checking the time, he returned to the truck for the remaining groceries. Picking up the last grocery sack in the truck bed, he heard a brittle snap coming from the direction of the pines by the road. He glanced up, paused for a moment, but couldn't spot deer moving through the trees. He had no fondness for any of the tick-covered beasts; they did a great deal of damage to a crop if they hopped their way onto a field. Another item for the list: check fencing.

By the time Hubbard made it to Emily's room, she was in bed wearing her favorite pink pajamas, her eyes closed. He stood in the doorway for a moment, marveling at how much she still resembled the toddler he bounced on his knee. He tried to step lightly to the bedside table and the small lamp with the translucent shade featuring the smiling visages of a dozen animated princesses.

"Daddy, do you still have nightmares?"

Surprised, Hubbard straightened abruptly, trying to disguise his embarrassment at the question. "I thought you were asleep . . . Why do you think I have nightmares?"

"Mama told me . . . She said it was because some people have dark secrets in their past. What're your *dark secrets?* Will you tell me? I can keep a secret. *I promise.*"

His jaw clenched. His ex-wife was the gift that kept on giving. Emily would have to deal with those terrible stories one day, but please, not now. He tried to force a chuckle of amusement. "I don't know what your mother is—"

Emily lowered her voice to a whisper. "Daddy, some nights I heard you . . . It scared me."

Reaching down to the floor, Hubbard pretended to straighten her bunny slippers. He came back up, forced a half-smile, and pulled her covers up. "I'm fine. I don't have *night-mares*. I have funny dreams. I laugh at them in my sleep. That's what you heard. Isn't that silly? Let's have a contest to see who can remember a funny dream. The funniest dream wins."

Emily stuck out her pinkie finger. "You promise?"

Hubbard ignored her tiny finger and lowered her hand under the bed covers. "I think I've made more than enough binding contracts with your pinkie this week. We'll talk in the morning."

"I have dreams, too . . . Sometimes."

Hubbard reached for the *Princess* light. "I know you do." He switched the lamp off, leaving only the nightlight burning.

"Maria will decide who had the funniest dream," Emily said.

Hubbard sighed. "We'll see."

He closed Emily's door, remaining outside her bedroom for a moment. *What else had his ex told Emily? . . . Why did he think he had the know-how to raise a daughter? . . . Why was it always so damn dark in this hallway? Stop thinking.*

Maria will be the judge. He should have fired that girl-woman when he had the chance. The longer she stayed, the more Emily would become attached to her. Tomorrow was Maria's last day, come hell or high water.

Downstairs he turned off most of the lights in the house, while discovering more things to add to his to-do list. His circuit stopped at the kitchen. He pulled a notepad from a drawer and sat down at the kitchen table. Taking a deep breath, he slowly released it.

Overhead, a milk-white globe put Hubbard at the center of its circle of direct light. The incandescent pool surrounding him was a stark contrast to the soft gray just outside the door. The rest of the house was silent, except for the faint ticking of a mantel clock coming from the seldom-used living room. Hubbard glanced up when the home's wood flooring popped, contracting due to cooler air circulating underneath the house.

He recalled sitting at the same spot at this table the summer his world fell apart.

After they buried his father, Mr. Carlos decided the allowance R.J. provided for the family's household expense was safer when given directly to the Hubbard boy. He didn't trust the pharmaceutically-fogged mother with a generous amount of cash.

Within a week, the twelve-year-old Hubbard discovered the kind folks at the liquor store were very accommodating; allowing the underage nephew to buy supplies for a get-together his uncle supposedly had in the works. The large number of greenbacks Hubbard held in his hand did much of the convincing.

"Anything to help the grieving family," the owner said. Even at twelve, Hubbard caught the underlying sarcasm.

Before he left the house on his late-night walks in search of ghosts in Shanty Town, he'd fortify himself with a few of beers. Back then, when he was drinking, he heard the floorboards squeak outside the kitchen doorway and thought his mother was approaching, finally wise to her child's drinking and his disappearances.

It was never her, just the strange creak of contracting joists.

By that autumn, older girls were showing the growing boy with a fistful of cash how he could buy moonshine and pot . . . and teaching him other things.

Until he left the house for college when he was eighteen, he had it pretty much to himself. His mother never ventured far from the safety of her bedroom. It was a solitary six years. After two weeks in a college dorm, he returned home with laundry and found his mother, as always, lying in bed. This time, however, she was unnaturally still. A pill bottle in one hand and a note gripped tightly in the other. The slip of paper, torn from his high school notebook read: *Please forgive me.*

It was a simple message that he didn't understand. Was she sorry she took her own life? Did she regret the past few years where she was little more than an apparition in his life? Or was his mother seeking his forgiveness for something that he wouldn't put words to?

That night, after they removed her body and all the neighbors had finished their solicitous, yet sanctimonious visits, he climbed the stairs, threw open her bedroom door, flipped the double bed over, and dragged it piece by piece into the backyard. The bed frame, mattress, box springs, and all the linens were tossed into a lopsided pile. He took a liter bottle of Jack Daniels and poured half of it all over the mound, tossed a match on top of it, and watched as it was slowly consumed by waves of yellow.

As he stared at the flames, he drank as much as he could of the remainder of the Jack Daniels while watching black smoke rise into the moonless sky.

The next week was a drunken haze. In that swirling alcohol fog, he stumbled into Anne.

Just like that it was over. College. The City of Lights. Everything.

The house was too quiet tonight. He needed a tall bottle and a short glass. *No, goddamn it. No.*

He shoved away from the table and banged out the front door, down the steps to the grass. He took a gulp of cool air and bent over, placing his hands on his knees.

Rising up, he took a few steps toward the road, seeking composure. He glanced at the dark ruts in the ground caused by Luis's truck. *You can tell a lot about a farmer by the condition of his front lawn.* He looked away and sighed.

An orange firefly, flitting in the air among the pines by the road caught his eye as it fell to the ground and blinked out.

He stopped in place.

It was too early in the season for fireflies.

A chill of surprise ran down his back. Hidden in the trees, a man had crushed a cigarette out on the ground.

Whoever it was; he'd been concealed there for some time. He felt his heart beating faster, his breath quickening.

He glanced up at Emily's second story window. Her nightlight gave the room a soft, warm glow.

You sick son-of-a-bitch. Hubbard's right hand balled into a fist. With an effort at casualness, he pretended he was in the midst of an aimless walk that was taking him closer to the trees.

The crackle of a brittle pine cone breaking under a footfall was clear in the calm night. Two cypresses in the distance, highlighted by the low moon, bent to the right and bounced back. Something small and solid soared into the air in his direction, bouncing to a stop in front of him.

With the need for pretense gone, Hubbard bolted for the line of trees almost fifty yards away.

Twenty yards from the trees, he heard an engine turn over. He pushed himself to go faster. *Get the license number . . . anything that would put that sick bastard away.*

Hubbard blew into the trees at full stride just as a rifle fired on the road. The narrow tree in front of him cracked open and wood splinters blew into his face. He threw his arm up for protection, as if this were a snowball fight. Distracted by the bullet's near miss, he tripped on a branch and stumbled forward.

He saw a barrel flash and heard a shot. At the same time there was a dull thump as a bullet pounded into the ground a step in front of his faltering pursuit.

"*Shit.*"

Losing his balance, he fell and rolled into the shallow drainage ditch that ran alongside the road. He was breathing heavily, in the grip of adrenaline and rage. Another gunshot and a third slug dug into the ground.

Despite the risk, despite the warning shots, he couldn't stay down. He lifted his head, and came off the cold ground as if he'd fallen on a hot griddle. The creep's car was peeling away, his lights turned off in the shadowy night. Hubbard caught a glimpse of the vehicle's dim form rounding the bend before it was concealed by thick foliage. A second later, he spotted a flicker of bright red through the dense branches as the vehicle's lights came on.

He spun around to race for his truck and continue the chase. But rational thinking returned, unwelcomed, with each of his strides forward.

He didn't know what kind of vehicle he was looking for . . . or the direction it had taken on 281 . . . he didn't have a gun . . . and he'd be leaving his daughter alone in the house . . . He slowed to a halt, breathing heavily.

He took steps toward his house to call the sheriff, but soon halted. Toil would simply call the state police. And the state police would be led by Connors. After his TV interview, he could expect little help from anyone wearing a Smokey hat. Connors would attribute the shooting to an off-season hunter and tell Hubbard to call the Arkansas Game and Fish Commission to complain.

He turned back toward the road and his eyes were drawn to the object that the intruder had thrown. It looked like a rock, but there was something more. He walked fifteen yards to get a better look. Rubber bands secured a small piece of paper to the rock. He pulled it off. In the dim light, he could still read the large block letters: *STOP NOW BEFORE YOU GET HURT.*

Hubbard felt his pulse race. This was about the Arab. The murderer? Why would he be more concerned with him than the FBI? His anger returned and he ached something to hit. *Don't push me. I won't run.*

The secondary plan was not as satisfying as finding the bastard and beating him senseless. He went to his truck and got his flashlight. He walked back to the trees and began a search in the pine needles where he thought he'd seen the firefly fall.

After a few minutes, he spotted the cigarette butt on the ground and picked up the stub. It was still warm. Two words, "Kool Menthol" were printed just above the filter. Without a DNA lab at his disposal, it would have to do.

Hubbard found the cedar tree that stopped the first bullet. The soft wood had shattered at the point of impact, which was head height. If the shooter aimed a few inches to the right, the bullet would have lodged in his skull, killing him.

The shallow drainage conduit lay in front of him. His momentum would've carried him there if he'd been hit; the second body discovered in a Hayslip ditch in less than a week.

The lethal coincidence would make interesting conversation at his autopsy.

He turned his back to the tree and slid to the ground. Sitting back against the tree that stopped the slug that almost stopped him, he drew up his knees, propped his elbows, and rubbed his hands across his face, remembering the past few minutes of pursuit.

What was he thinking? He charged into these trees without thought, unarmed. He even abandoned the relative safety of the ditch when the stalker, or stalkers, were firing at him. What made him act so damn stupid?

One day your anger will kill you. Mrs. Walsh's off-hand comment felt like a doctor's grim prognosis.

15

SPOTTING AN IVORY-BILLED WOODPECKER

THE NEXT MORNING, Hubbard became aware of another presence in his bedroom. He struggled to open tired eyes and focus on the small figure sitting at the end of the bed.

Emily scrutinized his face, her brow lowered in concentration.

Hubbard recalled their conversation from the previous night. Likely, she was looking for trace evidence of a horrific nightmare—or a funny one—still visible on his exhausted features.

She seemed to come to the conclusion that her father's face was a blank slate, and her attention shifted. "Daddy, why are you sleeping with a hammer?"

"Hmm . . . what? Hammer? . . . Oh, this?" He picked up the heavy tool at his side. "Um, I wanted to get an early start. Farmers always need a good hammer near them." He put the hammer on the bedside table. "What are *you* doing up so early?"

"It's not early. It's late. Maria and I have a project."

"Project? . . . What time is it?" Hubbard pulled up on his elbow and looked at the alarm clock. "Eight o'clock? God—" He caught himself, then repeated the censorship on his next word. "Shiittuuute."

He threw off his covers, muttering to himself.

"Did you dream anything?" Emily asked.

Hubbard pulled a fresh t-shirt from the chest of drawers and found a pair of jeans in the closet. He was required to weave around Emily, apparently seeking a junior bird's eye view on his clothes gathering, as he moved. "No. Did you?"

"I dreamed I heard noises. Did you hear noises?"

Hubbard looked at his worn jeans. It jogged his memory about his plans for this morning. He pulled his nicest shirt from the closet and replaced the jeans with slacks. "I slept like a baby."

"Where are you going? I thought you were going to use your red hammer?"

"I am, but a hammer's no good without nails, is it?"

"I bet I know where some are. Do you want me to find them? You won't have to go anywhere."

"I need special nails."

"Special?"

The doorbell rang, saving him from further interrogation.

"Oh, that's Maria at the door. Don't you both have a project?"

"Yeah!" Emily bolted from the room and bounded down the stairs.

Wait. It could be the man from last night making a house call. He grabbed the hammer and trailed after Emily. Already down the stairs, Emily shouted Maria's name and he heard his too-young, too-pretty, too-disconcerting housekeeper's reply.

He took a breath of relief, which turned out to be a fleeting emotion. *Maria.* He still hadn't fired her. *Another item for the list.* Tonight, he'd check that one off.

He headed for the shower. The sleepless night had left him groggy with fatigue. With every noise, he rose from bed; hammer in hand like a minor-league Thor, checking the front door or strolling to the pine trees along the road. In the cold light of day, his weapon looked pretty silly. He reminded himself that despite the tool's heft, the stalker's rifle bullet carried more weight in a disagreement. He put it on the floor of the linen closet. If a problem arose, he would use his fists. His clenched hands had carried him this far in life, no reason to change now.

A few minutes later, he bounded downstairs. He passed the two girls busy in his living room. He saw just enough of Maria to become disconcerted. No one could just throw on a t-shirt and jeans and look that good. What was she trying to do to him?

When he arrived at the hot house, he began to water his seedlings. The mindless activity allowed him to reconsider the previous night's discovery. Should he tell anyone that he knew Amir's identity? Was that the reason he was killed? What was his life like to have that family legacy? How do you live like that?

Hubbard shut off the water. It all felt too familiar. He felt an unexpected kinship toward Amir. Was that what was driving him to continue to his amateur investigation?

When he put up the hose, he felt as if he'd just gone a few rounds in a fight that ended as a draw. He would go to town and hear the latest news about the murder.

He went back into his house and headed for the living room to say goodbye to Emily. She and Maria seemed startled when he appeared in the doorway. Their uneasiness, and sideward glances, was enough to make him pause, one brow raised in suspicion.

The two young women stood close together, a human wall, blocking his view. Behind them, the furniture had been moved, jumbled together like ill-fitting jigsaw puzzle pieces.

"Ummm, what's going on?" Hubbard said.

A hound dog with chicken feathers protruding from its mouth couldn't have looked guiltier. "Nothing," Emily said, with over-the-top, little girl innocence.

"Y'all doing something in there?"

"We're going to make it look pretty," Emily said.

"This room? Nothing can help in here. Tell Maria it's a nice idea, but it's a lost cause. We spend all our time in the den with the TV. I don't think the fireplace even works."

"Maria says it does."

"And how would she know that?" Hubbard avoided looking at Maria; she stole his focus from what he needed to do. "Never mind. Just tell her I said it was a lost cause."

"Okay."

Hubbard decided he needed to give instructions to an adult, not a child. He turned to Maria. "Très diablo." Very devil? It wasn't what he meant, but Maria seemed like she understood and nodded.

Hubbard turned to smile at Emily. "Gotta run."

Before he got off the porch, the prominent tire ruts left by Luis's truck drew his attention again. He had to fill them in; another item for his list.

Nothing was going right today, and his luck didn't change when he turned into the square. After three round trips, he couldn't find a parking place at the square. It took even more frustrating minutes to find a lonely spot in the alley behind the pharmacy on the opposite side of the square.

Hubbard tried the back door of the *Shop and Drop* drug store, hoping to take a short cut through the business and shave some time from his walk. It was unlocked. *Ah, small town living.* He nodded to the girl at the cash register, who smiled sweetly in return, pointing to a poster on the wall promoting the tomato festival. Hubbard nodded and smiled. "Can't wait."

Hiking across the diagonal concrete path toward City Café, two people he barely knew stopped him and thanked him for his article in the *Union Democrat*. Copies of which were delivered in town that morning, thanks to the Little Rock printer and U.S. Mail. His copy would arrive in the afternoon mail.

Paula Dempsey, the pixie-sprite woman who owned the *Fresh Start* bakery, was the second person. "Why aren't the other news people telling us what's going on like you are?"

Hubbard was startled by the question. She must have confused his article with some other news report, but he didn't have time to explore it with her. Besides, his story was the most out-of-date version.

He shrugged. "I don't know, but I'm *so late*." He trotted down the sidewalk.

Her voice rose as she called after him. "I'm locking my doors and keeping a loaded gun by the bed. Well, come by sometime and check out my gluten-free buns." She winked and was off.

Hubbard nodded and waved his hand in acknowledgement.

The diner was crowded. The lunch hour began early in a farming community. Hubbard found an empty stool at the counter and swiveled around to survey the room. If he was lucky, Toil, Eddie, or someone from the FBI would be here and he could begin a casual conversation that might lead to details on the investigation.

"Hey fellas, here comes R.J." A voice, faint but discernible in the dining racket, came from the direction of the large windows at the front of the diner. Hubbard's felt a new heaviness on his shoulders.

Rick Copeland, an overweight rice farmer, stood by the front wall of plate glass and looked toward the square, both hands pressed against his big pot belly. He was informing three men at his table, all wearing denim overalls, that R.J. Hubbard was approaching. The plus-sized planter held onto a second spread, even larger, by the river.

Why did people feel compelled to announce an R.J. sighting like he was an ivory-billed woodpecker?

Some townspeople were looking at the entryway expectantly; others were pretending to be oblivious to the impending arrival of his uncle. But there was no denying the difference in the energy surrounding him. It was as if two hundred tuning forks had been struck at once. Jolted, the lazy dining gossip was transformed into the buzzing of a hive.

The diners seemed to hold their breath for the arrival of a man none of them really knew. Most were possessed by emotions difficult for Hubbard to define; adoration with a strong undertow of fear? Others were consumed by a quiet loathing they wouldn't dare express.

At any rate, R.J. was about to enter the diner.

Hubbard spun around on the stool and turned his back to the entrance.

16

HOW TO MAKE AN ENTRANCE . . . AND EXIT

FROM HIS STOOL AT THE CITY CAFÉ lunch counter, Hubbard's attention was drawn to a woman wearing heavy blue eye shadow and clothed in a drab brown outfit. She sat at a small table with two children, almost Emily's age; the kids were peering at the entrance to the dining area with apparent eagerness. The mother grabbed the arm of the older of the two boys and pulled him toward her, her head jutting forward accusingly. "Do *not* gape at the door. Our family does not look at the likes of him unless we have to. *Do you know what that man did? He—He . . .*"

The weight of Hubbard's stare must have stopped her. She hesitated; her eyes blinked rapidly, and then she slowly turned her head upward in his direction. When her eyes reached Hubbard, she twisted uncomfortably in her seat and stared at her plate, shushing her son who kept asking, "*What'd he do? What'd he do?*"

Hubbard's jaw ached from clenching his teeth. He looked away and his eyes fell on a blond woman in her late thirties, sitting at another table with a girlfriend. She had set aside her unfinished plate lunch. She flipped her long hair over her shoulder and opened a compact, with a surprising intensity. She examined her face, lipstick in hand. After making a corrective dab, she pressed her lips together and practiced a smile into the small mirror.

The blonde's friend, a tiny brunette wearing a tight pink t-shirt, appeared dumfounded by her table mate, and shook her head with an expression that looked like disdain.

At that moment, his uncle entered, and the room took note.

R.J. Hubbard, with salt and pepper hair, still trim with none of the protruding belly his contemporaries had acquired, cut an elegant figure in the small town. For most people, however, it was difficult to see past his smile; broad and confident, it swept the room like the beam from a lighthouse. It was the display of assurance by a man who believed that everyone should be thrilled by his arrival.

Hubbard wondered why he never saw any doubt on the man's face. He wasn't oblivious. R.J. had tremendous insight into people and their motivations, he must certainly be aware of the mixed, but always strong reactions, he elicited in his hometown. But now, like always, he looked like the guest of honor at a surprise party. He grasped hands and slapped backs at the first table he came to and seemed to have no doubts that the next table would be welcoming as well. Young and old, man, woman, or child, they all gave him their full attention. Hubbard thought that even babies in strollers seemed to be clued in, but he knew it was his imagination playing devilish games with him.

Everyone's relationship with the fifty-five-year-old man was as complicated as it was unique. For some of these numbers he had done a "favor" for at one time or another. His beneficence was well known, but secretive, a favor bestowed by R.J. Hubbard was something you remembered, but never spoke of. So these favors, like most his uncle's life, remained in the shadows.

R.J. was moving to another table. In a town where denim seemed to be the standard uniform for men, R.J. was the man garbed in expensive wool and custom made shirts. The only outlier was his boots. They were old and worn—a point of curiosity for people who wondered by a rich man chose to wear boots that seemed well beyond their useful life. But Hubbard's father had the same quirk, putting new soles on the same old boots repeatedly. Hubbard was glad the old boot preference gene had skipped him.

R.J. was getting too close. Hubbard focused on the counter in front of him, hoping R.J. would pass by.

"Hiya kid."

No such luck. Hubbard turned to his left as R.J. sat on the stool beside him. He had hoped it would take R.J. another ten minutes to make it through the supplicants in the lunch crowd.

"Hi. Um, haven't seen you in a bit," the younger Hubbard said. "Where've you been keeping yourself?"

"Here and there."

"Oh . . . Yeah, of course." Questions to his uncle never got a straight answer. *Why did he even try?*

Uh, say, I hear you've hired a housekeeper."

John Riley sighed. "How do you hear these things?"

"Here and there. Do you think she's going to work out?"

"I don't know. I think she's too young."

R.J. nodded, his face looked like he was mulling over something. Hubbard braced himself. Anytime his uncle chose his words carefully, there was usually something else going on.

"I want to talk to you about that article you wrote. Why are you getting involved with something like that? You've got a farm and a daughter to think about."

"Ah, you read the paper, I guess. Mrs. Welsh would be proud that the most important man in town reads our little rag. As far as the story about that poor kid, I'm stopping now. I just did it for extra money—like always, no difference."

"Well, it's a little bit more than a simple article. I know you. You don't know where it will lead. *What you might find out.* I know you. You don't give up when you got an idea in your head. "

"I give up all the time."

"No, you don't."

"Yes, I do"

"No—"

"Okay, you're right. *I don't give up.* See? *I gave up.* I do it all the time."

"Not this time. Not when you have such a crazy theory to stand behind. I don't believe you."

"What crazy theory?"

"Let's put that aside for a moment. I don't want to argue. I have something I need you to do. A favor, let's say."

It was a remarkably short turnaround time for payback. "Oh." He couldn't hide the disappointment in his voice.

R.J. smiled. "Don't worry, it's really simple. I think it's time to show you some stuff. Tell you how things work on my farm. How to keep things going. It'll just take a day or two."

Hubbard was momentarily stunned by request. His uncle wanted to show him how things worked on his farm. Why now? Didn't the old man realize he had a farm to run, too? "I am really behind with my planting. Can it wait a bit?"

R.J. smiled. "Don't worry, your crop will be in before nightfall—drip irrigation, your tomatoes, everything. I sent some men over this morning. I really need you to be able to focus on this."

"What? I don't understand. Do you know how many men it would take to get all that done before nightfall?"

"Of course. I'm the one that sent them."

Hubbard's cell phone rang in his pocket. He reached into his coat.

Before he answered, R.J. placed his hand on Hubbard's arm. "Oh, and I told my men that they could park on your lawn. No more than a couple dozen trucks, maybe a few cars, a working tractor. Not much. That's okay, isn't it?"

"What? My lawn?" Protest was futile. The ring of his phone telegraphed their arrival.

Hubbard switched on his cell. It was an excited Emily.

"Daddy! You'll never guess!"

Hubbard spent another minute calming Emily and waiting while she translated his instructions to Maria who was keeping the workers at bay until she knew Hubbard approved. He hung up.

A waitress appeared and set down a coffee cup and filled it, momentarily interrupting the conversation. After she went into the left, Hubbard turned back to R.J. He was momentarily surprised to see that his uncle was intently studying his face. He knew the look. R.J. expected the favor to be returned."

"O.K. I guess I can do it."

R.J. nodded. "I was thinking about what you said about your housekeeper. It's too important a decision, leaving your child in someone else's care; to let it all go to chance. I'll write up a list of suitable—"

Hubbard rubbed his forehead in frustration. "Wait . . . Just wait. I got this. I can make my own hiring and firing decisions."

"But, if she's too young, it won't work. *It just won't work.* Listen to me; I've been down this road. Let me help you."

"Just a second. Emily is my little girl. I think Maria might surprise us all. I'm just going to wait and see. Give it a few days."

"For once, will you just listen."

Hubbard took a sip of coffee.

R.J. sighed. "Well, there's no changing your mind . . . Call me and we'll set it up. I'm kinda in a rush. It's important."

Hubbard felt his chest tighten. "What? So soon?"

"Can't be helped." R.J. surveyed the room. "I see Reverend Harper. He wants to see me about *some big emergency*—he is always so dramatic. It's probably about the 'thank you' luncheon for the flood workers." R.J. put his hand on Hubbard's arm and squeezed. "In the meantime, let go of this murder thing. You don't want to get some nut job all riled up."

"Nut job?" Hubbard wondered if his uncle had heard about his visitor the previous night, but that would be impossible. His uncle continued to squeeze his arm, a bit too forcefully. "Ouch," Hubbard said.

R. J. smiled. "Sorry. I just don't want this murder to create problems for you."

It was an odd comment to process. "Um . . .It's not."

"Good." R. J. patted his arm and stood. "We'll talk."

"Yeah," Hubbard said.

He watched R.J. walk away; his uncle's progress was slow as several diners rose to greet him in turn.

"John Riley Hubbard, I knew you wouldn't be far away from your truck."

Hubbard turned to his other side to see the grinning deputy.

"Oh, hi Eddie. How're you doing?"

"I'm doing great! Guess who is back at home where he belongs?"

Hubbard nodded. "Well, I think I can guess just fine. Congratulations."

"Mona said that if anyone was going to kill me, it was going to be her, not some stranger. The White River Killer can just get in line and wait his turn . . ." Eddie's head rocked back and forth with contentment, closing his eyes as if he was savoring the memory of her comments. "*She loves me.*"

Hubbard tilted his head and his forehead creased. "Sounds like it . . . But, why did she mention the White River Killer?"

"*Oh, I almost forgot.* Sheriff Toil wanted me to fetch you as quick as possible."

The clang of the round bell sitting on the kitchen ledge sounded. Hubbard turned and saw what looked like his BLT sitting on the kitchen window ledge.

"Tell the sheriff I'll be there as soon as I can."

"Well, you come when you can. But remember; when you see your truck you're going to be hopping mad. So, come find the sheriff."

"Okay . . . Um." Hubbard's brow furrowed.

Eddie was quickly away, before Hubbard could react. He called after the deputy. "Uh, Eddie, what about my truck? Why am—"

Eddie didn't hear him and seemed intent on leaving the dining area at the speed of a cannonball.

Hubbard stood. He couldn't ignore Eddie's comment about his truck He threw some bills down on the counter.

Hubbard followed after Eddie. He progress was slowed by the Sloan family, who lived about a mile from his place. The couple stood in his path and told him that they read his article and wondered what the world was coming to. Hubbard hurriedly told them that he didn't know either. The reaction of the town seemed a bit over-the-top.

Hubbard wove through the tables, trying to make it out of the diner without being stopped again.

R.J. Hubbard looked around to see if anyone had heard Harper's emotional plea. Fortunately, their table was in the corner. No one was looking at them. This was probably one of the few times when the general noise and confusion of the café was a blessing. He turned to face the minister. "Keep your voice down."

"I asked you if we could meet in my office at the church. We can go there now—'"

"You know I don't do church."

"You want Henry to kill you. That's insane."

"Do I look insane?"

"You know, I've known you've for so long I don't think I would know. I do know that you've done some crazy shit—"

"Reverend. *Your language.*"

"What is going on? They think you've got a fifty-fifty chance with surgery, don't they. You've won with worse odds than that. Why give up now?"

"I'm glad the good doctor believes in the privacy of health information."

"We all grew up together. That trumps PHI."

"If he said that I wanted him to kill me and didn't explain the whole thing, I think I may have to go over it all again."

"Go over what?"

"Hear me out. This is how it will go down. They'll make a hole in my skull so that they get to that tumor buried deep in my brain. If possible, he'll cut the thing out. I'll have to do some physical therapy when I get out, but I'm alive.

The other possibility is that they won't be able to cut it out and it'll remain there. According to the Mayo Clinic doctors, I'll be dead in nine to twelve months. Now, how interested do you think I'll be in starting physical therapy to last out the last few months of my life? I'll be living the last few months of my life pissing on myself or talking like a four-year-old.

My solution is this. If the tumor is located where he can take it out and save my life, well, I want him to do. If it can't be cut out, then I don't wake up. It's really quite simple."

"It's not that simple. You're asking him to murder you."

"No, I'm not. I'm asking him to recognize when my life can't be saved. It's the same as writing DNR on a chart—Do Not Resuscitate. Doctors write it on charts all the time. I want to make the decision on how I die. Do you really think I'd play this any other way?"

Harper leaned back and looked at R.J. with pity. "How do you live with yourself?"

R.J. gave him a tepid smile. "Next question."

"Okay. Are you going to have a conversation with John Riley before you do this? You owe him that. You have something to tell him. Let him find some kind of peace."

R.J.'s have hardened and his voice lowered. "Harper, don't pretend to have knowledge that you don't have."

The Reverend leaned across the table. "I've tried to save your soul my whole life. You were my mission. How stupid was that. Okay, I failed. I failed in so many ways. But I can't fail in this. *You will have that conversation with him. I'll see to it. You won't go to your grave with secrets between you.*

R.J. stood. He felt the weakness in his left side. "If you think you know anything about me, then you know this. Don't cross me. After I'm gone you can tell him whatever you like. Make up a fairy story. *But you don't know anything.*"

R.J. walked from the restaurant trying to disguise his limp, ignoring all the eyes that were watching him leave.

On the square, Hubbard debated whether he should go to the sheriff's office or head for his truck, still parked, he hoped, behind the *Shop and Drop*. He decided that seeing the condition of his truck was his top priority and headed for the pharmacy and its short cut to the alley.

Inside the store, the girl at the register, who he had nodded to a half-hour before, looked up. Her brow knit with concern and she pointed toward the back door. "Everyone's out back looking at your pickup. I'm *soooo* sorry."

Oh, shit.

Hubbard threw open the back door and saw a group of nine or ten onlookers gathered at the side of the truck, facing away from him, all focused on his truck. They were abuzz with conversation, pointing and gesturing in dismay at something hidden from his view by the informal congregation. Surprisingly, he saw Mrs. Welsh in the crowd. It was very unusual for her to leave her post at the *Union Democrat* offices.

The cluster effectively blocked his sightline until Jimmy Rodgers, who owned the dry cleaners, bent down to examine the damage to the truck's rear fender. There was a long crease in the sheet metal that hadn't been there this morning.

Sheriff Toil turned and spotted Hubbard approaching. "Okay, here he is. Give him some room."

The rest of the small crowd wheeled around to face him, their eyes wide, anticipating his reaction. They fell quiet, and began backing away from the truck, revealing the damage. His vehicle looked like it had lost a prize fight. Someone had taken a club of some kind and started at one end of his truck and began swinging away, creating deep dents in each panel of metal and knocking off his side mirror which still dangled from a thick black cord. Hubbard counted the indentations, at least seven separate blows, high and low, left a trail of woe on the side closest to him.

Everyone was quiet; respectful as mourners at a gravesite. Shaking his head, Hubbard walked slowly to the rear of the truck. No damage was evident there.

Toil spoke up. "Whoever did this got this side and cracked the side mirror on the other side as well, but nothing else. I guess something must have scared him off."

Rogers, the dry cleaner, wearing a logoed blue polo shirt, patted Hubbard's back as he passed. "Sorry, man. You'd think that with a state police cruiser back here this morning, nothing like this could happen. This town sure is changing, and I don't like it."

Hubbard's mind was in a cloud. The damage seemed so mindless and vindictive. "State Police? *Arkansas* State Police?"

Rogers nodded broadly and smiled. "Well, yeah, Louisiana State Police sure don't work here."

"What were they doing in the alley?" Hubbard said. His brow creased as he tried to piece this together.

"Patrolling, I guess. If they just stayed here a little longer, I bet the trooper would have caught the guy. It was probably some teenager playing hooky, looking for trouble."

"Yeah," Hubbard said, softly.

Toil walked up to Hubbard. "We'll find the guy. I've got a call into Pete Druckman."

"Druckman? Why?"

Bill Lader, the pharmacist, stepped closer. "He went out the back door after he got his nose drops. He might have seen something."

"Oh . . . Maybe."

His eyes turned toward Mrs. Welsh. She was staring at Hubbard with an expression he had never seen on her face. What was it? Embarrassment? Why would she . . . He looked down at the newspaper rolled up in her hands. She had it wrung so tightly it looked like she was trying to wring the ink from it.

"Mrs. Welsh, um, is the damage to my truck going to be in the paper? I don't think—"

"That's not why I'm here. Have you seen the paper?"

"No. I'll probably get it in the mail this afternoon. I'll look at it tonight." He turned back to survey the damage to his vehicle once again.

"Maybe you should look at it now. *There's something I need to explain.*"

Hubbard had a new sinking feeling in his gut, and slowly turned back to her. The raw emotion on Mrs. Welsh's face concerned him more than the damage to his truck. He took two long steps toward her and held out his hand for the newspaper.

She didn't immediately respond. She took a deep breath, releasing the air from her lungs as she handed Hubbard the new issue of the *Union Democrat.*

It was twisted so tightly that it took Hubbard a moment to find the paper's edge and begin to unroll it.

Toil stood beside him. "Great story. You made Sergeant Connors look like a fool. The FBI informed Connors's captain that they'd be working directly with Hayslip law enforcement from now on." Toil rocked back and forth on his feet. *"I feel like a kid on his birthday.* I'm telling everyone in town that whatever John Riley says about the murder goes for me to. I owe that to you."

Hubbard flipped the weekly to the front page where his story and photos were laid out in four columns. Above his bylined article, a bold black headline seemed to shout; *White River Killer Hits Hayslip.*

What . . . the . . . hell?

Eddie burst out of the pharmacy's back door at a gallop and skidded to a stop a few feet away. He was breathing heavily, as if he had been sprinting. "There you are, John Riley. The FBI boss man said he wants the trouble-making reporter who's spreading lies and panicking the whole town. He thinks you must want to play hard ball." Eddie peeked back at the pharmacy door as if he was concerned he had been followed, and then back to Hubbard. "I told him I knew right where to find the troublemaker and he didn't need to send all those other agents."

Hubbard sighed. "Thank you, Eddie."

"You're welcome."

17

CHECK AND MATE

EDDIE'S BREATHLESS ANNOUNCEMENT of the FBI's intention to play hard ball with Hubbard cast a pall over the alley. The remaining onlookers began drifting away, as if they were avoiding guilt by proximity. Their exit left Hubbard, Toil, Eddie and an overwrought Mrs. Welsh alone behind the pharmacy. Hubbard discovered he couldn't get upset with the woman over the misleading headline, which was "panicking the town" in the view of the feds. The *Union Democrat* editor's anguished face suggested the judicious Mrs. Welsh was punishing herself far too much over the alarming banner without his adding to her distress.

"Okay, Eddie," Toil said, "you've delivered the FBI's message, but remember you still work for me. I need you to hop in the patrol car and get over to the Higginbotham farm. Take them the Star City police report. They'll need it to make an insurance claim on that blue work truck of theirs. I've warned that old man a thousand times that it's not like the old days when you could keep your keys in the car ignition and leave your front door unlocked at night. But hell, what can you expect from a farmer who's dumb enough to think he's going to make money planting cotton?"

Hubbard rubbed his forehead, trying to process the last few

minutes. He lowered his hand and turned to the sheriff. "What happened to Mr. Higginbotham's truck?"

"It went missing this past weekend. The sheriff over in Star City called to tell me they found his old pickup early this morning. Somebody pushed it down the embankment by the Highway 121 Bridge. It rolled into the White—total loss."

Hubbard's head tilted to the side as he considered the timing of the theft. "Last weekend? Do you think it could have been used in the murder?"

Toil's mouth turned downward. "Nah, probably just some kids out for a joy ride. You know how teenagers are. Parents should lock them up at night."

Hubbard wasn't convinced, as Toil seemed to be, that juvenile delinquents were the criminal kingpins of Hayslip. He shook his head in response. "But still . . ."

Eddie's forehead furrowed as if he was troubled by Hubbard's idea.

Toil swung back toward his deputy. "Eddie, do you want to do it *today?*"

"Oh . . . You bet." Eddie turned on his heel and was off.

Mrs. Welsh held a white lace handkerchief in her right hand and pulled at its embroidered edge with her left. Her eyes were watery, on the verge of tears.

Hubbard decided the morning was bad enough without making an old lady cry. He took a breath and tried to find some lightness in his voice. "Um . . . The White River Killer? Gee, how'd that make it into the paper? I didn't mention the White River Killer in my story . . . Or did I? Was the serial killer added to my copy? No big deal. *Just asking.*"

"No, of course not. The only thing Tony changed was the headline. He called the printer before they went to press. I saw it this morning for the first time like everybody else."

"Doesn't Andrews need to get your approval before—?"

Mrs. Welsh raised her arms helplessly. "He owns the newspaper. He can do whatever he wants." The old lady lowered her head, her right arm straightened and her hand lightly struck the side of her body again and again, as if she was whipping herself. "I can't believe this happened on my watch" Her voice broke with emotion. "My watch . . . my *res-spons-ibility*."

Hubbard had spent years trying to halt his mother's endless stream of tears. He couldn't bear any more. He put his arm around her shoulder. "Mrs. Welsh, the *Union Democrat* is a small town weekly newspaper, *not* NATO Supreme Command. Don't worry about this happening on *your watch*. It was out of your control. Okay? Please don't."

Mrs. Welsh dabbed at her eyes. "You don't blame me? Does the town?"

"No one thinks one thing about it." He squeezed her shoulders. "Say, that reminds me. Is Tony planning on being in the office to-day? I'd like to chat with him for a minute."

"Later this afternoon."

"Okay. I might drop by."

"I don't want this to cause a fuss. You know how Tony can get when he doesn't get his way."

Hubbard forced a half-smile, trying to convince Mrs. Welsh he wasn't mad. "Oh, I know. He can be quite petulant. *Petulant*, what a word! Wasn't that one of your vocabulary words back in the day? You see? I *was* listening in your class."

"Yes you were, dear." Mrs. Welsh wiped her nose with her hand-kerchief. "Well . . . I need to get back to the office and deal with all the calls. The phone is ringing nonstop." Mrs. Welsh patted Hub-bard's hand and then headed down the alley.

Hubbard watched his former teacher make her retreat; her head lowered in undeserved shame. A knot tightened in his gut.

Toil sidled up beside him. Although they were alone, he whis-pered out of the corner of his mouth like a bookie leaning against the rail at *Oaklawn*. "So, how do you want to play this? I can tell the FBI you gave me the slip. I've got a cabin in the deer woods if you want to lay low for a while. I bet your uncle can take care of this in no time."

Hubbard's back straightened in surprise. "You're kidding. *You think I should go on the lam?* I've got a daughter to raise, a farm to work, and after R.J.'s crew leaves today, a lawn to patch up. I haven't broken any laws."

Toil put one hand on his chest as if he was taking a pledge and leaned into Hubbard to emphasize his point. "I don't think they care if you've done anything wrong or not. These guys are dead serious. *This is big.* I know they had more feds lurking around town the last couple of days than the few they let me see. I told you, this is freaky stuff." Toil raised his head to survey the alley in both directions. He dropped his voice to a hoarse whisper. "A team of agents boxed everything up in the Arab kid's apartment late last night. It all left in an unmarked truck: furniture, personal effects—the whole lot. It's like he never lived there."

"Is that standard procedure? I thought they kept everything sealed up during the investigation."

"I don't know. Not this one, I guess . . . Of course, I'm not supposed to say anything."

"Sure, I understand."

Both of Toil's eyebrows arched. "But that's not all."

"There's more?"

Toil indicated a notice painted on the alley wall. "Just between you, me and the *Do Not Park Here* sign."

"Sure."

"The kid's body: They're going to bury him in the U.S. They're not shipping him home to Egypt."

Hubbard's jaw clenched at the news. He didn't know Amir, but was forming an attachment to a kid everyone seemed determined to erase. "Why not? His parents deserve—"

"The FBI told Connors that his family doesn't want the body sent to them. Must be some crazy Arab surreal-a-law."

"*Sharia law*, I think . . . But that can't be right. How did they reach his parents to find out they don't want his body? That phone number . . ."

Toil shrugged.

Hubbard scratched his chin as he sifted through the new information. "I know you're supposed to keep everything *hush-hush*."

"Under penalty of law."

"*Right* . . . Do they have any kind of theory about what happened to him?"

Toil placed a hand on Hubbard's shoulder and spoke to him like he was an exceptionally slow student. "He was shot."

"No. I mean, *who* shot him? Or how the murderer could put a shotgun right up to his chest without a struggle?"

The sheriff's reply did little to disguise his unhappiness with his role in the investigation. "Nope, they haven't taken the time to say diddly to me *and I'm the goddamn sheriff.*"

"What about the blue suit he was wearing?"

"What about it?"

"They still think he was killed early Sunday morning . . . *Right?*"

"Yeah. About nine a.m. according to the coroner. So?"

Hubbard took the sheriff by the arm and walked down the alley a few paces, trying to make the part-time lawman focus on his words. "If you were in Monticello, Arkansas, on a Sunday morning and saw a young man wearing a suit and tie, where would you think he was heading?"

"Church . . . But Amen, or Amir, or whoever was an Arab."

"Yeah, I know. But on *that* Sunday morning he was on his way to church. I can't think of any reason you'd dress up early Sunday in southeast Arkansas except for church. Can you?

"Um . . . But he was an *Arab*."

"Yeah. *I got that part.* Maybe he was a *Christian* Arab."

"Is that a real thing? *Christian Arabs?*"

"I got some leads who can give me more of his background."

"Who? What leads?"

Hank Peterson, the lanky owner of the hardware store, opened the brown metal door at the rear of his shop, stepped into the alley, and emptied a plastic trashcan into a larger bin. "Hi guys," he called. "You boys look like you're solving all the world's problems."

Hubbard raised his hand in greeting and forced a half-hearted smile. "Almost fixed them all." He lowered his voice to Toil. "I'll tell you later. I don't want our FBI man waiting any longer than necessary."

Toil agreed, but quickly had second thoughts. "Good thinking— *maybe*."

They took the long way down the alley and around the solid block of retail businesses. Hubbard battled a growing sense of unease. Ramirez had threatened to lock him up under the pretense of the Patriot Act. How many times could he rely on Ramirez not to play that card and refrain from tossing him in jail—if the lead agent, in fact, *could* throw him in jail without charges?

Hubbard was out of his depth. He believed he hadn't done anything illegal, but it was clear the U.S. government had a significant interest in the Egyptian student. Larger forces were at work here. He was playing a game with unknown rules and penalties. A farmer-reporter could be swept away in these murky waters without leaving a trace. *Why can't I let this go?*

At the door to the sheriff's office, Toil paused, his hand on the knob. "*Last chance.*"

Shaking his head, Hubbard made a show of bravado. "No, I'm good."

Toil nodded solemnly, and with an expression of regret, he opened the door.

Hubbard expected to see a scene similar to the one he witnessed on his previous visit, and was surprised to find the sheriff's office was almost empty. Two baby-faced agents, wearing government-issued blue polo shirts with the yellow initials of the FBI emblazoned on their backs, stood at the front of the sheriff's desk. They were motionless, staring down at Special Agent-in-Charge Ramirez, who was sitting behind it. Their superior was on a call, holding the telephone receiver to one ear, while his other hand rubbed the back of his neck.

All three agents pivoted their heads toward them as they entered. The feds glowered at Hubbard with surprising intensity. Their eyes narrowed like they were Melvin Purvis's men and they just spotted John Dillinger in front of the *Biograph Theatre*.

Toil's phone buzzed and his hand dove into his coat pocket. He looked at the phone's screen and then pulled it to his chest. "I have to take this," he mumbled. He spun around to exit the office through the door they had just come through.

Remaining in the center of the room, Hubbard shifted his weight from foot to foot, waiting for Ramirez to finish. He tried to ignore the other two federal agents who were quietly sizing him up. Their contemptuous silence was deafening.

The agent's attention returned to the phone. "No sir . . . No . . . Of course not . . . We don't shoot from the hip . . . *I just want to talk to the lad.* Due diligence . . . Yes sir."

Was he the lad that Ramirez referred to on the call? It was a surprising appellation; Hubbard didn't think the endearing term would have been the primary descriptor that the FBI's lead investigator in Hayslip would choose. Who was he talking to? His respectful voice made it sound like he was on the line with someone he considered a superior. And his reddening face seemed to indicate embarrassment that Hubbard was in the room to witness this exchange over the phone.

There were a few more "yes sirs" and "no sirs" before Ramirez was able to hang up and lean back in his chair. He rubbed his face, and took a few deep breaths, which appeared to be his effort to calm down. "In the past two hours, I think I've gotten calls from every member of the Arkansas Congressional Delegation. At least I haven't heard from either of the Clintons. I guess your uncle's influence only goes so far—thank God for small favors."

His comment about Arkansas's most notable political family was barely out of Ramirez's mouth when the younger of the two FBI men brows raised and his lips parted as if he just realized he forgot something important. The cub agent turned his head and seemed to direct his focus to a message pad placed next to the telephone on the small painted desk that Eddie used. A single pink sheet was detached from the pad and lay at the center of the deputy's work table. The agent looked stricken. He glanced at his irate boss and pushed his hands deep into his pants pockets while his shoulders crowded against his neck.

Ramirez swung his chair around to face Hubbard. "Your elected officials want me to handle you with restraint, and give due consideration to your rights as a citizen, while at the same time keeping the wellbeing of my government paycheck in mind." Ramirez leaned forward and pressed down on the desk with both hands. "But here's the interesting thing: They made several veiled references to a person I've interviewed for this investigation, but I'm not finished with—*your uncle.*

Hubbard brought his hand to his chin like he was a college professor considering the translation of a difficult phrase in *Beowulf*. He glanced over his shoulder toward the window at the front of the office. Outside, Toil paced on the sidewalk. He held a cell phone to his ear, nodding up and down like he was a human dashboard ornament, agreeing to whatever the caller was saying on the line. Only one man could elicit this subservient behavior from the town's new sheriff, a man more likely to raise his fists than lose his dignity. *Sheriff, make lots of notes. My uncle likes you to do that. It shows you're paying attention.* He turned back to Ramirez, ignoring the new heaviness on his shoulders, and produced a pleasant facial expression. "Well, I'd like to know him a little better, too. I think many folks would. He keeps his own counsel."

"That's what I hear. Apparently, your politicos are happy to do his bidding . . . and that cooperative spirit seems to extend to Sergeant Connors. He was in the state police evidence room during the time period your camera and the film inside of it vanished. What's on that film? Why is it so important?"

"It's my dad's old camera. It hasn't been used since he died. It can't have anything to do with your investigation. If there was film inside it, it dried up years ago."

The FBI agent's mouth twisted as his words slid out. "I can't prove it, but I believe that busted-up Nikon is now in your uncle's possession."

The revelation startled Hubbard. His head bent to examine the floorboards beneath his feet.

The room went quiet. Ramirez waited for Hubbard to look up before resuming. "I warn you, the only thing that those calls from your redneck politicians accomplished was to delay me a bit. Tell your uncle I'm not going to play his game of chess."

"What the hell are you talking about?" Hubbard was surprised by the anger in his voice. "My uncle's not responsible for the *White River Killer* headline. You need to talk with the paper's owner."

"Kid, you better keep your eyes open. There're lots of ways you can get hurt messing in this. You don't want to stumble into that kind of trouble."

Hubbard's face burned like fire. He reminded himself the three men in front of him carried government badges. *This isn't a street fight. Stay cool.* He made his voice sound reasonable, just a guy searching for clarity. "Um . . . are you *threatening* me? Remember I'm just a dirt farmer. We're a little slow on the uptake."

"Oh no, don't take my offhand comment as a threat. I just want-ed you to know—in case something happens to you. *The agency had nothing to do with it.* Understand?"

Hubbard's fists tightened reflexively in response to what appeared to be a roundabout attempt at intimidation. The town's newspaper headline was inflammatory and unprofessional, but Ramirez was overreacting: The *Union Democrat* wasn't the *New York Times.* This confrontation didn't make sense. Why did Ramirez think R.J. was behind the scurrilous headline? "Yes sir, I understand. I'm going to steer way clear of this from now on. I don't want trouble. That's not what I'm about." *In a pig's eye, you son-of-a-bitch. Stop poking me.*

Ramirez's eyes shifted their focus to Hubbard's clenched hands. He looked up again and raised one eyebrow. "If you think—"

The phone in Hubbard's coat pocket rang. Hubbard hesitated, but noticed the unexpected interruption had stopped Ramirez. He

shrugged sheepishly. Holding up his index finger, he then pointed
to the cell he was drawing from his pocket. "This could be my little
girl. You know how it is raising a ten-year-old daughter. You're a
dad, too." He put the phone to his ear.

The subordinate feds stiffened their backs, reacting to Hubbard as
if he was challenging Ramirez's authority. The two young men took
an ominous step, leaning forward like prizefighters, stopping only
after Ramirez raised his hand.

"Mr. Hubbard?" The elderly voice quavered on the line.

Hubbard recognized her voice instantly and then remembered
their appointment. "Oh! Mrs. Fincher! We were just talking about
you. I was just telling the fellows here that I was running late for an
important client meeting . . . Yes. I'm on my way . . . *Noooo,* it's not
inconvenient at all. The boys here are very supportive of my dream
of building a career selling insurance for final expenses . . . I'll be
there soon . . . Sounds *wonderful.*" Hubbard clicked the phone off.

The two agents looked to the senior man for instructions.
Ramirez seemed to be uncertain of his next step. He leaned back in
his chair. The well-timed calls from the Arkansas politicians were
having an effect.

This was Hubbard's best opportunity to escape. He began backing toward the office doorway. "See? I'm done reporting on Amir's
murder; got a client on the hook, got a farm that needs tending, and
got no time to waste here. Agent, I heard you loud and clear, and
this is the last you'll see of me." He reached behind him to find the
door handle. "Call me before you leave town and tell me how it
turned out. Oh, one more thing, I think there's a phone message for
you on Eddie's desk."

Ramirez glanced over his shoulder toward the small black desk.
The forgetful agent's face hardened into a snarl. Hubbard opened
the door. Ramirez stood, extending his arm to point challengingly at
the departing Hubbard. "Tell your hot-shot uncle the next time I
catch either of you near this investig—"

Out the door, Hubbard closed it quickly behind him, cutting
short Ramirez's warning. He began to speed walk away.

Toil called to him from behind. "I thought they'd be sending you to the federal pokey for sure."

Hubbard stopped, eyeing the sheriff's office door, expecting it to fly open, revealing agents in pursuit of their new public enemy number one. He jerked his thumb over his shoulder in the direction of his truck on the opposite side of the square. "Not this time . . . Well, I need to run."

"Wait." Toil approached closer, biting his bottom lip. "So, uh, if he asks, can I tell him you're going to leave this thing alone?"

Hubbard took a moment to respond. He tilted his head to the side. "If *who* asks?"

Toil made a weak attempt at a chuckle. "Well, uh, Ramirez, of course."

"*Oh yeah* . . . You can tell him I've dropped this thing like a hot potato. Tell him I'm running away like a scalded rabbit. Tell him I, I'm, uh . . ." Hubbard took a breath. "Yes . . . Tell him I let it go."

"*Good* . . . So, where're you off to?

"The Fincher farm. Mrs. Fincher wants to buy an insurance policy."

"The Fincher place? It's odd timing to be going all the way out there."

"Why is it odd timing? She's seventy. She needs burial insurance."

"Well, sure, that's what I mean. It's kind of late in the game for her to be thinking about buying insurance for that. You sure that's all she wants?"

Hubbard shrugged. "What else could she want? It's always a good time to buy insurance. Maybe it's time for you to consider it as well."

Toil's eyes opened wider. He stepped back, as if he wanted to avoid a sales pitch. "Guess so. Well, you be safe."

Hubbard nodded. "I'll try. Thanks."

Hubbard made his way back to his truck like a dazed sleep walker. The morning had created a sea of questions. Why was FBI interviewing his uncle as part of their investigation? Did they think R.J.

ordered the headline and Andrews delivered it like a pizza? What did the alarming newspaper banner accomplish, aside from spooking the town? How did R.J. know Amir, a twenty-one-year-old, foreign college student? Simultaneous to that thought, Hubbard realized that his internal questions meant he believed Ramirez's accusations were true. Somehow R.J. was involved in this.

Hubbard got to his truck. He examined the fresh dents along the vehicle's side and the dangling door mirrors. His deductible was sky-high. Repairs would have to wait. Was the vandalism a warning to stay away from whatever was going on? Or was it revenge from some long ago fight? He took a deep breath, blew out air between pursed lips and got behind the wheel.

R.J. asked him, almost ordered him, to stop his amateur, or at best semi-pro investigation of the student's murder. He remembered his uncle's words: *You don't give up.* What did that mean? He shook his head, trying to make the tortured thoughts disappear without success . . .

If his uncle murdered Amir, it meant he put a shotgun against the student's chest, looked directly into Amir's eyes, and pulled the trigger, oblivious to the sickening blowback of blood that must have sprayed against him. If true, his uncle was the monster that many in Hayslip believed he was.

The haunting memory of his mother, standing on the dirt road adjacent to the deer woods, pushing R.J. away, was as clear as if it happened yesterday. Hubbard fought a wave of nausea. His mother . . . his uncle . . . and the maturing adult features on Hubbard's face, pointed out by others in town, created a resemblance he ignored each morning when he shaved.

Hubbard tried the truck ignition. It still ran. He drove down the alley and stopped at the intersection with the street. Heavy mid-day traffic circled the town center. After several cars passed by, he spotted a TV van approaching. A return media visit was surprising, since according to Toil, there were no developments in the investigation that would make the long drive from Little Rock worthwhile. As the news vehicle sped by, he saw an unfamiliar logo, *Shreveport's Favor-*

ite News Team. Shreveport? Close behind, two Little Rock news trucks followed the out-of-state competitor down the street.

Why the fresh interest from the reporters . . . ? Of course . . . The murder of a college student was local news. *But* the unexpected return of the notorious White River Killer, a murderer who once left a bloody trail of dismembered female corpses along the banks of the White River near Pine Bluff could get wider coverage thanks to the reckless *Union Democrat* headline.

Ramirez wants to keep Amir's murder out of the national press.

He took out the FBI's photo of Amir distributed to the media. The image had been altered from the original he saw on the college student's driver's license. The kid's eyes were Photoshopped. Looking to his left in the DMV photo, they now stared directly into the camera. What other alterations had the feds made to mask his identity?

The narrow alley began to spin around Hubbard like a pinwheel. Becoming dizzy, he draped his arm across the truck's steering wheel. He lowered his head and took several deep breaths, fighting the darkness overwhelming him. His black mood was as familiar as family, a backdrop to this bleak homecoming to murder, lies and his obsession for the truth.

And like a distant summer from the past, R.J. Hubbard was front and center.

Hubbard raised his head, letting the sun bathe his face. The FBI's investigation was targeting R.J. If his uncle was capable of *one* ruthless murder . . . he was capable of two.

He wanted to hit something . . . He wanted a drink. *Let it go. You're sober. You're peaceful. Emily's home . . .*

One day your anger will kill you.

18

THE PAWN'S OPENING MOVE

DRIVING DOWN THE MONTICELLO HIGHWAY, Hubbard tried to keep his thoughts on the task at hand. After he delivered the necessary paperwork to Mrs. Fincher for her renewal, he'd make a quick dash to the college.

How did R.J. know Amir? Andrew's wife was Amir's friend. If they talked over several different afternoons in the diner—long enough to keep Sinclair late—then there was a good chance his uncle's name came up in their conversations. He needed to know how they connected to understand the FBI's interest in his uncle.

Approaching traffic that had slowed on the highway, he tapped the brakes of his truck, causing both side mirrors to rattle against the doors. *Is the damn highway department ever going to finish whatever the hell they're doing?* Traffic was slowed again due to a flagman and workers depositing barrels along the highway.

He got to the turn to the Fincher place. Just beyond a thick row of pines and oaks, lay the most miserable 200 acres of farm land in Warren County. The Fincher family had lived here, stubbornly, for generations, with each successive generation doing worse than the one before. Not only did the land lack adequate drainage, it was poor soil. The hard ground consisted of little more than a layer of topsoil blanketing a sea of rocks like oil on water. Mrs. Fincher's only son had given up on the place decades ago, leaving Mrs. Fincher to fend for herself on a farm that fell into disrepair and weeds after he left.

Now at the end of her life, the old widow just wanted to ensure she had enough money to be buried in the Hayslip cemetery next to her late husband. Since Hubbard had been working with her, she had started and stopped her small burial policy with the ebb and flow of her finances. Now, she was starting her policy up again, which meant she believed she had the money to pay for the premiums she missed as well as keep current going forward. It was a sad variation on Russian Roulette: Would her insurance policy be in effect when she died? The company agent before Hubbard had grown frustrated with the repeated starts and stops on her account and quit it. Hubbard persisted. There was no easy money here, just an old woman who wanted to be buried properly. He would keep doing this as often as he needed and would hope, along with her, that her policy would be in force at the right time and she'd cash in on her grim jackpot.

As he approached her dilapidated farmhouse, he saw Mrs. Fincher open the door and step on the front porch. She raised her hand in welcome and smiled. Hubbard nodded, but had the lonely thought that he was one of the few visitors to her isolated farm. He parked in front of her house, gathered his paperwork, and got out of his truck. *Please no silver dollar biscuits today. Please have mercy on me.*

As he approached, the frail woman wrapped her sweater around herself and folded her arms. "Mrs. Fincher, you shouldn't be standing out here. You'll catch cold."

"You're just in time. I've got a pan of silver dollar biscuits straight out of the oven."

"*Great.* I can't believe my timing." Hubbard felt his stomach ache in protest.

They walked into her overheated home. Hubbard watched the woman's old gray cat twisting its skeletal frame through his legs, wiping her feline face against his boots.

"Old Puss likes you," she said. "She's a good judge of character. She keeps me safe at night."

"I'm glad to hear that," Hubbard said, trying to sound pleased, but he had mixed feelings about her reliance on a rheumatic cat for both companionship and security. Hubbard tried to keep his focus on the woman and ignore the worn furniture. Every possible seating place in the living room was loaded with tall stacks of old magazines and newspapers. He guessed the yellowing periodicals were the same ones he saw on his previous visit almost a year ago.

Based on more clutter lining the home's hallway, the old woman's home life was restricted to the kitchen, bathroom and bedroom. "Let's go into the kitchen," she said, shuffling in front of him. "I hope you're hungry."

"Well, I could always eat one of your silver dollar biscuits. That's for sure."

A half-hour later they had consumed a meal consisting of rock-hard biscuits, fried salt pork, beans, and dark ice tea. In contrast to the dismal surroundings, she glowed through lunch, as if sitting at her small table was the social event of the season, gossiping happily and incessantly with Hubbard. She retold the same tales he had heard before, stories of her and her late husband living and loving, but most of all, struggling to make a success of this misbegotten family farm. As always, absent from this discussion was any mention of her son, Tom. The woman needed him now. She shouldn't be alone here.

"So, how's your son? Still living in Chicago?"

"Oh, yes."

She tilted her face down toward the table, hiding any emotion from Hubbard. He heard in town that it had been years since her son had contacted her. Didn't anyone have a normal family? If so, what did normal look like? Hubbard tried to get back to business. He reached down for his briefcase. "I've brought the paperwork—"

Mrs. Fincher didn't realize that she hadn't shared her news with Hubbard. She began as if he already knew the details. "Isn't it wonderful! *Someone buying my farm*. I can't believe I'm so lucky. A young man comes by one day and takes a bushel of pictures and tells me my place is beautiful. And then a week later an older gentleman drives his fancy car all the way over here to make me a top-dollar offer. It's an answer to a prayer. I'm just hoping they won't change their minds."

Hubbard was silent for a moment. Had the woman descended into Alzheimer's? It was difficult for any farmer in Arkansas to sell land without the bitter assistance of a foreclosure sale. Although she held a nice-sized holding, her property had little value. The luck of a spontaneous offer to purchase this barren farm arriving unbidden at her doorstop was difficult to accept as genuine.

"*Who* took photos of your property?"

"Let me think. He was one of those rap singers I believe. You know like Jay-Zee-Lo and what have you."

"A rap singer took photos of your property? Are you sure?"

Mrs. Fincher nodded. "His name gave it away. He said that folks called him "Double A".

"Double A . . . ?" Hubbard thought for a moment. *It couldn't be.* "He didn't give you another name, did he? Something that sounded like *Amir Abadi.*"

"No . . . I don't think so . . . Oh, I don't remember. He said that I should call him *Double A.* All the young people call him that. I guess he meant his fans. He was a very sweet boy."

"Mrs. Fincher, um, could I ask you about the older man with the fancy car? Do you remember who that was?"

Mrs. Fincher's brow wrinkled as she tried to remember. "It's uh, um, now what was his name?" She stood and padded in her slippers to the kitchen cabinets. Painted white, their latex color was yellowing with age. She reached up and pulled off a business card secured with a red push pin to the wood front. She turned around, holding up the card. "*This man* . . . He says it's important that I act now. I have to sign the papers right away to get this wonderful deal. I told him *I'm so ready.* This will allow me to start my burial insurance again."

Hubbard extended his arm and she handed him the card. He

took a breath. He flipped it over. "Are you sure this was the man that made you the offer?"

"Yes. That's my savior. Do you know him?"

"Yeah, I do." Hubbard examined the photo on the card. It was Chet Herring, a sleazy realtor out of Little Rock. Billboards in the city featured large images of the gap-toothed man, wearing a bow tie that spun in the wind. It didn't make sense that Herring was interested in farm land; he usually was involved in commercial or residential developments. Two hundred acres of rural property was not something that would interest him.

"He said the photos showcased the natural beauty of my property. I told him that this was the most beautiful view in Arkansas."

Hubbard imagined Amir's portfolio of images from the Fincher farm: photo after photo of wild grass, rocks and weed. "Uh . . . Yes. It's picturesque."

"Double A spent a lot of time on the ridge. Oh course, that's the best part of the property. Mr. Fincher and I used to have picnics there."

"The ridge?"

"Here." She put the paper towel that she was using as a napkin down on the table. "Let's go look. I haven't been out there in quite some time."

Hubbard helped her as she struggled with a coat. When they made it out to the front porch a chilly breeze swept over them and the woman shivered. She pulled her arms around herself.

Hubbard scanned the farm, looking for a ridge. On the long edge of the acreage there was a rocky outcropping, no more than ten feet in height on the far border of the farm. It was spotted with brush and a few scrub pines. He pointed to the distant barrier. "Is that the ridge?"

Mrs. Fincher nodded.

"I'll walk over there. Why don't you wait here while I go take a look?"

Mrs. Fincher shoulders fell in relief when she heard she didn't have to make the trek. "I could heat up some more biscuits. There's always more. They keep just fine for weeks and weeks and weeks."

Hubbard nodded and faked a look of delight. "I'll hurry back." With a tip of his hand, he headed out. He knew her farm was near the White River, but couldn't visualize how far the waterway might be from her property. No one approached the river from this side. The Monticello road followed the higher and more difficult to access north bank of the river. At the entrance to her fields, he forced open a rusted gate and trudged across former cropland, now choked with dandelions, pigweed, uncut rye, and Bermuda grasses, and dozens of baby pine trees reclaiming the Fincher land as forest.

After some difficult walking, he reached the outcropping, a short rise comprised of sandstone, shale, and a streak or two of coal. Grass, stray vines and one foolhardy azalea bush had made homes in its nooks and crannies. Hubbard found a foot hold, then a second, and was able to spring to the top of ledge.

He stopped short, stunned by the unexpected view.

Before him, stretching out to the horizon was the White River. The waterway, contrary to its name, was usually colored brown by farm runoff, but here it actually became white water thanks to the bedrock underneath the Fincher farm, constricting the river channel. Large rocks that had fallen from the canyon walls eons ago obstructed the river current, aggravating the water and whipping it into froth as it made a constricted turn to the southeast. It gleamed brightly in the sun, cutting through the Black Jack Pershing State Park forest on the opposite side, racing to join up with the Mississippi River.

Once the rocky ledge was leveled by bull dozers, this million dollar view would be revealed, a selling point for an upscale residential development. But where did Herring think the buyers would come from? No one in Hayslip could afford . . .

Andrews, you son-of-a-bitch! You got the highway commission to approve the Interstate extension to Shreveport. A divided highway would shave off almost an hour of drive time to Little Rock. This panoramic view would lure new weekend homes of Little Rock's wealthy.

Herring, probably in concert with Andrews and others, were buying land before the public announcement. When the new highway became news, this property would skyrocket in price. Profiting from this insider knowledge was a highly illegal move for Andrews. No wonder he didn't boast about his accomplishment when they talked on the phone.

Hubbard remembered the photo he had seen laying on the porch when he stumbled from Amir's apartment. That image was a different from this; empty like Mrs. Fincher's property, but with large oaks framing the field. Amir had been taking photos of other attractive parcels being considered for purchase. Who was funding this land grab?

Perhaps guessing was unnecessary.

He hopped down and made his way back to Mrs. Fincher's farmhouse, while considering the magnificent view. Hubbard had seen this part of the river before, approaching it, like everyone else, through the state park. He had no idea that the Fincher farm was located at the top of the sheer rock wall that towered over the narrow bank. Directly below it was the spot where R.J.'s best friend died in a fishing accident years ago. It was another unexplained death during the first month of that grim summer.

But that was then, this was now.

Hubbard was going to get Mrs. Fincher the deal of her dreams—dreams she didn't realize she had at the moment, but soon would. He strode back to the farmhouse with a sense of grim determination. Did R.J. think this was a game of chess?

Pawn takes castle . . . rook?

Whatever.

19

MOVING DAY

HUBBARD RETURNED ACROSS THE WEEDY FIELD to Mrs. Fincher's farmhouse to ask for her proxy on the negotiations and get her wish list for a perfect deal. Sitting at her kitchen table again, he was surprised by the expansiveness of her imagination. The old woman could dream big when she set her mind to it. Maybe dreams don't come with expiration dates. He took a deep breath and assured her that he would get her terms. The distinct possibility that he might not help at all, but only screw up a transaction that only required her signature, tried to work its way into his thoughts—but he pushed the negative thought aside.

Leaving her farm for Monticello, Hubbard telephoned the college girls who worked at the drive-in. They were both at home. *Cleopatra*, or rather Missy, was as seductive on the line as her party costume in Amir's photo implied. She told Hubbard she was *so* eager to see him that words *failed* her. Her endearment delivered in a sultry voice.

"Yeah, uh, sounds good." Hubbard told Missy he'd be there in ten minutes and clicked off. *Keep your wits about you, Hubbard. Don't get sidetracked.*

The three girls had an apartment on the same pricey street as Amir, but across the road and two houses away. A small U-Haul truck was parked in their driveway.

When Hubbard rang the doorbell, it triggered an immediate vocal reaction deep in their home, muffled, but with the snap of battlefield commands. He caught the words, "wait for me" and "no, he came to see me" and then the thump, thump, thump of multiple footsteps racing for the house's massive entry—then nothing. After a long moment of silence, he heard the click of the latch and the oak door slowly opened, revealing the two girls affecting an expression of cosmopolitan élan.

Missy smiled at Hubbard and flung her blond hair over her shoulder. Behind her, Carla Jo, almost hidden by Missy's mane, dodged the hair whip and peeked around her roommate's shoulder. They both wore shorts and sorority-branded T-shirts. Instead of shoes, their feet were clad in white athletic socks. The young women reached out and yanked Hubbard inside without warning, as if they feared he might escape.

They escorted him through a jumbled mess of cardboard boxes, scattered newspapers, and bubble wrap.

"Y'all moving? Aren't classes still in session?" Hubbard said.

Missy released his arm and walked to an ivy-green couch, which had been pulled away from the beige wall in their central room. She yanked two boxes off, let them both fall to the floor, and kicked them away. She then returned to Hubbard and pulled him along to sit down beside her on the sofa. "You'd think when Amy flew off to Europe without giving us any notice; she or her daddy would feel some sort of obligation to write a check for her share of the rent through summer."

Carla Jo joined them on the settee, becoming the other feminine bookend pushed against him. She tucked her long legs, tanned to a luxurious brown, underneath her. "There wasn't space for us at the Tri-Delt house. You should see the dump we're moving into. The rest of the school year is going to feel like an *en-ternity*."

"*E*-ternity," Missy corrected sharply, leaning toward Carla Jo.

Her long hair smelled like violets. Perfumed locks brushed softly against Hubbard's cheek like a sweet caress.

Carla Jo tilted back at her. "Don't correct me! You're always trying to make me feel like I'm *un*-sophisticated. *Hell, you're from Dumas.*"

Missy's appeared angry at the slight, her bottom lip protruded like a pugilist's. "And what's wrong with Dumas?"

The intimate closeness of their quarrel produced an unexpected rise in Hubbard. How long had it been since . . . ? He had to get down to business. "So, um, what can you tell me about Double A?"

Both girls froze, leaned back, and their eyes opened wide with surprise. Missy was the first to speak. "How did you know Amir? He was so quiet, we thought we were his only friends."

"I'm writing a story for the *Union Democrat.*"

Carla Jo lowered her voice to a whisper. "The *Union Democrat?* My mama just called. She said Aunt Juanita phoned her this morning to say that the front page story was that Double A was killed by . . ." Her voice trailed off.

Missy shook her head in confusion and then sighed with frustration. "By who? We can't hear you!

Carla Jo leaned across Hubbard and punched out her words in a throaty whisper. "The—White—River—Killer. It was the headline in the Hayslip paper."

Missy gaped at Carla Jo and then looked at Hubbard. Her forehead furrowed with anxiety. "Is that true? Why would they hide that little news flash in the Hayslip *want ads?*"

Hubbard's brow creased. "The *Union Democrat* is a *real* newspaper . . . But, uh, the White River Killer thing, um, that's just one man's opinion."

Missy reached for Hubbard's arm and pulled herself against him. "The White River Killer murders beautiful young women. Carla Jo and I fit that profile—*big time.*"

On the other side of Hubbard, Carla Jo squeezed Hubbard's bicep to get his attention. "Amir must have died trying to protect *us.*" Her voice took on a dreamy quality. "We're so vulnerable. *Anything* could happen to us right *now.*"

The girls felt warm. They smelled sweet. Hubbard knew he was just a few squeezes and presses away from losing his good sense. He gently removed their hands, stood, and took a few steps away from the couch. "Uh, girls . . . Let me reassure you that this wasn't the White River Killer. I think Amir was killed by someone he knew and trusted."

The girls glanced at each other and then back at Hubbard. Missy seemed alarmed. *"Do you think we did it?"*

Was she joking? Hubbard waved his hand for emphasis. "No . . . no . . . *no*. But I thought that you might tell me who some of his close friends were."

Carla Jo looked at Missy before she answered. "He didn't have many friends. He was shy."

Missy nodded. "He was a *dork*. Amy was closest to him."

Carla Jo put her hand on Missy's shoulder, looking as if she wanted to take the lead in explaining their absent friend. "You see, that was just her. Amy was always picking up strays. Whenever we drove past a dead dog at the side of the highway, she'd start crying. If our landlord let us have pets in this apartment, I bet she'd pick up every lost cat, dog, or opossum she came across."

"Is that all Amir was to her—a stray?"

Missy blinked with surprise. "What else could he be?"

"I don't know. A boyfriend?"

Missy and Carla giggled. The laughter seemed real, as if Hubbard had made a clueless suggestion. When Missy could finally speak, she said, "Amy is high society. She's the one who was paying most of the rent for this place. She can do better than some nerd *Arab*. Know what I mean?"

Carla Jo elaborated. "She dragged him around like he was her special project, always encouraging him to smile, and telling him to not let the past dictate the future—that sort of stuff."

"What past? What was she referring to—?"

Missy frowned and shook her head. *"Nothing.* Amy always talks like she works in a fortune cookie factory. The rich can afford to believe that shit."

"Rich?"

"Well, *she's* not rich exactly. But her *father* is," Carla Jo said.

"Who's her father?"

Both the young women looked surprised that Hubbard didn't know. "Dill Foxcroft," Missy said.

"The highway contractor?"

Missy raised her eyebrows. "Is there another Dill Foxcroft?"

"No, I suppose not. I guess I never got her last name. Sorry."

Hubbard remembered his encounter with Foxcroft and his veiled warning about R.J. staying out of the road business. It was all beginning to make more sense.

"How'd they get along?"

Missy seemed taken aback by the question. "Mr. Foxcroft and Amir?"

"Yeah."

"They didn't know each other. Why would they?"

"But certainly Amy's father came over here from time to time, met Amir somewhere or other."

"I never heard about it if they did. Her daddy never came here; she always went to Hayslip. He made her drive home every Sunday for church service. She could never miss since he's a deacon at the Baptist Church." Carla Jo's face took on a little smirk. "Everything's got to look right and proper. *Oh, no.* I don't think she'd introduce Amir to her father."

Missy nodded. "After all, her daddy's not too pleased about *us* being her friends. We're a bit too *common*. He keeps his baby on a tight leash."

"But I heard that Amir had a job taking photos for someone. I assumed he was working for her father."

"A job? Why would Amir need a job? Have you seen his place? The furniture? The artwork? He was rich—family money."

Carla Jo arched her eyebrows dramatically, as if she was on stage at the dinner theatre in Little Rock. *"Oil money."*

Missy held up one finger and chided her. "You don't know that."

"It has to be."

Hubbard didn't want to get sidetracked by another squabble. "Did Amir ever say anything about his family?"

"No . . . I don't think he was close to them," Carla Jo said. "They gave him an inferiority complex or something. He took photos of people all the time, but he'd never let anyone take his photo. He found out I took a couple of him when he wasn't looking and he got so mad you'd think I'd murdered someone . . . *I guess I don't play by the rules.*" She said the last part looking directly at Hubbard, as if that had special meaning for him.

"That picture in the paper didn't look anything like him, "Missy said.

"It was a driver's license photo. Nobody looks like their driver's license photo," Carla Jo countered.

Missy sighed, shaking her head at Carla Jo before turning to Hubbard. "He was different from us. I asked him about his parents once. He said they believed in things he didn't, so they didn't talk very much." Missy shrugged her shoulders with a '*what can you do?*' expression. "*Families.* Everybody's got one."

Hubbard cleared his throat. "Yeah."

The conversation with the girls continued along the same frustrating lines. It seemed that his best source for in-depth information about Amir was Amy, but she had left for Europe almost a week before the murder and wouldn't return home until the end of the year.

Missy failed to hide her jealousy. "Her father probably sent her over there to land some goddamn prince to be her husband. *It's not fair.* No matter how hard I work, I'll never have a chance at that kind of life."

A sympathetic loneliness for Amir pressed down on Hubbard's shoulders. His nominal American friend felt more outrage about the vagaries of wealth than for the Arab student's brutal murder. He wondered if Amir's relationship with Amy went deeper than his being her pity project.

"How did Amy take the news of Amir's death?"

Missy rolled her eyes. "She called us, uh . . ."

"Tuesday," Carla Jo said.

Missy nodded. "Tuesday night. She *freaked* out. Went off the *deep end*."

Carla Jo's eyebrows arched and she held up her hand like the guard at a school crossing. Her concerned expression made it seem that she thought that Hubbard would get the wrong impression about Amy. "That's just the way she is—too soft-hearted for her own good."

Hubbard was trying to weigh the implication of their words when Missy told him that they had been interviewed by the FBI. The feds had asked them if they had any photos of Amir on their cell phones. They had a few, which they had shared with the agents, thinking they would only take what they needed. But when the phones were returned to them, the two photos that included Amir had been erased; even the copies of the digital images they hadn't told the feds about on a web photo site were gone.

With a lot to consider, Hubbard left a business card with his cell phone number with the two girls, requesting they ask their traveling roommate to call him the next time they heard from her. The young women were uncertain when that might be since she was vague about her travel itinerary, but they would ask Amy Foxcroft to contact him.

At their door, he lied to the two girls by promising that he would visit them in their new place. As he walked to his truck, he noted a white Chevy Impala parked at the far end of the street. Bright sunlight reflected off the windshield.

There was one other person that might provide more background on Amir: Trish Andrews, the soon-to-be ex of the Boy King. She was probably working with her dance team this afternoon. Hubbard, like every male in the vicinity, knew where and when the college cheerleaders practiced.

That knowledge was instinctual, much like how migratory birds always knew true north.

20

THE EXES OF EVIL

HUBBARD LOOKED INTO THE REARVIEW MIRROR as he got behind the wheel of his pickup. The Chevy Impala, parked at the far end of the street, was the only other vehicle on the road. He glanced back at the front porch of the big house and raised his hand in farewell to Missy and Carla Jo, who were watching him depart.

Maybe it was paranoia, but he knew the FBI would be very interested in his activities. The same Chevy, or its twin, was behind him on the highway when he left the Fincher place. Perhaps his suspicions were triggered by his angry confrontation with Agent Ramirez, but still . . .

At the corner, he made a lazy turn onto Maple. When he was out of the line of sight of the Impala, he gunned the truck, drove to the next road, and turned the wrong direction on a one-way street. When he had gone the length of four houses, he made an awkward U-turn and stopped behind a large SUV at the curb. He was only partially hidden from any cars driving down Maple, but if he was lucky, it would be enough.

To his right, he noticed an elderly woman, wearing a floral smock and slippers, standing in a garden at the front of a turreted Victorian home. She had been busy with her roses until Hubbard roared down the street. The silver-haired lady took a small step in his direction and wagged a shaming finger at him for reckless driving.

Please lady, give me a break.

He returned his attention to Maple Street. A florist truck passed by and then there was no more traffic. Embarrassed by his melodramatic imagination, he was about to put his truck in gear when the Chevy flew by carrying two men who appeared to be in their early thirties. In the passenger seat, a man wearing sunglasses pointed to the road ahead of them. Then, they too were gone from view.

Impalas. Hubbard never liked the clunky vehicles. But they were the popular choice of rental car agencies and corporate motor pools. He had guessed that this apex of non-descript automobile design might be also a staple of federal fleets—especially the FBI's.

It's not paranoia if you're right.

He heard a small noise that sounded like the tapping of a miniature woodpecker. The paper-thin woman, who had been pruning flowers a minute ago, was now at the passenger door of his truck, using a cut branch to rap on the window.

Hubbard rolled down the glass.

"Young man, what are you doing? Are you *crazy?*"

Two questions without easy answers.

Five minutes later, he was driving on the narrow roads of the college campus. Every weekday afternoon in spring, the college stadium was home for the Monticello cheerleader practice. When Hubbard walked onto the field, Trish Andrew's team was hard at work.

The Boy King's wife, wearing tight pink shorts and a school sweatshirt, didn't look much older than her charges. Her blond hair swung gracefully across her shoulders with every step she took. Focused on her squad, her back was to Hubbard as he approached. The young women gathered in front of her were attempting a human pyramid, an impressive three-girl-high structure. Hubbard tried not to gape at the great wall of toned legs gleaming in the sunshine.

Trish shouted instructions as her team climbed skyward. One

girl's right foot slipped off its shoulder perch, but the cheerleader caught herself, found a new foothold and continued her ascent. Trish lowered her head and shook it with disappointment. She then stepped forward, beating a clipboard against her leg. "Ladies, keep your eyes on the horizon or you'll lose your balance . . . Stay focused . . . *C'mon, eyes front.* What's goin' on? You *nailed* this yesterday."

Her team continued to struggle, tottering back and forth until the pyramid crumbled to the ground. Trish cursed under her breath, threw the clipboard at the grass and stomped away.

Hubbard took a couple of steps forward. At first, everyone appeared to be all right, but then he noticed a pretty brunette cheerleader limping off the field. He trotted up to her. "Are you okay?"

Her bottom lip was pressed tightly against the upper one. "Yeah . . . It's just my ankle." She tried to take a few steps before stopping, wincing in agony. "It may be broken." She pointed toward the sidelines. "Could you help me get to that bench?"

Hubbard scooped her up in his arms. "Don't put any weight on it until we know how badly you're hurt."

"Oh!" she said. *"You're so strong."* Her arms wrapped around Hubbard's neck and she laid her head against his chest. Her hair smelled like honeysuckle in June.

Once on the sidelines, Hubbard helped the girl get settled on an aluminum bench and then kneeled before her to ascertain the extent of her injury. She rested her petite foot on his thigh, allowing him to examine the entire length of her leg.

Hubbard focused on her ankle. "Tell me if this hurts—"

Trish's voice boomed behind him. "Clarice! You're not foolin' anyone. Get with your squad and start on the new dance steps right now."

Clarice revived and stood. She bent down and whispered in Hubbard's ear before trotting back on the field. "We're here every afternoon."

Hubbard was surprised her pain subsided so quickly. He stood and faced the field.

Trish walked to him and folded her arms in front of her. "John Riley Hubbard, I should've realized you were the tsunami that crashed my women."

Hubbard's brow rose. "Tsunami? I don't understand."

"Of course you don't . . ." A sly smile spread over her face and she put her hands on her hips. "I think I know why you're here. You've heard about me and Tony splittin' up."

He didn't expect her directness. In the bright light of the afternoon he could see that any question he asked about her marriage would appear rude and presumptuous. Perhaps he should've thought this through more fully. "Well . . . um . . . uh."

"Are you here for *you,* or did *Tony* send you? If you're here for Tony, tell him the answer's no. I'm tired of his insane jealousy. I met the terms of my pre-nup agreement and I'm goin' to collect. That's the only thing he's good for—giving a dirt-poor girl like me a chance at somethin' classy like I deserve. And he doesn't have to worry about bein' alone in that big house when I'm gone. There will always be a sweet-young-thing waitin' in the wings to get her a nice slice of the Andrews family fortune."

Trish's back straightened as if she was accepting a challenge. "This time it's goin' to be different. He's not going to scare me off like he did his other wives. He can't frighten me. I'm goin' to do somethin' big with my life. Hayslip will be hearin' lots about me real soon." Trish's voice became as cold as a blue steel gun. "Everyone better stay out of my way."

"Um." Hubbard interjected the non-word as a placeholder, trying to interrupt her drawlin' mean-spirited monologue. "I'm working on a follow-up story for the *Union Democrat* about Amir Abadi's death and—"

"I saw the paper this morning. *Your part was hard to miss.* You really think he was killed by the White River Killer?"

"No. I don't. Not a chance in the world." Hubbard attempted to chuckle. "Long story about that headline . . . Um, I know you were friends with Amir and—"

Her eyes turned skyward and she released a loud groan of frustration. "*There was nothin' goin' on between us.* I don't think Tony ever believed that, but it's true."

"Did Tony accuse you of something?

"Tony suspected I was sleepin' with everyone—*yes, even you.*"

Hubbard felt a pang of guilt over his pre-wedding, backseat entanglement with the Boy King's future bride and his jaw tightened.

"Amir tried to tell me the last time I spoke with him on the phone. He said that he had gotten into some kind of dust-up with a rich guy in Hayslip. He was too scared to say who it was."

Hubbard brow creased and he stumbled over the word. "R— Rich?"

"Yeah. I think it was his roundabout way of telling me that Tony was threatenin' him. He warned me it'd be too dangerous to be near him, so he stopped takin' photos for our recruitin' brochure. He was afraid somethin' would happen and I might get hurt. He was afraid *for me.*" Trish wiped a tear from her eye with the back of her hand.

Hubbard was surprised at the appearance of a tear, but reached into his pocket and handed her a white handkerchief. After she had dabbed her eyes, she gave it back to him.

Hubbard tried to come up with something appropriate to say. "From everything I've learned about him, it sounds like he was a nice guy."

Trish began to sniffle. "He . . . was."

Hubbard returned his handkerchief to her. "Keep it. I go through lots of these working in my fields."

She held the handkerchief to her nose. "You and I both know Tony don't have near the guts to kill someone by himself. If he wanted someone dead and gone, he'd hire it done for him. Hayslip's too small a town to find a killer-for-hire just like that." Trish snapped her fingers. "The FBI needs to ask around. Somebody heard somethin'." She bent her elbows and raised her hands like machetes to add strength to her words. "Get the bastard who shot Amir—and you'll get the man who hired him to do it—*Tony.*"

"You really think your husband could do that?"

Trish nodded. "*Yes, I do*. You don't know him like I do . . . But I've told all of this to the FBI. It *had* to be him. I don't know what the agent's problem was acceptin' somethin' *so* . . . Trish's brow wrinkled and her eyes tilted down toward the field as if she had spotted a snake in the grass. Her face slowly turned up to Hubbard. When she spoke, her voice was low, almost a whisper. "Amir said 'rich'. I was so fixed on Tony . . . I didn't even think about . . ." Trish feigned a casual question. "Um . . . did your uncle . . . know Amir?"

"No. Of course not . . . No . . . I don't think so . . . Maybe . . . I don't know."

"John Riley, *why* are you here?"

"I'm just writing a story. That's all."

Trish looked at him for a long moment. Her brow furrowed. "Please believe me. Tell Mr. Hubbard that I don't know *anythin'* that could cause trouble for *anyone*."

"Trish, I'm not . . ."

Trish glanced at her team. "I have to get back to work. Regionals are in two weeks."

"Sure."

She turned back, her eyes intent on his face. "Be careful," she said, and then jogged onto the field.

Dance music blared from the field speakers. Hubbard stayed a moment longer and watched Tony's unhappy wife pace as her team became a swirl of motion. Her focus, as far as Hubbard could tell, was not on the young women, but on a section of empty stands.

Trish Andrews's suspicions reminded him how unformed his own were. When she brought up his uncle's name, he started to defend R.J. out of habit.

He blew out a long stream of air through pursed lips.

Heading for the stadium gate, he pictured Luis and the Rolex . . . or was it a Seiko? That led to thoughts about Luis's employer. How could he find out if his uncle knew Amir? R.J. Hubbard revealed little about his life. It was a safe bet he wouldn't be open about his connection to a murder with an unknown perpetrator.

Head bowed, dark memories began tumbling through his mind. The breeze at his back felt a few degrees colder than earlier in the day. He was all the way to his truck before he glanced up again.

"Shit."

The parking lot was almost empty on this weekday afternoon, only a dozen or so cars were parked near the north entrance to the football field. One vehicle, however, was making a tight circle to exit the lot through the east gate.

Hubbard had been so focused on the FBI's Impala, he didn't notice the second car following him—Tony Andrews' white SUV. *How long had the Boy King been following him?*

21

ANCIENT AZTEC CUSTOMS

ON THE DRIVE HOME, Hubbard mentally sorted through all the information he had gathered. When added together, it was tantalizing but inconclusive. By the time he reached his house, he had to admit; he wasn't much further along than when he began the day.

Hubbard turned into the long driveway leading to his farmhouse. Dozens of new tire tracks from his uncle's huge work crew from today crisscrossed his once-pristine yard in all directions. He sighed. *You can tell a lot about a farmer by his lawn.*

Hubbard parked his truck, got out, and did a double-take toward his house. The sky was darkening as the sun headed for the horizon. The only light from the house came from the living room windows. Their brightness drew his eye to the single source of light, since it made the home's façade look like a one-eyed buccaneer. Inside the house, he could see the freshly painted glow of yellow walls. *Yellow.* He hated yellow. Hadn't he told Maria and Emily not to bother painting the room?

He walked through the front door prepared to let loose—a terrible end to a terrible day. He threw the truck keys on the hall table and took three more steps to the arched entry to the living room.

He stopped abruptly, bobbing his head downward to trap harsh words before they escaped.

Before he could point heatedly to the blinding yellow walls, the rearranged furniture, or the army of knick knacks gathered from the four corners of the house and pushed together on every flat surface in the room—he saw Emily's face. It was so transparently excited, pleased, thrilled, or whatever over-the-top adjective he could think of that it outshone the amber warning-signal walls. His daughter was bouncing on her tiptoes, trying to contain her anticipation of Hubbard's reaction.

He needed a moment to regroup.

He glanced at Maria, who had a new streak of yellow paint highlighting her raven hair. Her bottom lip protruded a bit and she blew stray hair strands off her sweaty forehead. *God, you're so pretty, even now . . . Goddammit Hubbard, get a grip. She works for you.*

Holding up one finger, he made a small circle in the air and said, "This takes my breath away. Give me a second. I want to take it all in."

Emily brought her hands together, stopping just short of applause, her hands frozen in mid-air, as if she couldn't wait for what he might say next. In a moment of blind luck, Hubbard had stumbled on words that met her gigantic expectations. Maria patted Emily's shoulder.

How much damage had they done? Maybe he could learn to live with yellow. *Just ignore the room for eight years until she leaves for college.*

Hubbard took a step into the room, did a half-smile and nodded at the walls like they were new friends.

Emily ran to an end table and did a sweep of her hand over the crowded field of bric-a-brac like a game show hostess. "Ta-da!"

He guessed that the flotsam filling the room must have been Emily's contribution to the effort.

"Maria said that we might want to keep only *the most beautiful* of our art objects in here. I told her that I wanted daddy to choose. This is *everything I could find.*"

Hubbard believed her. He nodded. "It'll be tough to choose." He spotted a trio of framed photographs on the round table that held a big lamp, which was now positioned by the windows. He recognized them by their old frames, photos that he kept in a box in the attic. How did she get her hands on those?

He walked to the pedestal table. Frozen images from the time before: his mother in the kitchen, his father on an Easter morning. Behind the two pictures lay a third framed image that couldn't stay here: a faded color print of the twelve-year-old Hubbard, wearing a baseball uniform, standing on the pitcher's mound, while boasting a toothy grin. It was the season he was going to show everyone in Warren County what his strong right arm could do.

He stopped playing baseball that summer, but still, he showed them all. True, not many had the opportunity to see his blistering fastballs win a game; but they all heard stories about his fistfights or witnessed the bloody aftermath of a brutal swing from his powerful right.

Behind him, Emily was intent on rearranging her decorator items atop the sofa's end table. His daughter was occupied, so he took the opportunity to tip his photo over with a finger. He turned around, prepared to smile and say something appropriate. Maria was staring at the downturned frame, her brow creased. Her brown eyes flashed upward and locked into his. It was an uncomfortable moment before he looked away. She had seen the part of him that he wanted to hide. It was private. He felt his face flush.

Don't you ever blink?

Emily ran back to Maria and put her arm around her. It looked like she wanted to share this moment of glory. Hubbard didn't know if he liked how attached she was getting to Maria. Things were moving much too quickly. "It looks great." Maria and his daughter smiled back at him from the center of a room that looked as bright as sunrise.

He had to get out of there.

There was a brief silence before Hubbard could think of an excuse. "I need to check the fields while there's still light."

Hubbard left the room, ignoring Emily's pleas to remain for a more in-depth tour. Once he was outside, he could breathe again. He kept walking until he got to the place near the gate where he could survey the fields. It was quite a sight. As promised, his uncle's crew had completed work that would've taken him two weeks to complete. Now all he had to do was to pay back a favor.

Twenty minutes later, Hubbard heard Luis's truck horn at the front of the house.

Maria came out the back door and waved to him. "Señor Hubbirrrd."

Hubbard sighed. Of course she would have an endearing way of pronouncing his name. He waved back to her, acknowledging that he knew she was leaving. *If I could just keep this distance between us* . . . He returned to the house and was immediately hit a mesmerizing aroma from the kitchen that he hadn't noticed before.

In the kitchen, Emily focused on a digital timer like a bird dog.

"What are you doing?"

"Maria said that I need to tell you when the timer went off. That meant the Coke-A-Van was ready. I have to ask you to take it out—but I can do it. I know how to do it *safe*."

"Coke-A-Van?"

Emily nodded. She pointed to a cookbook on the counter, which was surprising since he didn't own one. Hubbard picked it up and examined it. It was written in Spanish; apparently the dish was Coq Au Vin—French. Someone must have told Maria that he once had a stupid kid's dream to escape from Hayslip and move to Europe. What was she trying to prove with all this painting and French cooking? He noticed that Emily was staring at him.

"What's wrong daddy?"

"Nothing," he said. But Emily didn't appear swayed by his denial.

Hubbard turned toward the countdown timer as it sped through the last minute of cooking time. Maria did all this in one day? What was she? A one-woman blitzkrieg? It would be too easy to read qualities into a woman who was little more than a question mark. Guatemala. What's in Guatemala? What remnants of ancient Aztec customs did she still follow? Or Inca customs? Catholic customs? Whatever. The point was they had nothing in common—nothing in common? Why was he even thinking this way? If she stayed here, he was going to screw up. It was just a matter of time.

"You know, um, I don't think Maria will be here much longer."

The timer went off. It was loud, and they both jumped a bit.

Emily turned to him. Her eyes were watery. "Why not? She has to be here. She's perfect."

"Perfect for what?"

"Just per-fect."

Hubbard tried to placate his daughter. "She's a very nice lady."

"She's great. She said she'd go with us to the Tomato Festival if you said okay. I said, of course you'd say okay. Everybody goes to the Tomato Festival."

Hubbard's eyes opened wider with alarm. "You can't do that. You can't invite her to something like that. It's the wrong message to send . . . *You see, you don't understand.* That's exactly why she has to go."

"B-B-Because I asked her to go with us to the Tomato Festival?"

"No, not because of that . . ." He tried to slow his explanation down. "We don't know her. We have nothing in common with her."

"I know Spanish, so I talk to Maria all the time. *I* have something in common with her. A thousand things in common. Millions of things." She offered proof. "*We both love the color yellow.*"

"Well, that's not enough. I knew this arrangement was wrong and it is. I can't be here with Maria."

"I love her."

Hubbard was feeling a fair amount of panic. Why did he let this happen? "No! No, you don't. You've known her a couple of days. Once we get somebody in here who's right for us—"

Emily started breathing heavily and her bottom lip jutted out.

"Young lady, don't you cry. Don't you even *think* about crying . . ."

The tears came anyway. Emily looked like she wanted to say all manner of things to her father, beginning to speak twice before stopping. Finally, she blurted, *"Maria is perfect. I want Maria."*

At least that's what it sounded like to Hubbard, her words were delivered in a loud wail of anger and he missed parts of it. Emily bolted from the kitchen shouting something completely unintelligible through her tears. Her small feet made sounds like thunder as she ran up the stairs to her bedroom.

Hubbard rubbed his temples and the buzzer went off again. He opened the oven door and tried to grab the pot without using the mitt. "Shit!" He pulled his hand back, kicked the oven door closed, and walked over to the sink. He ran cold water over the burn.

The cell phone went off in his coat pocket. He ignored it, keeping his hand under the water. The caller tried again. He turned off the water and pulled the phone from his pocket. On the display was a number he didn't recognize with an out-of-state area code. He set it aside. Then the kitchen wall phone rang. He ignored it, turning the cold water back on. Then his cell phone started up again. He gave up. He turned off the water and answered it.

"Hullo."

"Mr. Hubbard, I'm so glad I reached you. I hope this is a good time. This is Special Agent Lisa Longinotti with the FBI. Do you remember me? I was wondering if you could get away for a little while this evening and meet me for a drink so we could talk. Maybe go over a few things." Her voice sounded amazingly . . . pleasant.

It would be nice to have a moment of calm.

22

THE FBI AFTER DARK

IT WAS EASY TO FIND A PLACE for Emily to spend the night. The Hendersons had a teenage daughter that Emily adored and they were only a farm away. Hubbard was not as lucky with Longinotti's preferred meeting spot. He hadn't returned to *The Bandstand,* a bar on the outskirts of town, in two years. Not coincidentally, he stopped coming here when he ceased drinking. Agent Lisa Longinotti surprised him by insisting they meet here tonight.

The Bandstand had the good fortune to be a private club holding a liquor license in a dry county. As he parked, he could hear the pounding of low bass notes in the music coming from the dance floor. It was only eight p.m. and the lot was almost full.

Hubbard didn't quite know the purpose of this meeting. The attractive agent was openly flirtatious with him on the phone, just wanting to talk, a lonely girl away from home, the reason wasn't totally clear. Surely there must be some prohibition covering an agent's involvement with a person associated with an active case. But in the view of the FBI, Hubbard wasn't a suspect or a witness to Amir's murder, so maybe that rule didn't apply in this situation? But Lisa, no, Agent Longinotti came across as a young woman dedicated to her job. A farmer living in Arkansas would be a hard bump on her career path.

Hubbard remembered when he was in Toil's office, examining the photo of Amir released to the press by the FBI. After he set the image down, he noticed the comely agent was watching his reaction intently. He had tried to erase the troubled expression on his face and shield his thoughts. Perhaps he was too slow.

Walking toward the front door, his memories of the dive flooded back. As he climbed the stairs to the entrance, he battled the nerves that twisted his insides into a knot. A drink would help.

The long-standing Bandstand building had been enlarged multiple times over many years, each new extension not bothering to match any other part of the building. Its current incarnation formed an ill-defined "V" shape. The entrance was at the V's point, allowing patrons in both wings to see the arrival of newcomers. Hubbard stopped just inside the door to pay the fee that made him a card-carrying member for a night, and continued into the main room.

From the elevated landing, Hubbard surveyed the crowd. If he couldn't spot her from this vantage point, he'd be forced to walk the length of both wings to find her. He dreaded all the looks, the questions, and the natural assumption he was there to party. He walked down the steps into the crowd.

"John Riley," a female voice coming from his right floated above the buzz of the crowd.

Hubbard turned and saw Kath Baker leaving a group of admiring men.

"I thought you were trying to be a 'new person.' Looks like the old one won out," Kath purred. Like most men under the age of sixty, he was mesmerized as she closed in, not walking, but undulating toward him as if her body was made of liquid pleasure.

She put her arms around his neck, and pressed against him. The club disappeared for Hubbard, replaced by her body's warmth, the sweet press of her breasts, her blue eyes, and the scent of her flowery perfume. "You can't tell me you're not feeling what I'm feeling."

Standing with her leg against him, she could probably feel him and what he was feeling. "Kath, I really am trying to . . ." His voice had become a gravelly whisper.

"John? John? Over here," another female to his left called.

Over his shoulder, Hubbard saw Agent Lisa Longinotti, waving for his attention, standing by a table in the West Wing as locals called it, oblivious to the interest of the males surrounding her. Her professional garb, so different from the way the other women in the bar dressed, was attention-getting.

"Who's the bitch?" Kath tightened her grip on his neck.

"Um . . . Well, actually she's an agent with the FBI and she's on a case."

Kath pulled her hands away. "Yeah. Right. You son-of-a-bitch, you can't treat me like I'm a fool. Is she rich? Is that it?"

"No, she really is . . ."

"You're going to be so sorry. You've done this to me twice. Nobody does that to me."

Walking away from him, she strutted no longer. Her shoulders were hunched and her hands were balled into fists.

"Kath . . ." He was just making it worse. Men followed along in her wake and she was gone.

Agent Longinotti adopted a sheepish grin, shrugged her shoulders, and opened her hands toward the ceiling. As Hubbard headed for her, she crooked a finger, beckoning him to follow her.

They tacked right and left through a swelling tide of boisterous patrons. Hubbard saw countless men turn their heads, drawn in as much by her metropolitan exoticness as her toned legs.

Hubbard took a breath and surveyed the room to clear his head. He recognized many of the faces—probably not a good thing to be so familiar with the patrons of a honky-tonk.

Longinotti had taken one of the wooden booths that lined the back wall of the west wing. As soon as they sat down, a waitress appeared to take their drink order. The agent pointed to her drink. "I've gotten a head start. You're going to have to catch up."

Hubbard noted pink nail polish that had been absent earlier in the day. He looked at her drink. "What are you having?"

"Jack and Coke."

"I've lost track of a lot of nights in the company of Mr. Daniels."

"Me, too."

Something was off. Longinotti's assertiveness seemed more like a performance than hormones. Hubbard looked up at the waitress. "Just soda water and a lime."

Her lips pouted. "You're not going to let me drink alone. That's not fair. I'm off-duty, I want to relax." She reached for his hand. It was surprisingly cold. "Oooh, your hand is so warm. It feels good."

"I'm sorry. I'm trying to cut back." The waitress was still there. "Soda water and a lime, please."

The waitress glanced at Longinotti before she left them.

"So tell me, why does everyone call you by two names—John Riley? Are you so big that one name just doesn't do it?"

Hubbard's mouth curled up in embarrassment. "Nothing like that. My grandfather was alive when I was born. His name was John, too. They used my middle name, Riley, to keep things straight. I guess my grandpa didn't want anyone to think he was the one with dirty diapers. Anyway, it stuck."

Longinotti continued with questions about his life, his daughter, and especially about his uncle. After another failed attempt to get Hubbard to order a stiffer drink, she leaned against the seatback and tapped her empty glass with one pink fingernail as if she was contemplating the solution to a difficult problem. She engaged his eyes. "You know, you've got Ramirez really buffaloed. He's afraid you're going to screw up the investigation."

"Me? What am I doing?"

"Look at it from his perspective: There are only three people here who could get in our way: Connors, Toil, or you. Connors is an idiot. Toil just wants to be a farmer—"

"Don't I want to be a farmer, too?"

"No. You want to be anything but that. You think playing a reporter is your ticket away from this town? Parlez-vous français, Monsieur Hubbard?"

How did she know that? "Um, if you mean the 'White River Killer' headline on my story, that wasn't me, that was . . ."

"We know that. It's the story's content that's got us worried."

Longinotti used the word "us." It wasn't just Ramirez who thought he was trouble.

"I didn't have anything in my article that everyone else hasn't reported as well."

"No, you're right, you didn't. But the Hayslip newspaper is distributed on Wednesday, which is why it didn't get the notice it deserved."

"Why did it deserve—"

"When's your story deadline? Isn't it Monday morning? You knew all the facts of the case almost immediately after it happened. You were ahead of everyone else then, and we're still trying to catch up with you now."

Hubbard's mind raced, trying to come up with a reason that would make the FBI believe he was ahead of them on this investigation. He remembered his recent calls to New York. The only way they could know about that . . . They had his phone records. They knew who he'd been talking to and tonight was their reaction. "I don't think . . ."

"Mrs. Welsh is a character, isn't she? I like that term she uses, "brinkmanship." You're a man who lives on the brink, isn't that right? How many long nights have you spent holding a drink in one hand and a gun in the other, trying to find the courage to pull the trigger?

Hubbard sucked in his breath.

"Oh, don't pretend you're offended. We had a psychologist profile you. No one could grow up with a childhood like yours and be normal. You have a very dark soul and you know it."

There was a squeal of feminine voices at the bar entrance. Almost every man's head turned to watch them pull at their skirts and flip their hair.

Hubbard was reeling, his insides burned like they were on fire.

He pretended to watch the female performance at the entrance to conceal his anxiety. *What was the agent doing? How many people had she talked to? More importantly, what did they tell her?*

"Okay, that was a lot to take in." Hubbard turned back to the agent. "You profiled me like some sort of serial killer? Why are you so worried about someone screwing up your investigation? Shouldn't you be more concerned with finding Amir's killer? Isn't that the reason your team came all the way from Washington to backwoods Arkansas?"

"Let me be plain. If anyone harms this investigation, it's going to be you—plunging headlong into some place you don't belong. Why would a man take such incredible risks for a part-time job? What's fueling your obsession? Your father? You want to solve this murder because no one solved that one? Do you really think that will heal you?"

Hubbard tried to smile. "That's silly. Your profiler needs to get a life."

"You're out of your league, John. We have the resources to get you out of our way—one way or another."

"That sounds like a threat."

"Take it how you want. This can go hard or it can be easy. You're a man with personal issues trying to resolve them by interfering with a federal investigation."

"What the hell is in this profile of me?"

"Freud could have written a book about you. Daddy issues, mommy issues, and more importantly, uncle issues."

The past never dies. "That's enough."

"What's the matter, John? It's a small town. Everyone else knows the truth, why don't you? Your uncle and mother got away with murder. Then the guilt destroyed your mother. How does it feel sitting around the family table at Thanksgiving—all warm and cozy?"

Hubbard's fist crashed down on the table. "I said that's enough."

Longinotti jumped, her eyes showed a brief moment of fear, but she quickly recovered. "Yes, that's right. Just what the profile predicted: a quick temper, unresolved rage you can barely control. If I were a man, this is the moment you'd be lunging across the table at me. That's why I'm here. I'm a woman, all by herself. You can't start one of your legendary bar fights with me, can you, John? Your profile says you never run. Why is that? You seem to have no problems running from the truth."

"You're just repeating the lies I've heard all of my goddamn life . . ."

"I can see what you're trying to hide. It's on your face. You know it's true, don't you? Is your uncle going to leave you all his money in his will? Is that the going rate for murdered fathers? What kind of man are you? Or are you still that little boy running through Shanty Town all alone? Why have you never had the courage—"

Hubbard's voice sounded like a growl. "Don't rely on the fact that you're a woman. I'd kill you right now if you were a man . . ."

"Kill me? So, it runs in the family? You've betrayed your father and you're going to kill me? Why don't you take a good, hard look at yourself? I bet you don't like what you see."

A waitress carrying a tray came up to the table. "Everything all right here?"

Longinotti turned to the waitress and smiled sweetly. "Oh, yes. We're good. Just talking about Father's Day." She made a show of putting one hand to her mouth as if she was concerned about being overheard in the noisy club. "It's a sensitive subject."

The waitress was unconvinced. "Well, okay. Just keep it down." She put a drink down in front of Hubbard.

Longinotti smiled at the waitress like it was a surprise gift. "Your timing is impeccable. Thank you."

The waitress looked at her and then at Hubbard. "Yeah . . . You okay, buddy?"

"He's fine. He just needs his drink to calm himself. Isn't that right, John?"

So this was the reason for the meeting at *The Bandstand*. She knew all the stories from his past. If he crawled into a bottle tonight, he'd be out of their way. Just a slight push was all he needed. He realized they were right. A slight push and he wanted a drink. He felt sick.

The waitress left.

"Jack Daniels and a little bit of water. Did we get your drink right? You know, one thought just occurred to me. John Riley and your Uncle R.J. Your initials are just the flipside of his. Did anyone ever point that out to you? I guess your mother had a sense of humor." She waited for some response from Hubbard. None came.

She didn't overlook anything. Hubbard stared at the drink in front of him. He wanted a drink the moment he stepped inside the club. If he didn't take it, she'd continue to pester him.

"The whole town was only too happy to give us the low down on you. People talk, talk, and talk about you and your uncle . . . C'mon John, take a drink, you know you want to. I made arrangements with the bartender. *You can have as many drinks as you want tonight and it's all on me.* How does that sound?"

Hubbard's brow curled. "All the drinks I want?" They were offering him a government-funded bender to stop him from pursuing this. Next time, they would try something else. Hubbard surveyed the crowd as if he was looking for an escape route. Something clicked for him and all the previous tension fell away. He took a drink.

"There. That's better, isn't it? Why don't you go find that slutty girl who was at the door and have a good time? I hear you're quite the lady's man—but only when you're drunk."

Hubbard took another sip. Longinotti reached for her purse to leave.

"Tell me something."

"What would that be?" Longinotti smiled, looking as if she was enjoying seeing his fall, getting him to climb into a bottle with only the power of her insight.

"You're the profiler, aren't you? That's your job with the FBI."

"Such a bright boy, too bad you're nothing but a farmer."

Hubbard nodded in agreement. "Yeah . . . You can see right through me. Can't you? . . . You knew I'd get angry when you insulted me and repeated stupid lies about my family. Anger at slander is such an *unexpected* reaction. But still you predicted it. Brilliant. Then you piled on insight after insight: Like I wouldn't hit a woman even if she deserved much worse. Again, you amaze me. Oh yes, and after taking a sip of bourbon . . ." Hubbard took another drink. "I won't stop until I'm unconscious. Bravo. You'll have to call me tomorrow morning to find out how that one came out."

Longinotti put her purse down.

"Thank you for tonight and the drinks. You've confirmed something that I've suspected, but had no way of proving: The FBI's not here to solve anything. That's not your assignment down here in 'Moonshine County', is it? That's why all your resources are being used to stop anyone from getting close to the truth about Amir. And why the state police are kept at arm's length and Sheriff Toil became your local contact."

Longinotti's voice was like the hiss of a serpent. "I'd be careful. You're heading . . ."

"I've arrived, agent. Didn't you say I get there before everyone else? As for you coming here tonight, a woman alone, helpless, and unaided . . ." Hubbard pointed to three men in turn, sitting at different tables, spread across the room. "I believe the 'trucker' in the penny loafers, that tired 'businessman', and that 'farmer' in the new boots and jeans are all getting a government paycheck."

The farmer was looking at Hubbard by the time his finger came to him. The undercover agent wore a surly facial expression familiar to Hubbard. He usually saw it just before a fight broke out. "You can hear me, can't you, Farmer Brown? We're wired for sound in this booth. Don't you guys have a budget? You must be burning through money."

The farmer averted his eyes.

"To be honest, Agent Longinotti, I'm cheating a little. Two of your men are new to me, but I've seen that guy in the suit before. He was sitting in a Suburban having a very heated conversation with someone on his cell phone on the morning you all arrived in Hayslip. At first I thought he was having an argument with his girlfriend, but when I saw the ring on his finger, I realized he was talking to his wife. Only a woman could make a man cry, beg and plead like that."

"He wasn't beg . . ." Longinotti stopped abruptly. Her mouth became a thin, cruel line.

The farmer's wide eyes went from the businessman, who seemed a bit unsettled, over to Longinotti.

"Tell me, Miss Longinotti, it is 'miss', isn't it? Are there any guidelines about inter-office relationships with married agents? I would assume so, but I don't know."

Hubbard stood.

"Don't get up." Hubbard grabbed his glass and finished the last of the drink. "You didn't ask, but as an expert in psychology, I think you should know this one rule about guys sitting alone in a bar. They always look up when the pretty girls come in the door. Always. After all, that's the reason they're here, hoping one of those girls ends up with them. They don't sit alone, facing the booths along the back wall *unless they're working*. Men are very predictable, even without a profiler in tow."

Hubbard was glad Longinotti wasn't packing her gun tonight. She looked like she would love to use it on him.

"One question—are you really going to play the recording of this conversation for Special Agent-in-Charge Ramirez? . . . Don't answer. I'm way ahead of you. Goodnight."

Hubbard wove his way through a crowd that had increased substantially since his arrival. At the entrance, he ran into Big John Dugan. The long-time proprietor served as his own bouncer at the club.

Dugan broke into a wide grin when he saw Hubbard. "John Riley, I was glad to hear you were coming tonight. We've missed you."

"Well, I've missed all the folks here."

"You're leaving too soon. I thought you'd be here all night. That lady said you could buy as many drinks as you want and we should put it all on her card. *The sky's the limit.* I told her, you don't know how many drinks John Riley—"

"Yeah, she said the same . . . Wait. What exactly did she say?"

"She said you could buy as many drinks—"

"Right . . . Okay . . . I want to buy a round for the house. Give everyone in the club a duplicate of what they're drinking now and put it on her card. After all, she said I could buy as many drinks as I wanted."

"Well, I don't know . . . I don't think she meant it that way. I'll have to ask . . ."

They both turned toward the agents, standing in a small circle by the booths on the far wall, immersed in an argument, accusatory fingers punctuating the air.

"Who are they?"

"Well, you probably don't want to mess with them. They're FBI."

"They're cops? In my bar? I hate cops."

"I think I've heard that before. Well, don't mess with them. They're tough. Play it safe or you'll get hurt. It'd take a hell of a man to stand up to the FBI singlehanded. People would be talking about this night for years. You don't want that."

"*The hell I wouldn't!* You'll back me up about her instructions about you and the drinks?"

"Of course, that's what the agent told both of us."

Dugan shook his hand. "Come see us." Dugan grabbed one waitress by the arm and started heading for the bar, picking up another waitress as he went.

After exiting the building, Hubbard headed to his truck. Agent Longinotti did have one surprise for him tonight. Something he never saw coming. She knew how much he wanted that drink on the table. It wasn't theatrics when he finished it front of her. He drank the booze because he couldn't control his desire for it.

In the blurry years since he started drinking, he had avoided the obvious.

He was an alcoholic.

Was that the only thing he refused to see?

He drove across the lot and stopped the truck when he got to the exit leading to the two-lane highway. If he turned right, he could make it to the liquor store on the county line in fifteen minutes. If he went left, he would return to an empty house.

Behind him, a driver tapped the horn, urging him to make a decision.

Hubbard turned onto the road.

23

THE OPEN DOOR POLICY

HUBBARD WASN'T HAPPY WITH HIS DECISION. Or the direction he turned on the empty roadway. If he had more self-control, he'd be driving the *opposite* way. He battled an almost overwhelming desire to stop and turn the damn truck around; exerting so much mental effort blood pounded in his temples.

It felt all wrong, but he was heading home.

Minutes later, he turned the pickup off the dirt road and onto the gravel driveway. When he drove around the last pine tree that bordered his property, the truck's headlights lit his farmhouse.

His foot hit the brake, slowing the vehicle to a crawl. His brow creased with concern as he surveyed the home's façade. Someone had been inside it while he was at *The Bandstand*, and then took great pains to make the home break-in so obvious that he would spot it from his driveway.

Hubbard never left his house without some light still burning. In the country, nighttime was too dark to stumble through, so everyone left some kind of illumination burning. But now, the floodlight at the barn was out, the light fixture over the front door was extinguished and the interior of the house was completely black. The front windows were like slate, dully reflecting the pickup lights back to him. Even the yellow room was opaque.

Most troubling, and most obvious, was the front entry. Whoever did this left the front door open, propping it with a mossy stone to assure it stayed that way. The entrance now looked like the opening of a cave.

He pulled onto the lawn so that his headlamps were aimed directly at the front door. The lights shot through the doorway and down the main hall; the stair banister and curved legs of the hall table cast spider shadows that stretched into eventual blackness.

From the cab, Hubbard looked around for signs of another vehicle or person. Nothing.

He considered the front of his house. Was the intruder or intruders still here?

What were his options? He could call the police. But there was just something childish about calling Toil to ask him to drive over here and walk through the house with him. If there was no one here, it would become a story told at the café.

But still, only an insane person would get out of his vehicle and check this out by himself. Anyone with a lick of sense would call and get some kind of help.

Hubbard turned off his truck and got out. From the tool box in the truck bed he pulled out a tire iron.

He wished he kept his guns. Even that red hammer would be handy now.

Hubbard stared at the bright façade of his home. It was an almost radioactive white under the high beams, turning the dark windows into dead eyes. He looked up, then down, going from window to window, searching for any signs of movement. He stood quietly, and listened for any sound that might be out of place in the cool night air.

In the distance, he heard the indistinct sound of a car door closing . . . or *a truck's* door. He heard an engine start up. It seemed to come from behind him and to his right, but in the country, sound can travel far and can fool you in terms of its direction.

To his left, there was a new sound, distinct and near, of a vehicle approaching from the direction of the highway down the rural road. It was moving fast.

Hubbard turned toward the road, gripping the tire tool. Somehow he knew the vehicle was racing toward him.

The car slowed only a bit when it turned off the road to crunch along his gravel driveway. Temporarily, it was hidden by the pines and then he saw its headlights, turned to high beam, emerge from behind the trees. He could tell it was a car, but it changed course before he could make out details and drove straight toward him across the yard.

Hubbard lifted the tire tool. It didn't feel like much of a weapon.

The car skidded to a stop twenty yards in front of him. Hubbard lifted his left hand to shield his eyes. He could see the dark form of a man getting out of the driver's door.

"Hello, kid. What's going on?"

Hubbard took a deep breath and then felt anger wash over him due to R.J.'s dramatic arrival. "What the hell? *What are you doing?*"

"I could ask you the same thing. What's going on? Why are you standing here holding a tire iron with the front door of your house wide open?"

"Somebody broke in. I guess the open door is some kind of message."

"I told you—"

"Yeah, you told me. But I'm not dropping this thing until I find the murderer . . . and I'm close. *I'm real close.* I want you to know that." It was a lie, but he wondered if it would trigger some kind of reaction.

R.J. was little more than a silhouette in the night, but he was quiet for a long moment. "I knew you wouldn't drop this . . . Well, I guess I can't talk you out of it . . . C'mon, let's check out the house." R.J. opened the door to the back seat and reached in.

Hubbard felt uneasy. He was aware of the solitude of this location. "Oh, don't worry about it . . . I got this . . . Okay?"

R.J. pulled something long and narrow out of the back seat of his car that Hubbard couldn't make out in the darkness.

"Well, there's no harm playing it safe." He came in front of the headlights with the item in his hands.

It was a shotgun. Hubbard held his breath.

"Okay, head inside," R.J. said. "I'll be right behind you."

Hubbard hesitated.

"Don't worry," his uncle said, "I know how to handle weapons."

"Yeah . . . It's not that."

There was a moment of silence as the two men stared at each other.

R.J. broke the silence. "Okay. I'll go in first. This would be a lot easier if you trusted me."

"Yeah, I know."

R.J. tilted his head as if he didn't quite understand the remark and then turned and headed for the house.

"This isn't really necessary."

"Humor me."

They got to the front door. Close up, Hubbard could tell that the bulb had been smashed; shards of glass were on the porch floor.

R.J. reached in and found the foyer light switch and flicked it up. It worked. A small circle of light appeared overhead.

R.J. walked to the living room and flicked the overhead light on. It worked, too and the yellow walls lit up.

"Jesus," R.J. said, startled by the brightness. This is new, isn't it? You've got to find another color."

"I don't know. It grows on you."

R.J. sighed. "Okay."

They continued on this way throughout the house, R.J. always in the lead. "So, what have you found out about the killing?"

Hubbard laid out the bait. "I think it all revolves around the new interstate highway."

R.J. stopped in place. "How do you know about that? It hasn't been announced."

"I have my sources. How do you know about it?"

Shrugging his shoulders, R.J. said, "I've just heard rumors." He walked up the stairs to the bedrooms.

Hubbard followed behind. "Somebody paid Amir to take photographs of land parcels adjacent to the new route. Somebody with insider knowledge could make a huge profit scooping up farmland that would soon be prime retail spots. There could have been several investors in that little enterprise."

"I suppose so. But using insider knowledge like that is a crime. If a group of men thought you were close to exposing their actions . . . well, there's probably a lot of money at stake. Whoever's behind this won't give that up easily. The White River Killer would be the least of your worries."

"I never thought White River Killer did it. That's Andrews's theory. No, it's all about that highway. I just got a little more work to do . . . and I'll know the truth."

R.J. was at Emily's bedroom. He suddenly turned. "Okay. That's it."

Hubbard took a step back, sucking in some air, watching the gun barrel swing off R.J.'s shoulder.

"You're right . . . No one's in here. Whoever did this is gone." R.J. cracked open the shotgun at the muzzle and took out two shells. "You okay, kid? You looked spooked. Do you want to spend the night at my house?"

"No . . . no, I'm fine."

Hubbard followed him down the stairs. The unloaded shotgun cradled on top of R.J.'s shoulders, pointing back at Hubbard.

"You know, kid. If something happens to you, it means that I'll be raising Emily." Hubbard felt his brow crease. "Yeah, I thought that might get your attention . . . Maybe that's what the rock at the door means. Think about what you're doing before you get hurt."

R.J. was at the door. Hubbard grabbed his arm.

"Just one question before you leave. Why is the FBI so suspicious of you? Agent Ramirez said . . ."

"Kid, the FBI is always suspicious of me. I appreciate your concern, but it's nothing to worry about."

"But what are they questioning you about—"

"It's late. I'm tired. Let's put a pin in this discussion until another time." R.J. was on the porch steps when he finished his thought. "Don't forget. You owe me a favor and I've got a tight timeline."

"How could I forget that?"

Hubbard stood on the porch steps and watched his uncle depart. When he could no longer see the lights of his car, he sat on the porch steps; looking at green space he once called a lawn. R.J. had managed to dodge his questions once again. *What kind of person drives around with a loaded shotgun in the backseat?* Even in gun-toting Arkansas, that was extreme. He remembered the coroner's description of the killer, "one sick, smooth-talking son-of-a-bitch."

Hubbard took a big breath and slowly released it. "I need a drink."

———◆———

It was two a.m. Hubbard sat on the edge of his bed, staring into the darkness. He couldn't sleep, or maybe he didn't want to risk another nightmare. He got up and flipped on the light. He had to do something.

Downstairs, Hubbard sat down in front of his ancient computer.

There were at least a dozen members of the media and many more law enforcement personnel involved in the murder investigation. Why was he singled out for special treatment? What did the murderer think he knew? The college girls said Amir was afraid to have his photo taken and the FBI seemed interested in altering or destroying any image of the student they could find. *Why?*

He replayed his dangerous encounter at the student's apartment. The two thieves were in the process of stealing photo albums and a computer from the residence. Outside, several photos had been dropped by the men during their escape and had trailed across the yard. The single image he saw briefly, lying on the apartment's deck when he was in a rush to leave, was a shot of an empty field.

Photographs, always photographs.

The Internet was a long shot, but it was the only research tool he had at his disposal. Over the next two hours, he typed in search terms that seemed to make some sense. They were all variations on 'terrorism' or 'Arab terrorists' or 'terrorist attacks', 'Egypt', 'Abadi' or varying combinations of those words. The search terms didn't have to be complex to bring a tidal wave of results. Growing fatigued, his eyes could barely focus on the succession of bearded extremists that appeared on the screen. *What do I expect to find?* Taking a last chance, he typed in a succession of terms, starting with 'terrorists', 'Egypt', and 'wealthy'. He remembered how they dispatched Osama bin Laden and added 'Seal Team Six' to the string. Before he entered the request, he added one more name: 'Amir'.

A news story from the *London Times* appeared at the top of a short list. He clicked on it, to see the image of yet another bearded terrorist accompanying yet another account of bloodshed and violence. This attack was in America. Hubbard remembered it, the Grand Central Station bombing five years ago. Almost one hundred lives were lost. As with bin Laden, a Navy Seal team was dispatched overseas and got retribution, tracking down the madman responsible for the attack, hiding in Malaysia. But this was not a narrow account of the New York attack, the headline read, "Egypt's Leading Family Divided between the West and Fundamentalism." The thrust of the story was that the psycho, *Abbas Alfarsi,* was part of a well-established Egyptian family, one of Egypt's ruling class.

It was very late, but his attention was drawn to the photo of the fanatic, Alfarsi, who helped plot the bloody assault. The man appeared to be in his late 50s, and his eyes were dark and narrow, crazed with hatred. There was something else . . . Something familiar. Hubbard's mouth opened wide with surprised recognition. He stood up, not believing what he was seeing. Son—of—a—bitch! Add thirty years and a beard to Amir's face and the image would be his. That's why the FBI doctored the photo. The Arab student's last name wasn't Abadi. It was *Alfarsi.*

Amir, the reserved student, the dork, as the girls called him, was the son of one of the most notorious terrorists in American history.

Energized by his discovery, Hubbard spent another hour researching the monster father, but no other account went to the trouble to list the names of Alfarsi's fifteen children borne by three different wives.

Hubbard released a deep sigh. *Did someone discover Amir's real identity and seek sick retribution on their own? Or was the kid's murder caused by something more mundane? An evil closer to home?* Whoever was behind all this thought they could push him out of the investigation.

He was ready to push back . . .

24

ROUND AND ROUND SHE GOES

IT WAS THE FLOWER GARDEN THAT DID MARIA IN. Hubbard agreed to till up his mother's old flower garden that had gone to seed for a new garden. Maria, through Emily's translation, had requested for a fun summertime activity.

Emily was a born salesperson. "It will teach me responsibility if I water it every day. *I need that bad.*"

The flower garden was followed by an irrigation request for the home's vegetable garden.

Neither of the planting activities was unusual for a farm. That's not what drove Hubbard to act. What troubled Hubbard was that Emily *now* referred to them as *Maria's* flower garden and *Maria's* vegetables.

There was no time to waste. From his tractor, Hubbard called Mr. Carlos and told him that Maria wasn't working out. After the Tomato Festival, they had to find new work for her. Mr. Carlos didn't understand the connection between Maria and the annual event, but he reluctantly agreed to look for a new opportunity for her.

Hubbard knew that he would eventually screw up with her. She was always within arm's reach and he was too damned attracted to her. Sometimes the pain of his growing desire made felt he was burning alive. It made him want to drink to deal with it. That's why she had to go.

Emily dashed to the Ferris wheel, followed by Maria, with Hubbard trailing behind them. It was an unseasonably warm night and they had stayed at the fair past Emily's bedtime. He struggled with an over-sized helium balloon, while carrying all the other fair prizes in his arms.

"The Ferris wheel! Can we go on the Ferris wheel next?" Emily called back to Hubbard. Hubbard looped the balloon string around his fingers to prevent it from escaping his grasp. "Emily! Please slow down."

"Daddy, can we ride it, pah-leeze?" Backpedaling now, Emily pointed up to the massive wheel as if it he couldn't see it.

Hubbard bobbed and weaved through a thick crowd, which was heading in the opposite direction, trusting Maria to stay within arm's reach of his daughter.

"Watch behind you, Emily." Hubbard grimaced as she crashed into an older woman wearing a full-length raincoat on this clear evening. "Sorry," he apologized to the silver-haired lady, who seemed annoyed by his lack of parenting skills. Maria had Emily in hand now, and got her headed in the right direction. Hubbard found an opening in the flow of people, dove through like a half-back, and caught up with them.

The heart of the Hayslip Tomato Festival was the Ferris wheel. All the other amusements were simple things—kiddie cars, mirror mazes, tilt-a-whirls—mere handmaidens to the majestic circle towering above the fairgrounds. Some people claimed the wheel had exceeded its useful life, but it was difficult for the town to let it go. The ornate ride was the last vestige of another era, a time when the event drew attendees from across southeast Arkansas, northern Louisiana, and western Mississippi. It rose more than sixty feet above the ground, the tallest structure in Hayslip, and provided a view of the lighted Star City grain silos in a nearby county. Each open car could accommodate two occupants, sitting on a single bench. The small seat was popular with couples (the unmarried kind) both for its view and the intimate proximity it required.

It was almost eleven, and most of the fairgoers were headed to the grandstands to see who would win the drawings and watch the festival's closing celebration.

A young attendant wearing greasy overalls barked out in a voice that mixed boredom and relief. "Last ride of the night."

"You know, every year I forget how tall that thing is," Hubbard said. "Emily, you don't like heights. Let's go to the grandstands and see if we won a trip to St. Louis."

Emily gazed upward and seemed to reevaluate her interest in riding. She grabbed Maria's hand and she bent down to listen to her. They both gave sideways glances at Hubbard as they whispered.

"What? What is it?" Hubbard said. His eyes examined the front of his shirt, thinking mustard had dripped on it.

Emily put her right foot behind her, balancing it on the toes, rocking it from side to side. "I want you and Maria to go. She's never been on our Ferris wheel."

Hubbard felt his face turn red. He remembered how tight those seats were. He had used them to his advantage in high school. They were designed for romance—not employers and employees on a work-related outing.

Maria said something, and Hubbard tried to translate. It was about no passengers riding by choice and Hubbard's name was included in the sentence. Once again, Emily was forced to serve as their intermediary.

"She said you don't have to ride," Emily explained. Before Hubbard could respond, he thought he understood Emily tell Maria that he was in love with the Ferris wheel. That can't be right. Hubbard believed his years studying French were hampering his Spanish. Perhaps because it meant abandoning his last childhood . . . fantasy was the best word to describe it. *Grow the hell up.*

Maria nodded as if she understood how a man could fall in love with an inanimate object. She turned to him and smiled. Her smile should be illegal. It clouded men's minds.

In previous years, it had been easy to deftly steer Emily, but she was getting older, wiser. "Sweetheart, I can't go. I've got to hold all your prizes. Why this big balloon might carry you away."

"Daddy, I won't float off. That's silly."

"There was a little girl last year. She didn't think she'd float off either. But if you look up on a clear night . . ."

A woman's voice from behind interrupted him. "We'll hold everything, John Riley. Emily will be safe with us."

Hubbard swung around to find Margaret Gibbons and her brood of four girls. Her husband was at the rear, serving as paternal pack mule. "My family's not going to be able to get on anyway. And Emily and Zoe can talk while you're on the ride." It was a superfluous offer since Emily and Zoe were already in a clutch, whispering and giggling. "Besides," Mrs. Gibbons nodded at Maria, "it looks like you two could use a turn or two on that big thing. It's a beautiful night." She winked at Hubbard.

"It's not what it looks like. It's not a date. I'm paying her."

Mrs. Gibbon's brow furrowed.

Hubbard didn't know how Jim Gibbons could see Maria through the mountain of fair paraphernalia in his arms, but apparently he saw enough. "Wow, what are her rates?"

"Jim, hush," Mrs. Gibbons scolded him.

Hubbard tried to correct the misunderstanding. "No, I mean she's my employee . . . domestic . . . uh, housekeeper."

Mr. Gibbons snorted, and the explanation didn't seem to aid Mrs. Gibbon's confusion either.

"Next, please." Everyone in line had boarded except for Hubbard and Maria. The ticket taker motioned impatiently for them to get onboard.

Maria took a step forward, but stopped when Hubbard didn't move. She seemed embarrassed by his reluctance. Maria turned to

Emily and said something in Spanish about the Ferris wheel and Hubbard.

"Of course he wants to ride. It's his favorite." Emily answered her in English, realized she used the wrong language, and repeated it in Spanish. For good measure, her friend Zoe added something more about boys and slow moving . . . trains? Did everyone but him know Spanish?

Mrs. Gibbons took charge and began liberating the items from Hubbard's arms. She whispered to him sternly, "You can't leave the girl standing there. You'll embarrass her."

Hubbard was outgunned by the opposite sex working in unison. Maria seemed to be trying to decipher what Hubbard wanted to do. She pointed up at the wheel, shook her head "no", while shrugging her shoulders. Yes or no?

Emily cheered like she was on a pep squad. "Go Daddy!" She was joined by a chorus of Gibbons girls chanting in unison. "Go, go, go . . ."

Hubbard gestured toward the wheel and then placed his hands over his heart like a suitor. "Let's go . . . Vamos. I love the Ferris wheel."

They walked up the metal steps and lowered themselves into the small compartment. Hubbard tried to give her as much room as possible, but there was no extra space available. They were as tight as chocolates in a Valentine's box. The attendant brought the metal safety bar down on their laps with a loud clang. Obviously surprised by the lack of space, Maria couldn't hide her discomfort at sitting this close. Her back was ramrod straight and her knees were clamped together. She stared into the night with a blank expression.

Hubbard tried to become less aware of her: The warmth of her body, the trace of citrus perfume in the air, and her pert breasts . . . were . . . right . . . there. Employers and employees should not be pressed together under any circumstances.

Without Emily present, he would have to converse with Maria without a translator. He slowly constructed a sentence in Spanish in his head. But when he turned to her, prepared to say, "El fête est fun mañana," his eyes were drawn to her raven hair brushing against the nape of her neck and he lost his train of thought. He turned away to gather himself. *I've become a Pavlovian dog.*

The Ferris wheel lunged forward abruptly, throwing them backward as their carriage rocked in response. Maria grabbed Hubbard's leg to right herself, and he twitched in reaction as if he touched an electric current. She yanked her hand away and whispered a few words. Her eyes focused on the empty space over his shoulder. He couldn't hear her soft voice in the crowd noise, but it sounded like an apology. It really wasn't necessary.

The wheel was spinning at a brisk clip now. A little faster than Hubbard remembered, and he was relieved that Emily was safe on the ground. The ride seemed to be too much for Maria as well. She gripped the safety bar so tight, her knuckles turned white.

They rode in silence, making three circuits. Hubbard's mind was racing, trying to come up with something appropriate to say in rudimentary Spanish. Maria continued to face straight ahead, ignoring the expansive view. As they rode upward to the top of the wheel for a fourth and final time, Hubbard pointed toward the blue lights on the distant Star City grain silos. Pointing had to be an international language. Maria seemed to relax as her eyes followed his arm to her right. At night, the lights on the giant silos on the horizon made them look like high-rise buildings planted in the middle of delta farmland.

They had no time to react when a shrill alarm rang below and the wheel jerked to a dead stop. All the individual cars on the ride, however, had no brakes and spun forward and back with surprising force. Hubbard was able to catch Maria with his left arm before her head hit the front edge of the car. Held only by the safety bar locked at their waist, they were whirled to face the ground one moment, and twirled back toward the stars the next.

The on-lookers below reacted in alarm, expecting the old ride to fling cars into the night sky before their eyes. Maria cried out in fright and her arms covered her face as Hubbard shot a glance below them as their car spun to face the ground again.

The ride workers were darting from side to side like rodeo clowns, trying to find an opening through the rocking cars and make it to the central post holding the Ferris wheel. Hubbard wrapped his other arm through a guard rail on the back of the seat and used his free hand to support Maria's head to protect her against whiplash. Her dark eyes wide, she dropped her arms and spoke Spanish so rapidly that he caught none of it.

The wheel, undaunted, seemed possessed by evil, intent on discarding its passengers. It moved again unexpectedly, knocking the worker wearing overalls off his feet when he attempted to dodge through an opening between the cars. The ride spun in reverse a quarter-turn, jerked to a stop, and then advanced once more like a mechanical bronco.

Below them, the panicked crowd continued to yell ineffectually at the men, who seemed unable to stop the crazed contraption. Hubbard's heart jumped when he heard Emily's tearful voice among the others.

In front of them, Hubbard spotted the heavy hand rail atop the back of another carriage separate from one side and then the other, spinning to the ground. Hubbard could only watch as the back of the old fiberglass seat of the carriage below them continued to splinter. The two teenaged girls inside the car clung to the safety bar like a life raft, shrieking as another section of their seatback gave way. How much could it take before the remainder split apart?

In their car, Hubbard felt the railing behind their seat begin to vibrate as screws began to detach. Maria leaned forward, but jumped back when the foot rail collapsed beneath them. Their seat tilted a few degrees to the right as brittle fiberglass drifted away from metal fasteners. Hubbard looked down. Sixty feet looked like a mile. *Get Emily away from here. She can't see this.*

Maria held on to him, her nails digging deep into his arm in desperation. Surprised by the strength of her vice-like grip, Hubbard was in some pain as he tried to calm her.

"El . . . uh . . . Je vous ai. Je ne vous laisserai pas partir." (I've got you. I won't let you go.)

"Que s'est-il passé ?" (What's happening?)

"Je ne sais pas." (I don't know.)

"Se cassera-t-il à part?" (Will it come apart?)

"Non. Je vous ai. (No. I've got you.)

Hubbard saw the younger of the two workers crawl on his belly like an infantry soldier under the malevolent ride. He made it to the center post, stood, and pulled the red emergency switch down with both hands. The big wheel ground to a halt.

A woman's voice from below them floated up. "Thank God." It took some time before the individual cars stopped swinging.

Hubbard and Maria were stuck at the top of the wheel where their car came to rest. He called down to Emily, telling her they were okay. He held Maria in his arms as she wept softly. He wanted to comfort her, but didn't know what to say. He made a weak joke. "Encore?"

His head tilted to one side. His brow arched upward, and then down as he replayed what just had happened in his mind. In his panic to reassure Maria, he confused French with Spanish.

Wait a minute.

She had answered him. Hadn't she? In French? That couldn't be right. He was hallucinating.

"Parlez-vous français?" He asked in a tentative manner since the idea of an illegal immigrant from south of the border being conversant in French was far-fetched. Maria slowly lifted her head from his chest, looking as surprised as he felt.

"Oui. Faites-vous?"

"Oui."

She sat up in the seat, looking at him as if he had announced he was a visitor from Mars. Perhaps finding an Arkansas farmer who knew français was equally unreal to her? They fell silent facing each other, stunned by the recent and literal turn of events. In the night sky directly behind Maria, Hubbard saw a roman candle soar into the sky, followed by another and another, each one exploding into a different shower of primary colors.

"Ladies and gentlemen," a voice from the grandstand loudspeakers echoed across the fairgrounds, "the fireworks have begun!" It seemed like a totally unnecessary announcement. How could you miss the fireworks?

Now that the Ferris wheel had stopped, the men below brought out an iron bar, about five feet long and shaped like a square "S". "This will take a few minutes," the older of the two called up to the riders. Ignoring the heated questions to explain what had happened and what they were doing now, they inserted one end of the "S" bar into a hole in a large metal box at the base and turned the bar like an oversized key. The wheel began to turn, almost imperceptibly, accompanied by a metallic, tick, tick, tick, sound as gears inched forward. The men stopped turning the bar when a car had travelled far enough to unload passengers. As each pair of riders got off, they seized their moment to berate the hapless ride crew. This would be a slow process.

In the lower cars, Hubbard noticed a few heads crane upward to see the source of the animated French conversation.

"How do you know French?" Hubbard asked in a tone that sounded as if he was still a little uncertain that she did.

"Luis and I went to a private school to train for government service. Graduates would represent Guatemala in countries across the world . . ." Maria stopped speaking, swallowed hard, and then she shook her head and smiled. "Everyone was choosing English as their second language. I thought being one of the few who spoke French would help me stand out. What about you? Why does a farmer know French?"

Hubbard's explanation was simple. "Back when I started in middle school, they still offered French as a foreign language. I only knew I wanted to be as far away as possible from Hayslip when I grew up. Paris is—"

Maria smiled like she understood. "A world away."

"Yeah, that's it. I had some crazy idea that one day I'd escape from here and sip coffee under the Eiffel Tower. And all this," his hand indicated the miles of farm fields stretching out to the horizon, "would be a dream." Hubbard shrugged. "Kid stuff, I guess."

"Did you ever go to Paris?"

"No . . . um . . . Life happens, I guess. I did go to Montreal for a summer to study French."

"I did too!" Maria exclaimed.

Hubbard's mouth turned up in a half-smile to see her so pleased at this shared connection.

The conversation became quieter when Hubbard asked her why she had left Guatemala. Maria described her father's sad fate at the end of her country's long civil war. How one day soldiers came to their home and took him away. Her father was a ranking government official on the wrong side of history. They never saw him again. Instead of offering support, their friends abandoned them, afraid to be associated with the losing faction. Her mother became despondent, and her brother Luis wasn't the same again—always angry, always in trouble. When her mother died, of grief, Maria thought, they were farmed out to relatives who didn't want them. Luis told her that America would offer them a chance to start over. So she agreed to follow him here.

Hubbard then gave her the short version of his life. He couldn't bring himself to tell her everything, not here, not now.

The hand cranking clicked noisily along, but it took time to revolve the giant wheel. Occasionally, Hubbard glanced down and waved to Emily and the patient Gibbons family.

Once he thought he spotted Luis and his bespectacled buddy observing them as they slowly descended. The pair was hard to see, though, almost hidden in the shadows of a far-away concession stand. Even from this vantage point, her brother and his pal were suspicious. If it was indeed them, why hide in the dark? Why not walk up and wait for Maria to reach the ground? After all, it was an opportunity to give him their version of the "evil eye" yet again. Maybe it wasn't them and he was just being paranoid.

When they exited their car, Maria was telling Hubbard a charming story about Emily baking her first cake. As Hubbard stepped out, he offered Maria his hand and was surprised to realize his awkwardness was gone. Emily ran up to them and Hubbard scooped her up in his arms and spun her around in a circle, trying to lessen the effects of the frightening scene she had witnessed. He laughed and said, "That was so much fun."

"It was?" she said hesitantly.

"Sure."

Maria's smile seemed to confirm her father's interpretation of the wild ride.

"Daddy, you were talking French! We heard you," Emily announced it like it was a newspaper headline. Her second thought was added like a subheading. "You found somebody who speaks your language—in Hayslip."

"Oui, sí, yes." Hubbard tried to wave it off. "Small world."

Several couples remained at the ride entrance to see who the foreigners at the top of the Ferris wheel were. Their faces were varying portraits of surprise when they saw Hubbard, Maria, and Emily emerge.

You'd think they'd never seen a farmer speaking French with a beautiful Latino woman at the Hayslip Tomato Festival.

25

THE KILLER ON THE WHITE

R.J. PARKED ON THE NORTH SIDE of the old stone and brick church, which stood one block away from the town square. For almost five minutes, he remained in his Cadillac and gripped the steering wheel like it was a lifeline, taking several deep breaths in an effort to find new strength. It was past ten p.m. and these days there was almost no energy left in him by this hour. His hand went to the gun in his coat pocket, touching it for reassurance, as if it was a talisman. At one time, R.J. thought that he could handle anything unexpected that might come his way.

Now, he wasn't so sure.

He didn't know what he'd be dealing with tonight. Harper had lost his mind. The pastor's drunken phone call thirty minutes ago confirmed it. "You wouldn't listen to me at the café . . . So, I'm going to talk to John Riley. Expect him to come looking for you. *He has to know the truth before your surgery.*"

R.J.'s caller I.D. provided Harper's location: *First Assembly*. Now, he had to stop the fool minister before he ruined whatever remained of his life. What did Harper think he knew? How could he know anything? It was impossible.

He opened the car door and got out, hoping the cool night air would revive him. In his peripheral vision he saw movement, barely visible in the night. He spun around, putting his hand on the pistol. There was the outline of a man in the gloom, walking unsteadily toward him. When the figure neared the light over the door, R.J. recognized the minister.

Raw emotion was obvious on Harper's pink face, distorting his features, driving his words. "Don't shoot . . . *or go ahead and shoot.* Take your pick. I knew you'd try and stop me."

He felt his pulse begin to race. This was more than the ramblings of a drunk. He took slow steps toward the preacher, his eyes darting to the shadows, checking to see if anyone was lurking there. "Small towns don't take kindly to their church leaders becoming public spectacles. Your drinking is no secret as it is, let me get you back to the church's first aid room. Is there still a cot back there? You can sleep this off."

Harper held up his hand. "Stop right there. Don't step any closer until I've said my piece."

"You've said more than enough already."

Harper looked at him for a long moment and seemed to be debating his next words. When he finally spoke, his words cut deep. "I know who killed your brother. I know that Tom Cole didn't die in a fishing accident on the White River seventeen years ago. *I know everything.*"

He felt his throat constrict in response, as if he was choking.

The minister took a wobbly step forward. "I've got the evidence sitting on my desk. If you want to see it, come inside. These church walls won't tumble if a sinner enters. After all, this holy house has seen worse than you . . . *I'm here every day.*"

He watched the reverend stumble to the side entrance, fling the door open, and enter. R.J.'s body was numb. He stood there, dumbly, and watched the door slowly close behind the preacher.

His mind was thick with questions. Was this a trap? Had Harper told this to anyone? What evidence did he hold? *Evidence could mean only one thing.* How did Harper find it when he couldn't? In his nightmares, the red metal box was floating along the White, being pushed by the current toward the Mississippi River.

His hand reached into his pocket and felt the reassuring cold steel and then he followed Harper inside.

Small ceiling spotlights burned in the large sanctuary, thin fingers of yellow light that touched the hardwood flooring, but the remainder of the interior was murky and hard to discern, rows of pews in a misty gray darkness. If he remembered correctly, Harper's office was behind the altar, accessible through an unobtrusive door next to the pulpit. R.J. hadn't been inside the church in more than a decade but he guessed the layout remained the same. Things were slow to change in Hayslip.

He walked down the aisle to the front of the chapel and climbed the steps to the platform where Harper stood each Sunday to harangue the congregation about the torment awaiting sinners. R.J. felt his heart pound and the weakness grow in his left side. If he didn't sit down soon, the room would begin to spin.

He got to Harper's office door and saw light spilling out from underneath. He turned the knob and pushed, letting the door swing open.

Harper was slumped over the desk, his balding head propped on one arm, staring down at the metal tackle box, expressionless. A large door to a storage closet, just beyond the desk, stood open at a ninety-degree angle, blocking R.J.'s view of its inside.

R.J. struggled to slow his breathing as he sat down opposite the minister and his eyes fixed on the red case as well. Tom Cole's dried blood was still caked on the upper corner of the box.

Harper didn't look like he was going to break the silence, so R.J. prodded him. "Are you going to tell me about it or are we going to play twenty questions?"

The preacher leaned back in his chair. "Two weeks after Frank died, Tom Cole came to see me—*in this office,* as a matter of fact. He looked like a wild man, several days' worth of stubble, bloodshot eyes, and filthy clothes. *But you know all that, don't you.* You saw him that Saturday."

R.J. forced himself to stand. *Was anyone else here?* He walked to the closet door and looked inside. The shelves held stacks of gold-colored collection plates and three cardboard boxes. One of the boxes, marked "Personal", had been cut open, its seal broken; gray duct tape was wrapped into a ball on the floor beside the empty box. R.J. turned back to the reverend, "Are you recording this conversation?"

Harper closed his eyes and compressed his lips, as if he was embarrassed to answer the question. "No. I'm not. And we're alone by the way, if you were wondering about that."

He studied the preacher's face, searching for signs of deception. His shoulders relaxed when he was satisfied Harper told the truth. "Why do you think I saw him before he died?"

"Cole had something to say, so I sent him to you."

"*You sent him to me?* You knew what he was going to tell me and you *sent* him to me? Why the hell would you do that? What do you think would happen?"

Harper drooped forward and both his hands went to either side of his head, squeezing it like a vice. "I'm sorry. *I'm so sorry.* The guilt was eating Tom alive. He couldn't take it anymore."

"Oh, I'm so *sad* to hear that shooting my brother was *hard* on him."

"He knew you were getting blamed for what he did, but he was too scared to come forward," Harper said. "He was going to kill himself, but he wanted God to forgive him. You've got to understand what he looked like, how desperate he was."

Harper pointed to a chair as if Cole was here, sitting with them. "He had a loaded pistol in his hand. He was seconds away from putting a bullet in his head and I couldn't stop him. *And you're the one who always knows what to do.*"

An ache grew at the center of R.J.'s chest. For years he had worked with this son-of-a-bitch on public projects, fending off the constant invitations to his church to lay his burdens down in front of the Lord but not a word about this. Not one word until now. The anger was burning through him, so hot, it was overwhelming. He fought the urge to pull the gun from his pocket. "No . . . No. You can't put this on me."

"But don't you see, by then the whole town had made up their minds about who killed Frank. I thought if he told you, then you could . . ."

R.J. sat in the chair across from him and leaned forward. "I could what? . . . Could what? What did you think—?"

Harper exploded in tears. "I didn't think! Okay? I screwed up *your life. John Riley's life . . . Alice's life . . . I didn't . . .* Tom said he couldn't take life in prison and everyone in town looking at him the way they were looking at you. The only thing that reached him was when I said God would turn his back on him unless he talked to you."

"*What profession are you in?* Why didn't you call the State Police?" R.J.'s head tilted back and he grimaced with painful insight. "No . . . It makes sense now. You called Sheriff Conklin, didn't you?"

"As soon as Tom left and I had time to think, I realized what I'd done. I got hold of the sheriff and he said that he knew the spot where you always fished. He'd head Tom off before he got there. He cursed me out for sending Tom to you. Conklin said you'd kill Tom if he didn't get to the river first and stop him."

"Too bad that thought didn't occur to you." R.J. leaned back, looking at the ceiling, remembering the tragic afternoon on the White.

"What happened when Tom got to you?"

"*Why should I tell you anything?*"

Harper lifted both arms, pleading. "Because I've lived with this as long as you have. Because it never leaves me either. Because . . . *please.* I have to know."

R.J. inhaled then slowly released a deep breath. "I was fishing off the bank down by the big rocks when Tom came running up like the devil was chasing him. At first, he was incoherent. I told him to slow down so I could understand him . . . And it all spilled out. He said he went into the woods that day to practice his marksmanship because *I told him* he had to become better with a rifle or he'd . . ." R.J. had to pause for a moment, saying this aloud was more difficult than he anticipated. His hand went to his throat, trying to coax it to relax.

"Do you want some water?"

R.J. shook his head. "Tom was shooting at anything that moved, using up three boxes of shells, and when he heard a truck coming down the road, he turned toward it. He lied to me and said the gun went off all on its own. *He wasn't to blame. It wasn't his fault.* He was out there *because of me* since everybody does what I say . . . That's when I hit him. He fell and his head hit the corner of my tackle box . . . Just like that, it was over . . . In less than a minute, he went from being my best friend to somebody I killed."

R.J. looked at the incriminating box that haunted his dreams. "When I saw what I'd done, I went blood simple. The town already thought I had killed my brother. No one would believe that Tom confessed, *oh so conveniently for me,* before I hit him? I'd be put on trial for both murders . . . So I got out of there . . . Later, I regained my senses and I realized that I left my tackle box at the river." Hubbard's brow wrinkled. "How did *you* get it?"

"Conklin brought it to me."

"Why?"

"He told me what happened and showed me the blood on your tackle box. He said that if *I hadn't sent Tom to you* none of it would have happened. My testimony at a trial about what Tom said in my office wouldn't do any good. A jury would think you were forcing my testimony, just like always, getting favors returned. Everyone knows you were responsible for convincing the deacons to let me keep my position here after . . . *you know.* You've got to remember what the world was like back then; Governor Parker was signing execution orders right and left. You'd get the chair . . . Conklin wanted to *save you.*"

"How?"

"*He needed my help to cover it up.* He said I could never say anything . . . not even to you. He wanted me to hold on to this," he pointed at the tackle box, "until he could figure out what to do with it. So I put it in the closet in a sealed box by the collection plates . . . and time passed and here we are."

"And you did nothing? Just had a drink or two, passing the time away?"

"Conklin said it had to be—"

"*Conklin*. How can you be that stupid? The minute you hid my tackle box you became an accomplice to murder after the fact. You were guilty, too. He could use that to stop you from coming forward if you ever developed a conscience. No church would hire a co-conspirator to a murder, no matter what the circumstances. *Don't tell me that thought never occurred to you.* Maybe that's what helped you stay quiet all these years."

"No . . . I, uh . . ." Harper looked down at the desk. "I don't know."

R.J. shook his head. "Why didn't anyone in this town ever wonder how the town sheriff could afford to buy part-ownership in a radio station? Or ever question how he could add so much new land to his farm on his salary?"

Harper's mouth fell open. "Why? . . . *Oh, dear God. Conklin was blackmailing you?*"

"Conklin said he could get his hands on that tackle box whenever he wanted. I hired men to break into his house to look for it—*and* his office, *and* his car; his mother's house—every place that I could imagine. But I never found it . . . So, I paid."

Harper tried to say something, but no words came out. Tears began to roll down his cheeks.

"Stop crying! You don't have the right" R.J. stood, his strength was returning and he decided to use it here. "*Listen to me carefully.* You're not going to say anything about this to John Riley."

Harper's words were blubbery. "But he deserves to know the truth."

"Why do you think he'd believe you? Think of what you'd tell him: 'Tom Cole shot Frank from an incredibly great distance into a moving vehicle and hit him dead center in the chest *all by accident.*' No one would believe that. *I* was the one who was the crack shot. Tom Cole couldn't hit the broad side of a barn from ten feet."

R.J. circled the desk and spun Harper around in his chair, leaning in to him, getting a firm grip on Harper's shoulders. "And why would you think John Riley would take the word of an alcoholic preacher *or me?* The truth told now would just seem like the desperate ploy of a dying man."

"You don't know that . . . *Please, you're hurting me.*"

"You don't know how it would turn out either. Remember it didn't work out the way you thought seventeen years ago. Look, I made a decision a long time ago. If John Riley asked me the question directly, I'd tell him whatever he wanted to know . . . *and it's not pretty.* But until that time, I won't risk it. He's the only family I have. Let *me* die in peace *or* I'll see that *you* die in peace. Got it?"

R.J. released him and returned to the front of Harper's desk. He knew Harper was beat; he was almost prostrate in his chair. "If I don't make it off the operating table you *may* think that you're free to say whatever you want. But remember what happened with Tom Cole. If John Riley thinks it's a lie, *another damn lie,* then you'll only make this horrible thing worse."

R.J.'s cell phone rang. He drew it out of his pocket and looked at the display. He mumbled to himself. "So many loose ends and I'm running out of time."

"What's wrong?"

"John Riley's got to stop. *I've got to make him stop.*"

"Stop what?"

R.J. waved off the question and put the phone back in his pocket. "I'll get this outside." He walked to the doorway.

Harper stood abruptly, causing his chair to roll back against the office wall. He pointed to the bloody tackle box. "But what about this? What do you want me to do with it?"

R.J. looked at the foul object. "If I'm dead next week, just bury it with me."

26

THE NUCLEAR OPTION

IT WAS MONDAY MORNING and the skies were clear, perfect weather to get something done. But Hubbard had compelling reasons to stay out of the freshly planted fields and near the kitchen where Maria was. Since the discovery of a shared language, he found there was more to her than met the eye—although what met the eye was plenty.

Casting about for something to do that kept him near the farmhouse, he took a short trip to town to buy a new overhead light for the porch to replace the one destroyed by the weekend's trespasser. After he tightened the last screw, he came down the step ladder, and reached inside the door to flick the switch. He stood for a moment on the porch staring up at the new fixture, admiring his handiwork. *You know, some extra security lighting might be—*

The milk globe above him shattered violently. He cried out in alarm and his arm rose to shield his eyes. He froze in place for a moment, and then he lowered his arm, brushing bits of glass off his shirt to the deck of the porch.

"Daddy?" It was Emily's concerned voice from the kitchen.

Hubbard took a quick breath to settle down and called back to her. "It's okay; I guess I crossed the wrong wires."

The top pane of the living room window broke apart, glass clattered to the ground, and the wood siding over the front door splintered. For the first time, Hubbard heard gunshots behind him. Instinctively, he spun around and into a fighter's stance, his hands turned into fists.

Two men marched toward the house from the tree line at the edge of his property. Both of them wore ski masks and the paper painter coveralls they sold at the *E-Z Fix Hardware* store. The masked men broke into a sprint toward him, raising their rifles. Hubbard was so dumbfounded by the bizarre spectacle that his first reaction was only to open his mouth in shock. Once again, the men fired. The bullets slammed into the porch roof just over his head.

Frightened cries of "Monsieur Hub-birrrd!" and "Daddy!" came from inside the house, bringing him to his senses. His heart pounding, he turned to the door in time to prevent Maria from coming onto the porch with Emily trailing behind her.

He held up his hands. "No, no, no! Go inside. Go inside." He spun them around, while looking back to see the progress of the twin shooters on his lawn. His heart went to his throat; they were closing the distance to his house too quickly. He slammed the door and locked it, just as two more bullets shattered the front windows and thudded into the living room walls. The woman and child looked up at him, panic in their eyes, waiting for him to tell them what to do.

He slung his daughter over his shoulder and grabbed Maria's hand. "C'mon, this way." He carried Emily through the house, towing Maria along.

"La police," Maria said, as they passed the kitchen.

He heard a foot kick against the locked front door. "No time. Keep moving. We've got to get out of here."

They burst out the back door, went down the three steps and into the backyard. Hubbard glanced back and forth across his flat fields. There was nowhere to run that a bullet couldn't reach. He took Emily off his shoulder. Maybe Maria and Emily could make a run for it while he held the two men at bay. *No.* They would make short work of him and then take them both down with rifle fire. He had to think. *Of course.*

"There!" He pointed to his grandfather's old bomb shelter which served as storage space for his vegetables. *If it can lock out an atom bomb . . .* "C'mon!" They ran to the small, partially-buried structure and Hubbard yanked open the solid, cast-iron door.

Maria took Emily by the hand and they scrambled down the three steps to the dank interior. They turned around when they realized that he hadn't followed.

"Keep this door closed," Hubbard said. He pointed back at the house. "When they come out the back door, I'm going to—" Maria and Emily bounded back up the steps to pull him in. He pushed back. "No. You stay safe in here . . ."

They now appeared more frightened than ever, eyes widening, pulling Hubbard toward the steps. "No," they cried out in unison. Hubbard didn't know what he planned to do when the masked men exited the house firing their rifles, but hiding was cowardly. The females ignored his instructions and attached themselves to Hubbard, Emily grabbing one leg, Maria wrapping her arms around his chest.

Two bullets smashed into the back door, splintering their way outside. Hubbard gave in to reason. "Okay, okay. Let's get inside."

Not trusting him to follow, they got behind him and pushed him down into the bomb shelter. Once they were inside, Hubbard reached back, closed the shelter door, and latched it, keeping his hand on it for security. They stood there a moment, breathing heavily, listening for more gun shots or any other sounds coming from the two men. Only silence. Hubbard squeezed Emily's shoulders, and brought her closer to him.

With a start, Hubbard remembered his cell phone. He pulled it from his pocket and looked at the screen. No service inside the thick concrete walls. Maria took hers out and looked at it. Her eyes met his and she shook her head.

Emily began weeping, her shoulders trembling.

Hubbard searched for comforting words. "You're okay, Emily. This old shelter has a *written guarantee* to withstand . . ."

Maria started speaking in an agitated French-Spanish-English gumbo of languages. "Quit sont-ils? Esos hombres? Who mauvaise gentlemen? Tears streamed down her cheek. "Il s'agit d'un enfant!"

Hubbard looked around the tight confines of the shelter and felt a new sense of dread. *What if I'm wrong?* He didn't quite get all of Maria's questions, but he knew the Arab kid's murder was behind this. He wanted to shout out to the men, 'I don't know anything,' but that would be a futile gesture. His hands became fists, he hated this helpless feeling. He ached to fight.

Two rounds slammed into the cast iron door, startling him and causing him to drop his hand from the latch for a moment, then he reached back to grasp it. Emily cried out, covering her ears. Maria pulled Emily away from the door and encircled her in her arms. Again and again, bullets crashed into the metal door, each strike echoing in the small space. The two men had to know that their bullets had no effect, but must be sadistically enjoying the terror they created inside the shelter.

The firing stopped. There was an eerie quiet. *Did they give up?*

Hubbard felt an upward pressure on the latch in his hand, as if it wanted to be released. Someone on the outside was pulling up on it, trying to open the door. He pressed down, marshaling all his strength. The old latch was thick and heavy, but it was covered in rust.

It might break apart.

He leaned into it, making a small noise of exertion as his effort increased against the upward pressure. He heard Maria gasp as she realized there was a real danger that the door handle could give way.

Emily buried her face into Maria, wrapping her arms around her. Hubbard fought to ignore his emotions welling up inside him from his daughter's anguish. He had to think clearly if they were going to get out of there alive.

He looked up at the gray concrete roof. The only natural light in the shelter came from two air pipes that allowed a small view of blue skies. A long time ago, the lead pipes had the ability to be sealed air tight, but the gaskets were long gone. Even if he could take his hand away from the door handle, a glimpse of blue skies would tell him nothing.

After an agonizing minute, the pressure on the handle ceased. He thought he caught some muffled words from outside. The exchange was rapid, but indistinct.

The thugs' excited conversation could mean they had hit upon a new plan of attack. He kept his hand pressing down on the handle and waited. In this pause, his head bowed with guilt. *I'm responsible for this. I didn't listen to anyone. I didn't give up when I should have.*

His head rose. No time for this. His eyes went to Emily. "Don't worry, baby. Daddy's got this." He prayed she bought into his bravura.

"Who are they? Why are they so *mean?*"

"I don't know. But when I find out, they'll never do this again. I promise."

There was a noise above him in the air pipes and the concrete interior grew darker. Hubbard leaned forward, trying to see what was happening while keeping his hand on the latch. He pointed to a light switch by Maria. She turned it on and a single bulb burned overhead.

Maria patted Emily's shoulder, and broke away from her to look up into the ventilation. Her hand went to her mouth, and she turned to Hubbard. "Tuyau d'incendie", she said.

Fire hoses? *No.* They were putting the *irrigation* hoses into the air intake tubes. A new feeling of horror came over him as he realized what would come next.

Water cascaded into shelter, pumped from his stock pond, the pressure steadily increasing. Emily screamed as the icy water splashed against her legs. Maria lifted her up on a bench and tried to shield her from the freezing water.

Hubbard's chest tightened as he saw how quickly it covered the entire floor. The powerful irrigation pumps could deliver hundreds of gallons a minute if turned up to full volume. The small shelter had concrete walls three feet thick—watertight. The pumps would overwhelm the small floor drain and water would rise to the ceiling in minutes, drowning them inside.

Maria's eyes met Hubbard's. He could see from the alarm on her face that she understood the motive behind the water flooding the compartment and the probable result.

He had no other choice.

It was impossible to be heard over the roar of water. He beckoned to Maria to come to him. She nodded and took Emily by the hand and they slogged through the rising water and root vegetables floating on the surface, released from their wicker storage baskets. His arms encircled them both. He pressed his face against Maria's soft cheek and spoke into her ear, hoping she could hear his French through the deafening cascade of water.

"Okay. We have to go out before it rises any higher. They'll be expecting me to run away from them, *not charge them*. I'll draw their fire—"

Maria tried to say something, to object to the suicidal plan.

"No. Please, listen to me. There's a path on the other side of the road at the front of the house that leads to the Gibbons's farm. You can't find it unless you know where it is. It's hidden by tall brush. Emily uses it all the time, she'll show you. Once you're on that path, keep running."

Maria leaned away to face him. Her face flushed with emotion. "No, I won't leave you."

"You have to. After all this, um, after it's over, please tell Emily to not think about this day, just all the other days. She'll miss so much if she's always looking back."

His brow creased at his own words. What was he telling her? Who was he to talk? His life was just the echo of a gunshot delivered years ago . . . now it was over.

Maria must have seen the pain in his expression. She touched his face.

He couldn't explain his actions; maybe it was because he had nothing left to lose. He took Maria in his arms and he kissed her.

Momentarily surprised, she soon returned it with the same urgency.

He forced himself to stop. He took her lovely face in his hands and held it like it was a precious jewel. "I promise you. I won't go down until you're out of the yard and on your way. You can count on me. No matter how many times I'm . . . I won't fall until you're both away from here. A .22 bullet is like a bee sting. It's nothing."

He bent down and pulled Emily to him and kissed her, switching to English. "Emily, we're all going to run to the Gibbons's farm. We'll be safe there. You're going to lead the way. *You've got to lead Maria.* I'll be right behind you both, keeping those bad men away, so don't worry about them. Keep running as fast as you can until you get Maria to the Gibbons's farm. She needs *you* to show her the way. Without *you,* she's lost. *So run, run, run.*"

Emily's eyes opened wide, unsure that she could do as asked. She looked up a Maria, but her new responsibility didn't overwhelm her, but actually seemed to help her manage her fear. She took Maria's hand and nodded that she understood.

Hubbard blinked a few times.

Maria wailed a loud, "Noooo," of protest, raising her arms, swinging them broadly in frustration. She waded through the rising water and shouted upward defiantly at the roaring waterfall. Her words were in Spanish, something about a child.

"They can't hear you over the water," he called. Even if they did, they wouldn't care. We have to do this now!"

Maria's face was twisted by her distress. "No!"

Under pressure, Hubbard had trouble finding the words in French. "You—have to—help my daughter survive. Please! I beg you!"

She stood there motionless, breathing heavily, and then her shoulders dropped and she nodded with grim understanding. She waded back to him by the door.

He turned away from them and reached for the door handle. *C'mon, they couldn't stop you when you played for the Timberjacks. The two jokers outside are blocking the goal line. This is no different . . . No different.*

A new noise, sharp and metallic, filtered through the rush of water crashing down from the ceiling. Hubbard's brow creased, and his head tilted up. *What now?* The water pressure began to falter. Their heads focused on the ceiling as the water slowly decreased in force in stages until no more came down. An unearthly calm descended in the shelter, punctuated only by the sound of their nervous breathing.

Minutes passed. Still nothing. Maria turned to Hubbard, wanting to understand.

"It's over," he said. "I don't know why, but it's over."

------------◆------------

It was almost three hours since the attack. The first of a legion of law enforcement officers to arrive on the scene was Eddie, who nervously called Toil when he saw the damage to Hubbard's home. Toil arrived, angry at first from being pulled from his fields, but he quickly calmed when he saw that Eddie wasn't exaggerating. The state police arrived twenty minutes after that. Hubbard was pleased to see that Connors wasn't among the squad of troopers. Somehow Ramirez heard about the incident, sending a symbolic FBI agent to poke around impotently on a case where they had no jurisdiction.

After they were interviewed separately and together, Hubbard received permission from the troopers to call Mrs. Gibbons. She arrived, and whisked Emily away from the crime scene to the safety of her house and the healing companionship of her three girls.

Hubbard and Maria sat on the front steps and watched the state police take photos, mark bullet holes with tiny flags, and dust everywhere for prints.

Hubbard's relief when he knew the shooters had left slowly evaporated. As he sat on the porch, he could think clearly without the prospect of imminent death. He replayed the sequence of the attack on his home again and again in his head. It didn't add up.

Maria shifted her position on the porch. A trooper with the state police seemed to pick up on her nervousness, shifting his position to stare directly at her. Hubbard realized with a start that he hadn't considered her immigration status. He slipped her his truck keys, whispering to her in French. "Why don't you . . ."

He let the words fade away when the Latino trooper approached her and bent down, whispering something in Spanish into her ear. Maria nodded. After he walked away, Hubbard asked her what he said.

Maria glanced around her, afraid of being overheard.

Hubbard smiled. "Don't worry. I don't think any of the troopers speak French."

Maria nodded. "He said they wouldn't ask for my papers. That's not what they're here to do. If I'd be cool, everything would be okay."

That was great news, if it was true.

The state police seemed to be wrapping up, which gave Hubbard the opportunity to walk to the center of his lawn and see the scene as the shooters saw it. He stood at the approximate point where the first shots had been fired. His eyes went from the broken living room window to the bullet holes on his porch roof. He was so immersed in his thoughts that he didn't notice that Eddie had walked up and stood at his side.

"Did you hear about what happened to the female FBI lady?"

"Hmmm? No, I guess I haven't."

"She ordered a whole bunch of drinks at John Dugan's place, *almost fifteen hundred dollars' worth*, and then she refused to pay for 'em. Big John called the sheriff to come settle it. Toil said she was crazy wild, refusing to pay anything, so the sheriff had to call the state police. She wouldn't listen to reason so the state police had to fetch Special Agent Ramirez from his motel. By the end of the night, Dugan's place was full of cops and federal agents."

Eddie shook his head and raised his eyebrows to emphasize his meaning. "Ramirez wasn't too happy with her. The sheriff said their boss turned as red as a boiled lobster. He ended up ordering the FBI lady to go back home to Washington. I guess he wants her to dry

out. *Boy*, some people don't know when they've had too much."
Eddie grimaced at his choice of words. "No offense."

"None taken," Hubbard said. Eddie's words reminded him how
eager the FBI was to stop his investigation.

Eddie stood shoulder to shoulder with Hubbard to share his view
of the farmhouse. "You're lucky they didn't get you with the first
shot," Eddie said.

"Maybe."

"What do you mean?"

Hubbard pointed at his home's front door. "Eddie, imagine there
was a ten point buck standing on my front porch, right at the door.
If you had your rifle, do you think you could hit him?"

Eddie raised his hands like he was aiming a gun. "Yeah. Sure
thing."

"That's what I was thinking."

"Those guys didn't know how to shoot straight."

"I think every bullet landed exactly where they wanted. That's the
point."

"I don't get it."

"Where's that FBI agent that Ramirez sent over here?"

"I think he's leaving. That's him heading to his car." Eddie pointed to the farthest car of the seven vehicles parked on Hubbard's battered lawn.

"I have to catch him, Eddie. I'll talk to you later."

Hubbard waved his arm, trying to get the attention of the young
agent heading for his vehicle. The sandy-haired man was thin and
wore a tight fitting jacket that revealed the outline of his shoulder
holster. It was the same message-taking agent he saw in the sheriff's
office earlier in the week. The agent scowled back at Hubbard, who
was trotting toward him. The agent put his hand on the door handle, as if he intended to get into the car before Hubbard could reach
him.

"Agent!"

The fed put both hands on his hips and looked at the ground as if he was enduring the biggest inconvenience of his week. When Hubbard was a few yards away, the agent looked directly at him.

"So, Hubbard, you got a jealous husband hunting you down? Some kind of lover's triangle, pretty boy?"

Hubbard stopped in front of the agent. "Is Ramirez in the sheriff's office?"

"I don't work for you. *You* find him." The agent pretended to check some notes from his pocket.

"Look at me," Hubbard snapped.

The agent ignored him.

"I—said—look at me."

The agent slowly looked up and arched an eyebrow at Hubbard. "You want to begin something with me? Assault a federal agent in the performance of his duties? Is that what you want? *It's a felony, tough guy.* So step right up and take your best shot."

"No. I want you to deliver a message for me."

"I'm not your errand boy."

"Today you are. Tell Ramirez to get all the other agents out of the sherriff's office. I'm coming to see him in a half-hour for a private visit. It's just going to be him and me—*no one else.*"

"*Special Agent-in-Charge Ramirez* is not going to take orders from some hillbilly who—"

"Yes, he will. Tell him I know Amir Abadi's real identity. Tell him that if he doesn't have that office cleared when I get there, I'll call my friends at the Arab News Network and clue them in. They'll let the whole world know who the kid was. All your work here, trying to bottle this up in the backwoods will be all for naught."

The agent maintained a stoic façade, but the color drained from his face and he became a pasty white. "I don't know what you're talking about."

There had been a large probability Hubbard would look like a fool with this wild bluff. He tried to hide his relief at the newbie agent's reaction. The junior fed's boss, Agent Ramirez, was too experienced to be caught off guard like this. Now Hubbard was confident his speculation was close to the truth, although he still had no proof of anything. He looked at his watch. He would play this out and see how far he could go.

"Agent, you're using up your half-hour talking to me. Shouldn't you be on the road?"

27

TRUTH OR DARE

IN SPITE OF HIS DRAMATIC thirty-minute deadline, it took Hubbard some time to get on the road to Hayslip. First, he had to tell the young Latino trooper several times that Maria would *not* feel safer if he stuck around for a while. Second, he had to ensure that the dawdling officer, taking time to check the air pressure on all his tires, actually left his property.

When the trooper was gone, he offered to drop her at the trailer she shared with Luis, but she preferred to stay at the farmhouse. They needed to talk, she said. That was hard to argue with. After the kiss, their relationship had entered new territory. Hubbard assured himself that this was nothing to get nervous about, they would take it slow, get to know each other better, and not rush into anything. It might take a year to sort things out. Maybe longer. Slow and steady. He was sure she'd feel the same way.

Maria was intrigued that Hubbard thought he knew who was behind the attack and what their motive was. He needed to go to town, meet Ramirez, and confirm his suspicions.

Standing by his truck, there was an awkward moment when he didn't exactly know how to leave her. Kiss? Handshake? Tip of his cap? She must have sensed his uncertainty. "We'll talk when you get back."

Now he was on the road, wondering how he was going to handle this meeting with Ramirez. When Hubbard had first considered the identity of the two masked men, his first thoughts were that Luis and his pal Pablo were behind it. His on-and-off belief that he saw Luis wearing a Rolex had briefly returned. But even though he thought Luis was capable of almost anything, he recognized that Luis truly cared about his sister. She was the only family he had. Luis could have easily timed an assault on the house for an evening hour when his sister was gone. He didn't have to risk firing bullets in her direction.

Hubbard pulled into the town square. There were no vehicles parked in front of the sheriff's office. He got out of his truck and took a moment to look around the square. Everything seemed normal, just another quiet afternoon in Hayslip, a man leaving the hardware store with a small paper sack and Susan Gordon, a girl he had a thing with one night that he didn't clearly remember, and her new husband, window-shopping in front of the *Blessed Event* baby store.

The agents were either gone, or Ramirez didn't get the message, or his crew was waiting inside to pounce on him as soon as he came in the door. *Which is it?*

Hubbard approached the office door and he could see through the glass into the office. Ramirez was sitting behind the sheriff's desk, obviously waiting for him to arrive, no paperwork cluttered the desk. There was no one else in Toil's office.

He opened the door and held it there for a moment. "I'm surprised you didn't leave the office door open for me. Doesn't the FBI rely on a big, mossy stone to prop doors open? I guess that tactic is reserved for special occasions."

The intensity of Ramirez's glare proved that his bluff had hit a nerve. Now he had to make his wild-ass speculation pay off.

"First, some ground rules," Ramirez said. "Everything we say here is off the record."

"Sure. I'm not much for the record anyway."

"Good. We understand each other. Now, whatever you think you know, you're wrong."

"You don't know what I'm going to say."

"There's nothing *for* you to say. The kid was Amir Abadi. Do you want to see his birth certificate? School records? I can get them. That's it, end of story."

"Sounds convincing. Excuse me; I'm going to make some calls to the media."

Hubbard made a move toward the door.

"Wait . . . wait. Sit down."

After a moment of consideration, Hubbard sat in the oak chair in front of the desk.

Ramirez leaned forward. "Your speculation could do a lot of damage to American interests."

"I don't see how it can if you have Amir's birth certificate and school records. I bet you can even produce a family member on demand."

"Certainly, we could. No problem."

"Sure." Hubbard nodded in agreement. "Um, by the way. Can you tell me why his family doesn't want his body shipped back home? What did that young man do that was so offensive to his family that—"

Ramirez's brow creased and his hand hit the desk. "Who told you that? Your friend Connors?"

"I'll deny it if I'm forced to testify."

Ramirez rubbed his forehead. "I hate small towns. Is he your fifth cousin or something?"

"Don't pull family into this."

"Okay, who do you think Amir was? Let me ease your mind."

"Well, his identity had me confused for a bit. Why did young Amir Abadi rate all this attention from the FBI? Was he a suspected terrorist? It didn't seem likely after talking to his friends. And why did a guy who loved photography hate to have his own picture taken? Also, why did somebody whose family could afford to send him anywhere, send him to small college in Arkansas?"

"And I bet you came up with a fanciful explanation for it all."

"Yeah. *He was hiding.* Not from some shadowy overseas group, but from his fellow students and the good people of Monticello, hiding in plain sight. Hiding with the help of the FBI and the United States embassy in Cairo."

Ramirez took a deep breath. "You're on very dangerous ground."

"How can this be any more dangerous than what happened at my house earlier today."

Ramirez stood and leaned across the desk, supporting himself on two straight arms. "You're kidding. You think my agents did that? Are you accusing agents of the Federal—"

Hubbard stood in response, his hands turned into fists. "Of course, it was your people. That attack wasn't intended to kill me. If the two men wanted me dead they would have simply drove up, rang the doorbell, and killed when I answered the door. They wouldn't have taken a long stroll across my front lawn, aiming their shots over my head. Both of them missed me when I was a six-foot sitting duck. No, it was *your* people. You terrorized my daughter and my housekeeper just to make a point."

"We don't do that. That's not who we are. That's not who I am."

"So what was that exercise at John Dugan's bar or the break-in at my house, leaving my front door wide open."

Ramirez stood straight and walked a few steps away from the desk, keeping his back to Hubbard. After a long moment, he turned back to him. "We had an agent who went beyond her scope of authority . . . Agent Longinotti had a very useful capability to manipulate people. It's very valuable for interrogations. Unfortunately, she used that talent on her fellow agents. She mounted her own rogue operation in some misguided effort to advance her career. *I didn't authorize it.* Longinotti is back in Washington with three other agents. Their careers are over. Once the investigation is complete, my career may be over as well."

Ramirez's face had lost its anger. "I apologize. I didn't know . . . But, I want you to know this: my apology is off the record. It never happened."

"Your words warm my heart. And does your apology include shooting up my house?"

"We didn't do that."

"And how would you know? Things happen without your knowledge."

"The three agents left here yesterday. I had a meeting with all my field agents this morning. All of them. That slack-jawed deputy was here for most of it. He can attest to that . . . to the best of his ability to attest to anything."

"Your agents are the only ones who would benefit—"

"Oh, and no one local stands to profit from the new interstate highway if it stays under wraps for a while longer . . . No, need to look surprised. You're not the only one who can uncover secrets. The Bureau has a little experience in that arena."

"Why do you think it would be related—?"

"Oh, come on. We know you're helping that old lady on the farm. So you must know that her land is now worth a fortune. A variety of shell corporations are buying up property all along the new route. Whoever is behind this is getting bargain prices now, but in the next few weeks the land value will skyrocket and the opportunity is gone. You're threatening the whole deal by poking around."

Ramirez walked around the desk to face Hubbard. "Are there any names of locals who might be involved in this land grab that pop into your mind? That's who Amir was working for. Maybe he found out what was happening. Maybe that's why he was killed. We've turned it all over to the Arkansas State Police."

Hubbard tried to manage a calm exterior, but it was difficult to maintain. The memory of his uncle's interest in stopping his investigation sent a chill down his spine. What was the man capable of? Maybe now he had his answer. He had to focus to get what he came for. "I don't know what to believe, but I'm willing to make a deal."

"A deal? What kind of deal?"

"I won't contact the media and tell them what I know. But in return, I want the FBI to leave Hayslip. I don't want anyone following me anymore. I'm not risking anything more happening with my little girl in the house."

"You have nothing to bargain with."

"I forgot to finish, didn't I. Why would the government and Amir go to such lengths to hide his identity? The good people of Monticello have many fine qualities, but knowing the subtleties of Arab politics is not one of them. In fact, I think there's only a few Arabs so well-known that they all would recognize the name. And only one of them is the spitting image of Amir. That's why you altered the photograph, so no one would make the connection. Before he was killed by Navy Seals, he had eighteen children by three wives. Who would have thought that one of them would end up in Monticello, Arkansas, thanks to the United States government?"

"That's insane. What a crazy, far-fetched theory. What have you been smoking?"

"Maybe so, but it sure explains the reluctance to have his identity revealed and the lengths you guys will go to keep him hidden—even after he's dead."

"It's stupid. It's wrong. It's fantasy."

"Thanks for your time. I have a call to make."

Hubbard turned and headed for the door, trying to keep his shoulders up. His theory now sounded crazy, even to him. He made it all the way to the door before Ramirez spoke.

"Wait."

Hubbard stopped. He slowly turned back to Ramirez. The expression on the agent's face told him what he needed to know.

"We were planning on leaving anyway. So you have a deal. I'm not confirming anything."

"Okay, we have a deal. But, theoretically, why would the U.S. government care about the education of a mass-murderer's son?"

Ramirez walked back to his desk. "Americans are all so naïve. We're going to be fighting one group or the other in the Middle

East for decades. It's in our national interest to have good relations with one of the most important families in Egypt. They're not *all* terrorists and we believe we can build a relationship with a powerful, well-connected Egyptian family. That's why we helped Amir go to college in America under an assumed name . . . It just went horribly wrong." Ramirez shook his head. "Look, I love my country . . . Sometimes you just have to trust that someone in charge knows what he's doing. And things that look bad on the surface are being done for a greater good."

"That's a nice thought." Hubbard took a step forward. "Why didn't his family want his body?"

"Hell if I know."

Hubbard studied Ramirez's face. He believed the agent was telling him the truth. He didn't know. Hubbard nodded and turned to leave. He stopped to hear Ramirez's parting shot.

"I want you to know one thing. If this crazy theory *that I'm not confirming* gets to the media, I'll know where it came from. An INS team will hit your farm and your lovely housekeeper will land in a holding cell in El Paso for a few months before she's deported. Her stay in a cramped jail *will not* be pleasant . . . *Housekeeper*. That's what you call Maria, right? That's what she is to you, your housekeeper?"

Hubbard felt his body tense and he spun around. "Don't come near her."

"Then you keep your mouth shut and pray no one else comes up with the same uninformed idea that you did, because the effect on your *housekeeper* will be the same. Do you understand?"

Hubbard fought the rage that was tearing at him. There was only one thing he could do to protect Maria. "I hear you."

Hubbard left the sheriff's office not knowing if he had really won anything from the encounter. He did, however, know what Ramirez had gained.

His silence.

28

Sins of the Father

RAMIREZ'S RECENT THREAT echoed in Hubbard's mind; *'Then you keep your mouth shut and pray no one else comes up with the same uninformed idea that you did, because the effect on your housekeeper will be the same.'*

Hubbard's phone rang. He drew out his cell and saw a number he didn't recognize.

"Hullo."

"Mr. Hubbard, this is John Steward with Arkansas Radio News. I'd like to interview you about the murder in Hayslip. Why do you think the White River—"

Hubbard clicked off the phone and jammed the accelerator to the floor. It was only a matter of time before the media discovered the truth. Now, thanks to him, Maria would pay the price.

As his truck sped down the road, he tried to concoct some plan. He could spare about a thousand dollars from his meager bank account. He would give it all to her. It wasn't much, but it would help her relocate. Mr. Carlos had many contacts in the north; he would ask him to give her some names of people who could help her settle into a larger city where she might disappear.

The turn of events was so abrupt Hubbard had trouble processing it as complete thoughts, rather than as emotions. *Maria. Maria gone. Maria, what have I done?*

The highway was a blur of pavement and cars as he tried to conjure a plan for her escape that contained more practical thought than panicked desperation. When he got to his farm and rounded the line of pines, he was immediately yanked back to reality when he saw the violent altercation taking place on his front porch.

Luis was pulling his sister out of the house by her arm, trying to force her down the porch steps. Luis's friend, Paco, Pablo, or whoever, was standing by a surprisingly new truck parked on the lawn, waiting for them. If the vehicle was Luis's, then the recent immigrant's fortunes had taken a major turn for the better.

On the porch, Maria fought back and connected with a roundhouse punch, giving Luis a good blow to the jaw. *Wow, she's a natural.* Luis staggered back and Maria kept it up, swinging away while tearfully screaming at him.

Luis's buddy turned toward Hubbard's truck as it skidded to a halt. He began to stroll casually toward him, keeping one hand behind his back.

When Hubbard turned off the engine he could hear Maria's rapid Spanish, colored by what sounded like fiery accusations he didn't understand. Hubbard flung the truck door open, his heart pounding. Brother or no, no one could treat Maria like that. He started forward, his fists ready, eyes focused on the fresh bruises on Maria's arms. He was aware of the teenager approaching him from his right, hiding his hand, and the knife he probably held, behind his back.

How stupid do you think I am?

The two men's paths would intersect in four steps. Three. Two. One.

The Latino's knife flashed in the sunlight. Hubbard took a quick step back and swung his hand up to catch the pint-sized thug's wrist as he reached the tail end of the thrust, when most of its force and speed were spent. Once he captured the young man's wrist, he locked on, spinning the kid face first into the ground. Hubbard, still holding the arm, dropped and let one knee fall into the center of the Latino's back. The teenager cursed loudly as Hubbard used the advantage of his superior position to force the boy's arm upward in a way unanticipated by nature. The bone would have snapped in the next moment, except the kid, now screaming in agony, let go of the knife. Hubbard stood and pulled the Latino up by his shirt collar and booted him away like an angry placekicker. The teen collapsed a few yards away, grabbing his crotch while writhing on the ground.

Hubbard looked up to see Luis hurl Maria down the porch steps to the lawn. Enraged, he charged forward. Luis looked up and saw him closing in. He reached behind his back, and pulled out a .38 from his belt, and pointed it at Hubbard.

Luis cocked his head and smiled tauntingly at Hubbard. "Keep coming and you die."

Breathing heavily, Maria managed to turn back toward Luis and his gun. "Luis, no!"

Hubbard forced himself to stop his charge. He slowed to a walk, reached Maria, and helped her to her feet.

"Are you all right?" Hubbard asked in French. "How could he do that to you?"

"Stop that goddamn French," Luis roared from the porch.

"He wants us to leave. He says he's made enough money . . ."

Luis seemed incensed that his command was ignored. "I said stop!" He came off the porch and down one step. He shook his gun broadly as if he thought Hubbard hadn't seen it.

Hubbard looked back at the new truck. "Money?"

Tears began to stream down Maria's cheeks and her face flushed as she pointed at Luis. "It was them. It was Luis and Pablo."

"What?"

Luis must have recognized his name in Maria's French. He shrugged his shoulders and lifted his chin. "Go ahead. Tell him. Let's see what the big man will do."

"They were the men in the overalls and masks this morning."

It took a moment for Hubbard to absorb it. "But they were shooting at you too."

Luis said they weren't trying to hit us. Just scare you enough that you would stop. He said no one would suspect them if I was here. He was paid by some rich man in town who didn't want you or Emily hurt."

Rich man. It felt like the earth collapsed underneath his boots. So many years of uncertainty, now he knew. He remembered his childish pledge to kill the murderer of his father. He would make good on it today. He felt his chest constrict.

Maria turned quickly around and screamed. "Pablo!"

Hubbard turned around in time to see that Pablo had retrieved his knife and was coming for him. He set his feet, trying to anticipate how Pablo would use the knife on his second try.

Maria blew past Hubbard toward Pablo, her arms raised like she planned to claw him like a grizzly bear.

Luis bounded down the steps and onto the lawn. Both he and Hubbard cried out simultaneously for Maria to stop. "No!"

Pablo seemed stunned by the unexpected counter-attack from Luis's sister, and he hesitated, knife still pointed forward, frozen in place. At the last possible moment he turned his back on Maria, afraid of the damage that her fingernails, now raised overhead like small knives, could do to him.

Maria leaped on Pablo's back and locked her arms around his head and began to twist it, making a sharp groan of exertion. Her angry words were too fast for Hubbard to understand. The only thing that he made out was something about a frightened child.

Pablo yelped in pain, dropped his knife, and used both his hands to try and pry her off.

Luis came forward, pointed his gun in the air and pulled the trigger. The .38 was deafening.

As the shot echoed in the countryside, Hubbard realized that Luis was distracted by his own gunshot. He bolted to his right and caught Luis's arm before he could lower it. Surprised, Luis pulled the trigger again, firing over Hubbard's shoulder.

Luis couldn't match Hubbard's strength and each time he tried to yank his arm away, Hubbard snapped it back. Hubbard's fist struck the right side of Luis's head. Again and again, he connected as Luis was unable to block the bigger man's attack. Finally, the Latino dropped the gun to the ground.

Hubbard's anger was undiminished by the surrender. His vision narrowed into a dim tunnel that only saw Luis's face a stand-in for his uncle.

Hubbard released Luis's arm and took him by the neck and tossed him against the front of his new truck. "I know who paid you. I just want to hear it from you."

Luis slid to the ground. His front teeth were knocked out and his words were difficult to understand with blood streaming from his mouth. "I *han't*. I *hook* money."

Hubbard sank to his knees, grabbed Luis's neck and held his face directly in front of his. "Look at me. You want to live? 'Cause I'm going to kill you if you don't tell me.

Luis shifted his eyes, trying to find his sister. "Maria."

"She can't save you. No one can."

"He'll hire men to *hind* me if I *halk*. He crazy. "

"He won't have a chance to hire anyone because I going to kill *him* after I finish with *you*."

Hubbard smashed his fist against Luis face and heard the crack of more teeth under the blow.

"Mr. Hubbirrd!" It was Maria voice. He couldn't stop. Nothing would make him stop.

Luis winched, preparing for another blow. "I'll *hell* . . . I'll *hell you. Flease*."

"Tell me. If you lie I'll start again. *I know who it is*."

"Then why?"

Hubbard brought his fist back.

Luis covered his face with his hand. "It was *Foxcroft*. Dill Foxcroft. He wanted you to stop before you found out *hat* he was the one who *hilled* that kid. He wasn't afraid of FBI, but he said that you wouldn't give up."

"You're lying." Hubbard struck him again.

Luis shook his head as tears rolled from his eyes. "No, I'm not. I *wear* on my mother's *hrave*. The Arab hurt his *haugher* somehow. He said he couldn't *hand* by and see her destroyed. A father has a right to protect his *haughter*. He paid us big money to dump the body. Then he paid us to torment you."

Maria ran up to them, crying. "Please, Mr. Hubirrrd. *Stop*. Luis is my brother. I beg you."

Hubbard studied Luis for a moment, and then he pulled open the Latino's coat. He reached into an interior pocket and found what he was looking for. He drew out a pack of menthol cigarettes and tossed them away.

Hubbard fought a wave of nausea. He stepped away and picked up Luis's gun from the ground and pointed it at him. "Get out of here. I'll give you a ten-minute head start and then I'm calling the police. I'm only doing this because you're Maria's brother.

Luis used his sleeve to wipe the blood from his face, rising to one knee. He reached out to his sister. "Maria," he said. What came after was in thick Spanish. Hubbard caught only parts of it. "Come with us . . . money . . . a better life . . . a servant for this man?"

Maria's turned to Hubbard.

He could see the uncertainty in her face. Maybe she thought that Luis, despite his brutality, offered a better chance for a good life. He also remembered Ramirez's threat. If she stayed here, they would come for her and deport her. *She had to flee.* He had to let her go. There was no other way. Unless . . .

He turned to her, switched to French and took a deep breath. "Will you marry me?" *What did you ask her? Where did that come from? Are you nuts? . . . Wait, no. This is right. As soon as she marries me, immigration can't touch her . . .*

Maria seemed as startled by his proposal as he was.

"What? What did you say?" Luis said.

There was a moment of silence, as if they were all waiting for someone to lead them out of this unexpected impasse. Finally, Maria tilted her head and her brow creased. She pointed to the ring finger on her left hand.

"Yes, a ring. Of course."

"No!" Luis called out, the horror clear in his voice.

She nodded her acceptance with a smile and turned to Luis and dropped the smile. She spoke so rapidly, and with such contempt, he caught little of her Spanish. She pointed to the truck as if she was telling her brother to leave.

Okay. Admittedly, they had ignored a few steps in the courtship dance. *Oh, what the hell. Given more time, I'd just screw it up.* Hubbard grabbed Luis by his coat collar, picked him up and shoved him toward the truck door. "Now, get out of here. Never come back to my farm."

Luis tried to muster as much dignity as he could while wiping the blood from his mouth with his sleeve. Pablo came around the truck, both hands bracing his neck, and he slowly climbed into the passenger seat.

Luis started the truck and backed up a few feet. He braked, rolled down the door window and leaned out. "You *ho* if you *cuuz* Foxcroft, he'll deny it. He'll *hust* say we were *hi-ing*."

Luis pulled away and drove across the lawn to the driveway. Did he see a bloody smile on Luis's face?

Hubbard felt a wave of uncertainty crash into the center of his chest. Did Luis con him about Foxcroft? Did he know just enough about the highway man to make it all sound plausible? Did he make up a lie to help him escape *and* protect the *rich man* behind all this —R.J.? Amir was putting the highway deal at risk. That's why he was killed. Luis worked for R.J., *not* Foxcroft.

Hubbard rubbed his forehead and paced forward. How could this happen? He was back to *not* knowing . . . *Lies.*

He raised Luis's pistol and fired the remaining bullets into the afternoon shadows stretching toward him. What was the truth? What had he become? He had been prepared to kill his uncle.

"Mr. Hub . . . John Riley!" Maria was behind him.

Hubbard fell to his knees and cradled his head in his hands. "Was Luis telling the truth?"

Maria's voice was filled with anguish. "I . . . don't know."

Hubbard felt his face flush and became aware of the dull buzz in his ears from the gunshot. "I can't do this. I *have* to know this time. Luis is right. Foxcroft will deny it . . . I don't have any evidence. It can't be like before. Not a second time. *No. No. No!*" He pounded his fist into the ground.

Maria dropped to the ground and put her arms around Hubbard, trying to ease a pain she couldn't understand.

"I'm got to find Foxcroft. I've have to know." Hubbard stood abruptly and looked down at her. *"Rich man* . . . Don't you understand? Don't you see?

Maria rose, clutching his arm, pulling him back. "No! What? How can you make him tell you? Nothing could make him confess to a murder."

Hubbard pulled free. "I can make him. He'll tell me. No matter how long it takes, I won't stop. You see, I have *one* thing that I'm good at . . . I'll going to beat the truth out of him."

Hubbard headed for his truck, ignoring Maria's pleas for him to stop.

I'm sorry, Maria. You're a good person . . . I'm not . . . Someone will be dead before nightfall. I just don't know who yet.

29

EVERYONE NEEDS A HOBBY

THE DRIVE GAVE HUBBARD TIME to reconsider Luis's forced identification of Foxcroft as the Arab's murderer. Foxcroft thought Amy needed protection from Amir?

It didn't add up.

Carla Jo and Missy had told him that Amy had a close friendship with Amir. Also, Amy had been devastated upon hearing that Amir had been killed. Not the reaction of someone who had been hurt by him in some way.

Protecting his daughter? She was in Europe at the time of the murder. If Amir had posed any threat to Amy before, she was safeguarded by her extended visit to Europe. There was no hint of a motive that would compel a deacon in the fundamentalist Baptist Church to fire a shotgun at point blank range.

The contractor's home was outside of town. Dill Foxcroft was of the same generation as R.J. He was a big man, with thick white hair that he combed back over his head. Hubbard didn't know Foxcroft well. It seemed that Foxcroft and R.J. were always at odds about one thing or the other. Whatever the reason for that conflict, Foxcroft had expanded his contempt to include his nephew, making Hubbard's previous interactions with the contractor brief and somewhat brittle. Of course, it was typical for Hubbard's relationships to be colored by the doppelganger of his uncle.

As Hubbard turned onto Foxcroft's long, brick-paved driveway, he anticipated the first question that the older man might ask upon the intrusion at his home by R.J. Hubbard's nephew. He expected a warm greeting such as 'Why the hell are you here?' He didn't have a ready response. 'To accuse you of murder,' wasn't the best conversation starter. He realized grimly that if he was going to make any headway with Foxcroft he would have to take a more direct. . . more forceful approach. It would be messy. Hubbard didn't care about that, as long as it led to the truth. Truth, at least for this murder, might help him find peace.

He approached the final turn that would lead him out of the thick pines and reveal the Foxcroft compound. The grounds included a large home and three impressive outbuildings that housed all the old man's toys.

Hubbard's heart began to pound. There was part of him, the part that paid bills, kept promises, and tried and sometimes failed to do the right thing, which rebelled at what he was about to do. Hubbard felt his nausea rise, but not enough to stop.

He made the final turn and the Foxcroft estate was revealed in its gauche glory. The clearing held a faux Colonial-style home, partially encircled by three mismatched outbuildings. His eyes were drawn to the metal building that housed Foxcroft's workshop. Directly outside the door into the building, next to a green picnic table, Dill Foxcroft was bent over, working a power saw, trying to push through a thick board. The wood plank was clamped to a saw horse and extended to the table which helped support the board's weight. It looked like a surprisingly improvised solution for a man who owned a complete workshop. Immersed in his task, he didn't seem to notice Hubbard as he parked on the drive, thirty yards away.

Hubbard got out, closed the door and leaned back against the side of the vehicle, folding his arms across his chest. He glanced at the big house. It couldn't see anyone inside. Foxcroft was a widower, and his daughter was on the other side of the Atlantic. He returned his attention to Foxcroft, still struggling to push the saw through a board resisting the progress of the blade.

Foxcroft finished the cut, set the circular saw down, carefully separated the boards, and pulled off his protective gear. His hand wiped away the sweat on his forehead before he spotted Hubbard getting out of the pickup.

The old man met his gaze and took a deep breath. He didn't say anything; but simply returned Hubbard's steady gaze, his own face expressionless. He offered no words of welcome or irritated objections at his appearance. Just silence.

Hubbard felt a chill race down his spine. *He knows why I'm here.*

Foxcroft turned his head toward the ground. When he looked up, he made a weak attempt at a smile. "Had to get out in the fresh air. Been working all day, the dust is playing havoc with my sinuses. You need to talk to me?"

"Yeah," Hubbard called back. "It appears that I do. I think you know why."

Foxcroft feigned a brief quizzical look, and then pointed to the door of his workshop. "Well, you'll have to talk to me while I work. I'm trying to get something done." Without waiting for an answer, Foxcroft walked inside the workshop without looking back to check if Hubbard was following him.

The afternoon sun was moving toward the horizon. Sunlight highlighted the top of Foxcroft's white head with a gold-colored cap before he disappeared inside. *How old is he? Sixty? Can I really stomach beating the truth out of an old man . . . I've become someone I don't know. Someone I don't like.*

As Hubbard walked toward the building, he wanted there to be another way to get this done. He would try to talk to him. If that didn't work . . .

In the doorway, he stood for a moment, waiting for his eyes to adjust to the interior light. The workshop was big, perhaps forty feet by twenty. There were almost a dozen projects lining the walls, wooden boats, china cabinets, and other furniture waiting to be finished.

At the far end of the metal building, Foxcroft stood behind his work bench. White peg boards on his right and left held dozens of vintage tools, each tool labeled underneath.

Foxcroft leaned against the tall workbench, one arm draped over the side. "You know, just because your last name is Hubbard doesn't give you the right to just show up unannounced and uninvited."

Hubbard nodded, but didn't respond immediately. He felt an unexpected anxiety flood over him. This felt all wrong. Foxcroft stood at other end of the long building, waiting expectantly, a phony expression of calm on his face, like a spider waiting for a fly to feel safe enough to enter its web. "Sometimes . . . it's necessary."

"Well, since you're here. Let me show you my latest project. Come closer." He waved his hand at the wood stacked on the work table. "See these boards—old growth mahogany. You don't see wood with tight grain like this anymore, had a devil of a time trying to make a straight cut. "

"I want to talk to you about Amir Abadi and your daughter."

Foxcroft looked up from his precious wooden boards and his mouth tightened. He shifted his position, leaning back. "I don't know what you're talking about."

Hubbard began moving forward, taking his time to cover the distance between them. "I think you do," he said. "You paid Luis a lot of money to dump the body and then give me hell when you thought I was close to uncovering the truth." Hubbard tried a bluff. "He's making a statement to the sheriff right now."

"Statement?' Foxcroft seemed momentarily surprised, and then recovered his air of righteous indignation. "You've got a lot of nerve. Coming here and making an accusation like that. Doesn't Luis work for your uncle? Is that what this is about? You're trying to put the blame on me for something your uncle did? You never learn, do you? You'll protect him on anything. Even murdering your own—"

"Shut up."

"Okay. Sure. I'll shut up. Don't want you to go all crazy on me. That's what most people think about you, isn't it? Or do most people think you're just a pitiful drunk. I guess it's a tossup."

Hubbard felt his hand ball into a fist. He forced it to relax. Foxcroft was goading him, trying to distract him. He had to focus "What horrible thing did Amir do to make you forget a lifetime of Sundays sitting in the Baptist Church?"

Foxcroft's face twisted in scorn. "Who are you to talk to me about my faith? If that crazy Mexican *is* talking to Toil or the state police, which I doubt, let them come ask me their questions. Let's see whose word they believe. I had no reason to kill that student."

Hubbard looked down at his boots; they were coated in a thin layer of sawdust— covered like the rug Amir was wrapped in. *This is where he was killed.* He returned his attention to Foxcroft. "Oh, I think you had a motive. Or at least you thought you did. Why did your daughter take the sudden trip to Europe? A trip none of her friends knew about until she was on her way to the airport. No one goes on a long holiday overseas, for several months in fact, without making plans, talking to friends . . ." Hubbard stopped. Several months. *How many months?*

"It was a gift. A surprise trip to Europe for her graduation. Of course, she had to leave a little early, but the school was accommodating. They bend over backward when it's your name on their new Fine Arts Building."

Hubbard nodded. "Yeah, I bet. And she'll return at the end of the year. Or maybe a tad after that." It all made sense now. She would return in nine months.

"What are you implying?"

"You're a very traditional man, aren't you? Is that why Amir was here early on a Sunday morning, dressed in a blue suit? Was he trying to convince an old-fashioned man with family values that he wanted to do the honorable thing?"

"He was never here."

"Oh, I think he was. And I think he was on his way to *your church to convert to Christianity*—that's why he had that blue suit on. He was going to win you over by answering the call at the end of the service. How'd that make you feel? Not any better than his own family, I suspect. That's why his family wrote him off. They had no room in their life for a Christian, just like you had no room—"

Foxcroft's fist came down on the workbench. "That's a lie. I didn't know him. I told you."

"Well, your daughter certainly knew him, knew him in the biblical sense, which is kind of ironic. What's the matter? Were you concerned that he might tell the members of your congregation why he was turning his life over to the Lord? Tell everyone that your daughter was carrying his child?"

"Goddamn you and your lies. You have no proof of any of this. You're slandering my daughter's good name!"

Hubbard scratched his head. "One thing I don't get. Why did he let you put a shotgun against his chest without a struggle? Did he think you were bluffing? Did he think it was a test of his courage or character or whatever to prove he was worthy of the love of your only child? Oh, he was *so* young if he believed that."

"Get out of here, Hubbard. If the police have any questions for me, let them come and ask them. I don't have to talk to you."

"Okay. But they won't need to ask you any questions. Your daughter is carrying all the DNA proof they need in her belly. You sent your daughter to Europe so that she could have the baby, give it up for adoption, and then return here with no one the wiser. Isn't that right? Just like the old days. Because abortion is murder, but murder of adults is . . . justifiable? . . . Tell me, what are the depths of your convictions? Will you call your daughter now and tell her it's okay to get an abortion to protect you?" Hubbard turned toward the door; he only made it a few steps.

"Stop."

Hubbard heard the unmistakable sound of the hammer being cocked. He turned back, holding his breath.

Foxcroft pointed a sawed-off shotgun at Hubbard. Where the hell had he hid it?

"I carry a lot of money, and this rides with me in the truck. You wouldn't stop, would you?" Foxcroft's voice had lost its anger. There was a sickening calm to it. The old man came around the bench.

Hubbard took a step back. "People know where I am."

"No. I don't think anyone does. You came here on your own."

Hubbard caught himself before he blurted out Maria's name. The sick bastard would hunt her down and kill her after he had finished with him. He realized that anyone he named as knowing his whereabouts would be put in jeopardy. *What the hell have I done? I know the truth. Where's the relief in knowing?*

"Stay there. It will be quick. It will be easy, if you stand still." Foxcroft kept moving forward, the gun pointed at Hubbard's chest.

Hubbard continued to back away. "I'm not one to judge. But what the hell does your preacher say on Sunday morning? Have you been listening to him?" When would Foxcroft get tired of this game and pull the trigger? Should he charge the old man and hope for the best? He tried to keep his breathing under control. *Don't panic. Talk your way out of this.*

"The Lord knows what's in my heart."

"I don't doubt that. But do you think he'd be pleased at what he sees there?"

"Do you know who that Arab trash was? He's the son of a god-damn murderer, a terrorist. He's evil. No one can blame me. He deserved what he got. My daughter's life would have been destroyed if she married him."

Foxcroft stopped and shook his head with genuine sorrow. "I'm sorry . . . I told Luis not to hurt you. Just scare you off. You can't say I didn't *try* to save your life. There's no other way now."

"I have a daughter, too. Please, you can't do this."

Tears began to roll down Foxcroft's cheeks. "I'm so sorry. Please forgive me. I'll ensure that your daughter's taken care of. *Forgive me. Forgive me. Oh, Lord forgive me.*" Foxcroft sighted down the barrel.

Hubbard had to act. He would charge Foxcroft; at least he'd die trying . . .

The long blare of a truck horn from outside startled both men. After a moment of hesitation, they turned in the direction of the noise. When Hubbard turned back, Foxcroft had lowered the gun.

"John Riley! Where are you, kid?" It was R.J. There was another blast from the horn.

"Stay quiet. Don't answer." Foxcroft said, in an unnecessary whisper.

Hubbard's mind raced, trying to consider options. If he called out, Foxcroft would kill him. Then he would kill R.J. when his uncle ran into the workshop, drawn by the sound of the gunshot. If he stayed silent, R.J. still wouldn't leave since he saw Hubbard's truck on the driveway. After a while, he would begin searching for him. Eventually, he'd make his way to the workshop and Foxcroft would kill both of them at his leisure. There was one chance that might allow one of them to survive.

He called out, not knowing how many words he could get out before the old man pulled the trigger. "Foxcroft has a gun. Get out of . . ."

Momentarily surprised, Foxcroft hesitated then brought the gun up. His face was flushed and he was breathing even more rapidly than Hubbard. Pulling the trigger the second time around was proving to be hard for him to do.

Hubbard decided that he had little to lose. Foxcroft was visibly cracking under the strain of contemplating a second murder, Hubbard turned up the pressure. He turned and walked slowly for the door, his muscles braced for the shotgun pellets that he expected to tear through him at any moment.

"Stop." Foxcroft breath was now coming in spurts. "I said stop."

"No." Hubbard couldn't come up with anything else. He was at the door and he opened it. R.J.'s truck was on the driveway, right behind his. He heard Foxcroft's footsteps racing up behind him and then he felt the gun stock slamming into the back of his head.

"I told you to stop."

Hubbard's head snapped forward from the blow and he staggered a few steps. He reached up to rub his head. He weighed the odds that he could wheel around and grab the gun barrel before the old man pulled the trigger—nil, or close to it.

Standing by the truck door, R.J.'s eyes opened wide when he saw the barrel pointed at his nephew.

Hubbard tried to wave him away. "Get out of here, R.J. Take

care of Emily. Tell Maria . . ." What? That he was a fool? "I don't know what I want you to say to her."

R.J. opened the truck door, but instead of leaving, he drew out his own shotgun that he stashed behind the seat. "Dill, I'm not going anywhere."

Foxcroft knocked the gun barrel against Hubbard's head. "Start moving or die."

The knowledge that Foxcroft wanted him to move forward made Hubbard want to remain in place, he hesitated.

"I'll kill you where you stand, then take care of your uncle," Foxcroft said.

With a deep sigh, Hubbard began walking again. "Get out of here, R.J. He going to try and kill us both. How did you know I was here?"

"Maria called me," R.J. said. "You're lucky I know Spanish a lot better than you."

"Please, get out now," Hubbard said.

R.J. leveled his rifle in their direction. "Dill, that sawed off thing works great at close range. But you've got to know that it's pretty lame at a distance. I can hit you with both barrels of my gun from here. And I want you to know, after I kill you I'm going to take my hunting knife and—"

Foxcroft pushed against the center of Hubbard's back with his gun. "Keep moving."

"No."

"I said move." Foxcroft raised the shotgun to the back of Hubbard's neck.

Sweat began to roll down Hubbard's back. This is as good as it would get. At least he would die knowing that he Foxcroft would get his. R.J. would kill Foxcroft when Hubbard fell. It was cold comfort. He felt his heart thump wildly in his chest. "No. This is it, Foxcroft. It's all over. Pull the trigger and get it over with."

Hubbard watched R.J.'s eyes open wide and his face grimace in horror. "No!" he called out, reaching forward as if he was close enough to stop what was about to happen.

Hubbard attempted to spin around, but the explosion from the gun knocked him senseless. He felt the heat of the blast and then the world became silent as he fell forward. He grabbed his bloody head and felt his skull come apart in his hands as he hit the ground. He pressed his hands against his head in a futile effort to keep the brain matter inside. His eyes closed and he felt the cool grass on his face. The buzzing in his ears made everything seem so quiet and peaceful. *Take care of Emily. Please.*

Through a buzzing that didn't sound like angels at all, he heard R.J.'s muffled voice. "Are you all right? Are you hurt?"

It was a stupid question to ask someone whose head had been blown to pieces. *Am I hurt?* Hubbard wanted to snap off an angry response, but he wondered why he was able to think at all. He pushed off the ground to his knees and took his hand away to look at the bloody flesh and bone that had been his skull. He then looked behind him. Foxcroft was on the ground, the short barrels of the shotgun pointed toward his head. He still clasped the shotgun in his hands like it was a bouquet of flowers. Hubbard's eyes traveled up to where his head once resided. Gone. He suddenly realized he wasn't holding a piece of his skull. Revolted by the sight of the fleshy stump, he flung the goo off his hand and stood quickly. He then bent over and became sick.

R.J. and Hubbard were seated at the picnic table behind Foxcroft's house, waiting for the police to make it to them. R.J. looked at Hubbard, whose eyes were downcast, a towel wrapped around his neck. The operation was next week. *There's never a perfect time.*

He reached into his coat pocket. They were able to salvage only three photos from the roll. But they were enough. He hesitated. Maybe it was time to only show John Riley two of the photos. He put the third back in his pocket.

"You know, it turns out there was film in Frank's camera."

Hubbard looked up briefly. "Yeah. I heard. Probably all ruined."

"Not all."

He saw Hubbard straighten in his seat. John Riley's eyes focus on the two photos he held in his hand. R.J. reached across the table to hand them to him. Emotion colored the younger man's face.

"One picture of you and Frank, another of you and Alice, I guess you were at a ballgame."

Hubbard nodded. "I remember this game. The last one I ever pitched."

There was a moment of silence. R.J. tried to read John Riley's thoughts as he stared intently at the two photos. Finally, R.J rose. "I've got to get something from my truck."

He walked around the corner of the large house, turning to make sure he was out of John Riley's sightline. He opened the passenger side door and collapsed in the seat, tears forming in his eyes. The last photo, the one he withheld, was of R.J. and young John Riley, his arm around the boy's shoulder, both of them smiling before the final game of his childhood.

Stop it. You don't cry. He recovered quickly, using the back of his hand to clear his eyes. He opened the glove compartment, shoved the photo inside and closed the door.

It's better this way. R.J. heard the first faint sound of a siren approaching quickly from the east.

This moment had such finality; it was hard to ignore the realization that he would never tell John Riley the darkest of secrets.

Why John Riley Hubbard looked so much like his him. *I've got more money that I can spend, but Frank got everything I ever wanted.*

R.J. stood and tried to gather his composure. He got out of the truck.

It's spring, a season for new beginnings . There was always reason for hope.

At the horizon, the sun was setting behind the tree line.

30

POST MORTEM

MUCH HAD CHANGED DURING the scorching summer months. Eddie's wife announced she was expecting another child. Eddie had to give up his job in law enforcement for job at the paper mill. Trish Andrews left Hayslip without telling anyone she was leaving. Some say she ran off with a college student. Others were not so sure of that and wondered why she disappeared.

Hubbard had married Maria and was now living in R.J.'s former home, trying to run an empire. One thing that hadn't changed was the nightmares of a murder he still didn't understand.

In August the heat and humidity of an Arkansas evening is harsh, but when teamed with blood-crazed mosquitoes, the night becomes cruel. Anyone who leaves the comfort of air conditioning after midnight in August, to go outdoors and needlessly endure the oppressive conditions, could be classified as a fool, a drunk, or a criminal seeking the cover of darkness. At just past two a.m., Hubbard met the criteria for two of those three categories.

Satisfied he was alone on the dark highway; he slowed the truck and switched off his headlights to help cloak his turn onto the un marked dirt lane. On this clear night, a half-moon and stars provided just enough light to navigate his truck down the road. After he passed through a track of evergreens and crossed the meadow, he glanced into his rear view mirror for a final check of the highway, somewhat obscured by pines. The roadway was deserted behind him; no flash of headlights to indicate anyone was traveling at this late hour to spoil his comfortable sense of isolation.

Although the consequences of being spotted tonight were significant, the risk he was taking only managed a slight tug at his nerves. It would all end tonight.

Continuing on the winding country road, he stopped the truck before he came to the first dilapidated shack of Shanty Town and shut off his engine. He got out and walked back to the tailgate. He scanned the length of the road until it made its first turn, searching for movement that might indicate he wasn't alone tonight. He tried to ignore the chorus of cicadas, katydids, and crickets, straining to hear anything coming from a more threatening, manmade source. He barely noticed the mosquitoes swarming around him like an angry mob, held at bay by a thick layer of repellant generously applied before he left the house. Turning back toward the highway, he thought he could hear the faint rumble of an eighteen-wheeler on the paved road, heading toward Texarkana. A clean escape from here would be a matter of timing and luck.

For a final time, he reviewed the rotting hulks of Shanty Town, little more than profiles in the dark. He remembered Mrs. Welch's words, "Somebody should burn Shanty Town to the ground. It's nothing but a breeding ground for snakes, rats, and disease." Her words gave him a weal rationalization for tonight.

He could never explain to anyone his reasoning. For his new life to begin, the nightmares and Shanty Town must end. It was as simple and as unknowable as that.

He pulled two five-gallon gasoline containers from the back of his truck and walked to the first abandoned shanty, setting one can on the road. He crossed the road to a second shack facing the first and deposited the other fuel canister. Returning to where he started, he put on gloves and opened the nozzle on the can. He carefully poured a track of fuel down the length of the right side of the road, dousing the gasoline in a wet circle at the end of the row to serve as the launching pad for his fire. He tossed the can into undergrowth destined to burn and repeated the process on the left side of the lane.

Upon completion, he reached into his pocket. Leaving nothing to chance, he had brought three lighters. He hesitated. He knew he should leave now. Combined with the summer drought, there was a good possibility the accelerant would make the undergrowth catch fire on its own, "naturally." But he couldn't depend on chance. For this to work, he had to do this himself.

Despite his research on the topic, his plan was quite simple. There would be no timers or fuses for this fire. He didn't want to take the chance that someone would be hurt by his actions. He would ignite one side of the road, followed by the other. His mission begun, he would stroll down the lane in the company of two growing trails of fire, stopping only to help the fire continue its journey—if needed. If everything went according to plan, he'd be in his truck, rejoining the highway by a different road, and on his way home before the blaze was large enough to be seen from the highway or town. Perhaps his plan was too simple. According to Wikipedia, nothing was more common than an arsonist being caught in his own fire, a victim of his own crime.

Any question that reflected doubt was soon discarded. *Why was he treating this so casually?* There was a myriad of possible unintended consequences. A fire no one could control, for instance. Shanty Town was surrounded by irrigated acreage that would contain the blaze, he reasoned. There was little chance of the fire spreading. Another rationalization, he knew, and he had dozens more. They were cheap.

Hubbard had an uneasy feeling of being watched, observed from the darkness. A sudden chill ran down his back. His right hand rubbed his neck, pressing down hairs that wanted to stand. He took a calming breath, but it was no help. He felt the presence of someone behind him, and slowly turned toward a neighboring shanty. He wasn't alone. His heart froze as he spotted a tall man, arms folded, leaning casually against the frame of the front door of a nearby shack. How much had he seen? Did he recognize Hubbard? His observer didn't drop his casual pose, seemingly unfazed to find an arsonist in Shanty Town. Hubbard opened his mouth, searching for words that could explain his actions. In the next moment, Hubbard's mouth closed and his heart began again, albeit shakily, when he realized it was only a gray shadow taking the outline of a man, a ghost on any other night.

He had to get this done before his nerves were fried.

"Anyone here?" he called. "I'm about to strike a match and set this whole place on fire."

There was no response.

"Hay alguien aqui?" His Spanish was improving rapidly, thanks to Maria. For any Frenchman, lost in the bushes, he added, "Est-ce que qualqu'un ici?"

He bent down and struck his lighter. He placed it next to a branch that he had heavily soaked to serve as a wick. A warm glow appeared on the branch above his lighter, approximating candle light. He withdrew his hand and the fire began to flow down the branch like a yellow river. A small drop of firewater jumped its banks, falling onto a lower branch, transforming into a golden bud. More fire spilled to the ground, spreading into a self-lighted pond. Several lower branches glimmered in the foliage, channeling fire down the dirt road. Hubbard watched as the flickering trail lengthened, jumping from branch to branch, racing through the parched brush in mutating trails of light.

Satisfied this half of the job was well-started, he crossed the road to begin again. He found his fuel-doused spot next to a squat pine tree, no longer an evergreen, now taking the color of coffee and cream. Its lifeless remains still served, however, as a tent pole for a web of kudzu vines, spinning away in all directions. He leaned forward, holding the lighter against a branch. The plastic grew warm in his hand, but the fire didn't catch. He pulled away some clinging vines and searched for better tinder lower to the ground. He bent down where the fumes still lingered. A single flick of his thumb and flames shot toward him like a cannon ball. Hubbard fell backward toward the road, covering his face, dropping his lighter. Almost in response, the wildfire acted like a winning boxer celebrating his knockout punch, raising arms of fire toward the sky, victorious, parading away from Hubbard in showy display, dividing and subdividing as it bolted down the lane.

Hubbard stumbled to his feet, jerked off his gloves and carefully touched his face. Satisfied that he was okay, he tossed the gloves into the building fire, and appreciated his dumb luck.

He noticed his shadow stretching out on the road in front of him before he felt the heat increasing behind him. He turned, gaping at a wall of flames, chest-high, lining the length of the road behind him. The unexpected blaze was tossing red-hot embers across the narrow lane in a lazy arc, like a one-sided game of catch. Much too quickly, Shanty Town was becoming as bright as mid-day as twin conflagrations filled the air with smoke and ash.

Surprised by the rapid progression of fires on both sides of the road, he belatedly realized his escape route to his truck was now bordered by dual infernos.

"Shit!"

The air around him became noticeably thinner as fire consumed all the oxygen it could find.

Nothing was more common than an arsonist caught by his own fire . . .

He backed to the center of the narrow lane and considered his chances in a desperate charge forward. He had to get to his truck now to escape the scene of his crime; returning to his vehicle in a circuitous route through the surrounding fields would take too long. His vehicle was a smoking gun. Unless he got out quickly, his truck would be discovered by first responders or a model citizen turning off the highway to investigate the flickering light in the sky. His truck was one piece of evidence, but his clothes and body, reeking of gasoline and soot, were just as damning.

He dashed forward, but despite urgency and adrenaline, he began to slow unexpectedly as the fire stole oxygen from his lungs and his legs turned thick and heavy as tree trunks. He was fifty yards from his truck when he stumbled and fell on the road, breathless. His chest tightened as he grew confused and disoriented. *Was he was going toward the fire or away from it?*

Nothing is more common . . . something about fire.

He rolled over and lay on his back. In the night sky, there had to be air uncommitted to the flames. He pleaded with the stars to share.

There was movement on the road. Hubbard lifted his head, straining to see through ripples of heated air and smoke rolling skyward. Incomprehensively, a figure was approaching him—a man in work clothes. His features were unrecognizable at this distance, distorted by wavy heat curling the air. *A hallucination,* he dimly thought. Hubbard fell back and buried his face in the road to escape the high temperature.

Man or mirage, he strode to Hubbard's side with purpose, crouched down and put one arm underneath him and pulled him to his feet. For an insubstantial ghost, he was remarkably strong.

Hubbard's arm was draped over the man's shoulders and they began to move. He took a few stumbling steps until his legs gave up and the toes of his boots dragged along the road like anchors. He wanted to lift his chin off his chest to see whoever, whatever was holding him, but it was all he could do to remain conscious. Although his eyes were swollen from the heat, but he forced them to open into narrow slits.

He tried to be heard above the roar of fire.

Let me go. Get out. Save yourself.

He could only see blue-jeaned legs and boots, entering his field of vision and retreating as his limp head bobbed up and down with each step, like a screen door flapping in the wind. He realized he recognized those boots: A worn tan leather, scuffed and deeply creased from years of use, a splash of barn paint on the right boot. Wolverines with brown and yellow stripped laces, tied off at the second hook, never at the top, double-knot.

His last remnants of consciousness came and went as still images:

His truck. Far away and out of reach.
Black.
Boots striding forward, impervious to heat.
Black.
The family truck from a long time ago. A bullet hole in the wind-shield . . . The goddamn bullet hole.
Black.

The heat of the fire faded. He felt himself being lowered to the ground and propped up in a seated position against a solid object. He tried to raise his head but failed. He sensed the man leaning over him to kiss the top of his head as if he was a sleeping child.

Hubbard awoke with a start. He was alone, his back against the front bumper of his truck. Coughing harshly, he saw Shanty Town recast as the burning of Atlanta. The dry vegetation burned bright yellow, surrounding the neighborhood of shacks as clouds of billow-ing amber. The wooden skin of the crude homes had burned away, revealing the supporting skeleton of red oak two-by-fours, now wrapped in bone-white flames. The wood framing gave way in the shack before him, cracking loudly as the weight of its heavy tin roof became too much to bear. The metal roof, covered in rust and traces of red paint, fell down as one piece, burying the broken remains of the shack in the ground. The first shack was followed by others in quick succession as they all collapsed in asymmetrical sequence, giv-ing up their ghosts in a whoosh of air that sent glowing embers, dark smoke, and the shadows of Shanty Town soaring up into the clear night sky.

Hubbard looked up. Above the tree line there was a strong wind, unfelt at ground level. It caught the ascending debris of soot and spark, twisting it together to craft a braid of gold and black. It pulled the entwined mix skyward in a long train, as if the dark cloud was departing this world, soaring upward, toward the moon, the stars and whatever heavens that lay beyond.

Hubbard stood. It was time to leave this place.

He had family waiting at home.

CPSIA information can be obtained at www.ICGtesting.com
Printed in the USA
LVOW06s0358281015

459962LV00001B/237/P